ropeless

❖◆❖◆❖

Tracy Koretsky

PRESENT
TENSE
PRESS

Also by Tracy Koretsky

POEMS
Even Before My Own Name

BOOK INCLUSIONS
"Learning the Language" (story) in *Where We Find Ourselves: Jewish Women around the World Write about Home*; edited by Miriam Ben-Yoseph and Deborah Nodler Rosen (SUNY: 2009).
"La Poire Hautaine" (essay) in *Poem, Revised: 54 Poems, Discussions, Revisions*; edited by Robert Hartwell Fiske and Laura Cherry (Marion Street Press: 2008).

For audio poems, author interviews, and links to short fiction, essays, reviews, and more poems, visit: www.TracyKoretsky.com.

Copyright © 2005, Tracy Koretsky
Published by Present Tense Press, Berkeley, CA. First printing, May, 2005. Second printing, November, 2007. Third printing, September, 2009.

ISBN: 978-0-9841242-1-3

For my Kenny, who makes everything possible.

Yes, the newspapers were right;
snow was general all over Ireland.

JAMES JOYCE
The Dead

prologue

Ida   Jacob, my husband, may the Lord keep you well, you had many little sayings which I thought were true. At this moment I think of how you would always say that the minute you drop your tuchas into a chair, this is when the phone rings. This is when they gotta sell you their siding; this is when it's time to think about insurance. Twelve dollars a month this thing! I should call the men to take it away. I should sit alone.

So why do I answer? This, my Jacob, you don't already know? It rang! The thing rings; I answer. A trained dog would do the same. Never mind the kitchen looks like a train gone through. Never mind I got just one morning to make maybe six dozen eir kichlah for the family of Sylvia Kaufman.

Oy, did I tell you? Such tragedy. The son-in-law—killed! In an accident! All of a sudden three children got no father. And you should see these children now, Jacob. Not babies like when you got sick and left us. No, these are big boys now. They need a father. They need... *aich*! They need and need. This is what children do.

So you see why the eir kichlah, eh? In every step you put more sugar. You sugar the cookie sheet they shouldn't stick instead of the potato starch. You sugar your hand to work them. Then you bake so hot, it's hard to stay in the kitchen. And then you look at them, you say, so what? So plain and everyday they look—little branches the color of bone. But when you bite, eh? You gotta bite hard. They snap. They make a little cloud of sugar. It floats from your teeth. I think maybe such sweetness surprises away some of the numbness. A very good cookie for death.

So anyway, six dozen, this is quite an operation. I got Paully beating eggs for the glaze. Very important, you make a froth but not a peak. No froth, you get shine. It looks gaudy. Peaks, you get nothing. Me, I'm up to my elbow in sugar. But the darned thing rang. So help me, I've got my habits.

"Ma," she says.

So I say, "Who's this? Jody?"

She says, "Ma, who else calls you 'Ma'?"

What kind of tone is this she uses with her mother? "I got a son too," I say.

"Right," she says, big sigh, "and he calls you Mommy."

"This is true," I tell her, "but he says it so many times a day living here in his home with his mother that all I have to hear is 'mmm' before I'm there by his side."

So Jody, she gives the silent treatment. You know how our daughter can be. I figure there's money being spent all the way from her California, so I go on, "This is how a mother behaves. You wouldn't know."

"Oy, Ma," she says, and then again with the big sigh.

So I say, "In fact, I think maybe I hear him calling now." Though the truth is, I can see him standing right there in front of me.

"Ma, wait," she says.

"Me, I can wait for Elijah, Jody, but Paully, if I don't stop him, he's gonna sugar those sheets himself."

"Eir kichlah?" she says. You see how she knows?

"I don't got those sheets schmaltzed yet, Jody. I don't want him near that sugar." This much is true. I did not lie twice.

"Ma, who died?"

You see? A daughter can read a mother's habits.

"Wait," I say, "I take care of business first." So then, wouldn't you know, I drop the phone and it knocks over the egg. For six dozen, there's a lot of egg. It pours down the cabinet. It pours on my shoe. So wonderful, now I got a glazed shoe.

I fumble with the phone. My hands these days, they don't stop shaking. "Oy, Jody darling," I tell her, "I got a mess here."

"Ma, who died?"

"Sylvia Kaufman's son-in-law, if you're so interested." Just saying it, I got to lay my hand on the counter; it should give me strength.

So Jody, of course, she can't believe. "Jeesh, no!" she says. "Aw, poor, poor Evelyn. How—"

"Look, Jody, the shiva starts today," I tell her. "I got my work cut out."

"Ma, wait," she says like she don't hear me.

So I tell her, "I'll listen better when you call later."

"Ma—" she says, right over.

"Tonight," I say, "after *Wheel of Fortune.*"

"Ma. Now." 'Now!' she says! To her mother!

So you can guess what's on her mind. What's always on her mind? She's got her big deal training. Such a fancy-schmancy class they can't do it in New York. All the way to California she's gotta go. Can you imagine someone having something so important to say about selling ladies' underwear that he can't say it in New York? Two months, she's gone already. I don't need the details. "So, excuse me," I say over, "Who am I to stand in the way of my daughter's girdle empire?"

So she says, "Ma, don't start."

"Fine, then. I'll finish."

But she don't say good-bye and I stand there, holding the phone. I hear her take a big breath. "Ma," she says finally, "I've done something about Paully."

Done something about...? Did I hear her right? I do for Paully. What he needs, I do. I got egg on the burner; it's going to cook there. "Jody," I say. "Whatever this is, I just don't got time now."

"Uh-huh," she says, real snippy, real quiet, you know how she gets. "Fine then, Ma. So have a pleasant visit when she comes!"

"Fine then. I will!"

And boom she hangs up! Boom! Is this how they do it in her California? Because, in Brooklyn, I can tell you, we do not raise our children to behave this way!

I look over at Paully. He's biting on his hand and moaning like he does when he's nervous. His fingers cover his face so only his eyes show. So what's he looking at so worried? My shoe! Oy, my shoe! You see! This is what a nice boy thinks about. I hand him down the paper towels, better I shouldn't bend. The right knee, it throbs all the time now.

My sweet boy, egg over everything, he wipes up my shoe. I reach down and pet his head. What would I do without my Paully? Forget Jody. Forget this nonsense. I got pans to schmaltz!

So of course I schmaltz too thick and the bottoms cook too fast and Paully gets mopey because I won't let him eat no dough. So now I gotta make a bribe. I tell him he can take the cookies over to

Sylvia's. He's whining, whining until I say, "All right, go already." I know I should do this myself, but Jacob, I'm an old woman, not a machine. I got no strength left. I do go stand on the porch so that when Sylvia comes out, I can wave. I watch our son carry two big plates right across. He looks both ways. He knocks real polite. You would have been proud.

Sylvia takes the cookies and Paully shows her I'm standing, shvitzing on the porch, and she waves and he waves too and we're all smiling and acting like the Love Boat is gonna sail any minute. And what I see there I am glad you died, died and left me, before ever having to see.

He's got almost no teeth now, the poor boy. The dentist wanted to pull but he couldn't teach Paully to work the dentures and I got enough just getting him shaved. Could you see this? Mother and son sharing the same glass for their teeth. I'm looking across the street at my shana babaleh and I see an old man. God save us, he's an old man now, Jacob.

book one

❖•❖•❖

dead bodies

−1−

Jody I shake hands across the desk and take one of two chairs on my side. I'm looking right at a young black guy, college boy type. He's the personnel rep. Next to him is Sharon Moore, Head of Women's Wear. She's the one that's got to like me.

I figure her for my age, maybe a little older, but it's hard to say because she's not wearing any make-up at all—I mean none at all! Other than that, she's not dressed much different than I might be on any given day: big round glasses, button earrings, white hose. That's one sharp suit, though. Beige. I hate beige. Beige just don't say anything.

Apparently certain phone calls have already been made, so at least I don't have to sit there and fidget while they read the letter Mr. Parker sent me with. But they do ask to see the little résumé I made up. Not that it exactly moves things along. I've been head of Foundations almost nine years now. Before that, I just got promoted internal. My boss would know me and see I know my business and move me up. But the way I figure, I am up about as far as I'm gonna go in Brooklyn. Sportswear, Office, and General Women's, they all turned over since I been on the job and they took younger, chicier-type girls.

So while they look, I talk. "You can see I put there, 'Foundations,' not, 'Lingerie,' " I say, pointing to it. "If you ask me, that's what my work is about. Lingerie? Who can pronounce it? People either try to make it sound all fancy-Frenchy, like lounger-ree, like every piece of it is to lie around in upon your satin divan. Or they go the other way—which is worse—and make it sound like 'fingery' with an 'l'. Okay, you gotta admit, that is how the darned word looks, but it sounds like if you wear it, you'll never get to work on time."

This is old material—rehearsed. I've been using it on sales reps for years. Once I even got some of it back from a new sales rep who got it from the guy he replaced. I trust it. It can be very important in a deal, you know, who gets the first laugh.

Sharon Moore, she looks at my résumé the way you do when a kiddie draws you a picture and you don't know if it's a dog or a mountain. You try to be nice. You try to sound excited. She hands it off to the personnel guy. He glances at it, and sort of slips it underneath the papers on his clipboard. So, oh well, making résumés is not what I do for a living. And what I do—I think anyway—I'm pretty good at. I go back to my material.

"What's left?" I say, "Intimate Apparel? That just don't do it for me. See, with 'intimate' there's this sense that you got to have someone else there. This I don't like. Not everybody who's buying underwear wants it to look good for someone else, you know? And forget unmentionables. First of all, it's silly. No professional person could say 'Director of Unmentionables' with a straight face. You'd sound like you're with the CIA. Besides, I mention them all the time. Some days I spend all day talking about them."

This makes them laugh, which means it's time for me to get serious. "And this, all this lying about stuff, all this intimacy, this is not what I am about. Me, I'm about Foundations. Stuff that goes under. My work is about making look good—and feel good, that's important to me—the way a woman is going to look every day, not just some, you know, certain nights."

Now the way I deliver "certain nights" is with this little eyebrow lift that usually gets people. It does, right on cue, which means now it's time to go for my big finish laugh when, suddenly, I realize I could not have set myself up better for my secret weapon. What the heck, I improvise.

"Speaking of which," I say, leaning forward and making eye contact with each one, "I took a few minutes to walk your department, and, if you don't mind my saying so, your sexies? By this I mean, your satins, your see-throughs, silks, lacy teddies, that sort of thing—that's what you hang beneath those track lights. You aim those lights right at 'em so they glow like they've been polished. And then, see, you put something in front of that section so it's... well, more private; so you can't just see who's there when you stroll by. Understand what I'm saying? Discreet." I lower my voice. I got 'em. "That's what will make us different from Victoria's. That section, you know, that section's really for men."

He stifles a laugh. Caught, probably. And she looks like "Aha!"

I go on. "The stuff you got there now—sleep shirts, baby dolls—
you ought to be moving one of those every third customer—"

"Right," says the young man, tapping something in his notes
with his pen. "Your supervisor, Mr. ah... Parker. He did write that
you sell an impressive volume in that category."

I do at that. I swallow to hold back my smile. "It's like this," I
say. "That's something a woman will buy for herself, but usually,
she's not gonna come in for it. She gotta think of it. And better yet,
she gotta think, 'Oh, that looks like something I'd like to slip into
right about now.' So what you do is, you surprise her. You circle the
bras with them. You put them like everywhere you might happen to
notice as you were bending over a rack to search out the right size,
noticing that little nagging pain above your hip, whatever. You put
them in the dressing rooms, like, whoops, someone forgot to take
this to the counter. See how this goes? I tell you—this works."

He's got a big grin, nodding along. She's leaning back, thoughtful.

I look at my hands and say, real quiet, real modest, "At least
that's the way women buy in Brooklyn."

I can't look at them. I sit back and press my hands into my skirt
so they won't be clammy. She clears her throat and says, "Miss
Kochansky, I'd like you to take a look at my department." He busts
out laughing and then—I just can't help it, I'm so nervous—I do
too. He looks at her, she makes an expression like "obviously" and
he says, "When do you think you can start?"

I look at the ceiling. I look at the walls. When.

Nine years I've been manager. And before that, six on the floor.
It's gotten so's I can see a woman walk down the street and know
what size she takes. The stewardess on the plane leans over to serve
lunch; I notice her left strap's adjusted higher than her right. This is
experience. I can do it. I know I can. But then I think: can I do it?
Brooklyn, I know. But California? California's full of movie stars.
What do I know from how a movie star buys?

But then I think: so what if they want you, you stinker. You think
you're gonna move to California or something, fancy-pants? Then
what happens to Ma and Paully? You dreamer. You know, it's not so

very nice and honest to ask for a job you don't mean to take. They got people sitting out there in messes, waiting for someone to do the work. Macy's been good to you and you treat them like this.

And then I think: why am I thinking? What kind of big exotic adventure is this if you already got it all planned out? Who says they're going to offer you the job anyway?

But I hoped they would.

And then they did.

And now, now I wish they didn't.

It wasn't about the job. When I first saw it there on the fax, well, taking the job didn't even enter my head.

See, what I wanted, all I wanted, was to be asked. Give me a little interview, is what I thought, a little all-expense-paid junket out to sunny Calie-for-nie-ay, a little perk, a little reward for riding out all those salary freezes all those years that the corporate high muck-a-mucks played musical chairs with the place I draw my salary from. Ah, the eighties! I'd been with Macy's all through 'em. So what I thought—all I thought—was: payback time.

I mean, California. Who wouldn't want to go? It's like we all live here already. Thanks to *Entertainment Tonight*, I know more about Julia Roberts than I do the guy in the next apartment. Plus, everybody but everybody got an Aunt Sue or brother Bill who lives here now. Everyone had either been on vacation or was gonna go. Everyone. Everyone except me.

Me, I'd never been anywhere—well, okay, Jersey a few times, for school trips and once on business, but not like, *stayed* anywhere. So when I saw it there, lying on the fax: Department Manager, Lingerie, Santa Clara, California, well, I felt like the room began to spin, like when I was a kid and imagined I could see the earth turn on its axis.

There was a number where I was supposed to fax my résumé. This was very helpful, but, hey, what résumé? So I reached for the phone. Personnel. All I had to do is tell the lady out there what I do and right away it's "When can you come out?" Résumé-schmésumé.

Day after tomorrow, she says, that's all I got. She'll take care of the hotel, but I'm supposed to set up a flight like lickety-split. Where is this Santa Clara anyway? Near L.A.? Ooo, maybe a little trip to Disneyland? Oh, I don't even care. I'm going on an airplane! Me! And on "the company," no less! Fan-cy!

I think: I gotta get my hair done! And these nails! Jeesh! And what do you wear on an airplane anyway? And I hope I still fit into my gray wool suit. And oops! Who would have thought a suitcase cost that much? Better ask Ma about Aunt Lila's old bag.

Then I think: you'd better what, Jody? You'd better do what? I am stopped still, my hand still holding a price tag.

See, really what I got here is two choices. I can lie to Ma, which is only gonna work until she catches me, or I can whine and beg, which pretty much works all the time but makes me feel like a worm. Worm or liar, I think, letting the price tag flutter away, liar or worm?

In my lap I see that quick sloppy manicure I did on that lousy cold plane. The whole way, nothing but clouds. The guy next to me put a handkerchief over his nose and it's chipped now anyway.

I feel like it's gonna take all the energy in my body just to make words. Like those moments when you realize something has changed and that's that. Like after a funeral.

I look at Sharon and the kid from personnel. "I thank you for considering me," I say. "I'm really glad I had a chance to come out here and see about this, but, well, I've been thinking... " I meet their eyes. "I mean, it all happened so fast... "

"Uh-huh," she says. "Well, how much time will you need?"

"That's just it, Mrs. Moore."

"Sharon."

"I won't be able to take this job."

There. The sky didn't cave in.

"You're kidding," the college boy says.

"Aww," Sharon says, same time. "Why?"

"Um." I'm blinking back tears. What am I supposed to say now? Sorry I can't even consider this job because I got a brother who don't know how to make lunch for himself? Sometimes you tell people things like that and you never know, they wonder how good you are at making your own lunch.

"I just wanted you to know," I say, "what I thought you could do with the department here from like, one Macy's employee to another."

The college boy says to Sharon, "Tell me she's kidding."

I try to be polite while he tells me nice things about the place. He calls it "Silicon Valley."

Sharon cuts him off. "Somehow I don't think the Bay Area rainfall is what's on Miss Kochansky's—"

"Jody."

"—On Jody's mind."

"I can't do much with money," he says.

So I say to him, "Look, we're talking about moving across the country."

I point my finger. "How'd you like to move to New York, right away, right on a dime?"

He puts his hands up, like, "surrender."

"Look Mike," Sharon says—and it's the first time I catch his name—"Why don't you just let Jody and I talk. I'll buzz you then." She turns to me. "Is that okay?"

"Well, I. . ." I say. The worst that can happen is she can be mad at me. Parker, he's not going to fire me.

So Mike goes and it's just me and Sharon. I am not any more comfortable.

"Obviously you have personal reasons," she says.

"Right," I say to my lap, "family."

"Well, I don't want to pry, but I need to ask. Is there anything I could do? As your boss, I mean."

I wish I weren't here. I wish I had never looked at that fax.

I unzip my bag. Sharon thinks I'm going for a tissue because I'm gonna cry. She comes around the desk and sits by me.

I dig out my wallet, open the catch over the photo part, and flip a few. I pass it to her. And when I find my voice, I say, "That's Ma. That's my brother Paully. That's Ma's apple strudel."

Sharon looks real careful at the picture. I got it so the light on Paully comes up from behind. It looks like he's got more nose. Also, if you shoot him a little to the side his eyes look better. You know, more normal.

Sharon don't talk for a long time. Then she does. She says, "That's a beautiful strudel."

"Paully, he's fifty-five now. Still lives with my Ma. She's seventy-eight," I say. "Her strudels are slipping."

I see Sharon nod as she puts it together. I put my hand out for my wallet. She passes it back. I put it in my purse. I make to leave.

She don't stand. She looks up at me. "I won't keep you if you want to go," she says. "Just tell me you'll think about it."

Now she stands. I can see myself twice in her glasses. She says, "I've never been anywhere. I mean, just this coast, not like New York or anything, but Jody, most people like it here. I think you will too."

I don't know what to say. Everywhere you look, someone's trying to sell you something.

"Take a little time," she says. "Walk the mall. Stay another night if you want; I'll make sure it's covered."

I'm tempted. Of course I'm tempted.

"I'm sorry, Sharon." I dig my nails into my purse.

"We can hold off deciding a few days anyway," she says, going for her close, "maybe a week."

The thought of going over this and over this for a week!

But then she says, "Sometimes Jody, once you know an opportunity exists you get all kinds of ideas for how to make it possible. Don't say no. Say maybe."

Truth is, I couldn't say anything at all if I wanted to. I feel funny on my heels as I walk out—teetery. After all, this is California. There could be an earthquake any minute.

I don't need to walk the place a bit. Who walks into an interview without walking the place a bit? I've been trying to imagine myself being there every day. Two stories of white stucco shops over a big open plaza. I mean big. Everything big. The fast food court, eight-plex movies, and this one joint with a salad bar like from five of those steam table places they got all over mid-town all strung together and no two bowls alike. But here, instead of some sticky, rickety table that someone has shoved a folded-up racing form under, you sit and eat in a big comfy booth. They got no worries about running out of room here in California. Macy's and Emporium are the anchors. That's a strong match; we're just different enough. But darn if there isn't a Victoria's Secret. That place is killing me. I'll tell you what Victoria's real secret is—she's The GAP. That is, the chain's owned by The GAP. Best advertising in the business. Now what are you gonna do about that?

So I think I got the picture and more of a picture I do not need. No what I need is a bath. And not just a bath either, but a bath so hot it's like your skin can't keep you in anymore and you sort of melt in the water and you don't have to bother about having a body at all, just a brain and a beating heart, which, when it comes to making a decision, I mean, what else do you need?

Besides, the hotel, I love. *"La Pequita Quinta"* it's called, peach and gray, very pretty. They got this big TV I can order movies on, little complimentary bottles of shampoo, conditioner, bubble bath, fresh flowers. Fan-cy. I can't help myself, the whole cab ride over, I hear that silly old tune in my head, "Ca-li-for-nia here I come, right back where I started from."

So I make my big plan: I'm gonna use three towels. Now is this luxury? But first I check out the room service menu, singing right out "roast chicken, and side of peas, right back where I started from, a chocolate cake and milk and what the heck, beer, you only live once, da da da, la dee dee da." You know, like "to the tune of." I crack myself up.

I pour out the little bottle under the tap and watch it foam. Then I call the desk to set up some food and a movie for later: Bill and Ted's Excellent Adventure. Okay it's for kiddies and I already saw it on cable, but—what can I say?—it makes me happy. So I'm humming the whole time they got me on hold. I tell you, my whole life I've wanted to order room service, one of those rolling carts with the food all covered up with silver lids, like in the movies—live like the other half do.

But, like the other half say in those same old movies, "Tut-tut.

Business before pleasure." I switch on the heat lamp in the bathroom. The room fills with steam. Clouds again. My first flight ever in my life, right? The whole way—clouds. And all I wanted was a new view.

The mirror fogs. Soon I will disappear completely. Which, like I said, is what I really want. I breathe the clouds in deep as I sink down.

I watch my skin turn pink, sinking down and down. My belly makes a big pink island. My breasts float up, two small pointy islands. I sink lower to hide them under. I got my foot against the cool tiles, my eyes closed. Suddenly I am no longer the short, square lady with the support hose and the twelve-hour bra. Her I leave back in Brooklyn to eat pistachio pudding and watch the Sunday matinee at Ma's. My heart pounds. It's a drum. "Ca-li-for-nia here I come . . ."

Yeah right, like I'm ever going any farther than down the street to Ma's. This is not very nice, Miss Kochansky. Macy's been good to you and you treat them like this.

But then I think: okay, so who says that street gotta be in Brooklyn? Brooklyn's changed. Paully, he should be able to go for a walk himself, I think, like he used to. Maybe I could find them a little place out here, close to me. A smaller place that Ma could handle. No yard.

I swish my hand in the water and laugh. Imagine Ma not having that stupid yard to complain about. What would she have left to say?

Aw Jody, who you kidding? Ma's never gonna leave Flatbush. Ma is never gonna be anywhere but exactly where she is doing exactly like she does.

So let her. Let her. Why shouldn't I take the job if they want to give it to me? I can do it. And then I think: can I?

One thing's for sure. I'm not gonna know if I don't try. People move for jobs. They do it all the time. Why shouldn't I?

Why shouldn't I? How about because I can't just leave Ma alone with Paully, that's why. Ask her and she'll say she's got everything under control there. Well, she's got another think coming. I go by after work and half the time he hasn't been out all day, not even in the yard. He's not washed; he don't smell good. Ma's just not on top of it anymore; I don't care what she says.

Poor Ma. It's gonna be hard for her to schlep her garbage to the curb tonight.

I run some more hot water and sigh into the heat. The little silver bubbles break up and dissolve. For the second time in one day I come out of the clouds. I look down at my big round pink island of belly. I close my eyes and let my head fall back.

You know, pathetic though it may be—Ma is also like my best friend.

So, all right then, plan C. Ma stays in Flatbush in a house that's too big for her to keep nice being driven happily crazy by her yard, and I bring Paully out by me. That could work. I can see that. Assuming I could get somebody in to watch Paully—hey, it'd only cost a couple of limbs—then Ma? Ma could get up every day when she wants, take it easy, no big jobs to do. No little jobs either, for that matter. For that matter, nothing to do, watch her stories maybe. I stretch my legs up on the cool clean tile. Gosh, that would be the life.

Then it hits me. It hits me hard. It hits me like a bullet, like a sniper shot. I think of Ma, I see her standing in that kitchen her hands in some bowl. My whole life, Ma got her hands in a bowl. Take that bowl away—no Ma.

I sit bolt upright. I slosh bath water over the side. I say it out loud. "It will kill her. It will kill her, Jody. You take Paully away, you got one dead Ma."

What am I doing? What in the hell am I doing?

That's it. It is never never never gonna happen for me. Take out a contract on Eckhart from Shoes back in Brooklyn. That's my only chance. That's the only way I'll ever make something of my life. My head pounds from the heat. I hold on.

I feel something inside me break, like a ripping. I feel something inside tremble and give. I am lying in this beautiful clean rose smelling tub in my pretty hotel on my first expense account ever and I am crying, sobbing, like I never will stop. I drag my nails over my thighs once, stinging. What a waste. A stupid, stupid waste.

I am never never never gonna live like the other half. Even with what I know about the track lights and stewardess' straps. Nothing I know—nothing—makes any darn difference.

I can't stand it; I'm burning. I hate this stupid tub. I stand up. I want my skin back. I want the world to stop spinning. Water streams down my hot skin. I stumble out of the tub and stand panting, making big puddles at my feet. I am never. Never, never, never.

I open the door to the other room. Cool air rushes around me; my pulse throbs in my ears. There I am in another damned mirror. Everywhere you look in this place, another mirror! Look at me! Look! Nothing but fat. Rolls and rolls of fat, fat, fat! Round shoulders, two chins, pathetic droopy breasts, nothing but stretch marks. They fall sideways, flopping over my belly, my big fat belly spilling over my little triangle of fur. My hips got to squeeze into the seat on the airplane. I can't take a step, my thighs don't rub. I press my nails into them. They dig so deep. God, I'm so fat!

What a waste! What a body! What is it for? I'm a daughter; I'm a sister. From the neck down this body might as well be dead. I can count my lovers on one hand. I don't even gotta use my thumb. I am never. Never, never, never.

I fall onto the bed. I beat on a pillow. I have got to—got to—get myself together. If I don't, I'm going to… My nails dig again, deep into my squishy thighs. I drag them slow and burning, raising welts. I drag them again, hugging myself, rocking, trying to breathe.

And then I do. Then I breathe. And somehow, the world stops its spinning. It's not like this is news. I've been fat quite a while. It's not like the first time I've cried about it either. Okay, or scratched. It's just the first time I've done it in California. And it's been a while since I stood before a mirror. Look at this body. Jeesh, what's the point?

I make myself do it—stand there and look. I swallow hard and sniff and stare at my forty-two year old face, just as it is, no make-up or jewelry, deep set brown eyes, pug nose, wide jaw, my short hair going gray now, the stretched holes for my earrings.

"Not everything is a job, you know," I say out loud to the mirror.

So, there it is. There. You got what you wanted. There's your precious decision. You, Miss Jody Kochansky, are a person with a few responsibilities. Some people would be happy to be needed like that. Not everything in the world is a job, you know? There are plenty of people who got it much worse.

What I long to do—the only thing I can think of that would calm me right now—is to pet Paully. There's a way he lays his head in my lap like a puppy when I bring over a movie to watch with Ma and I stroke and stroke until he falls asleep. My Paully. He calms me down; I calm him down. My brother and I, we're a team.

I close my eyes and sigh. It's not enough. I sigh again letting all my air empty away. I feel like an old sack that's almost empty, just one thing left in it, a heavy thing. All I gotta do is just take the thing out and I'll float. I laugh to myself at own my private joke.

When did I make that up? That thing about the sack? I know I've been thinking of them that way for a long time now. When was it that I started with all that business? I sigh again and it comes to me. The day we laid Pa's stone, the year after he died.

The three of us stood a long time in the cemetery after the rabbi went home. It just felt like there was something else to do. You look at the stone, put down a few flowers, you say the prayer, you go home. Still, it feels like something's missing, you know? Something's incomplete. So Ma, she goes and stands on the other side of the grave, looking up at me and sort of stamps the earth. "This is my place," she says.

"Yeah, Ma, I know," I say.

"Your father bought me this place. Right next to him."

"Yeah, Ma," I say. "I know. He told me."

"So when I go. . . " and then she looks at me and I nod all right already. "And here," she says, "next to me, this is the place for Paully."

We both look over at him. He's kicking a clod of dirt back and forth.

"I know, Ma," I say. And then because I think she needs to hear it, "Listen, don't you worry. I'm here to take care of things, okay?"

But that's not what's on Ma's mind. Ma stands at the plot next to her and says, "This is Paully. Next to me." She meets my eyes. "For you, Sunshine, we still got hope."

Hope. Ha! It's almost too funny. Hope that some man would come along who'd dig me a plot next to his. Well, maybe she had hope, maybe Ma did. But me? I gave up with that a long time ago. Didn't she have eyes? Couldn't she see? Who's going to...? Ah, never mind. And I was pushing thirty-five then. What did she think?

I looked down at my Pa's new grave marker, a shiny, flat, black and gray stone. Who would think such a simple thing could cost so much money? I had to dip into his savings to do it so it'd be right. This is how I will spend my inheritance, I thought, filling their graves and laying their stones.

Ma stands there like she wants some kind of answer. Paully pulls at the seat of his dress pants because they've gotten too tight. I squint at them in the sunlight. My inheritance: Ma and Paully. My two stones.

And I look back at Pa's grave and think how he got there. How hard that man worked, every darned day, down at the dock lifting his sacks. And I think how Pa handed everything else to me, Ma, Paully, the house, the secret. He might as well hand me at least one heavy sack. So, in my mind, I load in my two stones, and throw it over my shoulder. Then I hike out to phone for a cab.

When I open my eyes again I'm back at *La Pequita Quinta*. Hope. Ha! What is there to hope for? For someone to hold me? I don't even have a grave to hold me when I'm dead. I don't even have a grave.

There's no future for me in Brooklyn. For me, Brooklyn is the place to put the dead bodies.

I don't stop to think. If I think I may never, never, never. Sometimes in life you gotta just do. I reach for the phone.

And that's where room service finds me, on the phone with Sharon Moore—my new boss.

–2–

Jody   Ten digits and moving men were scheduled. Another ten and a temporary place in California rented. A third call to my landlord and all of a sudden I was giving away the ferns in my office. Don't get me wrong, I love the phone—greatest invention ever made. You can get anything over a phone. Delivered. Yet this, somehow this—moving away from everything I've ever known—how could this be so easy? But there it was. I was going. When I caught my breath all that was left was saying goodbye.

Mr. Parker, my boss, he took his glasses off and looked up at me. "I would like to have done better for you here, Jody," he said sadly. "I've been looking for the right opportunity for you for years. I'd like to see you in Shoes."

"Shoes?" I said. Shoes is big.

"I don't see Eckhart leaving though."

"No," I said. "No." I had no idea he saw me in Shoes. I was shocked that he saw me at all.

He laughed, like he's trying to tease. "I threatened them," he said. "I told them that we can't possibly let you go before Christmas. Nobody can run the Christmas sale around here like you. If we lose money it's on their heads!"

Jeesh, I never knew he felt that way. Looking down on Parker like that, I see a lot of gray. He hired me. I reach across the desk to shake his hand. He stands and comes around. He hugs me, nice polite gentleman kind of hug. Who would of thought?

The other managers and I, we had a sad little lunch. We went to their usual spot, the one that I'm never invited to. That's another reason I do so much work on the phone. The best part is being able to talk to people when all they can do is listen. When it don't matter what you look like and no one can judge and put you down.

And speaking of being put down, well, that's the part of leaving that wouldn't be easy. I had to tell Ma something.

What I wish is that Pa were here. Pa would understand. He'd see I had this chance at a great job in Santa Clara, California, that I worked so hard all these years to deserve and he'd say, "Jody, you wait too long to dance, the musicians go home." He'd help me talk to her. See, the thing is, talking to Ma, well, it's like a talent. Pa was the only one I ever saw who could really do it.

First you got to know when to stop listening because she's just going on and when you got to listen harder because she's saying a lot more than she thinks and it might be useful. There's a lot of timing too, like when to move quick and get your word wedged in there. Not that she'll listen necessarily, but at least that way you don't pull your hair out. And forget about it once she gets into a story. You don't get your turn until "The End" comes up on the screen.

And then there's all the sidestepping you got to do so you don't get into any subjects you've already decided not to talk to Ma about. So many things not to tell Ma. What I'm eating, what I wear, what I buy. The last guy I told Ma about was my boyfriend in high school who wanted to know if what Paully's got runs in families. Ma didn't even know and she still wouldn't let me see him any more. No, I sure don't talk to Ma about men. Not that there's even been a man not to talk about in years. What can I say? The musicians packed up a long, long time ago. Still, I got eyes, don't I? But not that Ma hears about.

Forget "interview." "Training" is what Ma heard. Also, "California" is new. Before I said, "New Jersey." Bad enough I said "overnight." Ma can't deal with the possibility I'm not a couple streets away, stopping off on my way home to bring her the orange juice she forgot when she was out. And while I'm there, I could just take out the garbage if I don't mind and maybe look at the bank statement, they've gotten so complicated, and on and on.

And before you know it, it's time for Letterman. Ma likes Leno, so I head home in time to catch the monologue. Two blocks down and around the corner, three floors above the Long Life Kosher Chinese, pajamas and teeth during the commercials, and tomorrow's another day.

Every night, every one, since Pa died, and most of them before. I could hardly remember when it started and there's sure no end in sight.

Right up to the last day, I just couldn't seem to get the words out of my mouth when she was standing there right in front of me, her hands shaking, her sweater on crooked. Always in a sweater now, Ma, no matter how hot. And Paully, all upset by the boxes.

That's when it hit me—my friend the phone! On the phone I won't have to deal with that look of disappointment she gets when something don't go her way. On the phone I can set the receiver in my lap for a while when she's just going on. If I want to roll my eyes, who's to stop me? Okay, I know it's a cop out. I'm only glad I came up with anything at all.

"It's a temporary thing," I told her, "a management thing." I figured how could she object to me getting some school?

"What kind of school makes you give away your apartment?"

"I'm not giving it away, Ma," I said, as I taped a note onto the mattress for the Salvation Army guys. "I'm sticking my stuff in a storage locker and sub-letting so I can pocket the rent and save for the future."

Ma don't know from money. She don't even want to know. But "save for the future," that she knows is a good thing. See I made up this big elaborate plan—too big, too elaborate really—I'm going to tell her a little more each day, how happy they are with me at this training thing, how they're making a big fuss, and then, when I think she's ready to hear it, how they think I'll be the perfect person for this special new position.

And then somehow, amazingly, three days later, I'm standing there with this apartment lady in this little white stucco number in the Chaparral Ridge Apartments, right? And she's pointing out the "Craftsman" built-ins for the third time, which, sure, I like all right—they're like tidy little nests in the wall of the front room—but I guess I haven't kveled enough for her yet. Hey, it's the third place with a red tile roof I've seen that day. Might as well face it. Bus routes. That's the bottom line.

See, this is a rule for me, a very important thing I learned long ago from dealing with sales reps: you gotta know before you let them in the door what's your bottom line. You don't and these sharpies'll stick you with a crate of leopard skin support hose. You'll sell one. Maybe. But only to someone who lives in Brighton Beach. Okay, the reps want to give you thirty off on this and twenty off on that instead of the other way round, let them. They got a right to make a buck too. But they ain't gonna shake me past my bottom-line. They know it. These days, they don't even try.

I ask her what lines this place got.

"Lines?"

"Bus lines," I say.

"You're about three minutes from 101," she says.

"I can catch a bus there?" I say.

"A what?" It's like I'm speaking Greek.

See right then I should have known I was in trouble. I mean, in New York all the apartment ladies know right away what buses a place got. This lady here though, she's looking at me like now she's got to worry if I can really make the rent or if I'm going to set the place on fire or something.

So—mostly so I won't have to look at her—I give a tug on the living room drapes, and what I see, let me tell you, you do not see in Brooklyn.

It was a clear day, bright, hardly any wind, so it was calm as a mirror, reflecting back clouds. And the cement around it? It's that kind that sparkles. Ooh! Can't you just see the postcard? Miss Jody Kochansky of Brooklyn to winter in Santa Clara this year.

So the apartment lady, she must have seen my jaw drop, you know. She says, "Welcome to California, Miss Kochansky."

–3–

Steiner   When the call came, naturally I thought there'd been a mistake. For one thing, the DOI Services cover just the New York metro. She was calling from California. Then she says that her brother is an adult. I do intake. I transfer her.

Five minutes later, the call bounces back.

"This *is* an intake."

"But you said he is, ah. . . " I fish the call sheet out of the recycling.

"Fifty-five," she says. Apparently, while on hold, she'd lost her patience.

"So it's a transfer. . . "

"Is that necessary?" The thought seems to agitate her. "I mean, I'd sort of thought we'd be easing him in. . . "

"Okay, well then, where is he now?"

"At home."

"I don't mean at this moment," I say. "I mean where does he usually go?"

"Paully? Paully don't usually go anywhere except sometimes to the A&P with Ma."

All of this was delivered very rapidly and unremarkably, so I thought, no, it couldn't be.

"He's never been with anybody but us," she continues.

"Okay," I say carefully, though "uh-oh" would have been more apt. "And who is 'us'?"

"Well, it's just Ma now, but before that there was me, of course. And Pa. But he's gone nine years already."

"Just the three of you?" I say, still hoping there was something I was missing. "His whole life?"

"The family used to be bigger, but then there was a fight. You know how families can. . . "

I have no idea what to say. I grab a fresh intake form and a pen. "Okay then, Ms. ah. . . "

"Kochansky. And it's Miss."

Just to be sure, I run her through the checklist on the form: schools, day facilities, work programs, synagogue. One after another, Miss Kochansky says, no. Just as I am about to ask about sport leagues, she stops me.

"Miss Steiner," she says, "I already told you."

So she did, she did indeed, but really that's not what I do. I do babies, preemies even, almost never as old as five.

"Miss Kochansky, I am not entirely sure the Daughters of Israel Family Services is the right agency for you. You see, in general—"

"But you're over on Avenue J, right?"

"That's true, but—"

"So Ma's on Avenue M."

"I see, well the location of the placement agency isn't really that important..."

"You can't phone first, Miss Steiner," Miss Kochansky says. "You want Ma there, you'd better not tell her you're coming."

Ah, so that's how it was.

When I have recovered myself, I say, "We don't generally make home visits at the Daughters of Israel. We don't have the staff, the—"

"I don't understand. When you put me on hold before, I heard that little sales spiel—"

"Yes, but..."

She mimics our machine, not half badly, "full range of services," she says, "whole families with special needs."

"We're not selling anything, Miss Kochansky."

"Oh come on. Everybody's selling something."

"But in general—"

"In general, in general. You keep saying that. Well maybe my family's not 'general,' Miss Steiner, but you could say we have some special needs."

Then, she lists them.

I am to give her a day to let her mother know that I am coming and then I am to "drop by," which is to say, unannounced.

Aha. Now that really set the stage.

After which, to make the premise more worthy of farce, Miss Kochansky makes it clear that while there, I am not to use words like "group home" or even "independent."

Hearing this, my breath catches. How could they? How dare they? And also, *why*? This is just so unnecessary.

Well what I do know is, I have not chosen this work to become disingenuous. In fact, I have chosen it precisely because I don't have to be. I am proud of what we do and disinclined to hold back. But mostly, I am a trained social worker, with a specialty in developmental disabilities. I have never studied acting.

Ida   Visit, *feh*. The best thing I can say about that "visit" is that it
was short. Such a know-it-all, that one, such a maven, right
from the start.

For one thing, I don't like her 'cause her skirt is too short. Even
for July, this is New York and a young girl should be careful. For another, she got no sense of humor. She shakes my hand all business-
like and says she's from the Daughters of Israel. I tell her, I got no
daughters in Israel, I only got one and at the moment, she's training
in California, but I wish she were in Israel because there at least she
would meet Jewish boys. This Deborah person don't even smile.
She starts telling me what the Daughters of Israel is. What? She
thinks I don't know this? Could there be Daughters of Israel without mothers of Brooklyn? So I tell her I got no money anyway and
she tells me she don't want money.

So I say, "What then, my gorgeous body?"

All right. So this is cheap, borscht belt, not very original. Still
Jacob, like you always told me, when you make a stranger laugh,
you make a friend. This girl, I tell you, it's not my fault. She should
take smiling lessons.

That's not all. She got no manners. She does not really thank
for the eir kichlah. All right, if the bottoms weren't so dark I would
have given them to Sylvia. Still, for homemade, you kvel. Her tea,
she hardly touches. I know why she asked for it, Jacob, she thinks
she cannot talk to my Paully in front of me. So tell me, what secrets
he got?

But when I come out of the kitchen with this tea she does not
want, the maven is scribbling notes on a clipboard. "Mrs. Kochansky," she says, "I have been having a very nice chat with your son."

We do a little dance with the tea. I hand it to her. She moves
her clipboard, so the tea rattles in her hand. Paully gets scared the
tea is gonna spill; he starts to rock back and forth. So I try to take
the clipboard which she don't want. All right, I take back the tea,
but enough already! Finally I get the clipboard from her, but Jacob,
pulling three teeth would have been easier.

"So," I point her to the couch. "You always take notes when you
have 'nice chats'?"

She smiles as she settles in. You see? It's possible. But don't get too excited. It's only for a second. "No Ma'am," she says, so formal, "only when I am doing an assessment profile."

I got no idea what she means by this. I look at the paper; there's no drawing there. It's regular paper with words on it. Fancy words. I try to figure them out when she yanks the clipboard away.

"What's all that you're writing about my Paully?" I ask her direct.

"These cookies are nice," she finally gets around to saying. She got a voice like a little girl. I don't know. I don't trust. "What kind are they?" she asks me.

"Miss Daughter of Israel, you don't know a eir kichlah?" I'm wondering if maybe I got a Daughter of Israel impostor here. I know, I know. You think I got the TV on too much. But really what I figure is, she's just trying not to talk about those fancy words of hers. So I say again, "What's all that stuff you're writing there?"

"Mrs. Kochansky, as you are probably already aware, the Daughters of Israel connects needy individuals with a network of services..."

I tell her, "Very good. If I find any needy individuals I'll send them over by you." She looks at me like I don't get it. So I say, "Have you tried over by the Greyhound station?"

She clears her little throat. "We do have facilities for developmentally delayed adults..."

"Develop...?"

"Retarded," she says. I'm not lying here, Jacob. She talks like this. She brings this up out of the clear blue sky. Then she looks at me over her glasses to see if I understand English. "Now I've only talked to Paul a few minutes," she says. "You've probably had much fuller assessments from other health professionals."

"You mean doctors?" I say.

"Well, yes, and whomever else you might use."

"Oh Miss, what-did-you-say?"

"Steiner."

"Yes, Miss Steiner, I see now what you want and I think it's very nice of you to ask, but," and then I lean in close, Jacob, I do not announce this in front of the boy, who, by the way, is paying no attention anyhow, "there is no cure for Down's syndrome. That's the name for what Paully got. There is no cure."

So Paully, bless his heart, stands up all of a sudden and says "Va-coom now," and I think to tell him, "No, sit still, we have a guest," but then I figure, what the heck, maybe then she won't stay long. I nod. "He's such a good boy," I tell her.

"Housework too, huh? Just as I thought. Definitely TMH."

"No. I just told you." I look to see that Paully's busy. I lower my voice. "It's Down's syndrome."

"Yes, Mrs. Kochansky," she says, real know-it-all. "That's ev-ident." Then she looks past me down the hall. "Excuse me," she says, "would it be all right... I'd like to go watch Paul."

"He's just gonna run the sweeper," I say.

"Yes, I know," she says.

"You want to watch Paully with the sweeper?"

"Yes. If you don't mind." She's got her neck all stretched trying to see. This can't be comfortable. Also, I can't come up with a reason why not. I shrug. She heads down the hall to go be by Paully. He's in my bedroom, sweeping the way I taught him, back of the house to front. They can't be having much of a conversation with the noise. So, what kind of a conversation do you have with Paully anyway? I quick run a dishtowel over the TV stand. All that dust, it's not nice. I'm not so used to company in the house any more.

So then she comes back. Or at least someone who looks like her comes back. Something has changed about this girl, Jacob. She's all frown now. Before there was no smile, but there was no frown neither. Now there is definitely an expression, but it ain't a happy one. I don't know. Maybe she's got a tummy ache.

"Mrs. Kochansky," she says, very serious, all business, "if you wouldn't mind, I would like to speak to Paul's doctor."

So now maybe is the time I should start to suspect, but who sus-pects? "Paully got no doctor," I say. "I take him to my clinic for the flu shot, for this or that or whatever. Oh, and I took him to the dentist when he had more teeth."

She puts her hand on my arm, shakes her head and talks to me like I'm Paully.

"He'll need further professional assessment, of course, but Ida," she says—and I have no idea how we got so familiar, all this touching and such—"but Ida," she says, "your son seems to have completely normal neurotic functions," or some such blah-dee-blah.

I got no idea what she's talking. I ask her to slow down. So she does. She talks real slow.

"Do you remember before, when I used the expression TMH?" she says. "That's trainable—teachable. You understand? Even at Paul's age, there's hope for improvement."

I can tell—I can just tell—she's thinking that even at my age there's hope for improvement. And maybe she's right but that don't mean she should barge into my living room to let me know it.

Oh, and "MH," would you believe, means "mentally handicapped," which no wonder the mavens shorten. But then, you know, I got no idea; it's all just a bunch of words. What I do understand is when she says, "Of course, we'll start with a day program."

"My Paully?" I stand right up over her. Even sitting down she's almost as tall as me. I look her right in the eye.

"It will be no trouble or expense," she says. "We have a bus."

"What 'bus'?" I say. "What 'trouble'?"

I can tell she is losing her patience with me which is fine by me 'cause I don't got too much left for her neither.

"I got no 'trouble,' " I tell her, "no 'expense.' I live here with my son and we don't bother no one and we do for ourselves and we're happy. My son is happy right here with his mother, right where he's always been. You gonna come in here and say different?"

The whole time she's looking up, trying to interrupt, "Ida, Ida, Mrs. Kochansky." She can't make up her mind what to call me.

"Well who asked you, little Miss Maven of Israel? I don't call no one with no problem."

"Please, Mrs. Kochansky," she says, "there's no need for hostility."

I look up at her, good and long. "Convince me," I say.

She's got that little chin of hers tucked into her chest, like a puppy getting yelled at. And I am not yelling, Jacob, I swear. I know you would not want me to yell at a stranger in our house. But when it comes to our Paully, I watch out, eh?

"Look, Miss Steiner," I say, "you'll forgive me if about my son I sometimes get excited. But you know, my husband—my Jacob—he used to have a little saying: bad news is best at breakfast."

She sits looking at her lap. I move back next to her, she should know I'm not mad. "You don't understand this?" I say. "No? I'll explain. It means if you got bad news to tell someone you should do it early in the day so they got a chance to fix it before they lose a night's sleep over the thing, eh? What is this, four o'clock already? So, anyway, tomorrow then. You just tell me who and I'll go get it all fixed up—"

"Who? Mrs. Ko—?" Suddenly this little Steiner girl's teacup is rattling away. I take it from her and set it down. She should calm down already.

"Don't be sorry. It's not your fault." I think to tell her about that Stern family down the street. Remember, Jacob? They didn't want our Paully playing with their little boy. Some people, filth on their minds, is what they got. "So just tell me what house," I say. "I'll get Paully all fixed up, a tie, a belt. We'll go over; I'll introduce. I'll bring some mandlebrat, maybe a little apple strudel. Paully will make all nice with the kitty or something. That will be that. Neighbors, I think, should deal with neighbors. You don't call in the city people for this."

"You don't know who—"

"What? Someone thinks Paully's scary?" My voice is very even. I want she should calm down. "So Paully's not scary. They'll see. They—"

"Mrs. Kochansky," she says, "that's not it." She meets my eye, then looks away.

They want to take him, Jacob! I always knew they would try! I always knew! Well they won't get away with it! I will never let that happen. Never!

So Paully comes in with the vacuum and all I gotta do is look at him and he knows not now. He takes it out again. Maybe he's done something. No, no, he's been with me. I can't breathe! They want

Paully! They... Who they? What they?

I look at this little breath of fresh spring air that's suddenly blown into my living room and try to breathe, just to breathe. I have the strangest feeling looking at her, like I want to bite her. I think maybe I better not open my mouth. Who knows what a mother will do? What is there to do? *What* is there to do?

And then it comes back to me: "Ma, I've done something about Paully."

I had forgotten. What, with egg on my shoe; it's cooking on the stove where it spilled. Who can think? And then, this guest. It's not like every day I got a guest. So much going on, I didn't put it together.

My jaw begins to tremble. My shoulders. "Jody," I say. It is not a question. I know it's Jody.

The little mavenela, she's got nothing to say. She stands and looks down at me. I see her swallow hard.

Jody! Can't even wait 'til she's back. Uses a phone all the way in her California as far as she can get from her mama to send a trouble-maker to make trouble. Well thank you, but I'd rather have choco-lates, if you don't mind. I'd rather have poison. Jody. Jody, Jody, Jody.

I stare at this girl, this dry slip of a girl and because she is not my daughter, because someone else's daughter—Israel's daughter, of all things—is standing there in my living room, I find that I can not find my voice. And then I do. "JODY!" I cry, then "Get out! Out!" Paully shouts, "Mommy" and comes running. I grab up that little girl's clipboard and throw it out the door. Her papers float, some here, some there, in the bushes, in the gutter. And that little girl too, Jacob, out she flew.

Steiner As I retrieve my personal items from her bushes, my heels digging into her sloggy overwatered lawn, I asked myself why I let myself get talked into this... this... well if I had once thought farce, I must now revise. Intrigue. Intrigue is more apt.

What am I? I'm a social worker sent by her daughter! I have

questions to ask and information to offer. What is wrong with that?

I mutter as I wipe leaf goo off my clipboard. Hey, I'm not the one who's done something wrong here.

Why just consider what this mother has done! Chosen ignorance, failed even to notice the changing world. She stepped aside, ignored or refused. Deliberately resistant or hostile, or perhaps, proud, for whatever reason—this mother opted out. And in so doing, she deprived her son of *years* of social assimilation. He is now, in my professional opinion, so cripplingly socially retarded that, if he lost his mother now, I doubt he'd survive her.

So sad. So sad and unnecessary! For two decades—more than two decades—a system has existed. A system more civilizing than any library or park. One that I believe gives us, as Americans, something that, as we enter this last decade of our millennium, we sorely need: a source of pride.

Granted, the concept was born in Denmark, but we have embraced it with greater zeal and innovation than any people on earth. We have, in real terms, altered our physical world. Every street corner ramped, every public toilet since 1975. We have backed comprehensive social systems, from educational opportunities to transit conversions to medical and rehabilitation research to every building code changed—every one—even to opening the parklands; we have done it! We have created the most accessible society in the history of humankind. Travel the world, you won't disagree. We have a long way to go, yes, but we are going.

So when I meet with parents that have just received a negative result on the amnio and reassure them, I feel like the bearer of great gifts. I have so much hope to offer. Everybody likes me. They put me in the video.

I march back up the steps and lift my fist to knock. Something stops me. I have never seen anger like that. Fury! She could have burned me with those eyes. I could almost feel the heat rising off her.

Here lives, I think, lowering my hand, in a house all alone but for a very old woman, a man with few teeth and threadbare house slippers, a shirt so ancient it was impossible to make out what the pattern once was. I peeked in his room. I saw a lumpy chair next to an old TV with headphones attached and, by the bed, a record player like I haven't seen since grade school, attached to a second pair. A cell to keep him in, lock him up, put him away. After, that is, he has finished the housework. How many hours of each and every day must he hide there silent and alone?

"Don't you worry, Paul Kochansky," I say before that weathered door. "I have seen you. I'll get you out!"

—4—

Ida   Day Center, they call it now. You and I know better, eh my husband?

So many years ago now, I can hardly remember. Who got that doctor anyway? It was Mrs. Shilovitch wasn't it? Because she brings babies into the world, this makes her an expert. Some American doctor she calls, with the blonde hair, the blue eyes. What? She can't find no one from the neighborhood? For "problem" babies, she says. Words like that I need to hear, I'm still so tired, my baby one day old.

So this doctor I don't remember too much. I think I only saw him just that one time and that one time, it was enough. This I will say for him though, such a long examination he makes of Paully— thorough. I remember how he pressed the baby's little fingers into a fist and then smoothed them flat. Remember how smooth Paully's hands were? No lines like most babies. Like pink shells, Paully's hands.

I don't think I've ever seen a doctor do that much. He looks at Paully's tongue and in his ears and eyes and nose. He moves Paully's head this way, that way, every inch of his little arms and legs that doctor feels. All this he does in front of me, as I rest, still there in my bed, but he never talks to me, just like I'm not there. And me? A word could not have formed in my mouth. There was fear there, I'll tell you, and hope. And pride, too, I remember. Anyone could see what a pretty, pretty baby.

He finishes, puts his things away, closes his little bag, snap. Still he's got nothing to say. He calls my mama and gives Paully to her. I'm feeling like a little girl who wants the dolly from the high shelf, except maybe I'm a little more angry than a little girl knows how to be.

You come in and stand beside me. Remember how you were? To sit beside me on the bed with this stranger in the room, you would never do. You were a fine man, Jacob.

You stood beside me and we listened to that stranger in our home, so quiet and slow like he's speaking to children. "Your child is a Mongoloid, Mr. and Mrs. Kochansky. Do you know what this means?"

I don't know, but I know "Danger!" Oh Jacob, I'm thinking our baby will die! You take my hand and squeeze it. You nod, this doctor should go on.

"This child will be slower than other children," he says. 'This child'—like Paully's a thing.

"Mentally slower," he says. "His intelligence," he says, "will be sub-normal."

'Sub-normal.' This I will never forget.

You tell him to continue, to say all he has to say. Me, I would not have, but you always need to know everything there is. So on and on goes the doom-doctor, that barer of hope and good cheer. "Mongoloid children have problems," he says. "Many can't hear or learn to talk." On and on he goes about the heart, the lungs, infections. But when he says, "Some can never be taught to use a toilet," I hear your breath catch, like a little punch to the stomach. I am thinking, please, my Jacob, for me, now be strong.

"It is not possible," says this doctor, "to know what complications this boy has."

"Excuse me, doctor," I am shocked to hear my own voice say, "you can tell me what mother knows all her son's 'complications' when he is not even two days old?"

So to you, to you—me, I'm not even there—this doctor says, "Children like this are difficult to raise at home. There are places," he says, picking up his little bag, "with people who know what to do. These children are much better off there." And right then and there I know, doctor-schmoctor, this man is a fool.

But you? What excuse have you got? "Please, doctor, wait," you say, dropping my hand. "Tell me. Is it...We can have other children?"

"Oh, yes," he says, real quick, like he wishes he was the one to bring it up. "And with such a young couple, there is good reason to believe that the child will probably be normal. But please, Mr. Kochansky." He puts on his hat. "Next time, a real doctor, not just some neighborhood midwife." Like if he had been there, the baby would be different. *Feh!*

The two of you walk through the door to the front room and I hear him tell you what he thinks I can't hear. "It would be best for everybody concerned," he says in that American voice, "if you'd move your child into a facility as soon as possible. The mothers," he says, "sometimes get too attached. They can become irrational."

So, there. At least about one thing that doctor was right. What he did not know is that there are times when irrational is only the sane thing to be.

One week, two, I'm still tired, always tired, laying in the bed, running my finger up the belly of my baby and stopping on his little nose. I want you should see how cute, and I see you slip away, all the time in the other room, all the time in your paper. And when the baby would wake in the middle of the night, and there you would be, beside me, I would wonder, "When did he come to bed?" And in the morning? Out in such a hurry like suddenly the loading dock is the most fascinating place in the world.

But that's not where you were going so extra early, is it? You think I'm not going to find out? A wife finds out.

All right, so you wanted answers. It was hard for you, I know. So many questions. What will we be able to do for this boy? Will he talk? Feed himself? Can he be happy? And about me, am I strong enough? Will I have to carry this child in my arms?

I had no idea you had them too, so many questions, just like me, but also like me, no one to ask. But answers are important. Answers are a thing we cannot do without, like daily bread. Someone has to make them up, so for once, this one night, if you don't mind, I took my turn.

"At work," you tell me, "not one person has asked. A man's wife has a baby, people ask, eh? This is how it should be. But here it is like they know already."

I shrug. "Let them know," I say. "Whatever there is to know, let who ever wants to know, know it."

You shake your head. "Everyone is different to me. I hate what they don't say."

I stroke your thick hair. You were so young, Jacob. "Yes, not to say things," I whisper into your neck. "This hurts deep. I do know."

"At Mama's stand, and in the neighborhood... Yesterday they said, 'And what do you read about Mr. Roosevelt, Jacob?' but today, they don't even meet my eye."

When I am stronger I will take my baby to the market. I will show them how proud. But this I do not tell you. For once in my life, I don't interrupt. I am only so happy to have you beside me.

"Maybe, Ida," you say, "just maybe what that goyisheh doctor said was the right thing. What kind of baby is this? It should be with its own."

I drop my hand from your hair.

"And sometime," you turn toward me, your face so hopeful, so tired, "not so soon—later—when everyone has forgotten, then maybe we could have another... "

I wrap myself in my own arms. When did this room grow so cold?

"We could start over! We're young, Ida, and that doctor —"

That doctor! That doctor! I want to slap your moving mouth. You have not learned a thing! You and the goyisheh kop! Two fools I have to listen to! I watch you, or not you—I refuse to believe that it's you—I watch the crazy fool who is pretending to be my husband and I figure him all out. Hates to go to work, he says. Then where's he off to almost before dawn? Off listening to other fools, I'll bet. A wife finds out. You are saying something. I don't care. I stand up and look down at you. I see you now; I see what you are.

"Over my dead body." This I mean to yell, but I don't. My voice comes out like a hiss.

"These places," you say, "they got other babies like that." You take my hands. "See how this makes sense?"

I see you. I take my hands back. "Over—" I say.

"The baby with other kinds of babies like that?"

"my—" I say.

You look at me and I see the muscles in your throat swallow. Whatever you were going to say then, you do the right thing and swallow. I see you come back. It's like you were taking a little vacation from your body and then you came home. "No," you say. And then, "Ida. You're right." You pat the bed next to you, I should be your wife again.

I don't move. "Where do you go?"

You sigh and take the papers from your pocket, dirty papers, all folded and stuffed down in your shame. Two weeks you've been going. Long trips on the train when you are supposed to be working. Out to New Jersey, up to Connecticut, looking at the paradises the doom-doctor brings into our lives.

You tell me it's not that you want to send the baby far away.

"No?" I ask.

"No," you say. "Ida, I don't want this, so when I hear 'Staten Island,' I go straight away."

And then they tell you about other places and you have to go there too. Always you got to know everything. Got to have every fact.

Why didn't you throw them away? All those shiny booklets with those pictures of the smiling nurses on front? Rip them into pieces and throw them right in that fool-with-a-degree's face? You are too impressed by an education, Jacob. To me a fool is a fool. You hadn't done enough damage already? It is the morning and the morning again and we have a baby son! Yes, a living baby son who struggled into life.

"And Ida?" I can barely hear you; you are so busy looking down at your lap full of dirty papers. "That place. The smell! It smelled...ah...gray. Can a place smell gray? Like an old rag nobody washed."

I cannot think what to say. My baby in such a place?

"Ida, I saw their food." You look at me. There you are. I know that man. He is my husband. "I wouldn't give a dog," you say. "I never saw such...Ida, I sat on the steps, I cried and cried. I don't care who looked."

I put my hands on your shoulders. Cry now, my husband, I think. I will never tell.

"So I think, maybe out in the country. Fresh air! Maybe here, maybe there..."

"With his Mama," I say.

"Yes," you say. "Those places?" You wrap your arms around my middle. "Ida, all of them, the same." And then you do cry. Not like the first time, ashamed and silent, but deep from in you, and unafraid. Oh Jacob, why did you, how could you, wait so long? I sit on your lap, right on those terrible papers you brought into my bedroom and we rock together a very long time. You cry and I cry until there is nothing left in us. Until we are like one, no skin to make us separate.

I wish for Paully, that I can have him back from your mother and hold him there too and show you how sweet and how special and really, if you just look, how perfect. In his own way, in our own way. Perfect enough. I feel that he must be hungry. I need to go get him. I do not speak, but when I move your arms fall away. You know. I straighten my skirt, my apron, my hair and step to the door.

"Ida, wait," you say, and I do. I am happy. Can you know how happy? You are back and once again I know the contents of your heart, but this one time Jacob, I wish you could have waited to say. "Ida." You come to me, stroke my cheek. "Soon maybe," you say, "we can have another child."

And I see that the one I made will never be good enough.

Steiner   After panning my little debut and informing me that I was no longer trusted with any information that she did not want to share with her mother, and that there was a great deal that matched that description, she takes a breath.

"Now tell me," she says, "how long until he'll be ready to move? I kinda pictured him at ah..." and then she lists the two most desirable assisted care residences in the entire metro area.

Now it's my turn to hyperventilate. What hat does she expect me to pull that out of?

"Where did you get those names, Miss Kochansky?" I ask, but I already know.

"Yellow Pages," she says, proving me right. "I could tell by talking to them that they were the best."

"Look Miss Kochansky, the waiting lists on those residences are so long they don't even take new names. Why, even the day center programs have become choosy. They tend to choose people they already know, the people already in their system."

"They promote internal."

"You might say that."

"Yeah, I hear that."

"The programs—the good ones anyway—they're limited, way short of demand."

"It's a seller's market out there."

"Exactly. They insist on intake assessments."

"Paully has to pass tests?"

"More like doctors. Physical therapists, occupational, recreational, cognitive, speech—"

"All those?"

"Mandatory."

"Mandatory?"

"They need to know what he can do. What might be dangerous, what beneficial."

"Well, why can't I tell them?"

"These people are professionals, Miss—"

"I see."

"The Director has laws to comply with. It's not her choice."

She says, "Yeah, yeah."

"And I'm going to need your mother's signature, Miss Kochansky."

"How about mine?"

"Legal guardian."

There is dead air. Then, to my amazement, laughter!

"Oh, is that all?" she says.

"Well actually...Miss Kochansky, may I ask, has your brother ever taken a bus?"

"Oh, probably not in ten years. Probably never alone."

"Well you see, these appointments are scattered all over Manhattan."

When she does not respond I say, "What I'm telling you is, it doesn't stop with the signature. I'm going to need her cooperation."

More dead air. Then she says, "Remember, whatever you do, don't say 'group home.' "

–5–

Ida   Two days later it's "You-hoo?" Can you believe it? A glutton, that maven, she can't get enough. I look through the peep-hole, she's standing there with this glued on smile, holding up all these different colored pamphlets arranged in her hand like a Chinese fan. I put the chain on the door and open it. It's open enough.

"I brought you something," the maven says. "May I come in?"

"No need," I say. "You won't be staying long." You should have seen her, Jacob, like a kite when the wind stops blowing. Her little pamphlets got all droopy. She's not so good at smiling anyway. It looks all fakey on her. So she makes a big sigh. I tell you what this girl don't got in strength she makes up for in pathetic. You got to feel sorry. "Tell me, Miss Daughter of Israel," I say, "they don't teach you to call first?"

"I thought you'd tell me not to come," she says.

"So what then, you'd rather I told you in person?" I mean what does she expect me to say? We didn't exactly part on the friendliest terms.

"Look, Mrs. Kochansky," she says, not quite so pathetic anymore, like maybe I'm getting to her some, "I don't like to work this way either."

I can't see her eyes behind her sunglasses. Why do the young people think you can make a conversation this way? "Take off your glasses, young lady," I say.

She does and puts on her regular ones and looks hard at me, setting her little jaw. I can see that she looks very determined. She also looks a little scared. I close the door and take the chain off. I step outside onto the porch.

I point at those pamphlets of hers and say, "Put those away." She's does what she's told, puts them in her purse. "Very good then," I say, "Now you can shake hands."

I put my hand out and she takes it, not so firm but then I don't grip like a man either. "Young lady," I tell her, "I owe you an apology."

"Oh, Mrs. Kochansky—" she says, all polite.

"No, no I do." I give back her hand. "I owe you an apology. My Jacob," I tell her, "my husband, who has died and left me now, he had a way with words. One thing he used to say that I liked was that bad news makes boil what already simmers. You understand this? This anger I shouldn't have shown to a stranger, it was not about you."

"It was about your daughter?"

"That's right," I tell her. "About my daughter—who by the way, suddenly don't remember the phone number she grew up with—I already got going a low simmer. You understand?"

"Yes," she says. "Yes, I think so."

"So you'll forgive me if I get a little excited."

"Yes, oh yes," she says like one big sigh and this little flicker tries to make itself happen on Miss Sunshine's face. Well, she tried anyway.

"Very good then. It has been nice to make your acquaintance," I say. So all right, this is a lie, but it is a polite thing. I open the door, to go in.

"Please Mrs. Kochansky, can't we talk?"

"What? We got something more to say?"

"Mrs. Kochansky, Ida." Oh, she's sweet like sugar now, and talking fast like she don't know how long I'm planning to listen. "I bet you could never get a babysitter."

"I had my Jody when she was old enough."

"And you've probably never had a vacation."

Jacob, you know this is true. Every year I gotta listen to Lila go on with the cruise to here and the week at Miami Beach, and always I wonder, what would this be like?

She says, "Mrs. Kochansky, you've been a mother such a very long time now."

I look at this little girl carefully. What can she know about this?

Steiner   Was Jody right? Was I missing something essential? Was there something I could never know?

On the other hand, does the oncologist actually have to have cancer to know how to treat? Isn't knowledge enough? Isn't desire?

When I'd first started at the Daughters of Israel, I'd go home every day, *every* day, feeling energized, feeling as if I have done some good. And that, above all, is why I have chosen this profession. All I've ever really wanted was just to be doing some good.

All right, it's weird, I know, this thing I have about "Good, Good, Good." If there's anything I've learned in my almost quarter century of life, it's that the Good thing is weird. You are never trusted, never believed. The kids at school think you're smooching up; the teachers can't figure your angle.

There was a time when I was innocent enough to believe that education could light the way. I even said words like "light the way." That and, "All effort is glad when aimed at noble purpose." Right there in my essay for Brandeis. I noticed the guidance counselor had highlighted it green. She seemed charmed. Apparently, once again, I was "cute."

Still, I had hoped that in college...

Ah youth, it is a clean canvas for the palettes of others. But if they could not leave me my pure shining white, why did every touch stain such an opaque gray?

The counselor had once been a hippie, that much was clear. She'd probably hurled rocks through some storefront and claimed it had meaning. At least she didn't go the greed-head route and start a vitamin pyramid scheme like most of her yuppie peers. No, she'd gone academic feminist and pushed med-school like bennies because I am just competent enough in the sciences to barely scrape by. She'd preach that "We need more women in this field," never indicating who "we" were and never once listening when I said, "I'm afraid that's just not me."

Still, I took a year of the program and learned in Bio 101 about the Peppered Moths, *Biston belularis.*

In 1848 these delicate white creatures, for some mysterious reason, migrated from the mythical Sherwood Forest of England to Manchester. In that smoke-filthy town these resilient beings of nature performed their famous evolutionary adaptation. They developed wings of soot, or so it appeared, and thus survived the appetites of predator birds.

I declared a major in philosophy and never went back.

Mom coaxed law school like the good-for-me vegetables of childhood because she saw herself as missing out on a political career. Politics, uch, what a gross smelly bog. Dad chanted "MBA"; he'd buy me a seat on the exchange. Another pit—this one filled with gladiators. The philosophy counselor could only posit grad school. Academe: politics more mired than politics itself. Grandma wanted marriage and many many babies. My boyfriend dreamed of a gallery to take sixty percent off the top from his painters. Me, I wanted only to break into a sweatless sprint and find meadows and clean beaches and the food not poisoned and people not afraid.

There was nothing. Nothing to believe in. Nothing to be good at. I was born Jewish, the convent was out.

And then I met Molly Semple. She cleaned the locker room at the Women's Gym. She mopped the showers on her hands and knees and buffed the spigots until they shone. She emptied the garbage bags and put out more toilet paper. She actually sang while she did her work, "You are my sunshine, my only sunshine."

Molly had been loved, had been to school and taught to clean. Molly lived in a house near the campus with four others plus a social worker. They cooked supper in the evenings, played Go Fish, sang songs. She had a boyfriend, she bragged, who often brought her flowers. And when I said that's more than mine did, she laughed with a beautiful grin. That night I dreamed of her, and the next night too. Molly Semple, it seemed, was something of a miracle.

Though soon enough, I learned, that was just not so. Molly was increasingly common, more the norm than not. Everywhere people like her were astonishing the rest of us with how much they could do, and with what pride and excellence, teaching by example joyous lessons in human potential. And even this was not a miracle. It was just that the rest of us had underestimated them all along, because they look a little different and take some extra patience All that is needed is a few people to help them achieve. A few people like me. A win-win situation. A type of perfection. Molly, you are my sunshine.

Columbia has a program. I enrolled for the fall.

Ida   "Every day," she says. "Every day a mother to a man who's always a child."

I do not like her saying this. I have thought it myself, and you too, my darling, have held me while I said this very thing, but it is for me to say. Still, it catches my interest. I shut the door and lean against it.

"Your daughter loves you and her brother, Mrs. Kochansky," she says. "Jody told me so."

"Jody who?" I say.

"Jody told me she wants you to play mahjongg in the afternoon with the other ladies." So I should cry at such words so dear to a mother, but then that mahjongg crack. What now? Suddenly I'm supposed to sit around with those women with the blue hair and listen to them gossip. Like a bunch of little girls in school with the gossip, gossip. This is what Jody thinks I got to do with my life?

"So who I got to play mahjongg with?" I ask.

"At the DOI Senior Center we have mahjongg every Wednesday—big money prize," she says. "You could walk home with twenty-five dollars in your pocket."

"Twenty-five?" I'm thinking, hey, twenty-five?

Suddenly she got a big grin. A smart aleck this one. Ah, forget about her, already. I pull open the door again. Inside I can see Paully; he's rocking in his chair, he's got his hand down there in his lap again, you know what I mean. I don't want this Steiner person should see this, but she's trying to look around me to watch him too. I step inside and shut the door part way. She's talking to me; she can look at me. Mahjongg. The smart aleck. "No," I say. "My son will miss me."

"Yes."

"He needs his mother."

"Of course."

So finally this Steiner person speaks a word of sense.

"Very good then, you understand. I don't like Paully with no strangers. All his life he's been with me."

"Yes!" She steps back, squintings. "I couldn't have stated the problem more succinctly, Mrs. Kochansky." And before I can think what she might be talking about she stands right up on the step with me, right there. So she's taller than me now and she can see over. "Paul," she calls out—like she don't got the idea yet that his name is Paully, I haven't said it a million times yet—and I'm saying "Hey!" and this pushy little thing is standing above me saying, "Will you come here a minute, dear?"

Dear. Dear!

So our Paully, like the good gentleman you taught him to be, he comes right over. He's bobbing behind me, he wants to see better. What there is to see, I don't know. But I'm beginning to feel a little like the pastrami between the rye, eh? Right here in my own doorway. "Please, Mrs. Kochansky," she says down at me. "Please just let me talk to him a moment." And before I can say anything, she says, "You want to talk to me, don't you Paul?"

So of course he does. You ever see Paully turn down attention? I myself cannot remember such a time. He starts calling out, "Meee! Meee! Yeah! Yeah!" What can I do? I give up. I step aside.

"Paul," she says.

"Paully," I say. "Your ears give you trouble?"

"Tell me, Paully," she says, real low. "Do you know that you are different from other people?"

Well I go right up and try to shut her mouth, but this don't help. She—and you won't believe this now, Jacob—she walks over to Paully, and she touches him. Grab-grabby night and day, this one.

The poor baby, he don't know what to do. He says, "Sing. Sing. The record player," like he does.

"Leave him alone," I say. I take her hand off his arm. I still don't know who gave her permission.

She just talks over me. "Paully. Do you know what I am saying?"

He just stood there, Jacob, looking at his slippers. Such shame he felt that day. I wave my arms around. What should I do? I can't stop this woman. "Yeah," he says, real quiet. Then a few times more, "Yeah, yeah." He don't look up.

"It's okay, Paully." She's got that sugar-voice again. "I like people like you."

"Enough," I say. "Enough, enough."

"Just watch a moment, Mrs. Kochansky. Let me talk to your son." Then she pushes me into the easy chair. I mean this, Jacob. It does not matter that it was gentle. Gentle-schmentle, she pushed me. She keeps talking, real sugary, to our son. "I know a place," she tells him, "where there are a lot of people like you and they all do things together. Would you like to go there?"

Paully's so upset he's rocking back and forth, like you used to call dovaning. Then she looks at me and says real fast, the clock is ticking or something, "It's like a school. He'll love it."

"No," I say.

Paully's jumping up and down, clapping his hands, laughing. He would not listen when I told him to stop.

"Think of the day center as a babysitting service," she says to me, and then to Paully, "You want to try, don't you?"

So help me, Jacob, our Paully, he could not even stay on the ground.

book two

❖❖❖❖❖

arise,

–6–

Jody How I see it is, there are only two ways to get in. You can make an entrance down the grand sweeping staircase, open your arms out like you're inviting the court to dance, and flow in, perfect, graceful, cutting the water cleanly, skimming the surface.

That's one way. The other is to bend your knees, shoot your arms up over your head, take a big deep breath, and plunge.

Oh yeah, sure, we've all seen the other ways, the toe-tryers, the waist-deep-shoulder-splashers, the seated dive—up for air in two seconds like a beach ball. But if you don't mind a bit of strong opinion on the subject, I would say that folks who get in this way are not real swimmers. They don't seem to have a real sense, you know, of what the water can do. What it's best for. How to use it.

First off, water holds you up. It responds to your motions in smooth gentle ripples or white foamy bubbles. It makes you shiny and sleek and like a light flexible thing. Imagine—me—moving easy as a little seal, floating, spinning onto my back and over again. Get me—I'm Esther Williams.

All right, maybe I am going a bit, ah, overboard here. But this is nothing compared to how I was.

For the first couple of weeks, to tell the truth, it was mostly a bother. I was one of those people—like a really lot of my neighbors are, if you get right down to it—who kind of like the idea of the pool more than anything else. I liked to think of how I'd look in it, flowing from my waist like a smooth blue skirt. I was the wet-to-the-waist-shoulder-splasher variety of non-swimmer. For one thing, I wanted to get in there before anyone should happen to glance out their back window and get a peek at my thighs. This is because I am a good citizen and I don't want to cause widespread panic.

And then there was the nightly "should I let my hair get wet?" issue and, Jeesh, so much to buy. I tried every plus size suit Sportswear had before I settled on one I hated. Add a little cover-up, plugs for the ears, goggles for the eyes, waterproof sunscreen with PABA at ten bucks for three ounces, a bathing cap, thongs, special shampoo to deal with the chlorine, and whatever else they can convince you to pay for, and you've dropped a bundle before you even get your feet wet.

But you know, looking back, this part was good. If I had waited– like say, until I had a paycheck—I may never have done anything but look at that pool.

Besides, the pool gave me a reason to get out the door and not spend all night locked in Macy's sorting out old receipts. All right, I admit this might not have been a half-bad idea considering, but I didn't want the boss people taking me for a sucker. I mean, this job! There was no end to it!

That first day, when Sharon took me to my office, I thought maybe it was a closet until I saw the desk and computer against the wall. Then I thought maybe they aren't through cleaning in there or something. But when Sharon left and closed the door behind her, then I knew. This is my mess.

Everywhere there are piles of papers, every surface. There are even piles on the floor between pieces of furniture. There's a pile under the phone. For the first week or so, I try to pick up a pile to see what's in it but I have no place to set it down that doesn't have another pile, and if I get interrupted—like say, to sneeze, because the place is so dusty I get a headache just being in there for a solid hour—all I will have done is make a bigger pile.

I only got three and a half months to the Christmas sale. The last woman on the job, she got the orders in, but I've got no idea what they are. I can't order signs, allocate space, nothing. Plus I got spring orders to get in. I ignore the whole mess, pull my chair up to my computer to turn it on. It's not even set up.

Ten times a day, I'd pick up the phone. I was gonna call old Mr. Parker up in Brooklyn and grovel. But then, then I'd get to thinking, that big tub of turquoise, empty and all my own.

The problem is by the time I get home and get my skin all pro- tected, my hair all protected—no horrible danger can come to me— and splash around a little bit, well, it's getting kind of late on the coast. And if I call earlier, like when I've just waited half an hour to stand on a bus and trudge home eight blocks of parking lot after parking lot, well, I get tripped up. And Ma, I tell you, she's got a knack—just a sense—for catching me in a lie.

See, according to my little story, I'm supposed to be in a temporary corporate place, right? But then I slip up and mention I'm making tea in my favorite pot or that I got a photograph of her in the house or that I can tell her what we deducted for Paully's dental on last year's tax return and she's so sharp, Ma, never misses nothing. She always says, "What? You got your pot with you?" and I have to quick make something up like, "No, I bought a new pot and I like it even better," at which point she reminds me that I should be saving my money for the future, like the price of a tea pot is going to have anything at all to do with the price of the future.

But I'm glad she does this, because it gives me an idea. What I start to do, instead of calling Ma when she likes to be called—after *Wheel of Fortune*—I do it on my lunch hour with the excuse that I can use the Watts line for free.

Ida Where is Jody? She should be here. She should be making one of her fancy teas, and we should play some gin rummy and watch the late news. Jody. She sends this, this...pestilence, this plague upon her mother's house, does it while she's in California so I can't yell at her right. She's so busy with her big deal training but she's got time for this mishegas?

Monday morning, six times, eight, I don't know maybe more, I stand over that phone, I say "Ring!"

So the phone, of course, it just sits there. Then I remember. First I got to wait, the sun should come up on the other side of the country. Even for a girl who don't know when to wake up, I gotta admit, it's still a little early there.

I get Paully out of bed, give him his oatmeal, shave him, clean what he got left in his mouth. No call.

I grab up that phone. I put her number by it in pencil so when she comes back to New York I can erase it. I can't make the numbers go around fast enough.

There is a voice on the other end like a girl in a barrel, some voice like the check out they got at the A&P. I'm supposed to push "one" to do something or "two" for another. But I got nothing to push. What I got's a dial. So I wait and I wait. I hang up, fold my arms on the table and rest my head. I don't even know how to use a phone anymore, Jacob.

I sit Paully down and get him started grinding almonds in the mortar. This is hard for me now since my shoulder got the arthritis, so Paully is a help, but if you don't mind, I would still rather put him in his room and have a little chat with the delinquent.

I give Paully his chicken soup and almond brat. I put him out to go pull weeds in the yard, he should go make the neighbors nervous.

It's three by the time she calls. Three! So excuse me, I mention it.

"Now look, Ma," she says, "I don't make time zones."

This might be smart aleck if it wasn't so mumbled up. "What are you doing?" I say. "Are you eating? What are you eating?"

"My lunch," she says with her mouth full, which besides being not so polite, tells me she is eating something not so good for her or she would say.

"What? What are you eating?" She don't answer. Like you used to say, Jacob: Guilt is a silent thing. "I hope you're not eating that greasy fattening pizza," I say, "it's only good to make indigestion."

I can hear the line make pops and hiss. For a call all the way from California, I think, we got too much time not talking. I guess, maybe, Jody got the same thought.

"All right then," she says, "let's get to it." This is what she must sound like when she talks to her girdle salesmen.

"Get to what?" I say.

"Come on, Ma," she mumbles at me. "You had another visit from Deborah Steiner."

"This you call 'a visit'? An attack! That I remember. Like a little bug, that one, like a skinny little mosquito buzz-buzzing around, flapping her little papers. A mosquito with no sense of humor."

"She's skinny, huh?" Jody says.

"Yeah, well she stopped by to suck my blood, but I sent her back to her nest. So now I am thinking, if I don't scratch, tomorrow there won't be no more itch—"

"Ma—" Always interrupting me, Jody. No sense of timing.

"What? Did you find her in your Yellow Pages under 'trouble-maker'?"

"Ma, no," she says. "Don't be like that. She already told me she asked Paully and that he wants to go to this... ah, school place."

School! *Feh!* Such words they make up! And who they got at this school? Teachers? They got teachers with chalk and letter cards? They got spelling bees? Keepers! That's what they got at those, those... gray... places.

"Paully?" I say, "Paully wants the lady should be nice to him. That's all Paully wants."

"That's not the way she tells it, Ma. She says you're the one that's not sure."

"So if you got all the answers already, what are you calling me for? Let Deborah Steiner listen to you eat unhealthy food."

"Well guess what she did? She made a special arrangement for you to visit! How's that? Special for you! If you like it you can agree to let Paully attend on trial. On *trial*, Ma."

Jacob, you at least took a day off work. Jody cannot know what these places are.

"Paully wants to, Ma."

"Paully got no idea what he wants. We don't mention again. He forgets."

"Ma, they're pulling strings for you over there."

"So? Who asked them to?"

"Well..." she says, "I did."

"And who asked you?"

"Oh, Ma." She mumbles. It's not bad enough, she's going to eat garbage, but now she's not even going to chew?

So I figure, for the sake of mine only daughter's health, I'd better do the talking. "Look Jody, Paully ain't never been without his mama. You know what will happen there? He'll let out such a screech; they'll send him right home—"

"That's the thing! You're gonna go too! At least to get him started." Then she says, "Ma, hey, it will be an adventure. Like when we'd all go to that place in Staten Island for your extracts and stuff—"

"Save your sales talk for underwear," I say, but what I'm thinking is how every time we went to Staten Island I got worried sick for Paully, someone from that place there would see him and want to take him away. So much I can't tell our Jody.

"Ma, they're gonna pick you up and take you and show you around and treat you nice. You can ask all the questions you want. What's it gonna hurt, Ma? A day away from the house. One day. Just one. Come on, Ma, I got all these busy people to do things for you. You don't go, I'll look silly. Please, Ma."

She goes on, pushing, pushing. I set my feet solid on the floor and take in a big breath. And just when I am about to open my mouth and say, "No! No 'school' at all," she says—real different sound in her voice now—"Ma, please. As a favor to me. Ma, when do I ever ask?"

So you know that sound, Jacob. That whining, begging, please-Ma-please thing that Jody does. Nobody can want something like our Jody.

And, what she says is true. She don't ask much. She don't. All the way from California she writes out the checks and calls the boy to mow the lawn and sends someone to spray for bugs and someone else to inspect the roof. I should tell her why I do not want this. But I cannot. I cannot tell her and still be a good wife to you. You see, even now I keep your secrets. But, all right, I admit, even if this were not so, still, this thing I do not want.

I close my eyes and hold the phone in my arms for a second like the sweet baby she once was. I let out all my big strong breath.

"All right," I tell her. "All right, Jody. One day."

Steiner   At graduation, I'd felt I had a choice. Academe? Policy? But no, I had wanted to do real work. And what has that work been? I take the results from the specialists and match them with the criterion on the placements. That's my job. That's all it is. Rules and red tape. Programs, not people. And forms! Federal, state, city, Internal Revenue, Department of Labor, Department of Education, Social Security, medical. It's not like I can walk around the neighborhood and see work which needs to be done and tap the proprietor and say, "I know someone who can do that for you."

And even if I could, somehow, manufacture a job that Paul

Kochansky could do for more than a full year, just for the right to add his name to a ten year long waiting list for a new group home, what would this home be like? The city has a policy that says to keep our funding, we have to bid first for the cheapest lots in the city. The last two residences available to us were in Harlem and Alphabet City. That's across the bridge and in neighborhoods most of our families have never been and may be afraid to go. And the truth is, sometimes our residents do get preyed upon. Oh, the things they don't teach at Columbia.

There are options, of course. One: they could throw money at it. Go expensive and private. My guess though, is that the Kochansky's have not got a secret fortune. Even moving the mother out and selling, they couldn't keep that up very long.

Option two: Miss Kochansky could sue her mother for legal guardianship. Sue. Her mother. Next.

I could petition the state to sue. No less slow, arduous, costly, or traumatic for everyone involved. Assuming a DA would make a case, which is really a lot to assume.

Or, four: survival of the fittest. Cheat to win.

My colleagues look around when they talk about this, lower their tones—but they all do talk. Everyone knows of a case like this. It can be a good option some justify, expedient if nothing else. Others just lay out the truth. Option four: abandon Paul in an emergency room.

The abandoned person, my good colleagues explain, becomes a ward of the state which is then bound by law to house their charge within 48 hours, to find him or her a bed and three meals. It is in everybody's interest to do this once and for all. And so, as these individuals are moved to the front of the line at state institutions, the waiting list for those who do not abandon their family members grows longer.

Occasionally there has been some talk of prosecution for this, but upon investigation, the sad case is generally dropped. After all, what outcome would the state change? My colleagues caution me not to go on record recommending it.

Paul Kochansky abandoned in an emergency room! Frightened, grieving, dropped as if from the sky into a pleasant institutional room, to rock away the rest of his days. To "grunt and gibber" as Robert Kennedy said—as he said more than twenty -five years ago now. Is this the best we can offer? Is no one else appalled?

Today's frontline is a different place. Our battles are waged for higher ground: independence, assimilation, individuality. Today we aim to enable—just to enable—allowing the individual to do as much as possible for his or her self.

You see, challenges and differences, they cluster in patterns that are identifiable, or, they do not. They conflate in infinite variety. Limbs that can't be used, tongues, internal organs, memories, enzymes. Their causes are known, or, they are not. Classification is beside the point.

After all, many brilliant and successful men and women are utterly unable to self-feed and groom. Others create soul-stirring music though lacking the ability to acknowledge another person in the room. They require one sort of assistance. Someone without the ability to cross the street for whatever reason, another. Many individuals require only a sense of community and an acceptance of difference.

My job then, to determine what the person needs in order to be self-sufficient and then, make that possible.

In a typical case, intervention is undertaken as early as possible. Speech and physical therapy are especially important in infancy. Next, education through the age of sixteen is a right protected by the state. School evolves by degrees into training programs. Participants begin in small groups, which lead, when possible, to larger ones.

I am happy to say, I think Paul could manage this. From his sister I've learned he can do a great many things. He can feed himself, dress, toilet. He once needed vigilant reminding about his teeth, but they have since all decayed away. I hope to take him to one of our dentists soon.

So, in time, I expect, I will be able to find Paul some sort of job. If I can do this, then it is possible, at least possible, that in some years, I might be able to find him a group home. I see it as his only chance.

The good news is he already does most every kind of housework: laundry, cooking preparation, some yard keeping. I suggest to the sister that we might try dishes.

"Oh yeah," she says, "I tell you, he's a nut for dishes. Sings like Pavarotti. You should see—"

"Sing—?" I say.

"Oh yeah, all the time. He shakes his head while he's doing it. It's like his big routine."

Dishes is a big loss. I think I can find lots of placements if he can really do them. "It's not cute, Miss Kochansky," I say. "It's a problem."

"Yeah," she says, "I know it." Then she says, "But yes it is so cute." Then, quieter, "And Miss Steiner? Also—I think I should tell you—he, uh…he touches himself."

"Ah," I say. I put down my pen. "A lot?"

"A lot," says the sister.

Vocational skills, moot.

"The good news," I say, after some time, "is that he'll grow out of that in a group, Miss Kochansky."

"You think? I mean we've tried everything. We've never gotten nowhere with it.

"It begins with peers, Miss Kochansky. It begins with peers."

–7–

Jody It was too good to be true. I always knew it. I knew I couldn't have it all to myself. One day there's this kid. She's already in, kicking up a foam, chopping the water into big waves.

I'm annoyed. I've had a hard day. The figures came back for the "big" mall-wide back-to-school sale. The big sale with the little itty-bitty figures. I mean, what was I supposed to do with back-to-school in Foundations? I put sports bras on sale and kept my fingers crossed. I tell you, it's the worst kind of failure when figures sag in Foundations!

I wish Sharon Moore had thought that line was funny.

So it's gonna take more than some strange kid to stop me. I throw off my little cover-up real quick, slide off the side, and begin splashing. Not that it makes a difference; the kid is getting water all over.

My usual thing back then was to walk to the deep end and swish my arms. I'd hold onto the side and kick and kick. See, then I was just learning to love the pool, the way it smells, the way it makes a steady little gurgle by the drains at the sides, the way it slows everything down, hushes everything up. I still didn't really understand what a pool could do. And I didn't want to get my hair wet.

Which, considering the spray the kid is putting up, is not really a choice. I think to myself—like in those old Westerns: "This pool ain't big enough for you and me both, kid." I think I ought to quick-draw a water pistol! I can't find a spot where she's not. I can't enjoy myself. I don't want to get out—too cold—but I don't want to stay in, and then, hey, she was there first. I have to let her do what she wants. So I wind up just cowering in a corner, hoping her ma will call her in soon.

She's a good swimmer, not a great swimmer, but then, what is she? Eight? You should see how many times she goes back and forth, back and forth. And at the edge? Fuh-lip! Like a little dolphin.

I tell you, I forget to be annoyed. What exactly is it that she's doing? I mean, sure, I've seen people swim, the Olympics and all. But standing arms length from someone who's really doing it? It's been since childhood.

There's a lot. All at once. Feet and arms, same time, that's the first thing. Then the head this way and that. And somehow her back keeps coming up out of the water. She sure has the energy though.

I'm still there, in the corner, as the sun begins to set. My arms go goose-bumpy in the wind when the kid pops out. Just like that, lickety-split, runs off, no towel, no looking back. She leaves a little trail of water behind her, like a snail. At last I have the pool to myself.

I let the water calm. I walk to the center of the shallow end, make a big sigh, a big, "now let's begin" sigh, face the other edge, nod at it once, like I'm accepting a dance with a stranger, and slowly do my best queenly arm opening. I flow in. I am wonderful. And then

I... well, then I do something. I don't exactly know what to call that klutzy thing I do next. I chop and huff and try to keep my hair dry. By the time I get to that other end, my head is pounding like a pile driver and I'm gulping air, coughing, my eyes stinging. I'm scared. I mean that truly; I think maybe I'll have an attack or something. I feel foolish. I feel ashamed. I take the stairs out of the water. When I think I could have had Shoes.

Danny   Dear reader, arise. Stand, if you have them, on your own two strong legs, and if not, then in your imagination, please, follow on this journey.

Walk with me, reader—your eyes need not lift from this page— and carry me to that small room with its porcelain throne and founts of water, that room planned for the sake of good singing, and rest before its door. Press it open, go ahead. There! Congratulations! You have—unencumbered—arrived, at the solid space of normal.

Now enter, oh please do, and find what you have fastened. I know you need not look there. You have done this all your life. Zip and wiggle, stretch and pull, lift and gather, or unbutton, what ever once was done, dear reader, now undo.

And if you sit, be seated. And if you stand, take your place. Now, free your waters. Release. Abandon. Listen to the sound of you at your most human, your roar giving to tintinnabulum, lovely in the round resounding. Now imagine too, all the others, some reading this, most not. Peers of pee-ers across your street, your town, even your whole nation, joining the grand chorus of waters which free and proudly fall: the spouts of Versailles, Tivoli, Buckingham, Niagara, and you.

Stay awhile. Linger. Be comfortable. Be thankful for your ease. Your body is a marvel of design.

And now, gentle reader, understand, as I tell of a young boy's journey.

While prone in the breathless afternoon room, the caw sounds of boys at stoopball rude through the window—boys whom a lifetime ago—six months—shouted "Run" in my ear and set my feet flying— I held it and held it until I thought I would burst. I vowed no more water, nor drink of any type, but still it came pressing, demanding release. Then weak beyond suffering I would aim myself at the too shallow bed pan and hope that, this time, no spill or hand shaking would ruin the newly changed sheets. How I hated my mother as she took it away, like a sycophant, that low and unworthy. How she pretended she did not smell what anyone could smell as, twice daily, my father held me and she smoothed the fresh sheets.

Books they gave me! Sweets! A radio too! Teachers they begged shamelessly to come. How could they think I could think about these things, when fury pumped through me brighter than blood? No, just one thought possessed my whole being: me, throned like a ruler, the door soundly shut.

And when I could stand not one more page of even the most adventurous book, when I thought I would bite the next teacher who questioned, I railed for my father to bring crutches at once. I battled for mastery, stumbling, crashing, helplessly heaped. I might cry or clam up or curse my own fate, yet somehow, despite this, again I stood, and my arms became legs.

My parents, those dreamers, they woke for a moment, and let go the teachers who had let go themselves. They understood that anything gained was much more than nothing and lent me their arms, their wisdom and faith. They understood that I was afraid. They were as well.

At last the day came when I faced the short hallway, throw rug cleared, my way swept smooth. Pointed like a sprinter, my eyes fixed on the white sink through the wide-open door. Tha-dump, I thrust forward, and slid very slowly, tha-dump, once again, my parent's smiles stretched broad. Tha-dump and tha-dump and soon I was halfway, and on I went, sweating, arms burning, enthralled.

Tears came when I realized I no longer felt the smooth coldness of white tiled floor, but I bit back those tears as I faced me in the mirror. A nine-year old boy standing willful and tall. Ah, the sound of my urine as it fell on the water. Uproarious! Deafening! The unmistakable sound of a stout normal boy.

What I learned to do, dear reader, you might not call walking. It does not involve placing one foot before next, nor shifting the weight. It is a creep then a skitter, a skip, swing and landing, syncopated, inconsistent, it takes forever and some. I am certain from the strained expressions of others that it must be quite painful to watch.

It is, beyond a doubt, my glory.

Jody   It's called a "crawl," a baby thing.

All morning at work, I'm thinking: a kid can do this; I should be able to do this.

I'm thinking: Shelley Winters in *The Poseidon Adventure*, it's not like she was Twiggy or something.

I'm thinking: it's not calculus or chemistry or something hard, it's just getting to the other side of the pool without needing an oxygen pump.

And then I think: stop it Jody Kochansky, you're a grown up now. It's too late for you.

I do my work.

So we get the afternoon shipment, right? I got one box that's nothing but lace and torn silk. I'm looking at sweat shop floor sweepings. Now this shipment, it's stamped paid fifty-percent in advance but it has no papers from their end. But what really gets me is that I will never find the address of those crooks in that cramped, crazy office.

I pick up a teddy, the tear sort of skates away, very smooth. And what do I think? I think: this is what the perfect stroke through calm water is like.

I mean, there it is again. I can't push the thought down.

I'm staring at this beautiful stuff, flimsy and light, and do I think, "Oh! I know where I saw those papers!"? No. I think: this must be the most elegant, lovely thing a body can do.

I think: I'm not stupid. I can learn.

Then I think: what you'd better learn, Jody Kochansky, is just where the papers for this shipment got to. You don't learn that, the water's gonna be too hot to swim.

But there is no hope. Whatever system the last lady on this job— whoever she was—used to do her ordering, I can't figure it out. Okay, she estimated stock pretty good—I'll give her that—but her accounts—what I can find of them amongst the piles—look like the used up Keno cards that get left on the bus, a bunch of random numbers without labels or quantities.

And if I can't find the papers for this shipment, I'm stuck with it. On a closeout, you got twenty-four hours. I call the shipper and nag until the guy there gives up the number for the supplier. I get this lady with a little high voice, very polite, who explains real slow like I don't know what a closeout is. But then I blow it. I ask for the manufacturer's number; suddenly her English is out the window.

My office has towers of paper. My office is a like a city of paper buildings and I got no map. All the stuff I would keep on my computer—half of them faded, all mixed within piles. No computer is going to get me out of this. No, my only tool is what Ma calls shvitzshtern, brow sweat. Though it does occur to me that a small bulldozer might be of some help. Or even better yet, just one teeny-weenie match.

I get someone to cover me at the desk and lock myself in.

Now Sharon Moore, she's been great. Really. Patient, not standing over my shoulder, but then the other day she asks if I've been getting my catalogs okay, pretending like maybe there's a problem with the mail or something. What she's really asking here is where are my new orders and why does my office still look like someone threw a hand grenade in there. If I have to eat this shipment, I don't want her to hear about it.

The day goes on. It sinks in. I'm gonna eat it.

I need a break bad. I flop down in the break room, drop a teabag into water, flip through the magazines. What do I see? "Plunge In: Swim Yourself Into Shape this Summer." Cover of *Self*.

So I read about how safe swimming is. How it won't hurt your knees or back if you're out of shape. I read how good it is for preventing heart disease and high blood pressure and cancer and osteoporosis and all the other things they get you to worry about on the eleven o'clock news just before you go to sleep. I read how more and more Americans are doing it. How it can burn as many as 250 calories a half-hour. How good it is for the skin. How good it is for sleep. I read everything there except for how to do it. That they figure you already know. I read past my break waiting to find out how and all they tell me is "at least twenty minutes three times a week."

That's not how; that's how long.

I go back to my office. Darn, it's still there.

How, I ask myself, how did she—Nancy Riley was her name, for all that's worth—run this place anyway?

Then I think: funny expression, "run." When you run you move rapidly in a straight line. But when you run a department you do like six dozen things all over the place at the same time. I don't run a department; I manage one.

Then I think: Jody Kochansky, you don't have time to think.

I go "eeny-meany-miney-moe" between the computer and the piles, though I know the whole time I'm gonna wind up at the computer. I'm trying to make some sort of system based on counting what I've got on the floor and the stockroom. I plunk down. I sigh. I kick off my pumps. I manage. That's me: a "manager," not a "runner," and definitely not a "swimmer."

But you know, I'm sitting there, looking into my screen, and in that dead moment before the system comes up, I see myself. I see myself wearing the glasses I didn't need before I started to do books and I think, "I didn't know how to do accounts." I didn't know, but I knew if I was ever going to get out from the stock room, I was going to need to know how to do them. So I bought a book. I just bought a book and every night I went through it until I was ready to take the test in Personnel. That's it. I needed to know; I learned.

I bring up what I think might be the right file. I try to sort out the model numbers from the sizes. I type "250." I think: hmm, that's how many calories you can burn in a half-hour. I see "3x20." I think: hmm...

I cannot let this go. I am making myself crazy. I push back from the desk. Look, it's called "crawl." No one teaches a baby to crawl; they just crawl. This is a thing you just do. You just do, Jody Kochansky.

And I laugh, because of the Nike commercial. And I sigh, because I'm going to eat this shipment.

Danny   Most days I think: it could be worse. And when it's worse, I just try not to think.

Those are the black days when I flail myself for failing to hide a bottle of Uncle Jack under the bed. Those are the days we don't talk about, when both Mother and I remember why we still live together. When the pain is so total and my body so stubborn I cannot fold into my chair without her. When I can't get off the toilet myself and, furious, desperate, call her to help me, a hand towel tossed over my crotch, her quick eyes, bewildered and ashamed, anywhere but on me and what a grown man has just done.

Or the other times, when my hands shake so the milk sloshes frothy, undrunk, to the table. When I cannot spread the toothbrush with paste or bring it to my mouth. When Mom has to phone the Center for a substitute because I am beyond words in rage, ready to rail, to burst, to claw at myself. The black days.

I lie in my room and stare at the ceiling. I beat my fists on the mattress and clench pillows in my teeth. This day will be the day I'm going to give up. Give up this horrible helpless me. I lie there and chuckle over choices. I am lascivious, greedy, a fetishist. All my delicious guns-to-the-head and razors-to-wrist, oh, the elegance of ropes, the ease of pills, the sweetness of carbon monoxide and how final, how noble, the grand Brooklyn Bridge. I give them each due play in my hot brain, lurid, complete, taking time, laughing, laughing, deeply, madly.

And then I think of Mom, of fists on the desks of superintendents and signs held high, chanting. Mom, whom I have already disappointed enough. And as much as I am certain she would be luckier with me dead, I know that leaving her this way would be too ugly, too cruel, a final disappointment from which she would never recover—a ruthless paradox over which I can cackle myself giddy. And I am grateful to her beyond all sense for this: a gift of a reason to live.

For these days, they aren't most days, laughing and lucid and full. These days—unannounced, sporadic, dim—just make the others more dear. And I am glad I have not hidden that bottle. That I pass each liquor store sure I don't want to. For most days I count my joys like beads on a string, name aloud the delights, fleshy and various, of this gorgeous and fascinating world. Most days I remember to remember everything I love.

I love old MGMs and onions, slow cooked in butter, and to let a raspberry rest on my tongue until it dissolves and then drink it. I love my hands plunged in silk or angora, especially of a saturate blue. I love Matisse for making beauty through pain and Goya because he looked at people like me. I love the Beatles and Yo-Yo Ma, Far Side comics and the poetry of Rilke, aged Bordeaux. Nothing is more luscious than a summer tomato fresh off the vine and a woman with a hand's hold of flesh smothers with her passion. I adore the smell of sex and let it linger in my beard longer than I ought. I love the sound of children when they're being tickled. And the sound of cows, though I can't say why. I love an orange moon. It means my birthday's coming. I love the way dust swirls in the shadows of the slatted blinds. I love roses best before they unfurl, and the purple throat of pigeons in the deepest dead of winter.

And that I may bring these gifts to lips again. And that I may someday share them. Amen.

Ida   Such a big day, I get up extra early. Jody says I'm supposed to pack Paully's lunch in a bag, which is not such a simple thing when you got a boy who don't chew. So what I think is that I should bake oogiyot-tahina. For Paully, this is a favorite, and such a day, he'll need extra nutrition. But oogiyot, even when you're not trying to get the whole batch baked by nine, are a lot of work. Still for such a big day, you make fresh.

The sun has not come up yet; there are no cars going down the street. There are only the noises an old house makes when it is waking up. Jacob, you never got this old. At my age, I know about the noises we make waking up, the creaks and the moans that feel good and bad at the same time, in the knees and the pipes and the hips and the furnace, the shoulders and the gutters, the fingers and the roof. When I can hear these noises, the house's and my own, this is what I mean by "quiet."

I drop some bread into the toaster. I better quick go get in the teeth before it gets cold. When I have time to notice these things, the way the bread smells just before it pops up or the way the hem of my apron is coming loose, this is what I mean by "alone." And alone is something I almost never been.

I take bites of my toast while I climb the little ladder and get out the oats, the mortar and pestle, the sesame seeds.

No, "alone," that was something "The Baby" don't get, always protected, always watched out for. Well there were only three rooms, eh? No nice house where everybody has their own room like I got here forty years now. No, then there was Mama and Papa and Izzy and me and Aunt Sylvia and Uncle Sherman and their daughter Lila. Everywhere I look, Lila. All my clothes, hers first. For the baby, everything last. Everyone else gets potatoes first. Everyone else goes first to the bathroom in the morning. Always this makes me mad. Did I ask to be "The Baby"? No.

I'm not happy with these oats. A little too moist. When I grind they get pasty and then they will drop heavy. An oogiyot is right when it bends before breaking.

That Lila! I could never win. Always she got the sheets in our bed around her feet. And the way they was always mixing us up! "Lila" and "Ida"—both "i"s and all. A person wants to be their own person.

So, why not toast these seeds, too? A little more flavor if they're nice and brown.

There was always people there. So much family. No secrets if we tried. Even the most private things. You know what I'm talking, don't you? That morning, eh? February. 1935. I wake up; I'm not feeling too terrific. Okay, so I got a guess. I had seen Lila twice now. I didn't know, but I think—maybe. All I know is not to get out of bed. This my body tells me.

So for two days I do this. I say I am sick and Mama Kochansky takes care of my work at the stall. She does not say she minds doing this, but I know she has her own work. I don't know what to do; I feel so rotten. After supper of the second day she comes to me and tells me tomorrow she will send for my mama. I see then she probably knows what my trouble is. So I tell her no, I will go to my mama's myself; she shouldn't lose a day's work either.

Hai, mothers! How do we know things? We just do. If we want to. My mama knew things I didn't know how to know. She smiled and left her piles of clothes—this I could not believe—to fetch Mrs. Shilovitch, the midwife. We had a good talk. I understood many more things.

So that night, a big celebration! Both families around my mama's table. That was the way our lives were managed for us. I barely had time to tell you before we had to sit and eat. Poor you, eat you could not do. You spent that meal, and so many meals over the next many months, fussing over what was on my plate; I should have the freshest and the biggest. Everything had changed, especially for me. Now I was not just the respectable wife of a respectable man but soon I would be a mother! Someone who would be listened to. It was very important I do this right.

So of course, end of March, Lila announces she's going to have a third. Nothing for myself. Never. Nothing my whole life. Except Paully. Paully everyone left for me. You too. You left him to me.

Ahh, so this butter I am creaming is getting maybe a little too soft. Next I'll have liquid and then I'll have garbage. So calm down, Ida. Some things you got to let rest.

The smell of the oats in my kitchen gets strong. Mmm. Such a good smell. A smell like hugging my Mama—all starch and heat. Imagine doing all that ironing, for all those people, all day, every single day. Quiet work. That was my Mama. Hard to believe she raised me.

But she never stopped, even grown-up and living with my husband's parents she still took such good care. When my legs began to swell she started coming every day. When the back aches all the time started, she brought soup and bread and fruit and always a bottle of milk—which I know is not cheap—and tells me I got to drink all of it.

Then, at last, my belly begins to rise, high, hard as pumpernickel. Jacob, remember what you said? You told me I was like a flower blossoming. Some husbands—I know, I have heard stories—they would not be so kind. Mama said it would be a boy and later, when Mrs. Shilovitch put her hand on me to feel the kicks, she thought so too. Lila had only had girls and everyone thought the one she carried would also be. Mine would be the first boy in the family. Mine!

But do I got my share of trouble with all the weight. August in Brooklyn. I cannot get out of a chair by myself. I almost never want to anyway. The vegetable stand I forget about.

I was just too little, not strong enough. Lila, she was much better off. She would come and go with Aunt Sylvia, always those two talk, talk, talking, coming in, going out, walking Lila's girls to school, buying this, selling that. So much fun, my Aunt Sylvia. Always knows the latest fashion. She loved the world. Yes, this is it. Aunt Sylvia had the life I wanted. She loved three things, Sylvia: her family, her hat shop, and to be in the world. And all right, so? She liked a little too the Sabbath wine. But it made her funny and rosy. She made me laugh.

I sniff the air in my own house deep. So terrible she died so young. I would like to have known her better.

Sylvia, she would have liked working at the stand, the air, the people stopping to talk, the colors, the pretty piles of cabbage and carrots and potatoes. A simple thing, it made me happy. You used to tease: do I use kugel for perfume? So this might not be such a nice thing, if you didn't love your kugel. But oh, you did. And you liked to see me happy. How could I not be? Still a pretty young thing, married and respectable so I'm free to speak my mind. I couldn't wait to get back to the stand all ready, but this time, with my baby in a basket. How everyone would fuss, fuss, fuss!

Everyone says don't worry, Ida, with the first, a lot of women deliver late. I thought he'd never drop. But then he did. And he was so pretty.

Paully, Paully, Paully. Fifty-five years now I eat almost every meal with Paully. That or I watch him eat, standing above the table, telling him to chew slow, to stop playing. With me, Paully has never been alone. But I have been alone with him. This is a puzzle but it is true.

You were never this old Jacob; you were never this alone. I was here. Jody was here. But me? Ever since Paully, I've been alone, eh? Those first days eating in our room, Paully asleep beside me. I should wash my face before I saw anyone. Not that I had to do that too often. Nobody wanted to come near. Nobody. I did not want to see anyone anyway. Even you, Jacob, especially you. *Ai,* who knows what I might say? That I thought it was my fault? That I hated being a mother to a baby like that the way you hate all the bad things about yourself. To speak might be to admit that this boy was not just like any other boy a mother could have. This I would never do.

I open the door to Paully's room. His head is turned toward the wall. His body is a big lump of blankets. He sleeps good. He always sleeps good.

You wanted more, I know. The way you read to him, all those stories, and then you made him say numbers. You couldn't accept. So Jacob, my philosopher, my deep mind, my poet, sometimes my darling, more you don't get.

I go into the room and put my hand on the shoulder of the boy who will begin school today. He is wearing the striped flannel pajamas that Jody sent from the Macy's. I think he looks a little like a jailbird. So today the bird flies.

"Paully," I say, "it's time."

He opens his eyes and closes them, makes a crabby baby sound. Every morning, same thing.

"Paully," I say.

He opens his eyes again, blinks and sits right up. "Morning," he says. Two notes, like Jody. Every morning, same thing.

"Morning," I sing back, real soft. Suddenly I feel so sad.

I can see him remember. His face changes like a light bulb turning on. "Big day," he says. This is what we have been calling it. He starts clapping, rocking, "Big day. Big day."

"So," I say, standing, wiping my hands on my apron, "you better hurry or you'll be late."

He hops right out. This is different. Usually I got to tell him and tell him. But today he stands, looking down at me like he can't figure out what's next.

"Bathroom," I say and I point because maybe suddenly he has

forgotten where it is. I go back to my kitchen to fix him his breakfast.

I got my kitchen going now, everything at once. I got some cottage cheese with pineapple and banana in a bag. I got sausages browning slow, coffee dripping—a smell that wakes up the belly. The flours are sifted for the cookies; the oven is heating up. I just got to add the tahina to the liquids, that's all.

I set the table for Paully. Me, I'll eat out of the pans; still so much to do. I go to Paully's room and lay out a blue shirt and gray pants and socks and shorts and a tee shirt. I can't find his belt, but I got to be worrying about those sausages.

Suddenly I realize I have forgotten the raisins in the oogiyot and I am so crazy I almost put them in whole. I can't though. I just can't. I get out a board and begin to mince them. Paully comes out and I have him turn around for me. He is wearing his belt.

There is too much to do. There is not enough time. The oven dings. "Paully," I say, "come help Mommy mince."

"Bakin'? Bakin'? Okay. The cookies."

"We're baking cookies for the 'big day,' " I say. "Oogiyot-tahina."

He starts jumping and bobbing. Oogiyot—so much work and everything—I don't make so much anymore. He gets right to it. I break three eggs into the pan; sunny-side up, less trouble. I drop some bread into the toaster.

I have always been able to eat like this—two breakfasts if I'm hungry—not like my Jody who should learn to watch herself. I got the eggs sizzling in the sausage fat. I put two on Paully's plate. I put three sausages and two slices of toast. I pour him coffee, a little milk.

"Breakfast," I say, and fork a piece of the egg from the pan into my mouth. He sits, leaving me a board full of finely chopped raisins. I quick dust three sheets with potato starch and mix the raisins into the batter. Then I go to the cabinet and get the secret ingredient that makes these cookies mine—one heaping teaspoon cardamom. And done. I dust a spoon and begin to drop them.

Biting off the end of a sausage I think, what else can I give Paully for lunch? The cookies, of course. I put in an orange; he likes to suck on them. Outside someone honks for the neighbor's kid. We eat our breakfasts; like I never taught him about a napkin. I finish my egg and drop the pan into the sink.

"Come on, Paully," I say. "I still got to shave you yet."

Paully finishes and pushes away.

"Mouth," I say and he wipes up.

"All right now," I say, "go," and he marches off to the bathroom like he's supposed to.

He sits on the toilet as I wrap a towel around him and spread the cream on his face. Like this he is just my height so I got a good position. I wet the razor. Paully closes his eyes. He still misses you doing this. Well, of course he does. You let him put the shaving cream all over you. Me, I don't put up with such behavior. I start under his left ear. He tips his head. I wish he could do this himself.

My first.

All right, so there were visitors. So what? Most girls get *visitors*. They get booties and rattles and cakes. Who do I get? The family. The family with their empty hands, a boy like Paully don't need a rattle.

So the girls from the neighborhood don't come. Fine. The girls from the factory neither. Fine then too. Let them stay away. But Lila, I don't care if she was pregnant. So what? Lila was always pregnant, one, two, three, right in a row. Her apartment smelled like a diaper. Sends Clara to tell me she thinks maybe Paully's contagious! *Bubbe meises* ! Your mama made you tell me that people don't trust to buy vegetables from a woman with a baby like Paully. You were so ashamed.

This was something I didn't think of at the time, that you should hurt. Me, I was too busy thinking about how I hurt, how you hurt me, and Lila and God. I promised Him I would be a good mother. So I couldn't work at the stand? I'd find something. And I would keep my baby safe and happy, if only He would help me, if only Paully could do a little, I would do the rest.

We raised a happy boy, Jacob. What more can we want than he should be happy?

So, if I'm gonna be late, what's Lila gotta do? You know for yourself what she's like. Lila's early. Big deal. She has Sammy next

Shabbat. I get the rattles and booties that are left over. The cakes, she keeps for herself.

"All right, Paully. You're done," I say, and wet the washcloth; he should wipe up.

Two weeks come and go, three. I can see I know how to be a mother. I want to enter the world again. I want to enter with my husband, but if you're not there, I'm going anyway. My baby and me, we cannot wait. I join the whole family at the table for the first time since the birth. I stand before them and I say, "Say hello, Paully," and I hold him up and wave his little hand. "Everybody say hello to Paully," I say, and to you—who, by the way, should have already known—I say in my don't-you-dare-argue-back voice, "Paul Irwin."

You would think I said, "Everybody sit dead still and hold your breath as long as you can" instead of "Say hello." They go glassy-eyed starring at you. I'm the one holding the darling precious baby and they all got their eyes on you. You were still a young man, eh? Lots of hair. You were always pushing it back. A nervous thing, push, push all the time. So what you do is you push, then you close your eyes and nod, once, twice, nod, nod. Then you make like to push again, but you leave your hand there. In front of everybody! How could you have done that to me, Jacob?

So your mother, God love her, gets right up, gets out the wine and says, 'Say hello, everybody!' And they all do, one after another. Such a moment, so sweet. And then we drink l'chiam and say hello, hello, again and again and pass Paully's little warm body around, to his uncles and aunties and Bubbie and Zayde, my baby gurgley and sweet as any creature can be. Everybody does a little tickle-tickle and bouncy-bouncy, the baby comes to his papa. You with your face still covered, your eyes still closed. Your son hangs there in your sister's hands.

And then, at that moment , I see a thing I will never forget. I see a man become a Papa. You take Paully and you wrap him in your arms and sigh so deep it has no where to go but tears. It was funny in a way, eh? Funny in a sad way. You held Paully so close and tight the baby screamed and you yelled—yelled—you! So loud I am sure the neighbors stop to drink a l'chiam too! "Hello, Paul Irwin. Hello my baby son!"

I remember how we'd stand there—the new parents—and watch him in the crib. You told me babies, the way they breathe, so fast and hard and nervous, they always made you want to help them. But how? There is nothing you can do. This, you told me, is how babies teach the way to be a father.

Me, I never told you, what I worried most of all. The diapers, eh? How long? How big a boy? I didn't know. I would sit him on his potty and say a little prayer.

I say, "Come here, bubo," and we stand in the mirror and I watch myself kiss him and his big silly grin.

If he'll only just walk, I would say to myself. If he'll just call me Mama. If he'll just... Too much. Too much worry all the time. He stood, he walked, he followed directions, he called you Papa. So what did we want? Already so much more than we expected.

Look at him now.

Paully is bobbing and clapping all over, like he gotta pee all the time; he's so excited. He keeps hugging and hugging, every chance he gets.

And then I hear a car honk, but this time it's for mine own.

Danny   I am not bitter.

If only we hadn't dreamed.

If only they hadn't, my doomed dreamy parents, doing what parents must die or do. Striving to rise, through the son. Their sun. Dreamers revolving around the one who would deliver them forth into that Promised Land: Professional.

A son in college: sweet fruit.

But I am not bitter.

No, only fallen.

It was the wrong time for illness. It was 1958.

It was a time when boys without legs did not need educations. It was a time when this was believed. Who could blame them? Who were they? Teachers, not saints.

To come to the house of a bedridden boy? A surly, depressed and sometimes sarcastic boy. To take a subway after work or on a

Saturday? I would not do so if I were they. I am not bitter.

It was the wrong time.

But my parents, my dreamers, like sleepwalkers, shielded, they fought 'till they found the flat parochial school. There were the boys, forelocked and formal, in black coats and white shirts and thrice-pinned skullcaps. Good boys, sheltered boys, bent over torah, who could not include me, but never made me the fool.

Twice daily Dad pulled me up by the armpits onto the bus like the bone bag I was, my eyes closed, and dreaming that soon he'd be done. Pa gently talking, things learned in the office: Zionism, labor, the Yankees last score. Did he know I was dreading that last stop? The Waist Hoist. His face in my stomach as he swooped me back down. And then ten, and then thirteen, sixteen and bearded, my father's grunt as he lifted, each time my small death.

So when I finished, I finished. No one dared dream more.

Then, they passed laws.

Suddenly I'm trendy—a symbol, a cause—suddenly scholarships circled like moths. Suited recruiters called out to me: NYU, full scholarship, Genetics degree. Great grades, great fun, great friendships, great fucks, great years we felt grateful for, great rhymes, great drunks. Tra-la-la the luck that floats in the breeze. We all dreamed of better. We let ourselves dream.

But I am not bitter, no, only eye-opened. Jobs then were for men who could stand on two feet. Who peed standing up and took stairs like Astair. Who, without ramps and handrails, without increased insurance, strode to their places exactly at nine.

I'd do no different than these men from Manpower who eyed once my wheels and began the slow drumming. Fingers tapping atop my résumé. My letter overturned, sketched on. No tax breaks for trouble. Back then, no tax breaks at all. But I am not bitter, for this I have learned: all life, to be life, must grow, alter, evolve. And that society is a creature and, therefore, transient too.

For now, I am told, oft though unasked, that if I tried now, I'd discover how much things had changed. If I tried now, they'd photograph me at coffee with a woman of color for the cover of their annual report.

If I tried now—if they could pay me enough, and they certainly couldn't—I'd just need a few courses to bring me to date. If I wanted to. If I had even one ounce of heart left.

But I am not bitter. The opposite.

I am sweet fruit, fallen.

Ida   I quick go wash the face, take off the apron, and put on the smile I keep for strangers. One more time, I look Paully over. Ten minutes ago he looked neat, now already the shirt is coming out. I tuck it in; he hugs me. We just don't got time. I hand him his lunch and a plate of oogiyot for the kiddies—he should make a good impression. Also I got a little plate to hand in to the bus driver, who, even though he is mixed up with those Daughters of Israel, does at least know to kvel for home made.

"Incredible." This is the word that bus driver uses. I would never say such a thing. But "incredible" he says, and this after one bite. He got a nice smile. "A cookie with an aftertaste!" he says. "It's subtle, it's..."

And then, would you believe, he holds the cookie up. To the light yet! Looking at it is going to tell him what it tastes like.

Though, of course, a million years, he'll still never guess. So I tell him, "Don't waste your time, Mr. ah..."

"Cohen," he says. Then he puts his hand out through the window. But really he only kind of puts his hand out because I can see now his arms don't work in all the ways arms are supposed to work. "Danny Cohen," he says.

He's got the hand out there just a second. Just one second, I swear. He's wearing some sort of funny gloves. Okay, so it takes me a blink or two. He pulls his hand away. I put my hand out. It's gone.

Old as I am, I still got trouble with this. I see a person who is not the way they're supposed to be, I get all jumpy. I meet a grown-up person shorter than me, right away, I'm Nervous Nelly. Someone can't see, I got to cross the street almost, they shouldn't run into me. This kind of thing you regret.

So I wish I could say this Danny Cohen don't notice. He notices. I see the way he closes his eyes. He got nice eyes, too, this man, very blue. But he never stops smiling, never stops waiting for me. Like maybe he would do the same thing if he met someone whose arm didn't do what he thought it would.

"Mr. Cohen," I say, putting my hand safe on my hip, "you'll never guess what it is. Everybody tries but..."

"Aw c'mon," he says, "just one guess." He closes his eyes and chews a bite.

"It's no use, Mr. Cohen."

"Wait, I've got it! Orange rind?"

I laugh loud, like just the very thought of this is ridiculous, though, to tell you the truth, orange rind *is* the secret ingredient in my Erste-Steren, and I am not so delighted to have someone thinking along these lines. "My husband," I tell him, "is the only one who ever guessed."

"I bet you he guessed the secret was you." And then he laughs. Like it was his joke! I don't know, I always believe that in polite conversation you should make your own punch line and keep off everyone else's. So, forgive me, it wasn't such a great joke to begin with. Though you, my Jacob, you would have said "pure Ida," not just "you."

"I tell you," I tell him, "for a poppy krechen, my Jacob suddenly had time to sit."

"Smart man, your Jacob," he says, big smile, dusting the crumbs off his hands. Those funny gloves are leather. I notice him steal a little look at his watch.

"Well," I say.

"Well," he says, and turns that smile on Paully. "Ready?"

Paully says, "Big day, yeah."

"Well said, my man," and then, like it's nothing at all, "Hop aboard."

So, you'll excuse me, but Paully don't just go "hopping aboard" every day. Paully don't know what to do, and I ain't much help neither. This little bus or whatever got one door on the side, a big door, I think maybe a heavy door. I try to open; I try something else.

"Push the button," Danny Cohen says, "on the handle. Push while you pull it towards you." He is talking through another cookie.

I get nervous.

"It slides," he says. "Slide it."

It slides. What slides? The button? The handle? The door? Paully starts whimpering. Inside one of those children is laughing and pointing. "Please, Mr. Cohen," I say. I shouldn't have to say. What's he paid to eat cookies?

So he sighs. Such a big deal I'm asking, he got to sigh. I put my hands back on my hips.

"Danny," he says, then, "Be right there." This is not what I expect. There is nothing in his voice that sounds like maybe he'd rather not have to bother with an old lady who can't open a door. When I look at him, he smiles and winks.

Then I see. To get out of his seat he got no small mishegas. First he got to put long metal poles with some kind of braces on his legs. And then he got to get turned around, another operation. And then he got to turn on a motor and get on a moving step just to get down to the ground. So of course I am sorry. All this just to open a door. I tell you, if I were this Danny Cohen, I would make a good sigh too.

"I'm sorry," I say to the ground. I don't want to look at him walk. I can hear it don't come so easy, all uneven sounding, not good.

He leans on the side of the bus thing with one arm. "Push and pull. Same time," he says. Then to the boy inside who is pointing, "Thomas, calm down." I watch him press in the button and pull the door. It rolls open, easy. I can see lots of other children in there already. Some got wheelchairs. Some, I can tell, got Down's. Most of them watch us, but a few don't seem to notice nothing.

"I'm sorry," I say.

He slams it back. I can see that for him it's not so simple. He steals a little look at his watch. "Okay," he says. "Your turn."

I step up to do it, shy like a little girl.

"Ah, no," he says, "not you. I meant... ah... " and I can see he's looking at Paully.

"Paully?" I cannot believe.

But there he is, real sweet, real patient, leaning on those metal poles, putting Paully's hand on the handle. Opening and slamming shut again. Every time Paully makes it work he says "Good job!" or, "All right!" and Paully, oh, Paully looks like it's his birthday and Hanukah both at once.

Then Danny pushes a button and some stairs lower. He tells my Paully to get on and asks the other children to make room for two people. One girl don't seem to notice, so Danny asks another one to slide her over. The other girl just slides her over. Everything slides around here.

Danny says, "There's no room for you up front, Mrs. Kochansky." I climb the steps and squeeze in next to my Paully. Through the window I watch Danny walk back to the front of the van. It is only a few steps but he makes it feel like a long walk. Such a nice man, I am thinking, and, okay, sue me, I noticed, such a handsome one. What happened to him? So sad. I don't got no words. Over my shoulder I can tell he's got a whole rigmarole to get back into his seat. There is some kind of lift with a motor. I can see that up there with him he got a wheelchair. So this is good, I guess. Maybe it's more comfortable, maybe less work. When he gets himself all settled, he wipes his face. A nice clean hanky he carries. A good boy.

"I want to thank you, Danny," I say. I make myself look him in the eye.

"Aaah," he says, and waves a hand like it was no trouble at all, which we both know is a lie, but it is a polite one. "Every one's different."

"We sure are," I say. I am so relieved, I almost laugh.

"I, uh, meant the van," he says and turns the key. Then he says to Paully, "Okay, my man. Let's see you do it again."

You should see, such an expert suddenly! Paully slides that door shut from the inside.

Steiner   I wait until the coast is clear, then I make a break for it. I'm about to enter through the cafeteria entrance when my name sails out. It's Danny Cohen flagging me down by his van. "Is that you, Deborah? Why, I was just thinking about you yesterday."

I dash over and circle to the opposite side of the van. By the time he gets there, I am crouching by the door so I can't be seen through the windows.

"Okaaay," he says as he rolls up. "Why are we here?"

"I don't want her to see me."

"Who? The mother?" he says.

I bring my finger to my lips and nod.

"A bit reluctant, huh?" Then he says, "Look, I'm going to start getting set to leave here, okay?" He gestures toward the van.

"Be my guest." I'm still stuck on "reluctant." That would not have been my word choice. Even "difficult" would not have been my word choice. "Faltering," yes, and "stubborn," not the half of it.

"Well, I think she's a stitch," he says, opening the passenger door.

"You think that?"

"Oh yeah! Don't you?"

He begins jacking his lift down. He works patiently and, while he works, he talks. "She's just naturally and constantly and unself-consciously funny. I mean, she's just mumbling that her teeth don't fit well or something and she'll say it in such a way that you have to laugh."

Were we talking about the same woman?

When Danny turns around, we speak at the same time. He says, "Yes, but why are *you* here?" and I say, "You said you thought about me the other day." New Yorkers can do this, speak at the same time as listen.

Danny's gesture is chivalrous. "Please," he says.

"You mentioned that..."

"Ah yes! Did you see the last *Smithsonian*, that fish in Florida!"

"Yes! *Clarias batrachus*."

"The Lurch Fish."

"A catfish, I thought."

"My own name for it." He lurches a bit himself as he fits himself into his braces. "Those ridiculous fins!"

I smile remembering the photo. These amazing creatures walk overland on their back fins to reach another pond when theirs goes dry. The poor things looks like they'll surely fall on their faces a few times en route.

"Anyway, I thought of you. You know, that paper you gave."

I was flattered Danny remembered. Every new social worker at the Daughters of Israel is invited to give a talk on her thesis topic and meet the DOI community. Most people skip the talk and just come for the party.

"What was the name of that again?" he asked.

"*Adapting to Limitations: New Possibilities.*"

"Right. What you said."

Danny's chair folds with a little woofing sound. He positions himself to set it on the lift.

"Now my turn," he says. "What gets you out from behind your desk?"

By the time I've explained that I have one month, and that beyond this month, without assessments, Paul will not be allowed to continue, Danny has positioned the wheelchair on the lift and leaned up against the side of the van.

"I bet that wasn't easy," he says.

"No, it wasn't."

"And she doesn't know?" I realize he means the mother.

"She won't be disappointed if he doesn't make it."

"Ah." That's all he says, but I know he's heard me.

"It all comes down to her," I say. "Nothing happens without her signature."

"Well, that shouldn't be too hard."

"Are you joking?"

"No. Listen, she's reaching out. She wants her life to change."

"Danny, didn't you just meet her?"

"Well, you're right. It is just instinct, but think about it, Deborah. Mrs. K. was used to a household of people all waiting for their next meal, her husband, her daughter, her son. She was important. She was in control. And of course, Paully was the center of her life. She has no center now..."

Mrs. K.? Where did he come up with that? Then he hoists himself into the seat and shrugs down at me. "So if she's not on board, how..."

"There's a sister," I say.

"Yeah? What's she like?"

"A salesman, a talker..."

"Not a listener?"

"No, that's not it. She listens. She listens but she doesn't acknowledge it. And then the next time, she's got it all figured in, all the angles covered."

"Ah, strategic."

"It's not a game, Danny."

"No, it's not."

"I don't mean to scoff," I say, "but this woman, Danny. Well she seems to expect that over the telephone and from the opposite coast, she can get—oh, everything! By her fantasy Paully will be set for life in a matter of months. And heaven forbid I recommend, say, the second best facility in New York. She's not settling."

"Would you?"

"What?"

"Settle? What if it were your brother? Why shouldn't she want that, Deborah? That's what every family would want."

"There are no beds!" I say. I know Danny knows this.

"Tish! Supply and demand! Is that what they taught you in that fancy school? Is that all?"

"They taught me how to enroll babies."

He works at his seat belt for a while. Then he says, "Let me ask you something. If you're that fed up why don't you make a deal, trade with a colleague. You could take two new babies for one old one."

"Well, that's not really the way we operate. We get cases on a lottery. That way it's fair."

"Oh," he says, rubbing his chin, "fair." For some reason, he says it like, "Oh, that old thing."

He laughs to himself while he puts key in ignition. "Well," he says, "'least you'll learn the ropes."

−8−

Ida   All right, so it's not gray. It's beige. Everything "public" they
make beige. Jody's school, remember? Beige also. I just want
you to know this. I want you to know that not even for one minute
did I let my son go to a gray place. Truly, my darling, this was a
school. A *school* , Jacob! With the construction paper all over the
walls! I would even call the place cheerful. Except... well... except
for the children. What can I say? A lot of air out of the balloon,
these children. So many with the wheel chairs and the head things.
Or—rocking on the sofa in the corner—a boy is as old as Paully. Just
rocking.

So there's this big table in the center with children and one of
these teacher-ladies sitting around it. She's helping a boy fit numbers into a puzzle. Numbers, Jacob! A lot to take in. And all the time
Paully on me; he won't let go. I'm an old lady. So, if you'll excuse
me for mentioning, I don't hold my bladder so good no more. I have
Paully hanging on me like that, there could be trouble.

I say "Paully! Cookies! We got to give those cookies to everyone." At last he's off me. He can hardly wait; I should take the
plastic off the plate.

One girl comes up and says something or other. I don't know
what. She talks too slow. "Martha is asking how much for the cookies," the teacher-lady says.

Paully just stands there, blinking, his mouth hanging open.
What's she mean how much? All I ever heard about this school
is "free, free, free."

"Paully's not selling those cookies," says the teacher-lady. "He
brought them to share. They're a gift!"

"A gif?" says the girl, real slow and then real slow, points at
herself, "Fawh meee?"

I can see by her eyes she will take the whole plate, and Paully, he
don't know what he's doing. He's never seen nothing like this girl
in his life. He's just standing there, blinking, not paying attention
to holding the plate like he should. I think maybe I'd better step in
before they got a floor full of oogiyot to clean up.

I take the plate from Paully, who bends over putting his head on my shoulder like he hasn't done in years, the poor baby.

So the teacher-lady comes and takes the cookies and puts one in front of each child. Some of them, I can tell, are all happy—oh boy! We got some special treat now—but some, it's like it don't get through. The teacher-lady got to say "Here's a cookie for you from Paully. Say hello to Paully?" Like that. Like a question. Like she ain't sure whether the boy or girl she's talking to is actually gonna manage that, which considering how many don't, you can understand.

Our Paully, he don't belong here. Some of these children, Jacob... no wonder Paully's scared. These children scare me too. Jody says they go around with these children. So what is it she's saying? They go around with *these* children? Where do they go they don't get pointed at?

That little girl, that Martha, she pulls some change out of her pocket and is standing there, her hand out, Paully should take it. "Heh," she says, "Heh, Pawy."

"Enough," I tell her. "Eat your cookie."

"Martha, stop teasing Paully," says the teacher-lady and winks at me, I should see how cute this Martha is. Me, I don't think trying to give money away for free things is so cute, but young people, they got different thoughts.

"Martha has just started buying things for herself at the store," says the teacher-lady while Martha puts her change away real slow. "She's just showing she knows how. Right, Martha?" Martha makes a face, eyes closed, tongue between her lips. She's very proud of herself, this Martha.

I take a good look at the teacher-lady. She's wiping cookie off one boy's face. What kind of person is this that wants to do this all day long? She's young, like that Steiner girl, but this one, she don't make with the lipstick and the hair just so and the uptown outfits. This one's wearing a sort of apron, or a smock, maybe. And the hair, just back in a clip. This is a girl, I think, who could be pretty if she spent a little time. So what is it she wants with this "school" and these children, I cannot guess.

Then in comes another lady, straight for me, hand out to shake. She tells me she's in charge. She wants I should rush off; she can show me whatever it is they got here.

This principal or whatever-she-is shoots a little look to the teacher-lady who comes up and gets real sweet-talky to Paully. Like he's one of those little Frenchy poodles, she talks to him, little high voice, not straight out like that Steiner does. So what can I say? He's interested. He lets go.

The principal-lady takes my arm. Everyone's grab-grabby in this organization. I watch Paully as long as I can. "Please," I am thinking, "please don't be a bad boy and rub."

The other one makes a place for him at the table by that Thomas boy who pointed on the bus. And—I want you to know this, Jacob—Paully looks pretty normal here. Paully looks pretty good. All right, so maybe he doesn't look like a leader among men, but he don't look like a schlemiel either.

Steiner   He looks constantly for his mother. That's what it is. I check the second hand on my watch and record this in my log. This way he has of darting his head about. He's looking for her. I start a new page for this.

So now, instead of actress, I'm playing at investigative reporter.

The aide —or should I say, an undisclosed source—described him as "pensive." That's all she said; her attention was divided. But this does not approach it. No, he is looking constantly for his mother. I am sure of it.

They have placed him in a classroom with Thomas whom he met on the bus. Thomas, they tell me, is gregarious.

The mother is being shown a short video. Then she will be walked about, and invited to attend a meeting with all of the professionals involved in Paul's case. She still doesn't know I'm here.

Paul's group takes its turn in the yard. I watch through the window of his empty classroom. Once in the yard he is purposeful, trotting out to the one tree and squatting beneath it, merely squatting there, watching. An aide approaches him. She tries to interest him in a ball. He seems, at first, confused. Slowly she rolls a ball to him. He takes it, holds it, and keeps it himself a moment before rolling it back. He seems engaged, a little frightened. He certainly seems to be able to handle a ball.

Out comes the recreational therapist. She gathers the group into a ring. They know the routine and form quickly. The aide seems to need to cajole Paul into the ring but she is successful. Once there, she takes one of Paul's hands and places it into the hand of his neighbor. The other hand she takes into her own. I put my pen down.

They begin by swinging their arms. Paul laughs and stamps, laughs again. They pass a ball. Everyone gets it to the next person somehow. Paul's aide, sure he can catch, throws it to him. It flies smack into his chest and falls. He looks everywhere. Except down. He does not look down. This was a slow toss from a gentle person. It did no physical damage, but he is shaken. He retreats to his tree.

The aide approaches. She rolls the ball to him. He rolls it back. She throws it to him. Smack. She rolls it. Fine. Returned. She throws it. Smack.

Smack. Smack. Smack. Why doesn't he catch?

She rolls it. The ball bumps against him. He smiles, rolls it back. The ball bumps against him. The ball bumps... the ball bumps. Aha, that's it. That's it! The ball bumps! Ha ha! That's it!

He can't see!

He chooses shade. He darts his head about. He squints past people. This man requires prescription lenses. He's not looking for her. He just can't see.

I feel myself grow red. I am actually aware of heat rising in my cheeks, my breath coming short. How long? How long has he needed simple corrective lenses?

I want to knock on that director's office right now—right now—and confront her. How long? I'd like to know. I'd like to see her face.

And then she will ask that she and her son be driven home. And then I will have lost him. No. I need her to want to cooperate. I need her to bring him back here. I need her.

Then I think: that's it. I phone one of our doctors, a very friendly GP who lives a few blocks away. He says he'll drop by tomorrow and do some simple tests. An eye exam. Right here. Free. She won't be able to refuse that. And when she learns the outcome of those tests, that's it. I'll have her!

Ida   They got a little TV show that talks about how the school works. They want I should start with some meeting with the teachers. So all right, I think, this is the same with Jody when she was in school. Then I see that I'm wrong. Here they got like a whole army. Everything is therapist this, therapist that. They go around the table and say what they do. Someone for big muscles, someone for small. I'm telling you, this is a big table. When the show is over the principal or whatever-she-is sticks her head in. Am I ready for my tour? "Let me check my busy social calendar," I say.

She thinks to give me a hand out of the chair, which, you are lucky, my darling, never to have gotten old enough to need. Me? I am glad for it.

We go around. She shows me the place. And what I am looking at here, Jacob, is a school. Really. It used to be a regular school and now it's a school for children like this. I ask her what grade she put Paully in. She tells me it don't work like that. She says they just mix them all together. She just makes sure all the teacher-ladies get about the same. She talks straightforward like that. She talks also a little too loud, maybe I have a little trouble with my ears. So this is a thoughtful thing even though I don't need it. I let it go.

She shows me how they got the bathrooms fixed up and then— like at last she's gonna show what's in store for me behind door number three—the gym. Such contraptions Nadia Comaneci even would not know what to do with! But these children? They're bent over great big balls, they're spinning wheels with a stick. Everybody's doing something.

And then I see, there in the corner, a man moves the hand of this girl in a wheel chair. She's just staring out at nothing. She don't even notice. And he stands there, pulling her fingers long, then making a fist, then pulling them long. It's like—*oy*, such sadness—like she's some old doll, hanging there, slumped. She got a plastic hat , like the construction workers sort of. Maybe it's heavy; she's so slumped.

This girl—I can't see her hair, but even so, I can tell she's a girl, eh? This girl, she's a full-grown woman, if you know what I mean.

So how do they deal with that, I wonder? *Oy*, such, such sadness.

The principal lady says, "Seen enough?"

I nod. I like this lady and I don't want to be mean, but our Paully don't belong here. "I have to take care of my son," I tell her. " *I* have to."

She blinks at me. "Mrs. Kochansky," she says, "there's more to see." She pushes open the door at the other end of the gym and, mmm, there it is. The whole place smells like a nice pot of chicken soup. She takes my arm again, telling me how once a week each little class helps make a big lunch for everyone in the school who don't got some special diet or bring their own. Our Paully has never made lunch in his life. He don't belong here.

We go past the tables and benches to where they got their kitchen. Across the room, a boy pushes back double doors. "Here they come," she says.

And there they are. A big parade. Wheel chairs and little golf carts and all the others who can walk by themselves in two lines holding hands. They got a lot of children here. The girl who don't know she's getting her fingers pulled gets wheeled into a corner.

So in comes Paully, holding hands with some new teacher-lady. She's carrying the bag I packed. He's walking a lot slower than he does, his head turning fast, this way, that. He's scared, I know.

"He's scared," I say.

"I know," she says.

"I'll go," I say.

"No, no," she says, "wait." Then, "Mrs. Kochansky, please."

The teacher-lady with Paully gets him on a bench next to that Martha and unpacks his lunch for him. Paully sits there rocking and biting his hand. "He bites his hand when he's nervous," I say.

"First day of school," she says.

Paully—I don't believe—won't eat. The poor baby. "I'll go," I say.

"Just..." she puts her arm on mine, "let's see what happens, okay?"

So it's one thing to take an old lady's arm when you're walking and another to hold back a mother whose child needs her. I yank my arm away and start over.

Paully says something in the teacher-lady's ear. She rubs his back when he talks to her. Who said she could? Then she looks up, sees me coming and her boss coming close behind and stands. "Mrs. Kochansky," she says. "Would it be all right to give Paully some chicken soup?"

"It's what I give him every day," I say.

"We can do that," says the principal-lady. So big deal, they open a can.

The teacher-lady goes off. I grab a quick look at the corner. Another teacher-lady is spooning soup into the sad girl's mouth.

The minute the bowl hits the table, the hand comes out of his mouth. But still he don't eat. He's too busy looking at everybody. "Paully never had lunch with so many people," I tell them.

So then that boy, that tall skinny one, Thomas, he slaps Paully on the shoulder. "Here," he says, so loud everyone can hear, "like this." And he dips his spoon in his soup and slurps it up. "You! You go!" Thomas says.

So just like that, Paully dips that spoon. Next to me I can hear the principal lady sigh. Then that Martha reaches out to the napkin thing and hands Paully one, nice and friendly. Paully—I'm so ashamed—don't even thank, much less behave like a boy who knows what to do with a napkin. Martha pushes it towards him. He ignores. So what does she do? She stands right up and, real slow, opens that napkin and puts it right there on Paully's lap. Right on his lap! Never have I seen such a thing! Such a little mamaleh!

The principal lady and me, we both laugh. "Martha is very neat," she says.

In the corner, the teacher-lady wipes the sad girl's face. I look back at my Paully. He eats every bit of his soup.

Jody I rewind again. "Esther honey," I say, "you made some of the worst movies ever to hit the screen, but you sure could swim." I watch her again, dripping on my carpet. The arm comes up at an angle like a square. The head goes this way, then that.

When they bring out the sequin mermaids for the water ballet number I turn off the tape and scoot out to the pool. "Okay Jody,"

I tell myself, "crawl." I do something, arm at an angle, arm at an angle. Then I do it again. Somehow I wind up at the other end. Out of breath, okay, but I'm there. I try again.

The gate screeches. In trots the kid. She skips her skinny little self to the side, shoots up her arms, and splish, one motion, no hesitation, no preparation. At the other end, she comes up, shakes her little head and fuh-lip, she's off.

I try not to let her throw me but moving alongside her waves, I swallow mouthfuls of water. I plant my feet and just try to stand firm, feeling stupid, coughing.

When I walked into my office this morning, I found a note that Sharon left with a little smiley face saying if I wanted to work extra she'd let me have overtime pay. I try to hide the note under the heaps of stuff on my desk and pretend I don't see it. A pile teeters. I catch it just in time.

Sharon, she's been noticing me, when I come in, when I go. I noticed she glanced at my out box. She noticed I noticed. So I don't think I want her aware of just how much extra I'm working.

I hold onto the side and just hang. That kid's gotta run out of steam sometime. My eyes close.

At least the stock is ordered right. I cannot figure out even one transaction completely, but it's ordered right. And the girls got a smooth schedule they can live with. The register rings out even. The sales floor looks good. The last woman on this job was doing something right. All I got to do to keep me going a season until I can figure the place out is copy her paper. Except, what paper? I got catalogs, register tapes, personnel applications, schedules, notebooks with random numbers, account books with random numbers, pages from old calendars, customer complaints, everything mixed together, everywhere.

Everything, that is, except orders and receipts. Everything except what I need.

I plunk into my chair. I kick off my pumps. I turn on my computer. Why I turn on my computer, I don't know. My computer is useless. I turn off my computer.

It's Saturday. If I can't get the 1:37 there's not another bus until

4:04. Just the thought makes me bone weary. I look at the little smiley on Sharon's note and right out loud I say, "Help me."

Just then, like a response, the phone rings. It was for Sportswear, but just standing there holding the receiver... well.

I stare at it. What if it fails me? My secret weapon. On the phone, I can be pretty much whoever I need to, whoever I can pull off good enough to convince the other end. I can go undercover—which is, after all, my line of work. I can pretend I'm from Wal-Mart, for example, and find out if that last sales rep who swore up and down he was cutting me the best percentage really did.

No doubt about it, my best deals are not face to face. It can't help but affect the deal whether I'm talking to a lady in a wearable suit or a religious guy with ringlocks and a hat or some recent retail school graduate with a tie and one of those small computers they always got. I don't even want this information; I'd rather get to the numbers, plain, simple and fair. But I'm human; it affects me.

Plus, it affects them. I got to deal with whatever problems they got about looking at me. He probably thinks I'm a fat pig. She probably feels sorry for me. So, okay, I admit, once or twice I used this to cut a good deal —"Oh, poor pitiful me, feel bad for me and make it thirty percent off"—but there's no fun in it. I tell you, I'm a big believer in phones. Why don't they teach phone skills in school? They teach penmanship.

So what am I waiting for?

So I dig out the old store directory from a pile behind a dead plant. She'd written on the cover what looked like: "In case fo emergencie," and her name and home number. I remembered it because I thought it was some weird joke. The handwriting looked like the kind you use on Halloween, all scratchy and broken.

What if it fails me?

I have no other choice. I go for complete honesty. "I am the woman who replaced you at Macy's," I tell her.

Right away she's trying to get me off. So I compliment her on a well-managed department. She thanks me and seems a little more willing to stick around. But then I get to it. "About your ordering system?"

That's it. Her voice comes back like a closed door. Then a baby cries in the background, she says she'll call back and I wait and wait, but she don't.

I open my eyes. I see the kid underwater heading straight for my thighs. Jeesh, can't she look where she's going? I step aside. She pops up beside me. "Race ya'!" she says.

"Wha...oh!" I laugh. "Oh no, I don't think so."

"Aw, come on, why not? I'll give you a head start."

"I don't think that will help."

"Aw, come on, why not?" She dog paddles around me in a circle. I have to keep readjusting to see her.

"Because I can't swim," I say.

She drops her legs and stands. The water is almost to her shoulders. The ends of her straw colored hair float around them. "Aw, come on," she says.

"I can't," I say.

"I saw you."

"You saw me swim?"

Her head tilts to the side, considering. "I guess not," she says.

"I didn't think so." I sigh. "That's why I don't think a race would be fair."

She shrugs. They have such skinny little arms, children.

"So how'd you learn?" I say.

"My dad teaches me," she says.

"Well, see? My dad didn't."

"Why not?"

Kids and questions. Why not? "Well," I say, "I'm pretty sure he didn't know himself." The kid finds this funny. I guess to a little California girl it is.

She makes a muscle. "My dad was swimming champion."

"Well aren't you fancy!" I say. I think: gosh, she's adorable. "What's your name, Honey?" I say.

"Ryan," she says.

I expect her to say, "What's yours?" She doesn't. So I say, "Well Ryan, I'm Jody." No response. So I say, "You're a good swimmer." I expect her to say, "Thank you." She doesn't. She shrugs and does her little dolphin dive.

What goes on? Shoulder, arm, head, one piece. Okay, I can try that. And the legs just go and go. I set out. I get to one side, touch, turn around and get to the other, where I stand, my hand laid over my heart like I need something to keep it in there. But I'm thinking: "Hey! That was a whole lap!"

Ryan pops up beside me, dripping. She stands there looking up at me, her eyes wide. She doesn't have to say it. I would tell her to go away if I had any breath.

"You have to put your hand like this," she says, and tries to pick up my arm. I let it hang, heavy. "Aw, come on," she says. She bends over, puts her face in the water and shows how to bring your hand around over your head. Now I see how that angle works. She stands up, chin and eyelashes dripping. "Now you," she says.

I feel stupid. But I see her inhale for another big "Aw, come on" so I just go ahead, I bend—and I need to bend way more than she does to get my face in the water—and then I bring my arm up and in front of me. I stand again, looking down at her.

"Why don't you bend your knees?" she says.

So now I really feel dumb. I bend my knees and come to the right level in the water. This time when I do the arm thing, it feels different. I have moved water.

"Do it hard," she says.

It's my turn to get wide-eyed. I look at my hand. My hand that just moved my whole body forward.

"Way to go," she says, thumb up.

"Ryan?" I say, squinting down into her little freckled face. "Will you teach me?"

She picks up my hand and shapes the fingers into a little cup, sighing. "I am," she says.

book three

❖•❖•❖

Action News

—9—

Ida   "To fall down is only to learn. To suffer: stand back up." Every morning you would say this, like your dreams got such terrible things to teach you. So many times you say this, I don't even listen any more. But now I say it, my husband. Now it's my turn.

Paully, one thing about him, he wore me out. Used to be I got his oatmeal, then his hair, his teeth, his nails. Paully dusts, I make up the list, we can go to the A&P, people need sunshine. So we buy what we need, we come home. This is tiring, eh? We need a little rest, a little chicken soup and kreplach. Then we got the mincing, the chopping, the sifting, and so on. Then it's time for the *General Hospital.* Next we got the mixing, the washing. We take turns. I bake while Paully does the vacuuming; I don't want he should be near the cookies when they come out hot. And then we take a little rest. All these things I used to do every day.

But now? Now we got these mornings. Everything rush, rush, rush, he should look good, have enough to eat, and then... then the house goes quiet.

I change from my nightgown to a housedress. Why do I bother? They got no shape and they look the same. But the dress is fresh and cool. It smells of laundry soap. I put some bread into the toaster and take my red sweater off the back of the kitchen chair. It's got holes in the elbows now. So who looks? I take out a fresh apron—the one with the little violets all over it. I like this one. Cheerful. And then maybe I'll make up something simple, maybe some lemon krechen. And then I'll wait.

So Paully likes this school, but me, I'm not so sure.

Oh, Paully likes this school, all right. So all right, the truth—he loves the school.

From the very first day, he got a love affair with it. He comes home; he talks so much I can't get a word in. I have to follow him around from room to room; he's bobbing like a jack-in-the-box. I'm asking, was he a bad boy who rubs at the school? He bites his hand. He says something about choosing dimes and nickels. Also, he says he "put the stones in the bag." I don't know what this means neither. I don't know why the big deal. He likes dimes and nickels? I got dimes and nickels. And Brooklyn is full of stones. So all right, maybe this is good. I like he is happy, and the glasses, the glasses are good. But I miss my Paully; I do. Fifty-five years you spend with a person, and suddenly... well.

You didn't know, Jacob. You never looked at him. You never looked *at* him. Why? What was so bad? He used silverware months before Lila's boy. Does anyone say, Ida, look how nice he uses a spoon! He don't get the carrots all over like that slobby Sammy. Straight into the mouth, neat and slow. No.

You know what I'm talking about, that night, back in our old apartment, my turn for Shabbat. I made a nice meal, I think. The air smelled the way fall does and of my challa in the oven and my baby was walking and putting on his own clothes, even combing his hair. George Burns was on the radio. I loved Gracie Allen. So wouldn't you know, just when she gets to the part about the long-lost brother—and this is why I listen, I love this kooky story—this is when Lila and her lot waltz in the door. That hat! *Ai*, I'm surprised that big fruit basket even fit through the door.

"I'm celebrating," she says, right over Gracie. "Today I got the baby to tie his own shoes."

So you look at me. What'd I do? Is every little thing in the world my fault?

"Let's show them, Sameleh," says Lila, like this is some great entertainment. And three times—three—she unties his shoes. He ties, she unties. So no wonder when he grows up Sammy can't tell when enough is enough.

Then the rest all show up, in twos, in threes. Every time Lila, with the "Show us, bubelah." On and off all night with the shoe. We don't even stop for dinner.

But you, you just sit there, like a big lump of dough. Your brisket lies there. Even the wine you don't touch.

So all right. So he learned to tie. In his own time he does it. What more do you need? But this is good. You stop pushing with the numbers, the numbers all the time. You see he likes the ball. Very good. You had a good father, Jacob. That I could always see.

I wish you were here now, my husband. You see? You *see*? School yet!

Paully, sunny Paully, chopping up apples. His favorite—can a mother be so lucky?—is cleaning the stove. He even likes to do the grease cover. So fine by me. He was good company, Paully. He was better company than Mama. He knew when to be quiet for the radio. He loves the TV. Loves the animals and the cartoons and that wrestling—which I can't stand, that he can go watch in his room. He's a good boy who's quiet while we watch the *General Hospital*. And the "Michael Row the Boat Ashore" over and over while he washes the dishes! Like he's Pavarotti on the TV! Every time this got me, every time. I could never stay mad at him.

I miss him at the A&P, the high shelves and the schlepping he used to do. So Jody, she sends me one of those rolling carts that fold. All right, this is a nice gesture anyway, but it does not help me reach my strawberry jelly.

And now the house, Jacob, it makes noises I never heard it make before—and not just during the middle of the night neither. I'm just sitting there any time of day, listening to these noises, like I got nothing at all in the world to do, maybe I even got the TV going, it don't matter, and I wonder where I got off to. I wonder how long I been sitting there just listening and I try and try to think of someplace maybe I need to go. Maybe the A&P again? I don't know. And, would you believe, sometimes, sometimes I find myself wishing I could just stand there with my Mama again and my iron and my piles of damp shirts. Another person, Jacob, another body in the room. And I sit there and I listen and I wish. I am growing so tired, my husband, so tired, of standing back up.

Steiner   Oh, I may have won the first battle. Since then, it has all been uphill.

On the day Paul Kochansky began to attend the day care center, I called to congratulate her.

"So a fifty-five year old man gets on a bus in the morning," she said. "Go call up *Action News*."

Although I never did get him to all the specialists, I did get him to some. At least I saw to it that he had a thorough physical, surreptitiously removing him from the center to do so. Those visits, combined with my intense observations, enabled me to put some sort of file together for Paul by the end of the month. Conspicuously missing, however, her signature at the bottom of the enrollment form.

She returns neither the paperwork nor my calls. I concoct excuses to get in—unnecessary permission slips for swimming and the like. They are wearing thin.

I have thought of slipping the enrollment form in with the pile, but I can't bring myself to sink that low. Besides, the form is eleven pages long. I'd get caught.

Once in, I have tried several tactics. Remaining relentlessly cheerful, for one. "And though it might not sound as if there are many options, Mrs. Kochansky, at least more exist now than ever before—"

She said, "Rah, rah."

I offered her a video, a Nova special. Before I knew it she had me figuring out why the "clicker thing" didn't work and then running off to bring her back some batteries for it. She was grateful to have them, but passed on the video, saying she'd seen that show featuring the actor who has Down syndrome. If she wanted to watch fantasy she could watch *I Dream of Jeanie*. The papers lay on the TV, untouched.

I remind her repeatedly that I am there at the behest of her daughter.

She calls her a run-away, says we're in cahoots.

Obviously, there are only so many times one can be treated this way. Even a simple insult like, "A school they call this place!" and I become defensive.

Then, suddenly, sheepishly and during the last minutes, she acquiesced.

And so, each weekday from nine until three, Paul Kochansky attends school.

Apparently the mother, now that her son has entered the system, is more or less ready to let the system have him, but not to assist. Her attitude swings in a rapid pendulum response from apathetic resignation—as easy to move as a ton of potatoes—to pugilistic confrontation.

Her main interest in me at this point, it seems, is making me go away. And really, who can blame her? She can't figure out what I'm still hanging around for.

Meanwhile, from the daughter, an endless stream of, 'Now remember, don't tell Ma that your taking him'; 'Keep this between you and me.' A million things she was not telling her mother and me constantly in the middle.

I consider overriding her wishes, speaking frankly to her mother, laying it all out. That would be the end of it, though, no more access to the mother or information from the daughter.

I consider what Danny said, removing myself, handing this off to a colleague with more experience, or maybe to another agency. I consider it often, yet for some reason, never completely seriously.

At any rate, the situation can not continue. The house grows shabby without Paul's care.

And then one morning the mother calls the center to say that Paul will not come in that day because he is sick. I stop by in the late afternoon to check in, and find him dust rag in hand, the house very clean. I mention this to the daughter who says she will talk her mother into accepting cleaning help in the home. I counter that if her mother took that temper out on an in-home worker—and it's only a matter of time—the result would be constant staff turnover. All at significant expense to state and family.

"All right, all right," she says. "I'll have a word with her."

Despite this, Paul misses twice more in the next two weeks.

–10–

Jody   My so-called swimming.

I cannot get anywhere. I'm stuck at four laps before I'm ready to die. Four. Not four and a half, not four and a quarter. Sometimes not four.

I mean I just cannot get anywhere. I've been working so late that I haven't seen "my teacher" in a week and since I can't figure what the last lady who had my job was paying for things I have to guess at figures based on what I was doing in Brooklyn. So the sales rep from my two o'clock meeting walks out of my office with this smile on his kisser like he's gonna take the wife out tonight and celebrate the new sucker they've hired at the Macy's. It was a big order too.

I start in on my new workout routine that I got from those women's magazines in the coffee room. You know, I never read them before I came to California. What do I want with "365 Things to Do with Chicken"? But they get left around the staff room here and I pick them up and it's like having someone to chat with over your Diet Rite.

It gets hard lifting my leg at about eight. I do two more.

So I have no idea how she gets in without me noticing, but she does, popping up next to me while I try to catch my breath. "Well Jody," she says in this fussy, adult voice, "did you practice?"

Somehow I get the feeling that this is a perfect imitation of something Ryan must hear often. I laugh. "Play an instrument, Ryan?" I say.

"Piano," she says.

"Oh, how nice. I've al—"

"That's what you think," she says.

"Don't you like it?"

"Every night, the same thing, scales, scales, scales, scales. And then these dumb songs. No one—"

"I wish I'd had piano lessons," I say. "I wish someone had made me practice."

"That's what my mom says." She crosses her skinny wet arms.

Oops. No good. I think I must have convinced her once and for all that, in fact, all adults are alike.

Why exactly is it important to me, what some little kid thinks? All I know is that while I stand there, trying to think of something to say to make up for it, she heads for the other side with those pretty even little strokes of hers.

I start my leg ten times to the back. Ah, I have nothing to prove to this kid. I watch her over my shoulder. The show-off.

I guess that's the advantage of not having anyone in your life: you've got no one to prove anything to.

Thinking that sort of knocks the wind out of me. I put my back to the wall and begin to lift front.

I mean, I have people in my life. I got Ma, I got Paully, but I really just don't know that many other people. I know there are people at work, and they seem nice, but after the fiasco I had with Lester at the temp agency I got a rule not to get involved with anyone from work. Hey, I need my job.

It's other women, too. They just make me nervous. They seem to know things I don't. My own girlfriends—from school and all—well, they got so busy with their families. It's like when you start a family you lock up the windows and pull down the shades. One day I looked around and all those old girlfriends—gone.

I turn back to the wall and start my left leg—wouldn't want to be lopsided.

And if you don't have a family...well, it's like at my neighbor, Evelyn Kaufman's, wedding. We used to give her my fancy clothes when I outgrew them. And suddenly, there I am, at her wedding. And if that's not bad enough, I get put at this table of all these old friends of hers; I don't know any of them. They're all younger than me, and every last one's talking about their kids. And when they ask me about mine and I don't got any, the conversation—I don't know—they talk to me like I'm Paully.

My legs hurt today. I don't know about this stuff. I thought it was supposed to be good for you.

I get that leg up again. By now it's been so long, I don't even know what to say to other women anymore. Which, I may as well admit, is what's bugging me.

I drop my legs and stare at my feet, white and wavery on the pool floor. This morning I put a note in every one of my girls' time slots. It said, "Sign up for personal interview with Jody before Friday."

Jeesh, what have I done? I sigh and sink, holding onto the side. Well, I had no choice. In two weeks I'm gonna start receiving shipments for the Christmas orders Nancy Riley made and if anybody's gonna make any money on the Christmas sale, I've got to know what I'm getting. I've got to sit those girls down and ask what they've seen and what they've heard, not to mention who, and also when the orders come in and also, well...everything. I need answers and I need them like yesterday.

Ryan heads for my thighs and pops up. "Come on," she says. "Aren't you even going to try?"

I look down at her, my little coach. Yeah, God help me, I'm gonna try. I do something that's supposed to be like her little dolphin leap and set off for the other edge.

I'm not sure how she gets there ahead of me. She treads. She don't even worry about being in water where her feet won't touch.

"Are you all right?" I can tell she would rather have a more hearty playmate.

I'm out of breath, but I'm fine. I nod.

"I think I'd better show you how to kick," she says, then lifts her hands over her head and, oop, sinks. Just like that she pops up again at the edge. I huff my way over. There I am, still catching my breath, and she says, real impatient, "Aw, come on."

We take hold of the wall next to each other and begin to kick. She shows me that she is not breaking the top of the water very much. She tells me to use my whole leg, not just my knees. When I do, I am forced forward into the wall. I am beginning to see how this is done.

Danny A man like me has lost many chances. There is so much I do so want that may never be. I've fewer paths to forage, still I find the pickings sweet.

For a man like me is wealthy with time. I'm rolling in choices! As much luck as any, much more than some.

My small body down here, ever up-peering, rolling only forward after looking both ways. I wheel Willie, my chair, through the hoop of my week.

Willie, he makes me, more than I like, the man I am able to be. He shapes me. He's body; I'm mind. Willie, my keeper and beast. We fight, we fold, we bend, ever creaking, like wet wood to iron, coopered in, nailed.

At axis is Torture, circuit weights, daily lifted. The Veteran's rehab pool. Close to three hours, daily, not for improvement, but just to decrease the speed of decay. A little bit of what I think it means to be a man.

It is torture made communal—our little Brooklyn cross-section—me, Lemont, Rossinelli, Ciñaro, Evans, Riley, and Ho. Riley, in particular, will tell a well-timed tale. The running joke, of course, political correctness, though anything Letterman/Leno is game.

And when we have rotated one complete circuit, we help each other out and into our chairs. It's for Lemont that I choose "Veteran's" over "Y" or "J." We get each other looking right, maintain each other's gear. When one of us can't make it, the entire morning's shot. Yet sometimes, indeed often, it's not even that we talk, it's just that we know the other waits, daily, lifting.

I prefer my Sundays quiet, books and napping, supper home with mother. For even a man like me can not ignore mighty Monday's pull.

True, a week is but a concept, still, I think it best agreed to, that each day may be forward and full.

It is the wheel we roll in. At best we choose the trail. To follow the path of people, when you think you've found a friend, extend.

Lemont has two stumps where once his legs were, and beneath his left elbow, prosthesis. He has given up trying to match color in the models they call "Negro," and so resorts to shoe polish right up to his skin. As for me, with my weak arms and my ever-overloaded Willie, I'm always needing oil and often brake repairs. Willie, my keeper and beast.

Mondays I see Saul, blunt, sardonic, muttering, the runty little outcast of my middle school yeshiva. We'll drink coffee at his men's club, shoot a game or two of pool. The running joke, of course, Bet Shalom days. Something about Saul Rosen then, a certain... *je ne sais quoi*. He reminded of a cricket, something in his carriage. He turned out to be quite a fine man.

We talk about the families. I knew his sister well; we talk about her. He's having a hard time right now, talking about divorce. But I think at last he's finding himself—I think he's finding himself queer—I only hope he's brave enough. I only hope he's swift.

And then it's off to the earning, to the ever almighty, to my niches special yet substantial, to make my own way.

Yes, a week is a wheel to spin like the potter, wares for the market rising from mud. For city, and era, and fortune of birth, these we are given to make money and merry. And so I scoop from all I've been given and offer it up to the sun. The sons of the wealthiest secular homes.

Boys with drawers full of Calvin Klein and Ralph Lauren. Boys with their own computers, skis, cameras, stereos, color TVs. Boys who think they will have many chances, and who are probably right. Boys who have forever to be young. Boys from the wealthiest homes.

Boys who know more about Auschwitz than about duty towards good works, who are more familiar with Eichmann than David, after whom many were named. Secular boys.

He is assigned a certain passage, the grand I-am-man birthday party event, right? So I do my sweet deal.

A bar mitzvah dramaturgy, that's what I call it.

Three months, once a week, I charge a bundle but I'm good. My time's my own, I take it in cash, under the table. Word of mouth keeps me in business. Just call me wheeler-dealer.

For a week is a wheel to spin like a croupier. Set in silver motion by blind Fortuna's touch, a week is an opportunity each.

–11–

Jody She's coming. Tonya. The first one. Another person is going to have to fit into this office. I clear the piles off the little green chair and set it opposite my desk so she can peek through the space like I'm the lady who sells tickets at the movies.

She's at the door. Tonya. I run my fingers through my hair, casual, casual. I have been practicing and rehearsing. I don't want to let on how if I don't make good numbers on Christmas, then at least I won't regret telling Ma this job is temporary.

"Come in," I say, real casual.

This woman Tonya is thin as a rail with lots of hair and this hair of hers is always a surprise to me. It's completely different every other week. I mean, me, I haven't changed my hair in, I don't know, ten years maybe. But Tonya, she must make a little start every time she passes a mirror. Like, "Whoa! Who's that?" In my opinion, I think all this hair makes her head too big for such a skinny little body, but this is not my business. I wave my hand for her to sit.

She peers around my office nervous as a bird. Why, she's more nervous than I am! All right, all right; I can calm down. But she won't even look at me. Why? I can't say. Maybe she don't like white people. I wish I could use the phone.

I try to break the ice. "How long you been at Macy's? Always this department?" I ask this just to get things going; I don't need to. It's all right there in the personnel file I have spread on my desk so I won't misplace it in the clutter. She gives me quiet little one and two word answers.

I clear my throat. "Let me get to it," I say. "I've called you in here today to discuss a little problem."

So Tonya still don't look at me, but she does steal a peek at the file. So that's it. Well her name's right there on it. Several times in the past Tonya has been talked to about sneaking coffee behind the cash register, which she still does, far as I can tell, every time she works. No wonder she's nervous. But me, I figure, she wants coffee? Whatever. Just so she does her job, that's what I care about. I close the file and stick it between my wall and the garbage can. "This is my problem," I say, "not a problem I got with you."

She seems to relax, but still she's looking around, her mouth a little bit open, kinda dazed. Well, I gotta say, I've never seen too many places like my office either. If Tonya's been talked to about her coffee, it wasn't in this room.

I lay out the situation. Plus, I add, we got the mall-wide Columbus coming up.

"You mean they just left you?" she says, looking from pile to pile, "with this?" She sounds really sorry for me.

"Okay," I say, picking up my pen. "Maybe we'd better get to work here."

I have been thinking about ways I can take information the girls might know from stocking and work backwards. I tell her she might know more than she thinks.

But every question she answers no, no, no. She shrugs, her sharp little shoulders get lost in all that hair. "I run the register," she says. "I fit bras."

But then I do get something. I wish I didn't, but I do. See, I have still not gone to Sharon Moore and discussed how behind schedule I am. I want to understand first how much she knows and also how much she blames me for. I do know she has come into this office when I am not there—like to leave the little smiley note. It's the thing I wake up thinking in the middle of the night: Sharon standing in my office after I'm gone thinking, "Oh my, *who* have I hired?" I ask Tonya how often she used to see Sharon Moore headed for this office when it belonged to the pile lady.

That's when she says, "Oh, Ms. Moore used to meet her out by the desk."

"Meet her?" I say. Sharon and I, we don't meet.

"Yeah, almost every day. Lunch time."

"Lunch...?" I say. I think: I have never had lunch with Sharon. I think: Jeesh, they're chummy! So much for passing the blame. I'm all alone here. I'm all alone.

So Tonya, she's excited to know something at last. She's running on. "Um-hum," she says. "Those two? They had this power walking thing going on!" There is something about the way Tonya looks at me after she says this. I can just tell. She's thinking I could maybe use a little lunchtime exercise myself.

Skinny little Tonya with her eyes all over me. I don't blame her. Really, I don't. It's just that in New York, you know, I'm a little full, a zaftig juicy woman with a little more than a little spread below the waist, not a complete obese disgrace or anything, just seventy, eighty pounds over is all. But here, in California, it's like I should be making my living next to the tattooed lady instead of as Tonya's boss.

I roll my chair back so I'm hidden by the piles. If I don't want to see her looking at me, then I shouldn't look at her.

That's the problem, you know, right there. The problem begins, the way I always figured it—you'll forgive the pun—when you look around. Look around and you see all these teeny-twiggy models and all the nice clothes that stop at size fourteen. So what I do is, I don't look around. I buy my clothes from catalogs for women my size and try them on at home. I sit and stand a million times, cross my legs, schlep my bag and then go back and see if I've gotten bunched up anywhere. I pretend I'm bending down to get something off a rack for a customer so I can see if anything's showing I wouldn't like nobody to see. You know the old commercials where they torture the Samsonite luggage? That's where I got the idea. I dress myself nice, everything good, nothing tacky. And, until lately, I didn't even look at those magazines. When the ads would come on the TV, all that stuff about programs with fake foods, and diet pills and liquid diets, and especially that crazy woman who wants to stop the insanity, I sort of feel sorry for the people in the ad. I do. I know they aren't going to get past it. Hey, I'm fat, not stupid.

But I sure as heck don't say this to Tonya. What would she think of me if she knew that I look like I look but I don't feel ashamed? I don't need to look around to get something to be ashamed of. No, I got Ma for that.

I sigh. "I call my mother at lunch," I say.

But what do you know? Tonya sighs and shakes all that hair. "Yeah!" she says, real tired suddenly, like maybe she's missing her coffee. "Me too."

"Your Ma?" I say. It's funny. You never think of anyone having your problems.

I can't look at her. I look at the phone instead. I hear "Ma," I look at the phone.

Sometimes when I call Ma, I just put my head on my desk and listen. Ever since Paully goes the full day, tears. I say "uh-huh" sometimes. Sometimes I cry too. She don't even know.

"Every day," I tell Tonya, "lunch time, she makes up some crisis or other that only I can handle just to show me how it won't work, me being so far away."

I tell Tonya, "It's when Ma's sweet that it really gets me. She starts in with how much she misses the way I'd bring the Marx

Brothers' on the weekends."

"You two would watch movies together?" Tonya says, like hey! Daughter of the year!

"She's good company, my ma," I say, "and funny...? I tell you!"

"Your mama is funny?" It's like she's jealous or something.

"Ma," I say, just so she won't get the wrong idea, "she just refuses to learn the VCR. She won't even try."

"With mine," she says, "it's the microwave."

"Ma?"

"Jody?"

Every time when I call she says this. Like she gets so many calls she can't remember what my voice sounds like. Like she's got a dozen people calling her "Ma". I sigh.

"Jody, oh Jody, I'm so glad you finally called," she says. "It seems like forever I been waiting. Jody—you got to do something. This boy you got me, for the lawn? Jody, he's not working out."

When I finally got fed up with mowing Ma's lawn for twenty years I found a neighborhood kid to do it. Eight-fifty a trim, he brings his own mower, cleans up good after. But for Ma, this was never okay. No one can cut the lawn like Jody. I got magic powers.

"Why?" I say. "What's the matter?" Probably he left the grass by the back fence long again. Sometimes he does this. No one goes there anyway.

"He's taking advantage, a no good gonef, that one. Sees it's me who pays him, a little old lady, and not you, and he takes advantage. They don't know right from wrong, the children these days—"

"Ma," I run my hand through my hair. I sigh. "So?"

"He don't give me my change."

He don't give her her change. I better take the next flight home.

"*I* don't got change," she says, like who is she to have change.

"Aw Ma, just go to the corner."

"I should leave Paully to make God knows what trouble?"

"What's he doing home, Ma?"

That don't stop her. She goes on, I don't know, something about the kid or about kids in general. "Ma," I say. She is still talking. "Ma, look, don't give him nothing next time." Finally she quiets down. I go on. "Tell him he owes you. Then the next time—"

"Maybe he won't come back."

She'd like that. "Don't borrow trouble, Ma," I say, and then "Hey, Ma..."

But she don't hear me. She's going on about what happens when the grass gets too long and then they both start sneezing all over the place, and Paully's so sloppy with it. I could recite this.

Why is this so difficult? Why have I made this so difficult? There is like no subject that I can talk to Ma about now. I want to tell her. I do. I want to tell her that I like it here. I like standing beside my nice flower curtains where no can see me but I can feel the sun on my body. I like my bright white kitchen and my little shelves with the pot pourri and the glass cats and the picture cube.

Or about having breakfast out on my deck. I can't even tell her that. Not even that. First off, I can never say anything to Ma about food. I can't even tell her about the salad barn at the mall. That's what we call it. The animals to the trough. So much better than the greasy food court on Brooklyn. Ma is always telling me how to eat even though she knows I hate that. It's not that she's saying go on a diet. Then I could say, "You go on a diet, Ma and see how much you like it," and that would be that. No, Ma don't go on about how much food. She goes on about what kind. She thinks she knows what's best to eat because she's a mother, automatically, no other reason than that. When Ma's telling me what to eat she's not saying "Jody, you're too fat and you should lose some weight," she's saying, "Jody, you're not a mother, and until you are, you don't know nothing." Which, even though it looks like I'm never gonna be, pretty much settles that argument.

I told her about the pool once, she told me not to get fancy-schmancy out here. And about Ryan? I think I'll leave that can of worms on the shelf, thank you. I mean, I might as well sit there and listen 'cause there is not one thing about my life I can tell her.

"I give him a handkerchief," Ma's saying. "I show. Here Paully, here's how, but does he..."

–12–

Steiner   Once among peers he thrived. He joins the circle without persuasion. He is loudest in the singing sessions.
Nothing in the reports I receive bi-weekly is negative.

The others had only to tease him three or four times before he
relocated his fondling to the interior of his pockets. Though still
rather frequent, it is improving.

Paul Kochansky, quite clearly, was poised to stride; I had only to
open the door.

If only the sister would accept that less is feasible than she thinks.
One afternoon I tried to suggest that her family come join her in
California...

She cuts me off mid-word. "The way I figure it," she says, "if the
assisted living places are out, you've got to get him into one of those
group homes."

"Miss Kochansky! Just to apply, your brother would have had to
work a full year at a single job!"

"See, right there," she says. "That's the part I don't understand,
Miss Steiner, all that hostility."

"Parents wait years for these programs," I tell her, "and the programs are selective. And why not? They have plenty of people to
chose from who've received special ed their whole lives. I'm telling
you that not 25% of the waiting list are ever placed in a given year."

For a time she says nothing at all, and then when she does, she
says, "You don't know, do you?" she says. "I'm asking, do *you*—
personally—a brother or sister, a cousin maybe?"

I am tired of the question. In my profession, one is so often asked.
Oh, I know that for many in my field the answer is yes, but they are
no better at their jobs than I.

I have chosen a profession I can trust and believe in. One where
I could proudly tell the simple truth. Unlike many of my peers in
school, older women with families seeking to add on to their teaching degrees, I have chosen a profession. I have chosen *this*. I could
have chosen many things.

"I'm not sure it matters," I begin.

"Don't be so sure," she says. And then she inhales.

"A while back, like a year ago—before I ever even heard of Santa Clara, California—I was at my Ma's house one evening and she wants I should go down to the A&P and get her a few things. I figure I'll take Paully with me too, you know, he can help carry and also, that way he gets out."

"She doesn't let him out?"

"She's an old lady, Miss Steiner. She doesn't get out much herself. This is why you need to hear this.

"We get our stuff and we're just standing there in line and I notice the woman behind us gets this particular expression on her face. This look, Miss Steiner—well, let's just say it's not the first time I've seen it. It's a look like—how can I put this?—*horror*, that's it."

"Oh, now—" I say.

"No, no I mean it. You'd think Godzilla was weighing the apples or something. And it just gets worse, like a cartoon. So I think, first thing, oh Jeesh, what's Paully doing now? And it turns out he's not doing anything, just rolling some cans around like they're cars. I can't figure out what's this lady's problem. But I'm not gonna say, 'Hey lady, you got a problem?' 'cause that's just not something I'd do."

"I should think not," I say.

"Well I guess she sees me looking at her, wondering, and she quick reaches into her cart and grabs out her box of Kleenex, rips it open and hands me a couple."

"Well that was helpful," I say, though I'm not sure she's listening. Instead she changes her voice to something reminiscent of a "B" movie actress, broad and theatrical.

" 'He's. . .he's drooling!' this lady says. And I look over and sure enough, he is. Like a big so what. So I hand him the tissue, I say, 'Here Paully, wipe up.' And he does, and that's the end of that, but I will tell you, Ms. Steiner, they got a dentist's office in hell for that lady to work at."

She stops then and waits. I think perhaps I am supposed to laugh—the hell thing—but it's just not funny. It's just not. "She was an ignorant person, Miss Kochansky," I say.

"Ms. Steiner—you're gonna have to trust me on this. There are a lot of ignorant people out there. And something else, these ignorant people—that are everywhere, not just in Brooklyn or whatever, but everywhere—they hear you got a brother who drools and they wonder about your oral hygiene, you know. They wonder about you."

"No, Miss Kochansky, I'm sure—"

"No, Ms. Steiner. You are unsure. You don't know. I'm gonna guess no one has ever questioned your oral hygiene. Yet I sit here and I listen to you go on and all I can get—not from what you're saying, more like from what you're not saying—is this feeling that you're like mad at my family because, by your way of thinking, they didn't do right by my brother. They didn't enlist early enough or something. Maybe they did, maybe they didn't. I don't know. I'm thirteen years younger than he is. He's always been there, do you understand? He's always been there.

Jody   Every minute. Waking earlier than I do and singing in the bathroom; Pa could never get him to stop that morning singing. Ma set out his food first so he'd have something to do while she helped me with mine. He had a great big hug for me when I went off to school and another when I got home, which usually left flour somewhere on my clothes. Ma would let him out of the kitchen for a while then, and we'd play with my dolls or I would read him my books and he would put his head in my lap and sleep. When I got old enough to take him, we'd go to the playground. He couldn't get enough of the sandbox. He was jealous of my homework, jealous of my phone calls. I could never have friends to the house, never once a sleep over. And oh! This thing called camp! Two weeks in Connecticut where they did... I don't know. Camp things, whatever. Songs. Evelyn from across the street would come home with leather belts that said her name and orange painted boxes and potholders.

For me summers meant taking Paully to the pool. I'd walk fast as I could, dragging him by the arm, so's I'd be extra hot and the water would feel even colder and more surprising when I'd jump in. Paully was great at the pool, silly and happy. He'd try anything—anything I could think up—somersaults and handstands, submarines and cannonballs, stuff that other kids might get yelled at by lifeguards for doing, but they always left us alone. Me and my big white jiggle-bellied brother, spouting up like whales. Only problem was, Paully would not stand still one second while I tried. There was never any time for me.

No time of my own, ever. Even the most private things.

Like when I'm twelve, right? Just normal old twelve. But I'm a stupid twelve, you know, because I don't know. No one told me. My parents, well, they're a little older than most kids' folks, a little old-fashioned. I can even say a little shy. I guess they don't think.

Anyway, it's just an average day at the Kochansky house with everyone running around going nuts. Paully breaks something. What is it? Oh yes. One of Bubbe Rubin's teacups. The thing of it is, he breaks it on purpose. Paully picks this time to be going through this phase—always breaking stuff—but he picks the stuff. It has to be something he knows matters to someone else. I mean, what a brat! He's, I don't know, about twenty-five years old, I guess, and he's gotta get all the attention, all the time. Look at me! Look at me! And if he's gotta break something that you care about to get it, then he just will, you know? Bubbe's stuff is a real thing for him. He knows it will get to Ma. With me he goes after my dolls and my markers.

So then, for punishment, they make him go to his room. They say "You're gonna stay there all day! There's no one here to talk to you. No baking today!"

And he stands at the door, pounding, and moaning, "uunh, uunh, meee, maahmmy." Like an animal, like a...

Jeesh, he makes me so mad! Moaning like that! No one can think! Like he don't know why he's in there. He does. He knows. So they let him out, of course. He never has to stay in. He just gets louder and louder, "uunh, uunh, meee," and out he comes—a bright, happy boy. "Sing-sing the record player!" He comes into my room, like I don't tell him every day that he's supposed to knock, and he says, "Sing song, Jody!" And I want to say "Jump in the lake, you brat." But then, you know, I'll be in it. And me, they're not gonna let out.

So okay. So who said life was fair? Not me, boy. Not me.

Anyway, Paully has just broken this cup or whatever. Takes it off the shelf and smashes it down. I don't see him do that one, but I've seen him do others. And Ma is screaming, top of her lungs, "Paully! Paully you bad boy. Did I say never do this?"

And Pa comes in from the living room. "What? What's he done now?"

And Ma sees Pa and she knows, now she don't have to yell at Paully anymore; Pa can do it. So she starts wailing, "My mama's good cups! What have I got from her? Just this! What have I got for me? So little. So little and it's broken, broken!"

And Pa is like, "Paully, you get away from that," and, "Ida please," and, "Paully, that glass is sharp." At which point he calls for me. "Jody, come in here. I need you."

Like it's my job to sweep up the sharp glass. But me, I have never seen this rule. I have never seen where someone has written "All sharp glass will be swept up by Jody." So I ignore it. I go to take a shower. I'm hoping by the time I'm out, Paully will already have moaned his way out of trouble. And I figure, what with the water and a couple of songs, I can just block it out. Not that this is so easy. It's loud.

Ma is still with the "so little, so little." And Pa's saying, "Ida, enough is enough," which I don't know why he does, it always makes her louder. And he's yelling, "Paully, you get into that room, now! Don't let me hear you! Not one sound!" And Paully, well, you got the picture. Or not the picture, the sound. I turn on the water first, you know what I mean? Drown them out.

And then I take off my clothes and, well, there it is. Blood. On the panties. And, like I said, I'm like, hey! What's this? And I'm scared. I don't know. Blood. It's never good. I start yelling, "Ma, get in here. Ma, please, I need you. Hurry!" And I'm sitting and sitting, all the time it takes to get Paully pushed into that room of his, and all the time I'm like, just sitting there with my panties around my knees scared I'm dying or something. I mean I really think "dying." I don't know. Blood.

So finally in comes Ma with her hand out and this little piece of broken cup in it, like it's a butterfly or something. "Look what he did!" she tells me, like the whole neighborhood don't know by now.

And I say, "Mama! Look! Something bad!"

And she, like, falls, or no, not falls, she like drops against the sink. She lets the little glass piece go and leans on the sink looking up. She's got this expression—she still gets this expression—she closes her eyes and bites her lip and tilts her head up, like "Give me the strength to draw another breath. It's all so difficult."

And I think: oh God, this is it. This is bad. And I say "Mama? Mama, please talk to me."

And she waits and draws in a great big breath and I stare at her and stare until she turns to me and says, perfectly calm, "Why is the water running?"

"I... I was gonna take a shower," I tell her.

"So you gotta use up all the water in New York for that?" And then she turns around and shuts off the tap. That's it. Done. She stands up and turns around, her hands on her hips, like there's no big deal, and says, "Wait here."

So I wait. I wait and wait, and finally you know, I'm beginning to feel a little dumb, sitting there like that. I pull up my panties and I put on my skirt. I go looking for her. She's in her bedroom. She keeps her stuff in her closet, in this dark corner, it's a big secret, see, and she can't find this thing, this little belt I'm supposed to use, so she's, you know, on her hands and knees, searching.

Now Pa sees me leave the bathroom and he follows me in. "You don't come when I call your name, little girl?"

And Ma turns and looks up at him, great big smile, pretty smile. She's so small, Ma. On the floor like that with her sharp nose, she's like a dark little bird. She takes in a breath, real dramatic and she says, "Jacob, our Jody is not a little girl any more." Now I am just completely thrown.

And I say, I don't remember what, something like, "What Mama? Why not?"

And Pa says, "Jody? You don't know?"

"What's happening to me?" I cry.

And in the other room Paully is yelling, "Meeee, Meeee!"

Pa yells out, "*Sha* Paully!" and, "Jody, please enough," and, quieter, "What, Ida, you don't tell your daughter?"

"Tell me what?" I cry, a whole new wave of tears.

Paully must hear them. He gets louder.

"So, what?" Ma says, everything's a challenge, all the time. "So now I'm not a good mother?" and, "Paully, *sha* now!"

And I start in. I'm like Paully, rocking, crying, "Meee!"

And Pa says, "I just think maybe a mother tells her daughter a little of what goes on."

Ma finds the belt and she takes it and the pad and thrusts it at me. I don't know what I'm looking at. She says, "Here. Go put these on."

I take them from her. How they're supposed to work is not all together clear. I stand there waiting for more. Ma says, "Go. What are you waiting?"

"But—" I say.

"Go!" she says.

"I can't stand that noise," Pa says. "I'm gonna let him out."

And Ma follows him. "And you! Such a good father, you let him break things!"

And I go to the bathroom, and I sit.

–13–

Danny   Morning brings its misery medieval. Strap weighted leg to pulley; strap body to wall. Fifteen to the side, then crossbar to center. Inside, I'm aria, my suffering solo. Eyes closed, forbearing, just to decrease the speed of decay.

Each time, a throb deep in the hip. Change legs, repeat, this side, the pain worse. Then prone, and again, always water in my mouth here, and water up my nose.

Then Tuesday, when she can, I do my sweet deal with Sally. She slips a free "M" through the Met's admission booth. I actually *have* a membership! I've just never told her! Sometimes I'll savor just two or three paintings. Then, when she's off, I buy the bagels, and we discuss current reads.

Yes, friends new, old, unmet, friends fondly remembered, friends every possible day. Like spokes radiating, they make the spinning faster and fun.

Then boys who speak only when spoken to. Boys who have never been listened to before. Boys who mumble wisecracks just loud enough to hear.

Phase one I call "Cliff's Notes." What went down in the testament before that and then, what will follow.

Some still little boys, so far from manhood, they are probably still sleeping with teddies. With wonder richly running, they are caught up in the tale. Others comprehend with slick soap opera psychology; we know so much about each other now. In this age of shock TV, my work is boys.

We "deep read," like poetry. We consider every word.

With their sports or their rock stars, cheering and tribal, with their basketballs balanced between arm and hip, their minds out the window, tracking their brothers. They are not all special boys. Some boys are not bright; no amount of prep school will ever make them glow. Boys squeaking by. I listen to boys. Boys who can't seem to get beyond Willie.

We enter phase three, "direction," the meaning of the ceremony, all the laws to follow, a little bit of what I think it means to be a man. In fact, I have a set shtick. "Whenever you think you should thank God for something, you should. And mean it. And then get on with your day."

Most boys figure they can live with that. Then I teach the word "conscious" and how my little shtick applies; how it's learned through daily lifting. Most boys vow to try.

Next I'll plan to get to Kirsten just minutes before she closes up her shop. It's not that I don't want to visit, it's just that with Kirsten, a little goes a very long way. Something about Kirsten, a certain...*je ne sais quoi*. Who else can get emotional about a new dye for alpaca? But she was the first who showed my work, who got me ins at the chic consignments. She always offers me the best prices and a little too much advice. When you think you've found a friend, extend. And mean it. And then get on with your day.

For a week is a wheel you must set your shoulder to. A week is the face of a clock.

Ida   All right, all right, so I'm not alone *all* day. Every day, three o'clock, I got *The Steiner Report*.

This, I want to be clear, is not conversation. This is not "lunch." For Jody, way out there in California, maybe this is "lunch." I get myself a little plate of the cookies. So anyway, we eat, and Jody, she spiels.

"Deborah Steiner says they got lots of people Paully's age at this school place, Ma. Deborah says they give them little jobs. They give a paycheck, Ma."

All of a sudden Deborah Steiner can do no wrong by her. Deborah Steiner tells us all how to live now.

"A paycheck?" I say. "That will change my life."

I say this because I want Jody should stop with the wonderful wonderful Deborah Steiner already and get to the part I like when she tells me how our Paully is doing there.

Would you believe? They gave him fifty cents, he should go buy a Popsicle. This is what the mavens mean by an "integrational skill," he should do for himself, eh? All by himself he goes in and shows the man at the store what he wants. What does my boy come out with? A cookie! Of course, a cookie. Peanut butter. But he tells the teacher "oogiyot"! Is this my son, I ask you?

But this also I don't tell Jody. What I say is, "So why waste fifty cents? I got already a kitchen full of cookies loosing their chew." I don't mention I give them to the neighbors and send them to the school for the other children. I almost tell her about that nice bus driver who stays sometimes for a krechen or two, but not everything is Jody's business.

So what's she got to say? The whirlwind social calendar of the Daughter's of Israel. "Ma, you should go to the DOI mahjongg." Now it's "DOI" all the time; she's so familiar. "Ma, they got an afternoon movie there."

So, if you don't mind, I can take a nap here just as well. And here, you'll forgive me, I at least know where the bathroom is. Afternoon movie! *Feh!* I can just see Jody out there, sitting in her office, reading off a list that snoopy girl sent her.

"Okay, okay," I tell her, "so she was good for Paully. So I'm not retarded."

Every day it's like this, three o'clock, something to rely on. But then, one day, just as I'm getting used to it, she says something I don't expect. "Ma," she says. "They're gonna make a bake sale for Paully's school."

"Yeah?" I say, because she still won't admit how many times a day she finds time to phone her new best friend. "And how come you know all about it?"

"Ma, don't make like you're not interested," she says.

So Jacob, they take the boy for nothing. I got some debt to these people. And what are they asking? They're asking I should bake. This is how I add my share, huh? I didn't take from nobody, Jacob. Not even the family. Not until now.

"So I'm interested," I say. "I'm also interested in a million dollars, but I ain't planning my retirement."

"Get a pen, Ma," she says.

Since Deborah Steiner, my daughter makes orders at me. But I get a pen. She gives me the details.

Then she says, "Oh! Aren't you excited, Ma? Your cookies on sale again."

And so? Maybe I am. I open my mouth to say, but then I close it. I don't see why every little thing got to be Jody's business.

"You know what I wish, Ma?" she says. "I wish Pa was here, he'd—"

"He'd what, Jody? Make a big confetti parade down Fifth Avenue?"

"—be proud, Ma, Paully—"

"—That little van as the main float."

Silence. Jody, she don't want to fight. We're going to fight, she's going to go. And when she goes... when she goes...

I'm used to him. It don't feel right he's not right there in his room, listening to Mitch Miller, singing the way he does.

Now he comes home, it's maybe four-thirty already, and I can't keep up. Suddenly he won't sit still a minute. He gotta see how everything works. He takes all the cushions off the couch and then can't stick them back on. I'll tell you, those cushions ain't a small thing for me anymore. He keeps turning the radio on, off, on, off, opening and closing the living room curtains. All the time he wants to know why he can't do things the way they do at school.

And Jody, she says again, she wishes you were here.

"Jody," I tell her, the best that I can. "The house looks smaller."

–14–

Danny   No reprieve 'till Lemont's turn, when I unstrap gladly.

"Hey Danny," he'll say, "what's the word from NPR?" as he straps himself in that trap. Not for improvement, but when one of us can't make it, the entire morning's shot.

Comes evening I'll almost never miss The Thursday Night Old Boy's Club, currently in our thirteenth year. There's Joe with M.D. and Ray with C.P. and Ben, who, despite M.S., finished his Ph.D. I'm the only one without a set of initials and just one of the running jokes is proposing a set for me. We have laughed together since young men, stuck way out in our ghetto, our large "accessible" flat. More convenient to campus buses than to the campus, it was also clean, handrailed, and totally paid for—a special and very generous grant. When you think you should thank God, you certainly should. And then get on with your day.

But alas, it was just us, all the time, just us, until Joe talked us up to Pan Hel. Degrees or not, Joe's the brains in this group. Turned us into a charity concern. Suddenly sorority girls running through and down like water in the cups of a grist mill. Sweet smiling young women charmed to discover how we found so many things to talk about besides the game. And yes, a few stayed. Yes, quite a few! Those were the great days. Great.

I'm still filled with stories when I meet up with Andy in his favorite all night diner after the theaters go dark. Andy, a boy whom it was my great pleasure to tutor, interns at The 47th Street Rep. He's tells me his latest has a part based on me! I'm so flattered I fear I'll blush and be foolish.

For a man like me, I've lost many chances, there is so much I do so want that may never be. Yet seedlings I have scattered have sometimes come to bloom. And treasures too, I have gathered my few! Weighed and some tossed, others, tied-on.

Like spokes radiated returning to center, these knights in nothing, laughing and nudging whoever dares coast. These men of my a.m., who every day see this thing that I call "body." I only hope they're brave enough. I only hope they're swift.

Fridays, I think, are best to visit with older friends. Something about the coming weekend, they feel even more alone. We talk about the families. Or they talk; I just listen. Their stories can fill me like a nourishing meal.

On to boys in their green, hardening towards men. Boys teaching lessons of wonder and awe. There was the son of the veterinarian with his limpid room, glowing, walls of humming aquaria that he had watched for hours, his gentle explanations, his good eye for detail. And the boy whose brother died suddenly just one year before. There was the tortured violinist with his crazed ambitious mother. And there were several who never saw their fathers at all anymore.

Then, phase four, we write the speech. And if there's any time left over, we talk about girls. Boys who look at them and boys who are too frightened to and boys who are frightened because they don't want to.

Boys so sweet and dopey, everything a mystery at that age.

More than they have ever taken on, longer, deeper, harder than anything they've yet done. All eyes fixed upon them, relations flying in. Parents entertaining siblings they've vowed never to speak to again. The elders from the old country, perched to judge. Boys who are sleepless, so much laid upon them.

Saturday we slack our little Brooklyn cross-section. If there's any time left, we talk about women, or fall into conversations more one on one. These days it's Rossi I hurry to talk to. He's stumbling about now, talking divorce. Though I think that he's finding himself. We talk about her.

Lemont runs a booth in the Canal Street Flea Market. His stuff parks there permanently in an old wheelless van. I'm likely to join him if the weather is fine, hang out there, drink a few beers. I have a set shtick. I say once you buy it, if nothing else, you can have the pleasure of giving it away.

For hand over hand, passed, tossed, and lost, possessions, like time, are yours to use but not hold, to lose just as swiftly as gain.

For a week is a wheel of seven spinning circles. A mandala blown to the wind by our stride after prayer.

Jody June, well, she's into these groups—her Dad drank too much—so she goes to this meeting and that weekend workshop. And I listen to her, and okay, she talks about herself maybe a little too much, but, you know, I stand there and I listen, and when she says what questions they ask her in these groups, I gotta ask myself too. And it gets me to thinking. I can't say I'd want to be like her, always going on about myself, but I do enjoy listening. See, I always thought that it was just me, you know, and it made me feel like if I started to talk about myself, they'd thank me for giving them such a good nap.

Not that this is an issue. I would never say stuff like that, like about myself and Ma and Paully to some girl at work.

But before June goes on to tell me all about her own dad and how he was when her family had to move out of a house, or something— June's always got a story—I look at my watch long enough that she'll notice. It don't take long. June's a noticer. "But what did you want to talk to me about today, Jody?" she says.

I smile. It's me who should be asking the questions.

I give June the big picture. I'm willing to bet Nancy Riley bought right; last year's sales were healthy. So now all I got to do is figure out *what* she bought.

"One thing I have seen for sure," I tell her, "is that people buy different in California. They buy for business. They buy young. Other than that," I say, "I don't got data. I figure for ads I'll just go tried and true. I sure don't got time to get creative."

It's like I can actually watch her listen. "How do you feel about that?" she says.

"How do I...? I feel like I would like to be half way through the spring order forms by now is how I feel about it."

"I mean about not being able to 'get creative.' "

"I feel like if I don't get decent sales figures this Christmas, I'm outta here. This is not complicated, June."

"Maybe, but I've noticed the way you had the music in this department changed."

She's right. I dropped that dreary classical stuff third week and brought in some saxophone. More daring, high-end luxury stuff moves better with some slinky sounds.

"And I noticed how you had the lights redone."

Right again. On the sexies. Just as promised at the interview.

"And how you do the mannequins yourself."

Now that I wouldn't trade for anything. They're like life-sized Barbie dolls.

"I think that's all pretty creative, Jody."

I can feel the heat rise to my face. I can't look at her. "Do you feel you will somehow have to stop all that—all those pieces of yourself that you bring to this department—in order to keep this job?"

Now wait a minute. Who is asking the questions here? "Look," I say, "can we just talk about the ordering system already?"

I start in with my questions but June motions with her hand. Now what? She wants me to give her the sheet with questions on it. I can't believe this. I mean *who* is in charge here? But then, I don't know. I can see the point. A lot of our time is already gone and this will be more efficient. Leave it to June, if there's an efficient way to get something done...I hand her the paper.

She reads through the questions. Her head begins to shake. She reads through again. "I'm sorry, Jody, but really, I don't know any of this. When Ms. Riley had cases to receive she usually left me on the floor and had the rest of the girls work stock."

Of course she did. That's what I'd do.

"And as for sales reps, you know Jody, with my history of co-dependent relationships—and you know, this goes way back—my therapist has really suggested I avoid becoming involved with persuaders."

"What does that mean, June?"

"You know, people who don't respect bound—"

"No. I mean, what does it *mean*, June?" I say. "Can you tell me anything about the sales reps or not?"

"My therapist says I should avoid them."

I let out a big breath. I put my hand out for my sheet of questions. She gives it to me. I lay my head back against my chair for a second. Just a second, that's all.

"Jody?" she says.

"What?" I say. I put my elbow on my desk. I put my head in my hand.

"Maybe you could try calling her," she says. "Ms. Riley, I mean."

I close my eyes.

"Jody?" she says again, softly.

There is something about June. When she is talking, she is talking. Everything about her, her face, her body, is talking. And it's the same when she listens, only opposite. Even with my eyes closed, just hearing the sound of her voice, I can hear that she is listening.

I tell her about the call. I tell her about how I waited and waited and sat in my office all afternoon peeling off my manicure and never heard back.

"Probably she thought it was a stupid question," I say. "Probably she thought it was too obvious to even answer. 'I'm not going to stand here on a Saturday and teach this woman two semesters of purchasing when I worked hard to go to college and learn that.' "

See, that's why I didn't want to make that call. I didn't want to because if it led nowhere... if it led nowhere then...

"I started a secretarial school thing," I tell June. "It didn't work out."

Then I tell her how I started at Macy's, just a stock girl, and then worked and worked, keeping my eyes and ears open. I tell her how all of a sudden girls younger than me, and with college—that darned college. And prettier! And skinny!

"Those little skinny girls probably don't understand what most women want in foundations the way I do. So just keep that in mind," I tell her.

And I keep on telling her. I tell her a lot more than I mean to, a whole lot more, the entire time with my head in my hand like that, with my eyes closed, and her going "mmm" and "ah."

"When I started," I say, "they didn't even have college for retail!

"I should have gone," I tell her. "I could have. Why not? I'm not stupid. I'm not lazy. My grades were all right. I just, well... There were the kids who were going off to college and then there were the kids like me.

"Ah," she says.

"Well okay, I was needed. Bubbe Kochansky was getting on. She just couldn't do the vegetable stand alone anymore."

"Jody—"

I open my hands and look at my desk. "I knew it wasn't because of the baby. I knew when I hung up. I mean, that's why I didn't make that call earlier. The telephone: it's what I do best.

She tries again, real soft, "Jody?" I sit back and look at her. I'll say this; she don't look at all bored. I'm not mad at June. I'm just mad.

"I don't think I'll ever know half of what you know about retail," she says, and I start to break in, but I can see, June is talking now. And when June is talking, she's talking. "But I do know about what I know about," she says. "And one thing I know about is secrets and people who keep them and people who help them keep them."

"Secrets?" I say.

"Ms. Riley doesn't know if you have college or if you've been working at Macy's since the day you were born. And if she did, she wouldn't care. Ms. Riley was a good boss, Jody. I'm not saying I didn't like the woman or like working for her, but there was one thing about her... " June shifts in her seat. I get the idea she don't like saying what she's saying, talking to management about management.

"Speak freely, June," I say, and close the file on my desk and put it against the wall. "I mean, I sure did."

She lays her hands on her thighs, palms open, tense. "It's just that I know what I know," she says.

I nod so she'll keep talking. Suddenly I am aware that I am listening with every part of me.

"She was secretive," June says. "She didn't explain things to us—like why move this item instead of that—the way you do. She never had us back here in her office. She never had us schedule sales reps the way you do, or even answer her calls when she was in meetings. And there was just something about her, Jody." She shrugs. "I'm telling you, I know what I know," she says. "Ms. Riley pushed us away. She didn't look us in the eye. She had a secret going on, Jody. Me? With my father? That's just something I know."

A secret? She's a woman ordering intimate apparel. What's to be secret? What is she, an embezzler?

"Jody, her secret is not your problem," June says. "It's sure not your fault."

I stare at her. June is smart. She may be a little bit flaky, but okay, this is California. It don't mean she's not smart.

Not my fault. It *is* my problem, but it's not my fault.

I stand up and so does June. I can see she's a little embarrassed. I am too. I clear my throat. "Thank you." I put out my hand across the table. "Thank you, June." I have never felt more exposed before one of my staff in nine years of management.

June, wouldn't you know? She's one of those two-handed shakers. Her hands surround mine. "Thank *you*, Jody. Thank you for sharing all this."

And yeah, of course I wish she hadn't said it all California like that, but it don't change at all how I feel, lighter somehow, better. It don't change that I'm glad I did.

−15−

Ida So what they do is they get a little table at one of these Brooklyn neighborhood parties with the trucks that sell Chinese food and the high school band that raffles off a TV. It's the kind of day they call Indian summer, hot even though the leaves are turning. I get picked up by one of the other mothers and we all take money and talk. So what do you know? It's fun. I like to talk to these women. All the time I see someone from the block and it's "my son, the doctor," "my daughter, the mother of three." What can I say? "My son, the peanut-butter-cookie-buyer?" It gets so I see a neighbor coming, I pretend I got interesting shoes. But these bake sale mothers, they understand. And I tell you, Jacob, they are impressed.

I made up six dozen of your favorite poppy krechen. I should have made more. Except for the two I put aside special in case that nice bus driver from Paully's school comes by, every last one sells. Two times—two times!—people take one away and come back for more. There weren't enough for the second lady and she's unhappy about it so one of the other mothers says, "Perhaps maybe you would like to try some of these," and all together we notice this plate of what would have been sprinkle cookies if she hadn't waited until they were too cool already to sprinkle. So what we are all looking at is a plate of plain cookies sitting on top of a bunch of loose sprinkles. A good treat for the pigeons. Maybe. The customer, of course, she don't want. So we all take one, better this mother shouldn't feel bad. Little pebbles would have more flavor! This is what comes of these margarines.

So then what happens is everyone walking past the table squeezes left or right. The Red Sea didn't part that quick. And right away I know, oop, here they come—the chosen people. And just like that, there they are, Paully and eight, maybe nine children from his little school and one of the teacher ladies.

Someone got the bright idea the children should have balloons. They got them tied to their wrists or their wheel chairs and what happens is they keep popping into the faces of people trying to get past. I think that to crawl under the table until they are gone might be a very nice thing, but the other mothers—would you believe—start laughing. Laughing! Their children are bopping innocent strangers in the face and you'd think they were watching Lucy and Ethel! They make a big show calling them over. Suddenly I find myself fascinated by my very interesting shoes.

And then there they are, big grins all around. Some of the children need hugs, some make big silly laughs. And this, Jacob, I gotta admit, this gets me every time. Something about the way they laugh, so big and open. You gotta laugh too.

So I go around the table and give my Paully a hug, he should have like the others. Paully, I'll say this for him, he fits in. He's okay. He even looks good, his shirt tucked nice and neat, his up-to-date glasses. The lady who don't know when to sprinkle gives him one of her lumpy cookies and he gnaws at it and he's quiet and happy. You would think my son would have better taste.

But then this girl, this big toothy, tall girl, she walks right up to him, right up, and she takes off this little baseball cap she's wearing, and right there, in front of his mother, whap! She hits him with it. Right on the head!

"Hey!" I say. She don't pay attention. "Stop that, you!" I say. Still she don't listen. Paully, the poor boy, he puts his hands up, protecting. I don't know what to do. The girl won't listen. So I turn to the group of mothers and I say,good and loud,"Hey! Whose kid is this?" Everyone looks at me. So all right, maybe I don't need to shout. I start again, quieter. "Excuse me?" I say. "But who is the mother of this little girl that's hitting my Paully?"

I don't even get the words out of my mouth; there she goes again. Whap!

Just then this woman as big as our Jody in one of those floppy straw hats the Chinese ladies wear walks up to them. "Oh! You're Paully!" she says, clapping her hands together, such excitement. "Ellie has told me so much about you!"

So Paully does this thing that in fifty-five years with him day in and day out I never seen him do. He makes a sound, something like "Geeee" and ducks his chin into his shoulder, real embarrassed-like, blinking and smiley.

The lady in the hat says, "Make up, Ellie." The girl puts her hat on and Paully puts his hands down and everyone seems satisfied, but me, I'm wondering how many times a day this Ellie girl takes it into her head to beat up on my Paully. Then this Ellie sticks out her hand and Paully shakes it like a businessman. I'm thinking, when did he learn this?

The mother turns towards me and says, "It's okay, Mrs. Kochansky." Now, I have no idea how this mother knows my name. I don't even got time to think about it. She's making this expression, this big wink. Then she says—you won't believe—"Ellie *likes* him."

Ellie *likes*...oy. How can I describe this, my husband? "To fall down is only to learn." So in my mind, there I go, plotz. I stand right there and fall. In my mind, in my mind. I did not embarrass you. I'm stuck there, stupid as stone. Is this woman saying what I think she's saying? Of course she is. Even a stone ain't that stupid. Paully's making with the head ducking again, bouncing, loving all the attention. And Ellie, just like her mother, she claps her hands together.

Is this how any mother feels the first time she sees her son flirt? Frozen and alive and scared and proud, all very strong, all together at once? Ellie likes? I can't think. And it don't help that this Ellie's mother, she don't hush up.

"Ellie just goes on and on about Paully Kochansky," she says.

Still no words come. I nod. I can't figure how it is she manages such deep conversation with her girl when the only way I can figure out if Paully wants milk or Pepsi is to have him point.

I look over at Paully and his big goofy grin. You should see with the new teeth; he's such a sweet boy, so proud—all the attention.

Then the teacher lady says, "Paully's a cool dude, aren't you Paully?" So, now he's a 'cool dude.' So fine. I don't know what a 'cool dude' is and I don't care. What I know is my Paully is happy. A lot for me to admit, you, Jacob, know that more than anybody, but I ain't seen Paully this happy in...I don't know...maybe I've never seen Paully so happy. The teacher-lady stands and dusts off her knees. "Forward march!" she cries, and off our little army marches, and limps, and rolls, their balloons bouncing along. So many of them, so many children like this.

"What's so funny?" Steiner. Her hands on her little hips, spine stiff as a stick.

It was like the needle got pulled off the record. We screeched and went quiet, all standing there, sniffing, confused like when you wake up before you're ready. No one said anything because how do you explain that you're laughing because someone got hit in the face.

"Hello! Hello!" they all say at last. Would you believe? They like her! You could even say she's "in" with this crowd. Everyone got a question for her: "What's happening with this?" and "What's the story with whatever?"

All but one, a lady as tall as Steiner herself. She even got her hair cut the same way but hers is all gray. "Oh hello, Deborah," she says in this deep, beautiful voice, just like that Bea Arthur who played Maude on TV, and then goes off to sit at a table.

I follow her. "What? You don't roll out the carpet for Miss Steiner?" I say.

She says, "Oh, I see Deborah a lot."

Poor thing, I think, her child must really badly off, considering how often I see that Steiner.

Then, my lucky day, Steiner turns and comes toward us. "Everyone's been telling me how well Paully's fitting in," she says.

"He's getting hit on the head," I say.

She shakes her head and looks at the ground. "Okay, Mrs. Kochansky," then, "I'll see you at the center, Mrs. Cohen. You two have a good day." She walks away, her head hanging like a scolded puppy.

We settle back down and I sit next to Mrs. Cohen, who tells me to call her Sara. Across the way, there's a commotion. I don't even need to, but I look anyway. The children, of course, the children.

There are eight or nine of them, but they take up the room for twice that many, and it ain't all the chairs or balloons either. It's something about them, the space that each one has around them, like a bubble, no one gets too close. I hate the way other people look at them.

I lean over to Sara. "Tell me, which one of those children is yours?"

"Children?" she says, and then "Oh you mean..." and she sees what I mean, and then she says, "Well actually, none of them."

"None...?" I think I don't hear her, but I look and she's shaking her head. "So Sara, if you will excuse my asking," I say, "what is it you are doing here?"

"I work for the center."

"You?" Jacob, I'm sitting there with the enemy! "With them?"

"Well not work exactly. Volunteer. They're a good organization, Ida. One of the best in the New York area and that, that *is* something to be able to claim. Besides, I enjoying getting out, filling up my time—"

"So you want to spend your day with people like my son?"

"Like your...? Oh. No. No, Ida, I work in outreach. You know the DOI has a full..." And then her voice trails off which is a relief because I don't want to have to tell this nice lady what, in my opinion, the DOI is full of. She stands and waves her arm, big smile. "Why," she says, "here comes my 'child' now."

So I stand too because she's blocking my view and what do I see? That nice bus driver, Danny, who sometimes stays for a krechen! He sees his mother and he waves. He got something funny in his hand, I can't tell what. He rolls up. His mama leans down and gives him a kiss. "Mother," he says, "I see you've met Mrs. Kochansky."

"Yes, I was just beginning to tell her about my work at the DOI."

"Ha! Rescued!" he says to me. He makes a little wink.

I smile at him. He's got his mothers eyes. Then suddenly I remember the cookies. "I didn't forget you!" I say.

"Forget—?"

"The krechen ! You asked maybe I would put one aside."

"Oh!" he says, bringing his hands together with whatever it is he got in them. "My day is made! Bring it on! Bring it on!"

I make a little plate with a napkin and all, nice and pretty. I steal a few loose sprinkles from those other miserable cookies and toss them around for looks. "Here you go," I say, and stand back and wait. To watch this man eat a cookie is a pleasure.

Sara laughs at him, his enthusiasm. "How is it you two know each other anyway?"

"Oh Danny? He's good company!" I say.

"Same to you, Mrs. K.," then he breaks off a little piece—and I mean a little piece—and he says, "Here, Mother, try."

To Sara I say, "Sometimes I get Danny to stay and talk a while with a plate of poppy krechen."

Oh, does she enjoy! Chews and smiles, looks to see if Danny got any left. He don't. "I can see why, Ida," she says.

I take the plate away from Danny and he picks up that thing he had before.

"What you got there?" I say. And he hands it right over. It's like a potholder, a square thing, knitted thick.

All of a sudden, he's very intense. "Now what you're holding, Mrs. K, is a Lacey Maiden, nice strong basic pattern, right? You've got a nice wheat untreated linen there. Now here it is again, Lacey Maiden, but this one is pure Scottish broadloom."

He knits! Suddenly I wonder if he isn't a little, 'ya know.'

He goes on. "But, here, check this out. Here..." and he tries to twist back to get something from a bag, which is slow and hard to watch, but he does do it. Then hands me another square. This time it's the two next to each other in stripes.

"Just look what these two do for each other," he says. "If I juxtapose the textures, each appears more individual and the whole more rich." It's true, the tweedy one looks tweedier and the nappy one looks nappier.

And then he says, while he does that awful turn again, "Now, look at this!" He's got like a ring, like you'd put keys on, but bigger, and, instead of keys, it's got all these knitted squares attached on rings. "Flip all the way, Mrs. K. Get to the end. I'll show you what I'm up to these days."

So I move some cookies aside and lay the ring on the table, and fast as I can, get to the end. Jacob, in my life I have never seen such... He has left holes in the squares and bound them around the edges with winds and winds of yarn, so the holes are not really like holes, but sort of more like windows. In every "window" this Danny has done something. Maybe he got a bead hanging there, cut glass in deep colors. Or behind the hole, some kind of weaving, or a piece of mirror or a big awful knot or a foreign coin or a seashell, or sometimes even a feather. All so different. Somehow they don't belong there in the middle of all that knitting along, but still, it's like you're glad when you see them and you want to look hard.

"Some holes," I say.

"No excuse for shoddy workmanship," he says.

I meet his eyes. "None," then, "This kind of knitting, what's it for?"

"Sweaters!" he says.

"You make sweaters like this?"

"Uh-huh, I do. For very, very—"

"And he means *very*," Sara says.

"—wealthy people. But for my mother, for example, I make sweaters like this."

Sara opens her arms so I can see her sweater. What can I say, it's a nice sweater, but somehow I get a sense that she is tired of being his model.

"I tell him for me I just want them very warm and simple to wash," she says.

So all right, that's what she says. But I can see how this sweater is cut very Eisenhower. It suits her.

"But I can't help myself," Danny says. "I always give her beautiful buttons."

Sara shows the buttons, flat wooden ones with a border of tightly wound different colored threads.

"Those are some lovely buttons, Sara," I say.

"Guatemalan," says Danny, all involved with the rigmarole he got to do to put the squares away. How can his mother watch him do this? Anyway, she stands there, no expression in particular.

"I started with this stuff," he says, "because I wanted a sweater, Mrs. K. Other shirts could be cut down, but sweaters never seemed to work. So I took a class from the Y, and what do you know? Today, I'm a Hooker." He reaches for his wallet, no big problem because it's in his front pocket, and pulls out a card. It says: Hookers, a handmade sweater consignment boutique, Park Avenue at 87th. "I also show at American Folk in Grammercy, a few places in the Hamptons, and I just got picked up by a boutique on Prince Street." He winks. "Tell your friends!" Then he laughs.

Danny saw me once in my red sweater. I can't look at him.

"Gotta roll!" he says, which I can't believe. "Gotta hawk my wares."

"I thought you worked driving the van," I say.

"Oh I do this and that, Mrs. K." He reaches out his hand and Sara reaches out hers. She puts her fingers through his and he sort of shakes them side to side. A nice thing to see, a little gesture, affectionate, familiar. "Mother," he says, and then to me, a smile and nod.

Sara and I chat. I am so surprised by her and Danny that, for once, I let someone else do all the talking.

She tells me her parents were born here. She got some college, she says, but that much I guess I already got figured out. She didn't finish up though. She went to be a secretary or something, for the president of someplace or other. She said the name of the place like I should know, but what can I say? That's not the kind of thing I know. Whatever it was she did, I can tell by the way she talked about it that she liked it very much and that it was a long time ago. I don't ask her why she stopped. I know why she stopped. I know what it is to be a mother and I have seen her son.

"Alan was a loan clerk at a bank," she says. "Worked his way up from teller."

"A good judge of character, eh?" I say.

"The best. Yours?"

"No," I say, softly. I'm sorry. I know it's not a nice thing, Jacob, but it is true. "No. Too impressed by a college degree," I say.

"Ah. And Jacob's gone...?"

"Nine years now. I still miss him every day."

"Alan, five. I do too." She pushes her cup to the edge of the table. "Handsome though, your Jacob, right?" That you were, my husband. Everyone knew it but you. To Sara, I just smile and look at my lap. "I mention it because you can see it on Paully," she says.

"You can see what on Paully?"

"The beautiful thick hair. Strong shoulders."

Huh. Jacob, this woman thinks our Paully is handsome. I shake my head.

"And Alan?" I say.

"Charming," she says.

"I can see that in *your* son."

And finally, finally—you will forgive me if I am more than a little bit curious—I got Sara talking about Danny.

Ai, she got some sad story there, Jacob. Imagine, a normal boy. A boy with a mind, who liked to play stoopball and climb in trees—a fine boy. And then one spring day, an accident. His spine snaps. Then she got to watch him shrivel and twist. Those were her words. 'Snap,' 'shrivel,' 'twist.' I could not look at her after she said them.

For Sara, every little thing has been a fight. Not with her Alan, I don't mean. And not with the families either. Still for Sara, ever since the accident, she got fights for money to help her Danny, he needs a chair, a special toilet, a ramp, this, that. They got fights to get him in schools, fights with the health insurance. One big long fight this mother had.

I see what she means, and to show, I wave and say, "*This?* This is my life?" Sara's eyes get wide, and then she can't look at me anymore. I know why this is, Jacob. This is because Sara, she has been seen.

And suddenly—how can I say this?—suddenly I feel... Danny? Danny, all right, he comes by; we have a nice talk, this and that. He's a fine boy, Danny, but to him, I'm always just gonna be some old lady. But Sara, if she looks—you understand what I'm saying here, my husband—if she *looks*—if we look at each other—Sara can see me.

I tap her on the shoulder, she should come closer. "I was wondering," I say, "maybe, I could ask you?"

She bends towards me.

"I was wondering... that Ellie girl there. What do you think about her?"

"I'm afraid I don't know Ellie, Ida."

"Well, I mean her and my boy? What do you think?"

Sara takes a moment. "The teacher seemed to think it was all right. She sees them together all the time." Sara sits back in her chair, I guess she figures we're done.

But me, I still got no answer. I don't know exactly what the question is, Jacob, but I do know I want a good answer here. So I say, right out loud, she should see how I'm thinking, "You got to respect the teachers, I know, but when it comes to a son's flirting, I think only the mother's opinion should count."

She busts up. Don't ask me! I can't say what's funny here. She slaps my shoulder. "Oh Ida, you're wonderful!" she says, wiping her eyes.

Wonderful? Me? Such a thing to say! And then Jacob, next thing out of my mouth, "Sara, you know what makes those cookies like that? I scald the raisins in the milk first. Then I soak the poppy seeds in there. The poppy seeds drink the raisin milk, they hold the moisture and a tiny taste of burnt raisin, there's nothing else like."

This, Jacob, I'll have you know, is one of my most prized secrets. A secret like this, I wouldn't have told you. And suddenly, there it is. It falls off my tongue before I think. It makes me feel, oh, how to describe? It makes me feel like I want to lean on her, I shouldn't have to hold myself up and give such things away. Still today, I cannot believe I have done this thing. Sara? She just smiles, and says, "That so?"

She just don't get it—how special. So then I get a thought. It's a foolish thought, but it's something. "Look, Sara," I say, "maybe, if you got a little time, you would like, someday, to come to my house and we can make some krechen together for your son."

Sara, she don't miss a beat. She's taking out her datebook. So it's done. So I invite a guest special to the house for the first time since your shiva, my husband. Who can explain? Maybe they put something in that lemonade the Vietnamese dancing group was selling. Maybe, Jacob, it's because I'm wonderful. Sara says, "If I come Thursday, I can get a lift from Danny."

I raise my lemonade to her. "To a son who can drive, Sara," I say.

"From your mouth to God's ears, Ida."

We toast our glasses in the air. They make no sound at all.

book four

❖❖❖❖❖

Traffic

–16–

Danny Yes, I know, dear reader, you are human. You delight in all that is odd. And I have delayed now quite longer than either literary or polite. But you will forgive me, won't you, if on this particular subject, I prefer to not long dwell?

All right then, said, let us attend: the full physical inventory.

I am forty-two now, prime years by some standards, but am often treated as curmudgeon or child. Willie, he makes me. Much more than I like. Even in New York's insufferable summer, I wear full-length blue jeans and try to cover my arms.

My face, my best asset, I think quite pleasant, high-cheeked, straight-nosed. Blue eyes beneath such dark hair comes unexpected. I wear it short in front, a little tail behind, as is the current fashion. Lemont helps me keep my beard close-cropped, tidy, if I may say so, a soupçon sophisticated. And my dreamers, ah, bless them, they did pay for braces.

My torso, in time, has grown to resemble the concave cage of the severe asthmatic. Slightly stooped, slightly bowed, graceful as bent balsa, it's dip hidden beneath its glorious thick meadow of black and virile down.

And next, for my luxury, my full range of motion—dear reader, may I present: my arms. Wonderful working arms that circling, speak, and hug when they can. My arms, these arms—such as they are.

Ah, piqued? Yes, I know. And now, of course, I must tell. But why is it, dear reader, that to this it must always come? For what are limbs, anyway? Just extensions, inessentials. Not lungs, hearts, not stomachs—amenities merely. We must take care to not overly weigh.

Nor, the eyes, under.

For alas, my fellow humans with vision, we will think with it first, limited by our poor scope, imprisoned.

So, said. Let us attend: debit accounting.

My forearms, my hands, stopped growing at nine. Like slender twigs springing from the winter-pruned trunk of my wheel-strengthened muscles, they have a proportion, not unpleasant, but quite all their own. They are the slim sailless boom, the maestro's baton. They are perfect for puppets, so like puppets themselves. The hands, biker-gloved, leather protection from Willie's constant burn.

Next, appendages inferior: femur, tibia, fibula, patella—bone enshrouded in skin, a living lesson in anatomy. For even the graceful curve of flab, I would be glad. I had hoped that it would come with age. It has not.

They have their uses. I can crawl—in a sense—they afford me some balance. I can sit by leaning back on my heels. I can do this for hours and feel no pain, it is only the rising again for which I need assistance. And on very good days—which come now more rarely—I can manage the few steps from toilet to sink.

Yet they weaken. They decline. They mock the word "re-hab." My doctors have lectured, shown me the x-rays, blamed their useless dead weight for the agonies of my back which govern my every mood.

But alas, we humans with vision will think with it first. We'll recoil from others without legs—pure instinct, primal, beyond our control. It only takes a moment, but that moment's long enough.

Thus, dear reader—for inclusion—my bargain with pain. I am not bitter.

Is that enough now? Have you had your peep? Or does, audaciously inside you, your prurience still whisper?

I can fuck, I can lick, I have lovely little hands and I tell a good joke. There is only the small matter—the clear tube of catheter, constantly affixed.

Jody   "The buses around here," I tell her as I splash my shoulders. "Sometimes they just don't even show up!"

It's beginning to get dark already and Ryan has to go. She has already bounced out onto the side and is ready for her dash. But she holds for a moment, staring.

"You take the bus?" she says.

"You too?" I say. "The girls who work for me, they just can't believe it. They're like all telling each other. It's juicy gossip. 'Miss

Kochansky takes the bus. Wow! And she seems just like everyone else.' "

She stares, her mouth open.

"Ryan? Anyone teach you manners, or what?" Right away I am sorry I am so sharp, but I am burnt up. The salesman I'm supposed to see at two strolled in at three and then that stupid 49D...

She shrugs. "Traffic," she says. She says it just the way everyone around here says it, like, "so what are you gonna do?" From my stop to Chaparral Ridge they got parking lot after parking lot, burrito joints with neon signs, computer stores, insurance. No sidewalks, just traffic islands.

I turn away from Ryan, take the side and kick. Across the street, where the apartments are—no sidewalks either. And I don't live on a street to jaywalk on, especially at night. It's as wide as Park Avenue and there's constant traffic. When I finally do get to the one light, I have to push a button to get a walk signal. It's a big special request. Then the stupid signal lasts like two seconds. You've got to be a sprinter if you want to make it in Santa Clara, California, I tell you.

"I'm sorry," Ryan says, coming up beside me. "I just never met anyone who takes the bus before."

"Well, I don't see what they got them for if people aren't supposed to use them."

"They're for people who can't drive."

"Well," I say, "that would be me."

She rubs her eyes. "You can't drive either?"

I sigh. "You know, Ryan, where I come from most people don't drive."

"No way! When I'm old enough I'm driving everywhere."

"Well if you still live here, probably. But where I'm from we take subways, and buses, or now and then, a taxi, and we walk."

"Where's that?"

I think to say "the planet Zeron." Might as well be. But then I'd just have to explain that this is a joke. "I come from Brooklyn," I say, "in New York City." And then I say, "But I've moved here. For good." And to prove it, I say, "I've lived here almost three months now."

"Is that why you ahways tawk like dis?"

I sigh. Well, she's just a kid. "Yes," I say, sighing again, "that's why."

"And dis?" she says and makes a great big sigh with her whole body.

"Ryan, I do not—"

"All the time! You do it all the time!"

So now that she's got me feeling like a complete misfit, Ryan decides it's time to scram. This time she actually manages a "Bye" before she pads off. At the gate, she stops and turns to me.

"Hey Jody," she says.

"Yeah?"

"You're kicking from your knees."

And she's right. I am. I am making no progress. She trots off.

I should call Ma. I only got a few minutes left really before it's too late for her. She wants me to call her at night, I know. She keeps saying "we'll talk later." She always sounds groggy in the afternoons now, like I'm just getting her up from a nap. And I know she's not going to a doctor unless I take her myself.

I go in and pick up the phone. I put it back down. I click on the TV, pop in a potpie and change into my gown and slippers. It's only seven-thirty, I'm in a nightgown and slippers.

I pick up the phone and hold it, flip through the *TV Guide*. Nothing on. I put it back down. Eleven buttons away and I'll get to hear Ma tell me all about how I got nothing but work, work, work and how Paully dropped an egg behind the refrigerator. You know, just why the heck should I? I put it down. I go get my potpie. I poke in the crust; my face gets covered in steam. That's the best part of pot pies. I'm not calling Ma.

So I sit there and I watch and I eat and I think. And then I don't think. Just stretch out and watch until I feel like crying though there's no reason to at all.

I could call her. We wouldn't have time to say much but good-night.

This commercial comes on, the name of the school Marta is going to. One of my girls—going to school to be a cop. Says she wants to walk around her barrio in a uniform. A good sensible woman. She don't know anything about ordering, but she's a good sensible woman. Why does this make me weep? Why this?

I drop off to sleep, sniffling, and fall quickly into a dream.

I am little, maybe six, and still skinny. I had my long hair. I have a birthday cake in front of me. It is a chocolate cake and it has my name on it. It is covered in candles. It smells really good. The lights are dimmed and everyone sings happy birthday, Ma, Pa, Paully, some people I don't know, Lester, my first boyfriend Mark, Evelyn, Bubbe Kochansky, Bubbe Stern, lots of people, all very happy, singing and singing. And they won't shut up. They keep singing and singing, chorus after chorus of Happy Birthday. But all I want is to eat that cake. I just want them to stop singing and let me eat.

Then Pa says, "That's a good cake. Ma baked a dollar in it," and Ma says, "Go ahead, Sunshine. Make a wish."

But I don't wish. I don't want to take the time to think of one. I just want to eat the cake. So I pretend to make a wish, I just shut my eyes for a second and then I take a big breath and blow out all the candles. All I see is those candles going out, all the smoke, so much smoke it fills the whole room. And when the smoke clears, everybody's gone.

When I awaken, the TV is blaring hamburger ads until I find the darn thingy. I lay back and think. Who were those people I didn't know? Why were they at my party? And, where'd everybody go?

Suddenly, I know what I have to do. I have to take my photo book off the shelf and find my favorite picture of Pa. It's big; I had it blown up. He's in his chair in the living room. It was just no day in particular. His newspaper's in his lap. He hasn't gotten old yet.

My eyes begin to fill because I miss him and I love him so and I just wish he were here to help me talk to Ma. But then suddenly I stop crying and I say, right out loud, "You never asked me. You never asked *me*."

And I stand there in my living room, surprised by the sound of my own voice.

❖ ◆ ◆ ❖

Saturday afternoon, Ryan takes three little mincing steps and then a long slow one. She stops, opens her arm to show the cut of the sleeve, just like I taught her, walks center, nice pivot turn, puts her nose in the air, pretends to open the coat, and continues on her runway stride until she goes down, all elegance, right plunk into the water. She blubs up giggling. Me too. It's our favorite game.

"Watch this one!" she cries, and scrams out.

I step back. Usually when Ryan says, "Watch this one," it is followed by a huge splash.

She takes her start. She's really got this part down, real classy. But as she starts her runway walk, instead of showing her sleeves she starts waving her arms up and down, real slow, trying to be pretty. "I made this one up," she says, and lands puh-lunk in the water with those arms flapping up a monsoon.

At first I am laughing, but when she comes up, she don't stop with the splashing and she bothers me. I tell her, "Stop it! Now!"

I know. It's not her. I'm just not in the mood. That Meena today, she really got to me. What I would like to have talked to her about if I didn't have to talk about ordering, is how to be a little more courteous. But what can I do? Meena has this enormous family and all of them and all their friends come in for Meena and they don't really want to come in for anyone else. It's gotten so any one of my girls sees a woman in one of those saris, she don't even approach her, they figure she wants Meena. But what really gets me is the way she acts like she's above unpacking, stocking, receiving, all that. She acts like. "Why would I know anything?" But I do get something useful. Sharon, it turns out, used to come in Sundays a lot. Sundays! I mean, that's really odd. You never see management on Sundays. I should know 'cause I've spent a few there lately.

Ryan gives up and comes up nice and behaved next to me. "I'm gonna show that one to my dad," she says.

"He'll like it," I say.

"You didn't."

"I didn't like the splashing," I say.

Ryan giggles, which I wish she wouldn't do when I'm being serious. "It's not the same anyway," she says. "My dad sits on a chair next to the pool."

"But you told me he ducks under to look at your body the way you do to me."

"After he teaches me," she says. "*After*. Then he gets a couple of beers and sits in a chair and watches me do tricks."

Ryan has been bragging—like she does all the time—about her father. The amazing swimming father. Now Ryan has been bragging about this father the whole month-and-a-half I've known her and I've never seen him. The mother I've seen. I've never said a single word, but I've seen. She comes, hands on her hips, and gives Ryan a look that makes her scoot so fast she forgets to say good-bye.

The amazing swimming father though, there's no sign of him, and it comes to me. "Ryan," I say. "Your father. He's not here, is he?"

She steps away from me, sort of squinting. Well, maybe that was a little blunt.

"Nah," she says, kinda slow. "He's in Washington."

"Washington!" I say. "He's in the government?"

She laughs. "Everyone says that! Everyone." She reaches her little stick arms out and takes the side, kicking, over her shyness. "I mean the other Washington," she says. "Daddy's a fisherman. He's got a real fast boat and two crew guys. During the summer I go sell stuff for him. There's like a stand. With ice and fish. I take the money."

My heart sinks. Just think, that pretty little kid stands behind a smelly wet booth all summer making change, piling on ice.

"Then after, we do our practice. Daddy says if I can do the two hundred—that's the two hundred meter—" she says in the technical sounding voice she uses when she's telling me whatever it is I'm doing wrong this time. "That was Daddy's best one and he did it better than anyone in Washington and he won ribbons in college and I'm going to too someday."

"I'll bet you are," I say.

"And he says, this summer if I can do it in under four minutes, then he'll take me to get my ears pierced."

I think to say: Ryan, if you want to race, race. If you want to get your ears pierced, get your ears pierced. Don't go letting your daddy tell you what you want. But I don't say that. I'm not one to talk as far as that goes. I take the side too, and begin my kicks. What I do say is, "What's your ma say about that?"

Ryan looks at my ears, my empty holes. "I didn't tell her," she says.

Uh-oh. I think to say, Ryan, be careful. It's not so smart to let your father use you to make your mother mad. But I don't. I say, "I guess your ma don't go sell fish too?"

"Nah. Mom used to, but she hated it, all that fish, the smell. My mom likes computers."

My face is very close to hers. Really I am not used to being so close to another person. But the pool, it sort of swallows up sound. I say, "More than she likes your dad, huh?"

Ryan stops kicking for a moment and just sort of floats there, looking at me. "A lot more," she says.

I think to tell her, it's okay, lots of moms and dads don't get along but they still love their kids. Then I think: great, I sound like one of those ladies with the soothing voices on talk radio..

What I do say is, "Ryan, look, childhood is struggle. Everyone talks about it like it's some great big fun deal, but it's not. It's just not. People say that about all sorts of things, Ryan; they got all kinds of lies. There's a man for every woman. If you just work hard enough, you can fix your problems. Life begins at forty; that's a good one. Lots of lies. And you know, still somehow we grow up okay and live our lives. That's just the way it is."

Ryan's feet drop to the bottom and she stands there, big, big round blue eyes, blinking away.

"So it's nice then," I say, changing the subject, "spending the summer with your dad?" Aw, what am I so nervous about? That's months away.

Now when Ryan considers things, her head tips to the side. It's very cute. "Nah, not really," she says. "I don't get to see that much of him. He's out all day."

"And at night?" I almost don't want to ask.

She begins to kick again. "There's this bar he likes. I can go too.

They let me, but it's boring. I'd rather go back and watch TV."

"Not much of a summer, huh?"

"I'd rather go to camp with my friend Missy."

"Yeah," I say, "Me too."

She begins to giggle.

"I mean," I say, "I would rather have gone to camp too. I mean, when I was your age."

She crosses her arms, tips her head.

"Ryan," I say, "you ever tried skates?"

"Blades rock!" she says.

"Yeah? Are they easy?"

"I don't know. Mom says she doesn't believe I'll wear the pads when she's not looking and 'just who is supposed to pay the deductible then?' "

Well, her mother loves her. We had different skates, after all. It can't be easy to be a parent these days.

"Don't mind me," I say. "I'm always wishing I could do things in my childhood over." I don't know why I say this. It is the first thing that comes out. And also, it is true. Anyway, it interests Ryan.

"Like learning to swim?" she says.

I don't like the question. I turn and face the other side. This is my goal. I go through everything in my mind. The arm, shoulder, head, one piece, hand in little cup, over my head and down, kicks nice and steady from the thigh. I take a real good deep breath.

Ryan's father, though, he must be a very good coach, because Ryan is a good one. Thorough. First she shows me how, then she ducks under to see if I'm doing it the way she says. She'll stand next to me sometimes, her little arms folded, her head cocked to one side, studying me. I think I am doing much better; she wants more.

So suddenly she is up beside me, and what she does, I just can't believe. She reaches out and grabs my tummy from underneath. Grabs it—gets a grip—and pushes up. "Get your butt up," she says.

I am shocked. No one has touched me this way since...well, no one has touched me this way. "Ryan!" I say. "You don't—"

"Aw, come on."

So I get my butt up. What else is there to do? And suddenly

my feet are floating just under the surface and my kick is an easier, lighter thing. I break off and swim across. Fingers cupped, arm reaching like she taught me, kick, kick, kick, kick. Three laps. Three! I stand at the side, panting. From across the pool, Ryan is grinning. She dolphin dives and pops up next to me.

"Your little dive," I say between pants. "I'd like to learn that."

She does two, one right after the next, like a little skipping stone. She stands up, posing and show-offy. Then her face changes. She gets serious and begins to move her arms out away from her.

"What I want to learn," she says, "is the butterfly."

Ida   I'm used to the old ways. So the other day when Danny's over and he looks up at me and tells me flat out, "Mrs. K., I'd like to come by and fit you for a sweater," all over again, I'm surprised he knits. Also, I had a very different idea of how things would go.

What I figured was that this would be like when Aunt Sylvia would come the week before school started every year and take my measurements so she could cut down Lila's old dresses for me. Sylvia, she did this so nice. She didn't just make the dress fit, she'd put on a new collar or change the buttons so the dress would be all up-to-date and feel like mine. Which is why, even though all that standing up straight on a chair and getting pins stuck in my side was terrible, it was also a thing to look forward to.

But with Danny... for one thing, I'm a grown woman now, and Danny, well he's a man. So what? I'm supposed to stand there, holding my arms out from my shoulders and turning around and around, and he's gonna put the tape measure all over me? Could something be more embarrassing?

So what I say is, "Danny, you make sweaters for money. You got better ways to waste your time than making things for an old lady to wear."

I tell him, "I got other sweaters." He just keeps squishing the anise seeds from his springele onto his finger, and shaking his head. So who am I to argue? When he comes to measure me, I figure my job is to have something coming out of the oven. But Danny, of course, he's got all the time in the world, he has a whole ordeal before we get to this. He tells me he wants I should "pantomime motions." And what he means—you won't believe—is that I should play pretend like I'm doing this or that. And here I am, thinking being measured is gonna be embarrassing! But this ain't all, Jacob, no! He turns around in that slow way he got and digs in one of his bags and pulls out a pad and pencils like the artists use. He wants I should play make believe and he's gonna draw! I got my hands on top of my head. What a world today!

"One action I like to have people show me is ironing," he says.

"Ironing!" I say. It's not bad enough he wants I should play but I should play at something I hate? "Ugh," I say.

"Now, people fall into very characteristic positions when they iron, Mrs. K. I can see the way they distribute their weight, hold their shoulders, cross their legs. That way I can get an idea what kind of sleeves we'll want, how long a waist, how much drape—"

"You think about that?"

He shifts in his chair, a little sniffy. "That's why my sweaters are sold in designer boutiques, Mrs. K. They are designed."

I know I shouldn't, but I can't help myself. I look at the floor. "How much?" I say.

He chuckles. "More than you could afford."

"That much? *Ai*, Danny! I knew this about you. I knew it! From the first time I saw you eat a cookie—the way you studied it—I could tell, this is a person who thinks with his eyes."

"Yes. Now. My time is short, Mrs. K., and everyone does the ironing thing for me, even the Park Avenue ladies and some of them have never ir—"

"You make sweaters for Park Avenue ladies."

"One or two a year, anyway." Then he claps his hands, sharp and loud and says, "Okay dear, didn't I see an ironing board in one of those rooms back there?"

Leave it to Danny. We go to Jody's room. I pick up the iron and start to plug it in. He tells me not to bother, that we don't have time and this is just pretend. "Just look at it as your big chance to finally talk while you iron, Mrs. K."

"I should talk?"

"I want 'characteristic,' don't I?" He's grinning again.

So I make like I'm doing a shirt for Paully, and while I do this, I talk.

I tell him about the time after I left the vegetable stand I spent my days ironing with Mama. To this minute I cannot understand how Mama could want this dull work. Washing all the women did in the courtyard, together, a constant pouring from the rinse bucket to the suds bucket, from the boil bucket to the cool, the soft scrape of the washboards, the laughter—oh the laughter—and the chatter. Me all the while, inside, listening to Mama hum. Like being in the frying pan every day with her! She never wants to talk. She stands there with hot pins in her mouth. We got to stand; how can you do pleats right sitting? But why, why we got to wear a blouse, I don't know. A blouse and a slip, yet. Who's gonna see? The babies?

I tell him how I hated this so much that I started baking bread just to have excuses to stop for a while and knead. And how that led to the cookies and how your mama thought of selling my cookies at the vegetable stand, so I could give up on that boring bread and just do what I do best.

I tell him about the sign Mama Kochansky painted that said "Kochansky Family Bakery Cookies For Sale ONLY Here." And how people would go out of their way for them and once they were there, why not a few carrots, some nice spinach.

Danny sketches. He has an odd look on his face.

I tell him about the early days, in Mama's kitchen. What a crazy house! A little cheaper everyone eats home. Besides Paully I got also Sammy while Lila's girls are at school. This way I can make a chance for Lila, she can buy that hat shop. And then, she can run it into the ground. I don't care how much you tell me I should not gossip, gossip, gossip. Gossip didn't ruin Lila's shop. You also have to admit, Jacob, Aunt Sylvia's taste she did not have.

Poor Sylvia, all those years growing up, she could see it was me who had an eye for things. It was me who knew how fat a ribbon for how wide a brim. Lila, she never once showed a veil. Thought they were for hotsy-totsys. *Feh*! They make a woman a thing of mystery. All hats should have veils! Sylvia wanted that business should go to me. She didn't have to say. We knew. She would have waited. She was not in a hurry. We would have the money in time enough, she could retire. But then... then there was Paully. What could she do?

Me, I decide I'm gonna make good with these cookies, eh? So Lila gets the shop. Fine. I'll show Ida is good for something.

And then I understand. The look on Danny's face? This is the face of a nicely brought up young man being patient with a foolish old woman.

"Perhaps I've mentioned this before, eh Danny?"

"Well you have mentioned once or twice how you found yourself with your cookies."

"I what? I found myself?"

"Yeah, discovered your outlet, picked an instrument and joined the orchestra, self-actualized, got in touch with your inner child."

"Finding myself?"

"You've never heard that expression?"

"I don't think so! Finding myself. I like it! Finding."

"Oh, Mrs. K.! That's what I love about you," he says. "You're like Rip Van Winkle!"

"So you will forgive me, I don't follow trends."

I work quiet for a little while I show him how I do one of Paully's hankies. That Danny, he should know better. An old woman you show some respect. But then I think, Ida, since when you can't take little tease?

I make the last fold and have a look at him, working away in that notebook of his. "So," I say, "I 'found' myself. So where'd I get lost?"

And suddenly, it's Danny got no sense of humor, puts his pencil down, sits there looking at me, his head tipped to the side like the first time he saw a krechen.

"Doesn't pay to look, Mrs. K.," he says. "You're not going to travel that route again. Those courtyards? They've been filled with elevator shafts and hot water tanks. A young girl who doesn't want to do what her mother does, no longer has to. We live in the now, Mrs. K. The *now*. It is a thing to rejoice."

Jody   Beth I don't get. Okay, Tonya's got hair and a mama, June's
got her father, I can understand. But Beth, I don't get.

She don't talk. Why would a pretty young girl stick a ring in her
nose? And so much eyeliner, she'd scare a racoon. Plus, she's so
sulky. Of course her sales figures are nowhere. She's the best I got
for closing though, never off a penny—paperwork's neat as can be,
not in a rush to go. You would think a young girl would want to
rush off.

When I ask her about it she says nothing much goes on until
late night. That's like the longest answer I get from her. I give up.
She's not going to know anything about the orders anyway. She's
too part-time. I didn't even mean for her to sign up, but when she
did, what was I going to say? You I don't got time to talk to?

So she's making to go when I stop her. I just, I don't know—I
want to get through. I say "Beth? You like your job here okay?"

"Sure," she says. "It's funny."

I open my hands like, you mind telling me why?

"All everyone wants is push-up bras or minimizers or what
Madonna's wearing."

Well that's why people come to a place like Macy's for a bra; it's
a service. "That's funny?" I say.

So she gets this look like duh-hey, which really isn't the best look
to give a boss, and says, "Because it's *so* sad." Her so's got like three
syllables.

Well I'm totally lost. "Uh-huh," I say.

"It's like, no one's right with their body, okay? So they want to
go out and *buy* something—like you can *buy* something, okay? Why
don't they just change their bodies?"

I look at this young girl. She still thinks she can do anything.
"You can't just change your body," I tell her.

"Oh!" She rolls her eyes. This one's got a face that gives every
thought away. "That is just *so* retro," she says.

I fold my arms.

"Old-fashioned thinking," she says. She thinks I don't know
what "retro" means.

"That so," I say. One syllable.

"A woman can pump up! I mean, there *are* gyms. And they're making the diet pill you know. Somewhere in a factory in America at this very moment, there are guys working on the diet pill. You can get lipo. You can get a boob job."

Yeah, yeah, yeah. I don't even listen. That is, until she says, "Take you—you lost weight and you look great."

"Me?" It was like she woke me up. "I lost. . . ?"

I bought a scale on my way home. Eight pounds since I took the physical. Eight! I wasn't even trying.

Next thing you know I'm standing in the Walden's buying *The New California Diet* and *The Brand Name Calorie Counter*. I'm bringing my lunch to a bench at the far end of the mall lot for a brisk walk before and after. Suddenly I'm pinching myself here and there, the back of my arm just above the elbow, the neck, that little bit that puffs over the back of my bra. I'm shaking my thighs with my hand, I'm balling up my belly. I'm even doing this at work when the girls change shifts. I can't stop touching myself. I weigh myself every time I walk into my bathroom, sometimes twice. I even start asking the girls. They all have their favorites: bananas, fasting, eight glasses of water, hypnosis, fiber, sleeping in plastic, and Tonya, of course, she just swears by coffee.

I shock myself. Since when am I a woman who thinks like this? I take out every box in my freezer and read the labels. What the heck is "lecithin," I wonder. Well it's got "thin" in it, probably not too bad.

Then I notice a few of my things are a little looser. One night I take a good look at myself; I don't even dig my nails in. I don't even want to.

−17−

Ida Whatever her reason—however you want to judge what Sara Cohen did—there is one thing I can say beyond any doubt: that Sara Cohen never made a decent cookie in her life. Poor Danny. My heart went out.

I should have seen it. Right from the moment she walks in the door and I hand her the apron. She looks at it like it's going to clash with her outfit.

"We're going to make Schminkis," I say.

So all right, I know it's sort of a cute little word, but such a laugh she makes. Me, I'm not laughing.

"These are similar to krechen," I lie, as if anything dropped can be similar to anything rolled, "but there's much less room for error." A teacher, I think, has the responsibility to choose the right lesson at the right time.

"Schminkis it is!" she says.

That's what she says anyway, but what she does is she makes for the sofa; she's gonna have a little sit.

"Sara," I say, "the kitchen's this way."

She comes toward me, this look on her face like I'm the nurse gonna let her into the room so the doctor can do something unpleasant, it's not nice to discuss, then stops, halfway through the door. "Whoa!" she says. That's all. Whoa. You, my Jacob, know what she means by this. This is some kitchen we got here, eh? Anyone would say that. She don't speak, I don't know how long—for too long. Then, in this whisper, you would not believe how dramatic, she says, "But...why?"

"So?" I say. "I'm a baker."

"But it's so..." and she looks for a word, and this lady, she's good with the words, so I don't help her, I just stand there, she should think, it will be a nice surprise when she finally speaks.

Sunny? I want to say, someone should say something already. Cheerful, maybe? Two bright yellow counters, all the shiny hanging bowls. Big? So all right. We both know that's what she means, but so what? Anyone can see big. You don't need Sara's way with the

162 / Tracy Koretsky

words to come up with "big."

She shakes her head, still with the mouth open, "Cleeean!" she says and stands there squinting.

I watch her take it in, both ovens, both refrigerators, both sinks, the porcelain and the stainless, all pretty and polished, the hanging baking racks and the rollers and cutters all lined up on the shelves, and standing by the coffee maker in a nice fresh apron, me.

"Ida," she says, "is it always..." and she waves her arm like one of those girls in the used car ads, "like this?"

"Of course," I say. All right, so I don't mention I made Paully go over with the Windex last night.

"There's two..." she says, and I just stand there, she should figure it out herself. "Ida, why...This a kosher kitchen, isn't it?"

"What, Sara?" I say. "You've never seen a kosher kitchen?" Already I know she's never seen such a clean one.

"Well," she makes a little shrug, "no." This is the mother of the boy with the fancy yeshiva education?

"This kitchen," she says, and finally, I think, I'll get some of those fine and fancy words from Sara. "I tell you, Ida, it's like on those New School restaurant tours—"

"And why not?" I say, looking down, she shouldn't see how proud. That old green linoleum is cracking; we should have gone for the Armstrong.

"Forgive my surprise, Ida," she says, totally different voice now, a voice like a phone operator. "You do realize that the DOI center where you now have Paully is not Glatt Kosher. There are other programs—one in Crown Heights, for example..."

How we are suddenly talking about the DOI and not my kitchen I don't quite follow, but I tell her anyway, "Oh, nobody kosher around here. The cookies, Sara. This kitchen is for the cookies." She don't have to answer, Jacob. Better she don't. "Ida's *Cookies*," I say. "You never heard?" But I don't wait. I can see she never heard. "You never saw? Right here in this neighborhood? *Ida's* Cookies? At Rosen's? At Schimmel Brother's? I thought you said you live in this neighborhood?"

"I do. Yes, but...actually, you see, I've never really spent time in those, you know, Jewish shops."

No, I don't know. Where can you go around here if you don't go into "Jewish shops." And, what is this? She's got something against Jewish?

"Well, to Zabar's now and then." Her voice changes, it's like she's saying she's sorry all of a sudden. She pats her tummy "That food, Ida. It's so high in fat and not very—"

She don't even know who I am! I know when I asked her at the bakesale I didn't want to brag but I thought by now she'd be all excited because maybe her Danny told her, or maybe better she'd know the cookies already from the neighborhood and put two and two together. But she don't even know! So all right. So this nice lady don't even care if I am Ida's Cookies. This nice lady, all she wants is a little baking, a little conversation. All over there are kitchens full of women and conversation and baking. Why should this be a bad thing, I don't know. But I want she should know to who she's talking.

"You would not believe what a lot of money people will pay for a little cookie," I say. I say it quiet, but she hears. I force myself to look at her.

She makes a big grin. "Oh! But I would!" she says "For a really exquisite—"

I smile. I think maybe I suddenly understand something about her Danny, about the way he enjoys things.

I tell Sara how no one knew from Jewish cookies. That was half the fun. No one knew, so I had to do for myself. I started from my own bubbe's recipe book, I tell her. My mama, she didn't even remember she had it; it was up away on a shelf. But then one night I was clearing things out—I should have more room for flour, eh?—and what do you know? There it is! Remember? Such excitement! Everyone wants to look, to touch. All of a sudden, Mama, she starts to cry, her own mama's handwriting so many years later. Little notes on the pages, little thoughts, the ideas that come to you about how this or that thing could be better. Some good tips there, my bubbe left for me, though too much with the schmaltz all the time. For cookies, you should always use butter.

I tell Sara all this but I can see, schmaltz , butter, she don't care. So I tell her about the Yiddish and how I couldn't read because I learned to read American and how my Pa, he had to translate for me. And of course, everybody wants to try everything I make. What I'd do is I'd make the same cookie over and over, only one thing different every time. I kept it all neat in a notebook.

"Ida! How scientific!" she says

It was you thought up I should do that, my husband. Thank you, it was such good advice. But that Sara, she got the word for it, eh?

"We all had to discuss," I tell her. "Everybody got an opinion! Oh Sara, we had such fun!"

Sara laughs to think of it and sets down her cup. "I'd love for you to show me that book, Ida. I love old books." There it is again, Jacob. Again I can see that Danny is his mother's son. "Where is it now?" she asks.

I look at that stupid linoleum. I shrug. I know I shouldn't have done it, Jacob, but I never wanted to see it again, so much disappointment. "Gone," I say. "It's all gone now, Sara. Now I use this." I hand her my recipe box.

"Oh, well my, my! Look at this! Why..." she makes like it's much heavier than it is. I got a big paper clip for the place where the krechens begin. "Look how thick," she says. "There must be thirty! I never would have known!" She flips through, shaking her head. "You certainly must have made some special cookies, Ida."

When she looks down at me; something is different. Or not just "something." I know what this thing is. This is respect. And so? Why not?

I can't meet her eyes. "Well, I worked hard," I say. "I worked with what I had, and what I had was a small family kitchen and two little boys. Even the little ones can help. They like to mash things, and stir, and also to make little balls all the same size."

"But weren't they underfoot?" Sara asks.

"Oh sure," I say. "And the fighting! Who got to lick what. Always such a big decision, the spoons and beaters, or the bowl."

I laughed, remembering. Paully, of course, always wound up with the beater. They were more fun, but also the bowl would have more dough. And wasn't that always Sammy's trouble? Always grabbing for the dough.

Sara shakes her head. "Okay Ida, I guess you'd better give me something to do."

"All right then," I say. "You can start by getting that apron on and sifting six cups of flour into—" But then I see she's picked up a hand strainer, not a sifter.

"Sara," I say, "you don't know a sifter?"

She shrugs.

"Sara" I say, "what do you do when a recipe says sift?"

"I just dump it in there. Why get another dish dirty?"

That, can you believe, is the first time I see it, so much I did not want it to be so. She's not here for baking and conversation. What she's here for, I don't know, but baking and conversation, that's not it. She still hasn't put her apron on. "Sara," I say, "you didn't come to learn to make a krechen?"

She laughs, nods, laughs again. "Well frankly Ida, I think cookies are why God made Pepperidge Farm."

This woman, this Sara, standing here in my kitchen. What is she doing here? I like her, I do, her words, the way she's fast to see a joke, the way she's open to whatever may come. I like her, and I know that you, my darling, would like her too, the way she meets an eye, the deep way she listens. But I got to ask myself, why is she in my kitchen? This is the woman I gave one of my best secrets to? The poppies in the raisin milk—they don't get better than that. Fallow ground, this Sara! She don't care! As for my Jody, what can I say? She bakes like an accountant. Stingy. Everything exact and to the minute. She got no feel for it. I should put my recipe box in the oven now. This is what it comes to, isn't it? Fallow ground. Packaged cookies and ugly hats.

"Look, Sara," I say, "I think that what happens now is I bake, you sit."

"I...?"

"At the table."

"And do what?"

"Sit. Make me company."

"Oh really, Ida," she says, standing there, her hands hanging like a bad little girl who's been told don't touch, "come on. I *can* do something. I can chop something. I can chop those almonds."

Sara picks up a paring knife. A paring knife! I'm not letting her anywhere near my almonds. I fold my arms. I look at the chair.

She sits and puts her feet up. She don't seem too disappointed, she's not gonna make cookies today. Me, I start the cookies. Better this way, better conversation.

"My sister," she says, when I've gotten things under way, "lives in Florida."

"Miami?" I say. Jacob, you know I always wanted to go to Florida.

"No, not Miami," she says, "but not far."

Then I say, low, ".You'd like to go live there."

"Well, yes and no." She changes the way she got her legs. A mother, I know, she don't like to have to admit.

"But Danny," I say.

She looks at me. "Yes...but Daniel." She crumbles up a napkin. "I know he feels badly," she says. "Responsible. About me, I mean. He thinks I ought to be, oh, I don't know, working up a golf game."

The way she says this, Jacob, she makes Florida sound like some kind of quarantine. I'm thinking: every year, Lila with the grandkids out there. Once it would have been nice we could have gone.

"He just can't forgive himself that we live the way we do," she says. "He thinks he should be coming out to see me—you understand—with the wife and kids, summer break, that sort of thing." Then she sighs. "Perhaps in time," she says.

I wrap the cord around the mixer, it should stay clean. Perhaps in time, she says. Sure. And also maybe God will part the East River. "You will forgive me, Sara," I say, "but a wife?"

She sits herself up, good and straight, tosses her head so her bangs move from her face. "He's had girlfriends, Ida" she says, like "so there, you." And then, because she sees my face, she says, "Several."

"But he's..." and then I put the mixer cover down, put my hands by my side and make like I'm pushing at some wheels.

"Yes," she says, "he is." And she makes with the hair again. And then she says—you wouldn't believe—"I will admit that it has been too long since Daniel has spent a night away, though—"

"The night?" I say. "The whole night!" I open my mouth. I close it.

"He is a grown man, Ida," she says.

First I can't believe Danny can—you know what I'm saying—stay out all night. And then—his mother! His own mother *wants* he should!

And then she winks at me. She winks! "I just feel certain he's got something going on Thursdays though."

"You don't even ask?" I just can't believe.

"Of course not," she says. "He's entitled."

Well, if this were our Jody we were talking about here. . . *Feh!* Listening to men talk about underwear, that's as close to a sex life as our daughter got.

I turn and look at her, my hands on my hips, and that's when I see. Something about the way that Sara is looking at me, a little sideways maybe, one corner of her mouth up. She's bragging, Jacob! I should know what a normal, healthy son. Fine then. Her boy is perfect. "Well, I wish my son would talk to me and make me laugh and tell me about what he's reading—"

"But that's just it, Ida," she says. "That's just what I don't want. I don't want my son to be my companion. I want him to—"

"Sara, you will forgive me, I know what you don't want. You don't want your son to be the way he is. What is that, Sara, some big surprise? You want for your son to be normal—just normal—I know. Not great, not the very best of all, just normal., so that you can be normal, because as long as he is who he is and the way he is, you can't be normal neither. *That's* what you want.

Both hands come to her mouth, she knows when she's heard truth spoken.

"Sara?" I say, "Oh, Sara, what have I done?" I quick reach into the pocket of my sweater and bring out a tissue. She takes it. She puts out her hand for another one. When she hugs me, her arms circle me and some.

I mumble something about the milk and back off.

"Sit, Sara," I tell her, when I'm looking in the fridge. "I got for you a little story. "

I take a long time getting down glasses and pouring, she should have time to collect herself.

"One time," I say as I work, "many years ago now I had to throw away a whole batch of mandelbrat —six whole pans—all burned up because I'm so stupid, I'm listening to Mary Worth on the radio and I get all caught up. Oh, I'm so mad at myself, so mad—the morning's work, garbage. The family can't afford to lose money. And so I yell at Paully and I yell at Jacob and what does my Jacob say back? He says, 'Did you enjoy Mary Worth?' So I say, 'What enjoy? I cried.' And he nods and says, 'So? Did you enjoy these tears?' And I realized that, funny, but yeah. Yeah, I did. That Mary Worth, you gotta say, she was never bored. For myself, one day is like the day before that and the day before that. You let yourself cry, suddenly you got a habit. Who can take the time? But for Mary? How can it be stopped? So you see, Sara? A little luxury. And now, let's have some cookies."

I turn around, she's got lines around her eyes like the rays around the sun in a baby's picture. She is laughing like at the sweet child who has fallen but not been hurt, who you give a little bit ice cream, and is nothing but smiles again.

"Ida," she says, shaking her head, "I must say, it's been many years—I don't like to think of how many—since I've found someone whom... that is, can you imagine, finding someone—at my age!—a new friend!"

'Friend.' I went numb hearing it from her lips. She's standing there, her arms out.

"The, uh... cookies, umm." I step back.

She nods and puts her arms down and looks around like she don't know what to do next, so I say, "Sit, sit. I'll just... the cookies."

Then I get busy and what I don't know is that, Sara, she does too. When I turn around—what's this? She got the whole table covered with stuff, all kinds of papers and books. On her face, she got a big grin. "Well," she says, "I thought now would be a good time to get down to business."

"What business?" I say. I try to see what's written on those books she got.

"Well, as I said at the bakesale, I work to inform families with special needs."

What kind of woman? She's here to talk about the Daughters of Israel, Jacob! And how maybe my daughter don't think I can be a good mother no more since I'm getting on. Like I haven't had enough practice? I been a mother a while, eh?

"Oh," I say. I fold my arms. "Meddling."

"Ah," she says. "Maybe another time." Me, I'm thinking that once is enough. Sara is putting all her colored papers back in her purse. She's working fast, stuffing those papers and talking fast, same time. She's saying what a good time she had. In my mind, I hear the sound of seeds falling on concrete. *Feh*!

"So suddenly, what?" I say. "Suddenly I'm supposed to fall on my knees, 'Thank you very much, this is just what I've been waiting for?' I have not been waiting for anything, thank *you* very much. I don't want to say "thank you," I want to say, "Who asked you?" Why do they always think we should be so grateful?"

She stops with the papers a second and looks at me. "Well, Ida, I should say, I am. I mean, we are. Daniel and I. Very."

"Look, Sara," I say, "So Danny got a job with them. So this is good. So—"

"That's not a job, Ida." She turns to me, puts her hands on her hips, draws a breath and launches into this complicated mishegas about that van Danny drives around. A van like that, that you drive with no feet, this is some expensive thing we're talking. And that lift for the chair he got inside, that's a whole separate story and not exactly cheap either. Alone, Sara and Danny couldn't manage it. So some smart cookie over there got some money to buy it and made a deal with Danny where he schleps the children twice a day and keeps the van running and clean and they let him take it wherever he needs to the rest of the time. No money changes hands. Even I gotta admit, this is a kind and special trade.

"Have you looked at a New York subway map, Ida?" she says,

"Looked at it—for access?"

Well, to tell you the truth, Jacob, for many years now, I ain't looked at it at all. Sara folds her arms and frowns at me. "Danny would be stuck without that van. He wouldn't be Danny, that much is certain." She puts her bag down. "They're not the enemy, Ida," she says.

"I know, I know," I say, raising my hands over my head. "The DOI is wonderful. The DOI is perfect."

Her arms go back to her hips.

"Since the wonderful, perfect DOI, I'll tell you what we got. We got these mornings, crazy rushing around, and then he comes home, maybe four-thirty already, and I can't keep up. He won't sit still a minute. I follow him around," I tell her. "I warn him. I tell him I'm gonna lock him in his room like we did when he caused all that trouble, but he don't know what I'm talking."

"Oh Ida, I didn't—" she says.

"Throwing mine own mother's beautiful china tea cups—all I got from her besides the shabbas candlesticks—he don't remember. And those records he used to love so much that he cracked over his knee just to make trouble? Like they never existed. He got new records now. Now. That's all Paully knows from.

"And why? What for? So my son should earn a paycheck?"

She sighs and shakes her head. "No, Ida. That's not it. Can't you understand that Paul needs to be free?"

"Well Sara, he didn't cost anybody anything until that Steiner nosed in!"

"No, Ida, I mean 'free' as in 'at liberty.' Free to live his life."

"Oh, you mean *free*! Well isn't that pretty. And tell me, Sara, are you free? Are you? 'Cause me, I can speak for, and I'm not free. Free. What's free? If you're so free why ain't you in Florida?"

I see her gulp. She folds her arms across her chest. She looks at the floor, and then down at me. The expression on her face, Jacob, is something I just do not understand, bitter and sarcastic. "We worked hard," she says. "We never gave up on our son."

My husband, if only you could have seen her face. All at once I understand what it is she is saying.

"Get out!" I say. I do not say it loud, but I don't say it soft neither.

"What?" She can't believe. She's not like that little Steiner girl, all run-away-home when someone yells. Sara is a full grown woman and a mother. She knows how to fight. So before she gets the chance to, I repeat myself. "I mean it, Sara," I say. "Get out."

She picks up her bag of papers and zips it closed. "We gave our son the best we were able," she says, and not in a nice tone either. "The best we were able." She made for the door and slammed it after her. The whole house shook.

Danny   Your white dress, wind-lifted, madras and every-colored needlework. The sprinkles on a cupcake.

Ah, Sugar.

It was 1973. It was already an old song.

I sang it when you told me. "Ah, Honey, Honey." That shy sorority smile, how do you all learn that? Peppermint lips melting open. I just can't believe. I sing, "You are my Candy, girl!" Joe rolled over, knew a good thing when he saw one, said, "Like she hasn't heard that twelve times today."

It was already an old song. And maybe it was always a dumb one. Still, I could not stop myself singing, "You are my Candy, girl! And you've got me wanting... "

Those yards and yards of red, red hair. Maple syrup eyes, cinnamon freckles dusting that little Irish nose.

You in my lap, riding Willie 1. We were the pair in the chair in Washington Square. Someone took a picture. You waving like a May Queen. I just can't believe the loveliness of loving you. Autumn leaves drift and catch in your hair. My fingers, freeing them, caught themselves. The loveliness. I just can't believe it's true.

When I kissed you, girl, I knew how sweet a kiss could be. I just can't believe it's true. Let the summer sunshine pour your sweetness over me. I just can't believe it's true. Ah, Honey!

Your mouth on mine, not open at first...then! Ripe fruit! You are my Candy, girl, and you've got me wanting you.

After every class, after every dream, during every class, during every dream, enduring every class, rushing toward my dream. The four sweetest months of my life.

172 / Tracy Koretsky

I got down on one knee, right beside the fountain. I took both your hands and kissed them. I said, "Candy, will you?" I said, "I'm gonna make your life so sweet, yeah, yeah, yeah."

Your mouth around the word "yes": strawberry lollipop. I just can't believe the one I love, she feels this too. I just can't believe it's true.

"Yes" again, and again, laughing. "Yes" whispered into my ear, "Yes" written on my chest with your kiss-dipped finger. I take both your hands and I bury my face.

The forty sweetest minutes of my life: you, my confection, un-wrapped upon the chocolate hotel bedspread. Toes like melt-away mints, skin marshmallow white and smelling of the bath I just watched you take. My fingers in the butterscotch curls, drying now and springy. My lips drawing in your raspberry nipples like soda straws. The sound of your swelling. The loveliness. Ah, Sugar, the loveliness.

I stroke away your nervousness, my nervousness. All the others, empty bragging. I am virgin too. My other hand gropes the clasp of my pants. Any man might find this difficult. I fumble, a fool. Your eyes open, reverie disrupted. Your lips sigh a mother's coo. Long hands reaching, helping. I just can't believe. Your little painted nails. Jelly beans.

Your two hands working, not deft. You are not practiced at re-moving men's pants. We will teach each other. Honey, I'm gonna make your life so sweet.

I sing, "Pour a little sugar on it, Honey," my head against you, "Yeah, yeah, yeah." You laughing. That sorority girl giggle: penny whistle.

I take my hands from you and raise my hips high.

And that's when you see the tube... Your face...

You hadn't known. I'd thought...

Joe had told me you'd asked him privately if I could. He was touched by your shyness. It was 1973.

I pull myself toward you, my hands on your shoulders. We fall upon the bed, our trembling bubble, broken. I try to get it back. I sing into the softness of your hair, coconut scented from its fresh shampoo, "And you've got me wanting you."

But your hand is already reaching. The panties, the bra you are too upset to clasp and shove in your pocket. The shirt mis-buttoned, shoes untied. I can barely shift myself into my chair in the time this takes you.

Your hand on the knob. You running down the hallway. Hair streaming behind you: licorice twists. I don't even have time to... I grab the towel from your bath off the floor, throw it across my lap, try to follow.

You take the stairs.

Yeah, yeah, yeah.

It was already an old song. And maybe it was always a dumb one.

The room still smells of you. The bedspread holds your shape.

I just can't believe the loveliness of loving you.

I just can't believe.

—18—

Jody With this one, I can't get a word in edgewise. All I had to do was say "Tell me a little about yourself." It's sort of like with Ma, except with Ma, after forty-two years of listening to it non-stop, I don't have to listen so hard, but with this girl, this Amy, who knows what she's gonna say? She don't even know what she's gonna say.

She keeps me so busy looking at the page that I can't take a minute to look up at her. That's okay by me. It doesn't feel good looking at Amy, so tiny and pretty. Just a perfect teeny-tiny little china doll. She could be a model. She dresses like one.

She tells me she loves to work here because of the discount, giggle, giggle. She ends practically every sentence with a giggle. She tells me she spends her entire paycheck on clothes, and off she goes again.

Is that so, I'm thinking. All the time this one is calling in late because that car of hers has got something or other else wrong with it. And then she sits there telling me another belt around her waist is more important than one in her engine. I hold up my hand to stall her. "Maybe just one paycheck you could use on that car of yours," I say. I bite my lip. This is none of my business and I know it.

But she don't seem mad at all, just surprised to be stopped from speaking. She winks at me and says, "If I dress well, everything else gets taken care of. You know what I mean?"

I get a feeling in my stomach. I can't look at her. Only once have I heard "taken care of" phrased like that. Lester.

Amy's going again, on and on. How everything else gets taken care of. She's got three boyfriends, who it sounds like are well past "boy," who don't know about each other, and another one, that she gets all dreamy sounding about, young enough for her, who knows all about the other three and is tortured by them.

What isn't she going to tell me? Please, I am thinking, stop, just stop. Putting up my hand don't work. I have to say, "Amy, Amy, hold up here!"

Finally she hushes. I lay down my pen. I sit back. Hey! That's the blouse from the mannequin in the petite department. It was there a couple of days and then gone. It's probably the same one. I mean, how many size threes would Sharon buy? The neck plunges a little too low for the daytime and I recognize the lace trim of an Olga Bright Lights bra, color poppy red. I can't look at her.

"Amy, excuse me. I have to stop you here. Look, I know we don't know one another too well but I'm speaking here not as your boss, but as someone older than you, with more experience..."

Amy recrosses her legs. X-quisite sheer stockings, color, nude. Maybe she don't think I got enough experience to tell her anything. Maybe she's right. I clear my throat.

"You got to be careful with what you talk about at work. Especially with your boss." I say this, but I don't mean it. After all, it was just another girl who spilled it all with Lester.

Amy gets a little frozen suddenly, a little stiff.

"I mean, listen to what you've told me, Amy. Now I know—or I think I know—that all that stuff you give me about that old car of yours... Well, you got no problem with your car, do you? What you got a problem with is getting up in the morning after drinking too much and getting home to change from God-knows-where you've been all night."

Right away, she's looking at her lap. What there is of it.

"Are you sure you wanted me to know that, Amy?"

She looks up at me, blinking. She sure is a beauty. Nobody stays mad at her, I'll bet. Ever.

"Maybe we ought to go through my list of questions, okay?" I say.

She nods, still looking a little afraid.

Well, she's pay dirt. There is quite a bit she knows. A girl who shops the way she does? She snaps up the size threes before they ever hit the sales floor. She knows the days of the week the different manufacturers are received, and how many times a month. We go over this and over this, her standing over my shoulder, getting it right. When she stops giggling, Amy is sharp as a tack. And me, I'm close to giggling myself. I feel sure I can use this stuff to figure backwards when the shipments were ordered. Then I'll know if the shipments I'm receiving now are stock maintenance or Christmas supply. I'm gonna have dinner in this office tonight and tomorrow morning I'm gonna know a thing or two. At last.

Plus—and of course I didn't even have to ask for this—Amy's had a couple of dates with some of my sales reps. They didn't exactly talk about ordering margins, she said, again with the giggle—every time there's a man in the sentence there's a giggle at the end of it—but she didn't think they'd mind too much hearing from her again if I needed anything.

Mata Hari at my disposal. And there was something about the way she said it. The way she offered it up. Pretty impossible to stay mad at, Amy. A truly smart person. I told her I'd keep that in mind.

Then I thank her and thank her. She really has been a breakthrough. And I am already clearing a space for my keyboard by the time she winds around the piles for the door. Then it hits me, a strange vision. Amy with long red hair.

"Hold," I say. "Wait, Amy. Just one more minute."

Her hand drops from the doorknob and she turns to me. I try to collect myself. I do not understand why I am suddenly so mad, but

I am. I am practically shaking. She could probably see it on my face if she was looking at me, but Amy, like most very pretty girls, don't look at me. They look at my hair or my blouse or over my shoulder.

"You wouldn't know what happened to that little leather number I had on the mannequin by the *peignoirs*, would you?" That long-legged mannequin with the pouty lips. I'd given her a long red wig and a silver whistle.

Amy grins. "The one with all the zippers?" she says. That little scrap had zippers in places that—if you thought about it—probably weren't safe.

"Put it back," I say.

Now it's her turn to be mad. She thinks though. I am her boss. "But—"

"I bought that for display, Amy." I'll give it that. It's an eye catcher. But I never thought someone would buy it. I mean, I don't get how the sexy stuff went from satin to leather. You get close to someone and they smell like a cow.

Anyway, Amy puffs up. "I got a right," she says.

"Put it back." I flash on her standing there, all mad and bratty like that wearing that little thing and I can hardly speak; I'm so mad. It's got almost enough leather for a couple of wallets. "We'll see about your getting it at display discount after the sale." I say, every bit of control I got going into the sentence, "But I expect to see it on the red-head tomorrow afternoon." I meet Amy's eye. I *am* the boss.

How she has done this, I don't exactly know. How she has made me so mad. My hands shake as I boot up my computer. She leaves. We don't say good-bye.

The unfairness. The unfairness of it all.

I try to focus on the screen.

I was young once. And pretty.

I have been keeping the bills of lading in a pile since I started here. I can get a sense of a company's shipping time from them. I would not always have known to do that.

I was stupid once.

Just once.

Young and pretty and stupid.

I make a table, two columns, received date and, when I know it, shipping time.

Yep. Pretty stupid.

The information from Amy seems almost complete. It moves from my eyes to my fingers. I don't even think about it.

I'd leave exactly fifteen minutes after he did at lunch. I loved to look at my watch. Twelve minutes left to go, seven. I'd run the whole three blocks. The Lester Landau Office Temp Placement Agency to Uncle's, his usual bar. We could use a room there.

The door would be open. I'd turn the knob and come into the dark room where he was waiting. We'd press together just inside the door, me against the wall, crushed, God, so wanted. He'd rub me rough, through the fabric, up under my skirt, my shoes skitting off, then one-shoed. His tongue on my neck made me helpless. Nineteen and delicious, he eats me up.

And when he's ready, he throws me on the bed and rips at my hose while I hurry and unbutton my blouse. I fall back arching, wanting. He jabs at me until he's in, then right away grows locked, stiff, jerky. Then he's rigid. Then, all of a sudden, soft and heavy like a big puppy. He rolls off and starts to stroke and pet and talk to me. How long since he's been with his wife. What he was like when he was young, what sex was like, and I lay there and look at the gentle swirls in the pattern of the mahogany veneer bed board and think, now, touch me now. I strike pretty, stretchy, cat-like poses hoping he'll notice and touch me now and he notices, but that's all. He kept me wanting, all the time—coming so near. I could replay it in my mind that night and send my body off and off. Even just the light touch of my open palm, and I was traveling.

But then, with him there, I couldn't. I couldn't reach down and unlock myself. I couldn't tell him to. I could only lie there, panting, hot.

Oh, Lester, watching you, standing there. The light from beneath the door and off the clock radio, your body, fifty years-old, some gray pubic hairs, wiry, your penis, like a small fish. You never let me look at it enough, just hold it, when it was just small and regular. You put on your clothes, your polyester pants, your tie. You sit on the bed, beside me, tie your shoes. Then, dressed, you'd sit on your knees, your face between my legs, just looking, waiting a long time, and then moving in close and breathing, deeply, as much of my scent as you could and I'd want to scream AAAHHH! but then you'd stand up and blow me a kiss.

Can you believe I went through something like that more than once?

Four months. Four months I did that.

I cannot keep myself from it. I know I shouldn't. I am sitting there in my office. I am forty-two. I am the boss and my staff is out there. I dig my fingernails into my palms.

My hands fall to my lap, and then under my skirt.

Four months. Mondays and Thursdays. I just kept thinking next time we'll take our time. Next time we'll get it right.

My nail against my stockings, pressing, pressing then—pop—through to the skin, the rip widening. Eight dollar hose.

Then that other girl, my so-called friend, yeah right. My fault, I hinted to her. I shouldn't have done! Promotion time, she threatens to tell your wife.

My nails against the soft deep flesh of my thigh. Needles.

You know I won't talk. I'd die if my parents ever heard. You give the job to her.

I rip. Slow, burning. I can feel the welts raising, hot like scalded.

Outside the sound of the day's tape chugs through the register. Security will be around soon. They're taking away all the pumpkins.

A knock on the door, the Mexican janitor.

My head falls back against my chair. I bite my lip. I do not cry.

I didn't want the job, Lester. It wasn't about a job.

Danny   Your name on a card. Black on white, simple. Just the one name and a number, so clean, so neat, so easy. She says, "You're exactly what she's into. Rondee don't do the street."

Too many times, refused now. Too many times, denied. Concern for the extra time I'd take, concern for the bed, the smell. Concern for their bodies taking in the tube.

My hand on the pay phone, white on black, shaking. Your accent in my ear. I hadn't expected. No low rumble, no seductress, no games. Two o'clock. Alley entrance. Pick up a sterile catheter from the pharmacy on the corner.

Be careful what you say about them, these women of few choices, most of them harder than you'd want to make.

Your room on Ocean Avenue. Above a service garage. The constant sound of drilling and tinny top forty, REO, Journey.

You've done the place for access. Ramp to elevator, bathroom bars. So clean, so neat, so easy. Bucket by the bed.

Be careful what you see here. Be careful not to judge. Too many times refused now. Devices suggested, hand pumps and blow up dolls. Too many times just watching, taking care of myself from afar.

You shake my hand like a salesman. No low rumble, no seductress, no games. Black in white, I hadn't expected, your English accent in my ear.

Be careful not to look grateful. She doesn't need to know.

The smell of soap and rubber and pomade, bed liner and straightened African hair. The spicy kitchen smell of something. I ask, but you do not hear.

I speak of myself; you're indifferent. Your smile as put-on as your stroke. Hooker, whore, prostitute, businesswoman. Be careful not to love you. Of this, be most careful of all.

You do. I do not have to. You set the stage and run the show. The blinds, film noire lighting. Be careful not to say "virgin." She doesn't need to know.

Round face, round shoulders, round feet, round hair. You strip like a triathlon athlete, the clock running before your swim.

Round face, round butt, round belly, round boobs. You undress me like the ward nurse. No low rumble, no seductress, no games. No struggle removing my catheter. Drop the tube in the bucket, lay me out. The smell of rubber undersheet.

You show me black ass when you ride me. You do. I do not have to. I grip tight into your flesh and try hard to last. So wet, so soft, so black and gorgeous, your grip, so tight, I would have never known. Your smell. So human. Be careful. Be careful! She doesn't need to know.

Take my money, take my wheels, here: take my bone bag body. Take five twenties. Here: take more. Turn around my round Rondee.

Be careful what you ask for. Be careful how you ask.

Your head slowly shaking. Your explanation, the physics. So clean, so neat, so easy. I take your hand, squeeze it. I do so want to kiss you. Be careful not to love you, of that, most careful of all.

Your slow untangle, no seductress. You stand, then you re-mount. Your eyes somewhere above me. I ask, but you don't hear. So I take your breasts; I take them. You do not lower yourself. They respond, despite you. Thrusting slow, you pump—how strong! I never would have known! Your breasts clap together, round knees lodged, my arms pinned back. You do; I do not have to. I lift your breasts. I lose them. Beneath the left a small tattoo, a tiny butterfly in flight.

Constant drilling and tinny top forty, "This is not my beautiful wife," film noire lighting, the human smell of you. I know that I will cry out. I know that I must not. Hooker, whore. Do not love her. I am shaken, risen, dropped.

I want to hold you. Let me hold you. You bring a warm wet cloth. No low rumble, no games. You do. Your fingers rip the plastic package, clamp me to my tube. I tell myself, not again—do not do this. I know that I'll be back. My fingers touch your hair. Like polished leather, pomade.

You tell me what it's cost me, where to leave the money, how to leave. So clean, so neat, so easy. You flip the lights on as you leave. A dirty Ocean Avenue apartment, my clothes neatly folded on my chair.

I dress and open my wallet, count it out, lay it down. Be careful not to cry. Why cry? For what reason, tears?

I hate the way it looks there, green against the pillow. I fold; it looks no better. I arrange it in a fan. There is a table by the bed, a drawer, perhaps if I just tuck it...

Short hose. White vial. Syringe.

Ida   When I open the door, I see half his face black and blue, his
         beard he got cut off, there's a big open wound on his chin,
one side of his nose, swollen. Awful. Awful! But even all that's not
the worst. The worst is his expression, eh? This, Jacob, is an angry
man. So from you, my husband, I have learned how to tell when a
person don't want to talk about something, and Danny, well believe
me, I don't say nothing. I just step aside and let him in.

Real quiet, one after another, he puts his tape measure on me
from here to there, across the back, around the wrist. He writes it
down, then tells me how he wants I should stand next. If he can just
show without having to talk, he shows without having to talk. One
good thing is I don't have to stand on a chair because already Danny
is lower than me. We get this all over with.

I offer the mandlebrat, and you can believe I wish I had not chosen today to make my big point, eh? My thought was, I'm gonna
show Danny about his wonderful now. Now I can't grind or mix
because of the arthritis and Paully ain't here to do it either. So I
tell Jody this and she wastes her money on some kind of machine
she sends from her Macy's. Like paste these nuts come out, damp,
oily. So wonderful now I got to buy the nuts already chopped. You
would not believe how expensive!. I should rejoice?

But now, of course I wish I had something nicer, softer anyway,
maybe it hurts to chew, I don't ask. I make some tea. He can dip, the
cookies won't be so hard. I bring them out, he takes and dips. He
waits. Poor boy, he can't chew.

We sit quiet a minute. Then he says, "I had planned to be coy in
bringing up my mother, Mrs. K., but I am just not feeling too coy
today. Please talk to me about my mother."

He says this very seriously, calmly. There is no possible way I
could have said no. I say, "Did you come here to measure me for a
sweater, Danny, or are you here also to talk about those Daughters
of Israel?"

"If you don't want the sweater, Mrs. K. . . ."

I want the sweater, Jacob, so help me I do, and I don't want
Danny to leave here mad. He comes a little while on Fridays—I

look forward all week.

"You tell me," I say. "She's your mother."

"Well, I suppose it's not surprising that you don't have an answering machine, Mrs. K., but Mother told me she mailed you some cards. She says she phoned, many times, different times of day, and except from three to four, when the line is busy, it just rings and rings. Did you think it was my mother, Mrs. K.?"

I did think it was his mother. He can see that. He says, "Why?"

"She says she's coming here to bake. . . "

I don't mention the other part—the 'best we can do by *our* boy' thing ; maybe he don't know.

"I think she regrets that."

I have some tea. I think about this.

"Besides," he says, "I'm not sure she took that so literally. I think she just meant she wanted to come visit, talk. I don't think she truly understood your invitation."

"She came to talk about those Daughters of—"

"She thought you knew that. She seemed to think so when you asked her at the bakesale."

"I was just being polite," I say. "Asking about what she does for a living."

"I see," he says. He meets my eye. "I see." Then he says, "Can you accept that the two of you misunderstood one another?" He's probably right. He can see I think so. "I think you should talk to her, Mrs. K."

He won't take "no." I say, "She thinks she knows better how to be a mother."

"I think you should talk to her," he dusts his hands from the mandlebrat. "She says you're thought provoking." He starts to smile, but it hurts him. "Who's three to four? Your daughter?" He can see that it is. "You don't talk much about her, Mrs. K. Would you—" And then the phone rings, and I can see by the way he got his eyebrow up that it's her. He nods.

I grip the arms of the chair and raise the old hips up. It rings a few times more. I walk to the couch. I pick it up from the table.

It's her. Danny is already packing up, he can let himself out.

Danny   *Big Butt, Big Thighs, Titties,* so much more to the point
than I would ever choose to be. But a man like me, he
must do something. These women are paid, paid well. They're just
sitting there for a camera. No one's getting hurt here. No one's being
used.

I've got my place, my little hot house, green awning over clear
plastic drapes. Something about the lights. It adds to the tingle, like
a neon narcotic: Times Square.

Each time I promise myself I will choose well, the girls with the
gentlest eyes. Each time this is how I want it. It is never the way it
is. Hurried, saddened somehow to even read the titles, I grab what
I can at chair level, and roll right off to the desk.

Slick women, air bushed, shot with fire undertones. Women's
breasts, women's bellies, hips, thighs, necks, shoulders, pressed
against my chest.

I pay whatever it comes to; I try not to notice what they cost. So
much, too much, just to be left behind. I will not take them back to
my mother's home, a long wet bridge away.

The clerk takes them from me then comes back. The cash register
is not public. I don't tell him I want a booth; I don't have to. He
passes me a key with my change.

Big women, blonde women, and tiny Asian dolls. A pile atop
my throbbing lap. I carry them off.

I drop them open and random across the floor. Round women,
long women, brown, gold and rose fleshed.

I make like Salome.

A garden of flowers. A banquet.

First the sweater, slow unbuttoned, then swirled seductive.
Tossed.

Women corseted, women see-throughed. Women with teddy
bears to envy.

The shirt yanked and torn at, my virile meadow. I love to trace
my nipples lightly.

Women open, open women, mouths, legs, front and back.

My hands run over me, my breath comes short.

I turn to the corner, away from their eyes. I cannot let them see what it is to bare my legs, the process, the ordeal, the many-staged unleashing. The underwear! Banality! Oh, for a pair of scissors!

My chest hair, the nipples can send white lightening through me. The rib cage, rising, the sound of my hoarse coming breath, then down, slowly down. I lightly trace the erection, swaying even with this lightest touch. I want so much, I will die for waiting, but no, but first, the women.

I have pins in my pocket, duct tape, and a stapler. I quickly paper the room.

Women's hair, you can almost smell it. Women's hands, where they put them, where they do roam. Women's eyes, women's mouths, women's eyes. Women with women, women alone, curled women, stretched, on carpets, on beaches, on horses, in bathtubs, on hoods with ornaments of chrome. Looking right at me. Ready women. Ready women's eyes.

But—huh—what is this one? How did I get…Men? No, my God, not men. Men and women in…my God, they all use chairs!

Men with aching erections. Men with feather g-strings. A women, legs spread, fingers probing her butt. A man with a device that surely needs batteries. My God, here is a legless man in a leather mask, suspended. He hangs above a woman; his hard-on nearly home. I just can't believe—my God!.

Out. I need out. I need these clothes on. I need air. Sweater, pants, forget the rest.

Oh God, the clerk? That nebishy clerk. Did he slip that one in? Do I have to pass him? Oh, God—please—let me *run*!

Things fall, I think, on the way. I hurl myself into the street. That clerk! He must be laughing.

A man like me should not be out in this weather, a long wet bridge from home.

My bare hands cannot brake me. I skid. Right wheel goes over, thrown forward, nearly to the gutter. Rain falls hard on a dark street in a busy city. A strange, unnamable sound, rises from in me. It is not human; it is before that. Another mad man in Times Square. Like a drunk. In the gutter. In the gutter!

I try to rock the chair back. I cannot, the curb is steep and I am not yet capable. I will have to concentrate to do it, focus and struggle. My hands, they are bleeding. I wrap them in soaked sweater and can I see that my fly is opened wide, revealing my poor pink nakedness. I struggle with my painful hands to cover myself, cannot even do this, I am trembling so.

I throw my head back. Rain in my mouth. God? Like a bum! Like a bum in the gutter! Is this it? Is this what you have given me? Not like a fine—a fine—and loving man!

And though I cannot find You in heaven for neon, I cry God! My God! Why have you made me?

–19–

Ida   Don't worry my darling. Even in your grave your secrets stay safe with me.

Sara admitted that she'd been bragging and apologized. I said I was sorry I did not let her cry.

I told her, "We did the best by our Paully we knew how."

She said, "I know you did." Then she agreed to come again, this time with none of her propaganda. I agreed to have something coming out of the oven, she wouldn't even see the inside of the kitchen.

So you can relax, Jacob, we didn't talk about you.

Do you think I would want to? I have so much to brag?

So you were frightened, Jacob. So you thought it was your fault. You thought that a boy should be that way was the father's fault. Everyone knew it was men that made boys. Still, you could have touched me. I was still a young woman, and pretty. Didn't you want to touch me?

Night after night you would just roll over. Just mumble good night and leave me for sleep. You were everywhere but home.

It would have been nice that your answer to everything was not to go take a walk, off to the Union Hall, to your brother's. So much you had to walk about. That joke I made in front of Izzy about Lila and that stupid hat with green feathers. And why can't I just follow your mama's kugel recipe without getting all fancy. And how much for the dress, what to put on the radio. Everything made you mad at me, everything. I could not do one thing right. You don't like the program, the dinner, the dress? I know better. I know you did not care about such things. So? Neither did I. I know, but what could I say? You were my husband. You were my husband and you wanted another child but you did not want another one like Paully.

Our marriage had failed. Yes, that's what they would say now, how they would say it on that Oprah, the marriage had failed. But it was 1940. No one thought "divorce."

You couldn't wait to leave me. We didn't even join the war for another year. I know they were Nazis and some wars got to be fought. But I know why you left me, I don't care what you said. You left me with everything it takes to do Paully. You left me to pray you'll come back.

Pray. Ha. Pray! Pray I did not do, could not, and not just because I was a woman and didn't know the words. No. I could not pray because all I could do was rail. He didn't give me enough with Paully? I don't care what I did. I don't care how bad. Hadn't I had enough, he should take from me also the love of a husband?

But I did not understand. Five long years, did not understand how He could be so cruel. Until you came home, then I could see. God has sent me back a better man.

What happened to you over there, Jacob, you took to your grave. This is something I will never know. You've done good, eh? The other men, they like you. Suddenly my Jacob's the big macher. You never bragged, Jacob. We all whispered about it, but no one really knew. You had a medal; it spoke for itself.

Who could imagine that I would be glad for the problems we used to have. They made that marriage stronger. We were older; we had learned many things about each other. We had learned that we missed one another and that life was meant for sharing. How many are given a second chance?

Everyone was making more money. Me and Paully, out of my Mama's kitchen, we were making sixty dozen a day. Paully already he could do most everything I needed from him, chop, scrub, he was not so big for lifting yet, and his stirring and sifting were still sloppy. But those cookies wouldn't have got baked without him.

And oh! Was he happy to see you! His papa back! He'd wait for you to get home, so excited, all the attention you suddenly got for him, every night. You don't like the way Paully got without you. If Paully hurts his little finger, he makes a big boo-hoo, eh? And you think this is what comes of a boy always with his mama, all the time. So now you're gonna make Paully a little man. Paully is thirteen, and he's a big boy already, bigger than Sammy even though Sammy's almost gonna do the bar mitzvah, a strong boy, but he drops things, he falls down sometimes. Paully don't look where he's going. You're gonna show him. This is the way you run, this way you catch. Paully, he was never happier than those days, Jacob. Not before and not after.

Or me. Never happier. You were back, Jacob. Not back from the war, not only that! But you were back in my bed, my husband. And the tears of welcome spilled and flowed. My whole body was a tear of welcome. Jody was in me before two months had passed.

So now you want we should have our own house. Now that you are back I put Paully's cot in the living room, everyone got to step over him to get to the bathroom. But you say, enough. You say the government's gonna help us get our own house. My Jacob, you were so proud.

My husband back from the war acting like a father, another baby on the way, a home of our very own. I thought nothing could spoil this, nothing. And then Mama fell down one day. Lila found her hours later, pillowed in heaps of clothing, Lila always said, looking happy. A few days later in the hospital, she had a second stroke. That was it. She'd only woken up once or twice. She'd never been able to speak.

I missed her very much and cried every day. You held me and kissed my full belly and didn't say very much. You were good about visiting my pa a little in the evenings. You were better than me. I know you didn't mind this, you liked the company of men. It don't matter. I was still grateful every time, thinking of you there with him.

As my time with Jody grew close, you spent all your time at home, you and Paully playing something or other, keeping Paully as quiet as you could. Telling him two hundred times in a row when his brother or sister is coming.

But a boy is what you wanted. So? You wanted a son. And not a son like Paully who could never be like you. I try to remember, even now: this is no crime. What man doesn't want a normal son?

So? I gave you a normal daughter. So, in life sometimes we do not get everything we want.

You were gone again. This time, behind your paper. Oh you were home most evenings, but you were gone anyway. We didn't fight. I could see you loved me. You loved me and your little Jodeleh, and I could see you loved Paully, if, maybe, in a little different way. You loved me and you were there, but you were gone. And this time, a baby to my breast and Paully to watch out for, I did not try to follow. We did not fight. There was nothing to yell. You were too sad and your parents were trying not to say that the flat was too small and we should hurry and move already and I missed my mama a lot, and with the new baby, it was a while before I could sell cookies.

So then comes the day of Sammy's bar mitzvah, a day your son will never have. You were quiet for days.

You should have told him to be quiet too, Jacob. You should have told him, "never tell."

Up there at the bimah, making his little speech, Sammy starts to read little parts from the letters his Uncle Jacob sent him back from the war—all the stories, the men there, what went on. None of this, not one word, did you ever write to me. And to Paully, not one thin letter. Five years, not one letter! And to me only the food, the showers, the weather.

I thought maybe you didn't want to think, things were so sad for you there. I thought maybe you wanted to forget a little while. So I sent the jokes Aunt Sylvia told and a little bit of gossip and never pushed. But Sammy's letters! I had never heard you so! You told stories, Sammy should learn, and the names of things in other languages and how little towns looked. Long letters, and so many! I sat there in the synagogue, my Jody in my arms; I just can't believe! You, the whole time, your eyes on Sammy! And I see it, the love.

Never have I seen you look at our Paully that way! Never!

Then Sammy, he holds up the medal his uncle gave him.

I sit in that schul, the last one to know.

I pull you out of there, drag you by the arm, Jody at my hip. I shout, "Who is your son, Jacob? Who is *your* son?"

You look at the floor, you look at the ceiling, you fall to your knees before me, red faced, about to burst.

And then you do, your face against my hip, your arms around me. Once you told me you thought maybe He made oceans from tears wept by mothers. A pretty thought, but you were wrong. Still there would not be enough. He needed too the tears of the fathers, eh?

I stroke your head and wait. I wish I had more to give you but I am furious and your beautiful daughter sleeps on my arm—your normal daughter—a tiny and delicate child, anyone could see from day one, she had my mother's beautiful mouth. Why, Jacob? Why wasn't this enough?

Jody   I like the way they look, purple and Day-Glo green. I like the little brake thingys.

I can't believe I'm even considering it. But every day now, for like, two weeks—ever since I saw that golden-ager skating the mall—here I am again, two, three times a day.

No one would see me if I went after close. Maybe the janitors; they're busy anyway.

Oh, come on. When was the last time you were on roller skates? Kid stuff! What are you thinking?

I could afford this.

I go in, pick up the pads, put them down. The tile's smooth in the mall. There are ramps. It'd be easy. Forget it. You'd break your butt and there'd be no one to help you.

But then one afternoon—what can I say?—I've got them on. The salesman—young guy—stands by, grinning. I guess I don't look like your typical skate-person. What am I thinking?

And then I think about how cold that pool's been getting. The landlord sent a memo saying he'd be covering it for winter soon. I think, well I survived the pool...

I sit staring at those big purple contraptions, fascinated by my feet. Oh Jody, when was the last time you were on roller skates? I hand the kid my plastic.

When I carry them back, I'm like practically hugging them. I wouldn't mind that. I wouldn't mind just shutting my office door and looking at them for a while. No, it's silly. Roller-skates!

But oh, I do remember the last time. What I can't remember is the occasion. Some holiday, who knows? It was summer though, and hot. What was nice is that Aunt Lila and her family were out of town. I mean, Ma is nervous enough without having Lila show off her money and Sammy act like he's the only boy in the world who ever read a book. It was... I don't know, so happy. We didn't go places that much, you know. Not together, outside and all. I think Pa... well, Pa didn't like to be out with Paully. This was not shame. This was for Paully's own good.

So when I said, "Pa, what if we went out to Long Island? It's not like anyone will know us there. A little sunshine, some air. A nice holiday like everyone else."

Pa was like, "Ah, you got first the train, then there's the buses, all day, connections."

"No there's not," I say. "There's one train. Direct. No changes."

So Pa, he rustles his paper up. This is supposed to remind you that he's reading.

Ma comes in. She says, "And what do you know about it, Miss Transit Official?"

So I say, "I called, that's what."

"What? On this phone?" Ma says. She still does this. She acts like every time you use a phone you're taking something from the world that can't be put back.

"It's what they're for, Ma."

"Watch your mouth," Pa says, and that's that. No picnic. Over.

Every other family on the block, they get picnics. But no, not us. I'm gonna go back to school on Tuesday and the English teacher'll ask what we did over the holiday and I'm gonna say, "Nothing. Watched the TV," like every holiday of my life. I stomp back to my room, stomp, stomp, stomp. You think they notice? They don't notice. I start to slam my door, but then I think, no, maybe I'd better not.

I pick up pillows and throw them down. I open the window and shut it, open, shut. Why not just shut all the windows and lock them up tight? Why not nail boards across them so no light can get in? I stand there looking out imagining I am a prisoner allowed to see the sun for just one hour a day, but only through this window.

Just then, Evelyn from across the street goes skating by. She got those skates you strap your shoes in. And, so maybe I'm a little slow or something, but when I first saw Ev's, oh, I wanted a pair so bad. But Ma, you know, she thinks fifteen is too old for skates. Ev is maybe three years younger. Ma says Ev is still a girl and not a young lady like me. Ma says I'll just fall down and break my teeth and who do I want to pay for the dentist then? So that's that. But Ev, at least, did promise I could try hers. So I forget all my prisoner business and go out the back door. I stroll around and call out "Oh you-hoo," like this was some casual coincidence or something, and I go on over.

Ha! I figure I'm going to need a crow bar to pry those things off of her. But Ev, she's a good kid, and she made a promise and all. So she sits down on the curb and takes off the string around her neck with the key on it and hands it to me. She wants me to take her skate off! Can you imagine? Well, they are hers. So I kneel before her and unlock and, just to make conversation, you know, I ask what her family is planning on doing for the Monday holiday.

Central Park. Of course. I just turn that key over and sigh. I look up at Ev. She does look younger than me. Ma's right.

"Evelyn Kaufman," I say, "you are so lucky."

And she says, "Aw Jody, they're just skates. I'll tell you what. I'll let you use them all day Monday, if you want."

I mean, that was so nice, a little kid and all. I can't help myself; I begin to sniffle. Crying over skates and picnics at my age. Ev notices, of course, and she starts with, "What'd I say? Jody? You okay? Jody? What?"

I clear my throat and say, "You're just a very lucky girl, Evelyn. You are. You have your health and your youth..."

And she's looking at me now like I'm not quite right. She says, real drawn out, "Yaaah?"

"And you're comfortable and you have a nice family—"

"Ah," she says. "Oh, by the way," and then she takes the key from me and starts to take her skates off because I'm not putting my mind to it. And while she's looking at her skate she says, "Would you like to come with my family, Jody?"

Would I! Sure! A normal day with a normal family. Hot-dogs and potato salad. And oh, to be able to say, "Okay Pa, so you don't want to take the subway? Fine then. I can go myself with my friends."

That is so nice of Evelyn. I look into her face, ready to say, "Yes, yes, yes!" But I can't. I can't say nothing. I have never seen anyone pity me before. I look away.

I strap on the skates and carefully, slowly, stand up. I am taller than I've ever been, and Ev is way down there on the curb.

I look at her and say, "Why thank you ever so much for thinking of me, Evelyn, but actually, I would rather spend my holiday with my own family."

And just then Ma shouts in that voice of hers, "Jody Kochansky! What did I tell you about those skates?"

The look on that little girl's face! She don't want trouble. She gulps and shrugs.

I sigh and sit down. I can't work the key. Not with everyone staring at me like that. I try, it keeps, I don't know, slipping, it won't go in. I kick off my shoes and twist them out of the skates. And as soon as I have them in my hand, I stand up and run to my own house.

Ma stops me on the porch, right there, right in front of Ev. I think I'm in for it now. She reaches up for me—Ma's tiny and already I'm taller than her—she puts her hand on my shoulder. I think she's going to tug my ear. Oh, she can really hurt with that sometimes. But she don't. Instead, she says, "You want a little picnic, Jodeleh? Mama will make you a nice picnic."

❖ ❖ ❖ ❖ ❖

"One thing that I think is really unfair," Ryan says, "is that you know what it's like to be my age but I don't know anything about what it's like to be yours."

"Hmm," I say, drawing a circle in the water with my arms. "Well, what do you think it's like?"

She hops and lands her little keister on the ledge in one motion. "I think when a person is your age," she says, "then they can do whatever they want."

"Ah," I say. "Well, that would be nice."

She sticks her arms up over her head and dives, cutting a straight line to the edge. I bend my knees and start my huff and puff over.

There she is, right under water, sticking her goofy little grinning face right in front of mine. Blocks me, the little squirt. I stand up, hands on my hips, my heart pounding so loud I can hardly hear anything else, dizzy.

"Ryan!" I say, scolding and annoyed.

"Where are your bubbles?" She's even more annoyed than I am. "My...?"

"You got to make bubbles!" she says. "Here. Come under. Watch."

I forget to be angry for a second. I'm trying to figure what she's talking about. What she means is you got to exhale under water. I'm amazed. I didn't know.

"All the time I'm under water," I tell her, "I hold my breath. I like exhale and inhale all on the same stroke." I take my hand over my head and breath out and in to show her.

"No way," she says.

"Yeah," I say, and then like I've heard kids say on the TV, "way."

She takes off, trying it. A few strokes in she swallows water and starts coughing. Jeesh, I know that one.

"Yuk," she says.

"I go to her and put my arm around her. "You okay?" I say.

"That's what's wrong with you!" she says, her eyes big and wide and blue. "You don't know how to breathe."

So she shows me twice, inhale in the air, exhale in the water. I turn and face the other side. This is my goal. I go through everything in my mind. Arm, shoulder, head, hand, thigh. So okay. So here goes. I take a real good deep breath.

Oh my God! It's happening! It's coming together! And breathe and breathe and grab a new breath.! Light and then breath and then light and then breath.

Look at this! It's like I float! Whoop, better get the butt up. And then there's that rhythm. Ha! Look at me! Look at me! Hey! That's the side! Okay heart, stay in there! Lap two. Hey! Grab a new breath! Better use those thighs. It's not like rocket science, and hey! No—it's like submarine science! Ha! Look at me go! That's what's wrong with me! I didn't know how to breathe! I make four, easy. I make five. I make ten. I lose count.

−20−

Ida "Don't think I haven't asked myself," Sara says when we meet a few days later at her house. "Many times. Why me? Why my family?"

"What did I do to deserve this?" I say.

"I didn't say that."

"Yes you did."

"I said 'why me,' not, 'what did I do wrong'?"

"It's the same thing."

"I was about to comment on the pointlessness of such questions, Ida. What are you talking about?"

Just because she agreed not to bring out her propaganda, don't mean she didn't bring a big chip on her shoulder.

"You know what I am talking about," I say. "In your heart, you know."

"I'm afraid I don't."

"Whatever it was that you did."

"What *I* did?"

"I don't expect you to tell me, Sara, but you can if you want. I want you should know that what ever it is you did, I can understand."

"What I *did*?"

"He makes us pay, eh?"

"Who? Oh! You mean God! Ida!"

"He has His reasons, Sara."

"Tell me you don't think this way."

"Of course I think this way, Sara, and so do you!"

"I don—"

"You have asked yourself, 'Why me, why my family?' Of course you have. Also you have asked, 'Why didn't I pick him up that day?' "

I can see in the way she stands, stiff with tension, that I am getting through, that she knows these thoughts.

"If only he hadn't been walking," I say, "A good boy should be at home with his books. What do we care about the sports? Why did I let him go there?"

"I never thought—"

"Maybe if I'd had a better doctor," I say. "I should have gotten better for him. Maybe he'd walk."

"Ida, it was an accid—"

"And then later, you say, why should this happen to my Danny? Danny, he's a little boy, what could he have done? So you ask yourself, what have *I* done. What have I done to my son?"

"Stop it, Ida, it was an—"

"You didn't look over at your Alan and ask 'what has he done?' No, no, it couldn't be Alan, you think. I am the mother. It was me! It was me that worked at my fancy office in my pretty shoes with all the people everywhere thinking my work was so good. It was me that let the boy walk home."

"It was not my fault that my son was hit by a drunk driver, Ida, and I do not like—"

"Was it Danny's fault? A little boy? Alan's? Maybe Alan's? God has reasons, Sara, He—"

"Now just wait!" and then, this time calm, "Just wait."

She rubs her chin and paces.

I hadn't expected her living room. It's so nice, so finished. The furniture got the same design. The things on the shelves just so. And many, many shelves, full of books and photos. There is a big messy pile of books next to Danny's chair. That much I expected.

Sara looks at me and paces again. Then she comes to me, puts her hands on my shoulders and pushes me. Maybe not 'push.' A gentle thing. She puts me where she can look down into my eyes. She studies me.

"Poor, Ida," she says. "What did *you* do?

I cover my face with my hand.

My Jacob, you thought it was your fault! But what could you have done, my young man, my war hero? No, my husband, it was not you God had chosen. It was me! This was mine to carry. Mine to atone.

Sara sits so that she is looking up at me. "It's all right, Ida," she says. "You can tell me."

I bite my lip. Suddenly I feel trapped; it's not very often I'm in someone else's house.

"I won't judge you, Ida," she says.

I close my eyes. "But it is unspeakable," I say.

"No," she says real quiet, and takes my hand. "No, Ida, just unspoken."

"I was just eleven," I say, and she hands me a tissue. "I was a foolish little girl."

"And you've kept this a secret all this time, Ida?"

I nod. To her death Lila took it, and when her casket lowered into the ground, I buried it finally. "You're too young to remember how it was, Sara."

"How what was, Ida?"

"When I grew up, a little girl was a dangerous thing, eh? I was all the time helping my mama or doing my homework, all the time watched. So for me, how I looked forward to the last day of school. Oh, I had to work during the summer, I should pick up and deliver the bales; Mama shouldn't have to make the gossip with the ladies she worked for, but then...in the evenings? On the weekends? No lessons! Freedom! A little bit of time when they don't look so close."

Sara looks confused, but tells me to go on.

"So for once, having Lila in the family, it had its good side too, eh?"

"Your cousin, right?" she says.

I nod again. "They would send me off with my cousin, Lila. The adults, had no time to bother, and Izzy? He was a boy. He didn't want me around. Not that Lila always did want me around, but that's the way it was."

Sara shrugs her shoulders, "Okay, but what has this got to do with—"

"So every summer," I say, "for a few big Sundays anyway, Lila and I, we went to Coney!"

"Coney Island?" she says. "I'm not too young to remember—"

"Not like it was, no, Sara. When Coney was new, well, Coney, it was *the* place. Soon as May comes, I'll tell you who wants to go! Lila, and me, and the fun half of New York!

"Everything happened first at Coney, Sara, the fashions, the dance steps, the new songs. So maybe later it was Hollywood, eh? But then? Coney."

"Really!"

"Everybody wants to look. And also, to wear their best. My best dress I wore to bump down the Steeplechase and shoot the chutes! Oh, if Mama knew! She would never let me walk out the door! But Lila, like I say, being older and all, she wanted to look nice for the young men, eh? So what did we do? We snuck our dresses out in our picnic basket! So, all right, we didn't get no lunch, but did we care?

"See, this also gave me something I could use on Lila. If Lila's gonna stay out of trouble about the dress, she got to give me what I want. I love this feeling, that I got something on Lila. But really, this is not such a problem for her. Most times what I want is not so much different from what she wants—which is to do as much in one afternoon as we can before our money runs out."

"Ida, I'm sorry, I guess I don't understand."

"I'm telling you."

"You are?"

"You can't understand if you don't know this."

"All right, I know, I know," she says with a put-on accent, "you want I should hear a little story."

Is she teasing me? There is a gentle smile on her face, an expec-
tant smile. Like the sun that comes out after a rain, Jacob, her smile
made me hushed and sleepy. And to be telling this, to be saying
these things, this too felt like a dream.

"Here, Ida, put your feet up." She pushes the footstool next to
the chair.

"Sara," I say, "this really is a comfortable home."

"Ida, please," she says, "you and Lila..."

"Well what we loved—well, what everyone loved really—was
Luna Park. Everything there was...what? Exotic! Yes, that's what
the signs all used to say. Come see! Come see! The animals and the
people they got from all over the world in their special costumes,
and the music! But then—the line. The long, long line. Everybody
waiting to get into Luna Park. The longest line I've ever seen. But
don't think that ruined our time, no. See, they made everything
special there—even the wait. Like maybe they'd have a dancer with
veils, or a seal that could juggle. You could watch from your place.
Every year, something different."

"Why, I never knew," she says.

"So one year—"

"The year you were eleven?"

"I was still a little girl, Sara," I say.

"Yes," she says, "a foolish age."

"They got special people to entertain. Not foreign people, but,
well, they had these dwarfs for one thing."

"No!" she brings her hand to her cheek.

I can't help laughing remembering. "They had a big muddy wet
floor and these dwarfs, fighting, rolling around."

"Ida!"

"Everybody was laughing, Sara, the whole crowd in a ring
around them. This was the funniest thing. Another time, they had
also this man with no legs walking through the mud on his hands."

"No!"

"I was eleven, remember? I was still a little girl."

And that is all I say, for I have said too much.

"What happened, Ida? What did you do?"

Jacob, forgive me.

"Ida, what—"

"I was eleven."

"So you said."

I look at my hands. "They got these two men, uh, two boys—like my Paully, eh?"

She is leaning so close I can feel her breath on me. I speak soft. "They got them dressed like clowns," I say, "big funny collars and red noses. And they danced. The latest things, the Charleston and the Jotta. And then..."

"And then..." she says

"I stepped out of the line," I say, my eyes closed, remembering the hot day, the happy crowd. "I took the hand of one of the boys. I tried a little Charleston..."

Sara's breath catches.

"I tried a little ballet. I ran both boys in loops and twirled under their arms. I twirled them under mine, bumping up, falling down. I dipped them. I made them jump.

"The crowd, you should have heard, they were roaring. That huge crowd, laughing, pointing, holding their bellies, tears running down. The sound, Sara, it was like a wave breaking and then another. I wanted to be..." I look at Sara, she should understand. "I just wanted to be funny. Funny, Ida. Funny, funny."

She has a hand on each cheek, her mouth open, her eyes wide. I look back at my hands.

"I showed them how to hopak, you know, arms crossed like Cossacks, but they fell over squat kicking."

"Uh-huh."

"Other boys jumped in, showing off, doing handstands. Everyone started to look at them. I had to do something."

I glance at her. Her eyes are closed.

"I see over by the building there's a bucket. I run and schlep and send it flying over them. Shrieks from the crowd, they even made applause. Then I found the hose.

"I almost could not do it I was laughing so hard, almost doubled over, but the crowd, they chanted. Most of them, not all. Between the laughers with the red faces, I could see a few who just can't believe. They look angry maybe, or stunned. One of them was Lila, all pale, her head shaking slow, arms out to me, pleading me away."

Within the grave, Jacob, Lila knows also, this is why. This is why I was chosen for such punishment. Fifty-five years I have loved and hated a baby. I have watched my husband turn from me, and the world shun me. I have worked alone and lonely. I have tried. The other children, they grew. You loved them better, I know. They took care of themselves and they had you. This one, *I* loved. I kept him safe. I have made up for it, what ever I did, God, I have atoned.

I get this strong feeling like I should run out the door or hide in the closet so Sara won't find me. When she looks at me, there are tears on her face.

"I'll admit that's quite a story, Ida, but none of us get through childhood without regrets—"

"I have loved this boy!" I cry. "When did this become wrong? To love a boy and keep him safe?"

"I know you did your best, Ida." She stands and opens the window, rubbing her back above her waist, stretching, taking her time. When she turns back to me, she says, "This time, Ida, I have a little story for you."

She pulls a chair over from the dining room table and sits. "Ida, I went to a lecture, oh it was years ago now, but I still think about it sometimes. The speaker was a psychologist who had a specialty in something they call stress syndromes."

I'm not sure I like where this is going.

"This just means patterns that people go through who are sad or scared or something. See, the idea is that when the same thing is making a lot of people sad, they often go through the same pattern.

"She talked about Elizabeth Kübler-Ross. Do you know who that is, Ida?"

I do know. Remember I told you about her, Jacob—a very wise woman.

"A lady gave me something in the hospital, when my Jacob was sick," I tell her.

"Well I know that I felt those things," she said, "for Alan. I think what she says is very true."

But before I get a chance to agree, she goes on. "Now this psychologist, what she believed is that a lot of people, when they learn their child is retarded, they feel just the same way you did for Jacob."

"And for mine own Mama and Papa," I say.

"Uh-huh, but only this time, Ida, for a baby. A tiny, innocent, sweet baby that you made this way. You. In your body. A baby that will never grow up. But it doesn't die—the baby; your expectations do. And it's very sad, Ida, very, very sad, but that's not the worst part."

"No?"

"It doesn't stop," she says. "Your expectations die and die, again and again."

I put up my hands. I can't take no more. I can't breathe through all my tears.

Sara starts crying too. Between us, we keep the tissue people in business.

"I'm sorry, Ida" she says. "I'm so sorry for you." She puts her arm around me tight, I shouldn't have to sit up alone. "This lecturer had a name for it."

Sara comes close and whispers in my ear, no one should hear, "She called it 'chronic sorrow,' Ida."

I don't know how to tell what happened next. I can't hold myself up or breathe. I fall forward and pour the tears onto my lap. It has all been too much, all this talking. Too, too much. Every tear I have ever cried for my shana babelah, I have had to cry again. Every sorrow, I have greeted like an old friend.

Suddenly, I can't no more. I cried enough. Enough and enough again forever, I've cried. When I stand up, the wadded wet tissues unstick from my lap and fall to the floor. I walk through them and find the bathroom and wash my face with cold water. Then I do it again. When I finish, I comb my hair with my hands, my white hair stiff beneath my fingers. Sara is standing knocking on the door. She is asking if I'm okay.

I open the door and look up at her, good and long.

"So?" I say. "Chronic, maybe. At least they ain't fatal."

−21−

Jody Somehow I notice when Ryan swings open the gate; I don't always. I turn and call out to her. She don't call back. Something is different. She walks, not trots or skips like usual, but walks over to me. She don't dive, she sits, right next to me, dropping her legs in one at a time.

"Hey, Sunshine," I say. "What's up?"

"Aw nothing," she says.

"So if it's so 'Aw nothing,' how come you didn't come running in here for one of your famous dives and splash water all over me?"

"I'm not supposed to get wet tonight."

She's sitting there on the edge where the water laps up. She's wearing her bathing suit and she got her legs in the water.

"I'm not sure you're doing such a great job of that," I say.

"Jody?" She looks at her knees and starts to swish her legs. "My mom's been seeing a lot of doctors lately, like one every day." She sounds tired saying it. I notice her eyes and mouth are puffy. I notice her shoulders are bent.

"Yeah?"

"She's got a disease. It's called cancer?"

Ryan looks at me shyly. She's not sure she's got the right word.

"Cancer," I say.

"She's got to have this operation? Um, a hysteria-ectomy, I think they call it. My aunt is coming out to stay." Ryan closes her eyes and keeps them closed. I've never seen her do this before. "My aunt is going to stay in my room?"

When Ryan does this, when she makes everything a question, she usually wants me to know what she's talking about without her having to say it.

She meets my eyes. "I have to go to my father's," she says, and then, in case I don't get it, "Now. To live." She is fighting so hard not to cry, so I fight too. Ryan is saying good-bye. Ryan.

She draws up her little legs and hugs herself. "I don't even know what they're doing," she says, her eyes round and scared. The words spill out of her faster than I have ever heard them. "What if they're ahead of me in math? And then the teacher thinks I'm dumb and all the kids will make fun of me and think I'm dumb too."

I don't know what to say to her. Getting teased in school we grow up and recover from, but the mother? There's Cisplatin and chemo yet, nausea, pain, hair loss. Pa had Ma and me and Paully. Who's this lady got? But here's a kid and she's all worried about starting a new school which, I know, is a real deal and a problem for a kid. Probably she don't even get to talk to anyone about it because everyone's more interested in the mother. Even me, and I never even met the mother. Aw, poor Ryan.

What I think, about the new school that is, is that what Ryan says is certainly possible. But I don't say that. I say, "The teacher will understand, Sunshine. She'll know what to do."

The poor little thing is sitting there, swishing her legs to and fro and waiting for me to say something adult and I'm doing nothing at all, feeling nothing, like I have nothing to give for all these years of life. She's saying good-bye?

"Ryan, I don't know if you'll understand this but I want you to know that I don't think I can even remember the names of more than one or two kids I was in the fourth grade with. See, when you're a grown up, the fourth grade don't matter no more." I can see she's not buying it. Well maybe that wasn't so good. I try again. "You know Ryan, from what I remember, in the fourth grade the most important thing about being accepted is being pretty and you're a very pretty girl, Ryan."

I know that as a representative of the race of grown-ups I'm really supposed to say something more like, "If you're open and friendly and honest people will always like you." But in the first case, that's not true, say for example, you got the wrong clothes, and in the second, when I was nine I would have rather someone told me I was pretty. Jeesh, anyone.

She begins to cry. Well who could blame her? "No, I'm not," she says.

"Hey," I say. I gently lift her chin. "Hey, look at me."

She does.

"Haven't I been straight with you all the time?"

She nods.

"Well, I'm still being straight with you," I say. "You're a beauty now and you're going to be gorgeous when you get older." She is flattered; I can see it. I know this is cheap, not advice at all, just a quick fix, but I want her to smile. Something inside me is breaking. I feel so sad. "Especially," I say, "when you smile."

She does.

"I bet you sell a lot of fish when you smile," I say.

"My dad says that too!" she says.

I wish I could tell that man to sell his own stinky fish.

And then, drawing her legs out, she says, "I watched you swim for a while before I came in. You've gotten really good."

"You're a good teacher," I say. I bow to her. "Thank you."

She shrugs. "Maybe some day you'll teach me something."

My mind goes blank at this. If I ever see you again, Ryan. Will I? I look at this little girl, skinny bird shoulders and long, long neck, and I blink back my tears. Too little to be my friend, too, too little for everything I think may happen to her very soon. Come on, Jody, there must be something for you to say here. But I am empty. Empty and stupid and empty. I shrug.

Then she turns on a grin I know by now. It says, "I'm going to wi-in, nonny nonny boo-boo." I get ready.

She doesn't have to, but she says, "Race 'ya." We do three laps. She wins. Easy. I don't have to throw it, but I would if I needed to. She hops up on the side and waits for me, like she always does, but different too. Usually she's all grinny and braggy. But now she looks very serious, very still. She breaks my heart. "See?" she says, too quiet. "You're not even out of breath!"

And then—I can't believe it—but Ryan is about to leave. I see her suddenly very clearly, the yellow tank suit with the pink seashells on it, her hair loose and messy, the summer blonde streaks faded but still running through, two scabs on the left knee, a skinny little girl framed by star jasmine. She is saying good-bye. I can't let her.

Suddenly she is in my arms, my face in her chlorine tasting hair, rocking numbly in a pool that was once not big enough for both of us. I don't know who gets self-conscious first, but we separate. I look in those smarty-pants little blue eyes once more and I think: well, it's over. And then it occurs to me that I have thought that before. Cancer. Then I am ashamed of this thought because it is about me and not about Ryan. Sometimes I think it's a good thing I never got to be a mother. And I'm all caught up, thinking like this, thinking me, me, me, when Ryan just reaches out, just reaches right out, and touches my breast. I am not kidding. My left breast. Sort of pushes it to watch it float back into place. At first I am so stunned I don't stop her from doing it again. "Ryan!" I say. I don't know what to say.

"It..." She rubs her chin. "Floats?"

"Ryan, you know better than that!"

"I..." she says, then nothing.

I am very angry. I am much more angry than this thing should make me. "How would you like it? Someone touches your body and don't even..." I stop. I don't want to be this way with her now.

"You just grabbed me off the side and hugged me," she says, all puffy the way she gets.

Did I? I might have.

"Ryan." I want to grab her shoulders but I realize just in time how dumb that would be at this particular moment. What I do instead is change the tone of my voice. "Ryan, you know what? Maybe you're right. I think maybe there is something I got inside me to teach you." And I smile at this because it is true and because at last I have found a way for this truth to be good for something. "I'm sorry I yelled at you, okay? It's just, well, I didn't expect you to, ah, do what you did."

I can see her lighten up. Okay. I go on. "Honey, what I want you to know is that you..." I stop. I want to say this the right way. I know that even if this is all I have to give her, it is enough, but I want to do it right. "Sit up here, honey." I pat the edge of the pool. I don't want to look down at her now. She hops up, light as anything. "One day, not very long from now," I say, "you are going to be a very beautiful young woman—"

"Ah," she says, waving it away. Already she knows how not to take a compliment. Where do we learn this?

"Trust me, Ryan. I spend a good part of my week looking at pictures of models in underwear."

She looks at me funny.

"It's my job," I say. And then, seeing she's okay with that, I say, "You've got the bones and skin and the eyes. And you're going to be tall and skinny. And men, Ryan, nice men and not nice men, are going to follow you down the street into stores and classrooms and parks. They're going to stare at you in restaurants. You're going to feel sometimes like there are men everywhere who got nothing to do with themselves but follow beautiful girls, and you know what? You'll be right!"

Her head has that little tip to it. She don't know why I'm saying this. But I couldn't stop myself if I had to. "But you can't let them touch you. You understand me, Ryan? That's very important, what I'm saying here. Unless you want them to, unless you're ready for it, and comfortable with it, they got no business touching you."

I'm not sure I'm getting through. I am desperate. I want to, more than anything. I am getting louder. "Do you understand me? Never, now listen to me, *never* let anyone touch your body unless you say it's okay. You got to respect your body and then everybody else will too. This is the *most* important thing! If you really know this—not just words but really down deep—then everything will be all right. Do you understand me?"

I don't wait for her to answer. "Say it," I say.

"Say?"

"Come on."

"Don't let anyone touch my body."

"Unless..."

"I say it's okay."

"Why?"

"'Cause I got to respect my body."

"Yes! Why?"

"'Cause then everyone else will too."

"Yes! Good girl, Ryan. Smart girl."

"Jody?" she says.

"Yeah?"

"It's okay." So I hug her so tight I think I'm going to squeeze the stuffing out. "Mom says I can write you," she says in my ear.

"I'd love that, Honey," I say.

"Will you write back?"

"Come on," I say, just like her.

She laughs, we separate, she slowly stands herself up. "I wasn't supposed to be gone so long," she says.

"You want me to walk you back?"

She thinks for a second but then says no. "Mom's resting," she says. And so I watch her go, her little wet bottom leaving a trail behind her.

Ryan. Good-bye.

I rock as I cry. I cry and hold my middle and cry and cough and try to stop. And then, another wave, gulping for air and then breaking again. There is not enough space in my body to hold it all. I jerk and shake. I don't want to be so loud. What will the neighbors think? What neighbors? I don't even know the neighbors! I don't know anybody. I know Ryan. Oh, Ryan!

Water down the wrong pipe, I choke, and panic and make the choking worse, sputtering, frightening myself. I can't catch my breath, and then I do, and my legs lift back. I float, holding the side, my head resting on my hands, coughing, numb, empty. I begin to weep, but this time it's not for Ryan.

After I left Lester's and started Macy's and still had a few friends, we used to go out to clubs. Discotheques. We'd dress together for two hours, should I wear these earrings or these? Neither, wear mine. Does this make my butt look big? A big important decision. We'd practice a little hustle, in case anyone asked did we know it. It was the best part of the evening.

Then off we'd go. We'd always try to scope out a spot where there were lots of extra seats around just in case anyone would want to join us. We'd sit around and nurse a beer and bop to the music so that someone might say, "Hey, now there's a girl who wants to dance." We'd drink a little, dance a little, sometimes go out with a guy afterward for breakfast. If we liked him, we might slip him our phone number.

This is how my friend Lisa met her friend. He was a bouncer at this club uptown, the kind of place Lisa and I would never get in usually, you know. I mean, Lis and I, we went shopping for this occasion.

Great night. The people there, they're all like gorgeous. Nothing trendy, almost no one drinking beer. Same music, but the d.j. don't interrupt. Lis and I, we're not looking 'cause we already got dates after so we dance together on the corner of the floor. A couple of guys ask us, but it's no big deal. It's a great night.

So then after, we sit in a booth as they close the club, people cleaning up, Lisa's friend running a vacuum, my date's doing something with boxes somewhere. Then we have this big confab, I get introduced and we decide which diner we want to meet at. Both guys even got cars.

This guy and I, we go off together. I get in his car. I start fumbling with the seat belt. He don't even start the motor. It was like, boom. He was on me.

I got my clothes on. Somehow I'm on the floor of this car and he's above me shoving his pants down. He pushes my head towards his thing. It seems huge. He's a big man, over six feet, definitely lifts. Hair on his chest, sandy hair to the shoulder, slicked back. Back of my head, two hands on the back of my head.

"Hard, baby, suck hard."

How do you breathe with a thing like that in your mouth? I sucked hard. I sucked like to pull the thing off, his hands forcing the back of my head, his long legs wrapping my back, boots. He has boots on. Heavy legs, the car seat cuts into my breasts. I'm gasping, grunting, not MMM, MMM, I'm enjoying this, but gagging, trying to breathe, to say, stop it, you're hurting me, but I can't say. It's in my mouth. It's in my mouth.

He drags me up by the armpits until he can grab under my ass then grunts and hoists me and drops me against that seat. Back he goes, in the mouth.

"That's right, hard. Yeah, great. Hard."

All I could do was suck hard and hope I wouldn't die.

And then, oh God, it's like he sneezes in my mouth! Ugh. I want to spit it back. Uch. I swallow and swallow. I swallow and swallow and swallow and swallow.

It's not even a rape, is it, if it's in your mouth? It's not even rape. It's nothing. Uh, my mouth. My mouth! It's not even rape unless it's down there. I would give anything, it would of been down there. Not my mouth. Not gagging. It's not even a rape. No one made me get in that car with him. They'll say well, she wore that red silk blouse. She got in the car with him.

"Shit," he says. "That was great."

He grins at me. He's got blue eyes and a sweaty forehead.

"You're great," he says, and moves back against the seat, looking at the car roof, sighing, completely in awe of how good he is at coming. "Now go back to your little friend," he says.

His name is Jim. What a great thing to know, and anyway, is his name Jim? I thought I caught it but they still had the music going.

"We were..." I say. I was going to say, "We were going to meet them."

He opens the door. I get out. I take a cab to the diner. I don't know why.

They're sitting there, already, sharing some fries. He wants to know where his buddy is. I shrug. He goes to make a call.

Lisa says, "What's wrong?"

I say, "I'm all right."

She points out that I got a button missing on my shirt and gives me a bobby pin to close it. She asks what happened.

I say, "Everything's fine."

I try a fry. Mmm, the taste in my mouth. Warm and filling, substantial. I put on some ketchup. Mmmm.

Even before Lisa's date drops me off home, I'm thinking about Ma's kitchen, the counter top full of white plastic Tupperware, batch after batch, you lift the lid and the smell! Mmm. I'm gonna take one, maybe two, from every batch; she'll think she miscounted when she's through packaging. And Ma's got marzipan; I can take a teaspoon, she won't know. And Ma's got raspberry jam for the rugelach. Maybe there's strudel. There is! Mmm, better with butter on it. Butter and raspberry jam! Plus, I luck out: two logs of paglech dough in the fridge! She won't notice if I cut off the ends. Maybe that's what sits heavy and begins to make me ache, low in my belly and constant, I don't know. Ma's got heavy cream and chocolate; I bet that's good together. I crumble in a little poppy krechen. Maybe that's what sits, heavy; I can't say. And before I know it it's dawn. I'm on the floor of my mama's kitchen, my back against the counter under the sink, my chin on my chest, crumbs and raspberry jam on my red silk blouse. I roll myself over and force myself up, sick to my stomach and weary. I hide the evidence, sweeping the crumbs into my hand and eating them. I take one more macaroon with chocolate glaze and head for my room.

I'm going to my room but I stop at Paully's door. My sweet Paully, snoring a little. I pet him when he feels bad. He rocks and whimpers and I stroke his back. I love to stroke it, the way he calms down and breathes slower. I can feel it in me.

I put what's left of my macaroon on his big soft hip when I climb in behind him, fitting myself to him, propped up on pillows. I stroke with my left hand and eat with my right, slowly, chewing carefully; it's hard to get more down. And when the cookie is gone, I sit up and get all the crumbs from his hip, and then I lick my fingers, and then I sigh and lie back down. Paully, I can tell, has come awake. I say, "It's okay, Paully. It's only me." and he just grunts. I rub his back in circles, my eyes closed. When Paully starts breathing funny, I open my eyes, and there in the dawn light I see: he's rubbing. He's big and red and pointing straight out.

My stomach is so gross, I'm almost afraid to move. Paully next to me, jiggling the bed. Uch! I hit him with a pillow. "Paully, stop that! Now!" I say. And he whimpers and whines and makes too much noise and I'm afraid he'll get Pa up. So I reach out both my arms around him from behind and hold him tight and force his hands off and rock him until he is soothed and heavy. "Sha, Paully, Sha. Time to sleep now." And I rock him until he drops off with a shudder and pull out my arm and shake it awake. I roll on my back and stare at the ceiling. I am flat on my back; I lost my pillow to Paully. I run my fingers down my blouse. The silk feels so supple, my breasts beneath the silk, springy and full. I touch them gently, the silk growing warm, as my eyes fill. Tears tickle my ears as they flow to the bed, steady, like streams. I bite my lip so I won't make noise. Between my legs I am growing wet. I reach down. Through my pants I can feel heat. I rip at them, opening. I shove my hand in, past my panties, to my thigh. I dig. I dig until it stops feeling good. I don't want to feel good there. I don't want to feel anything. I dig with my nails and pull, the nails against my thighs, slow, burning. I shudder beneath them, my back arcs up.

It wakes me up—like a Pepsi—alert. I quick stand and zip up, tiptoe back to my room. Pa will be up soon.

Pa! Oh God, Pa!

My tears splash into the pool. A whole new wave takes me and I can't hold on any more. I tried, Pa. I did! I didn't mean to get this way, so fat. I'm sorry! I didn't know! Where do you look for a nice sort of man? And then it got too late! And I got so... I'm sorry, Pa!

I cry until there are no more tears, just dry swells of gagging and moans. There are odd lucid moments where I worry about me and think I should get out of the water. Then my vision blurs again as my body finds more. I cry so much my jaw hurts. I cry so much I feel again like I'm going to be sick. But then that passes and I'm not sick, I am just there, whimpering against the side of a pool. It's over. How is it that it's over? Ryan!

I let go the side and sink. Like I do in the tub, I let myself sink, letting go of more and more air. Down to my shoulders, down to my chin, and then, like a sigh, like a sigh that starts from my toes, to my bottom. This is something I have never done, letting my bottom drop to the floor of the pool. It's like blue glass all around me, very weird and very silent. My skin is pale and fishy. I can hear the thump of my heart. My feet lift, toes first, toward the surface. And up I come—couldn't stay down if I wanted. A woman who's built like me, well, I guess she don't sink. Up I come, face in the water, eyes open looking through that deep glass.

Then real slow, thinking about it, I open my arms. I open my legs. I am like a star, floating, free, carried, maybe spinning, I don't know. Drifting. Unattached. Yeah, that's me. Unattached, spinning maybe, who can say? Oh, it's so beautiful—that's what it is—floating this way. Carried. I could stay this way forever. So calm. Forever. If only I didn't have to breathe.

Danny   The sound of liquid? My head? The swirl of fever, sirens, a filling and rising, the unending ringing of far telephones, a blur that is light, cool drips of water running like streams down an open shirt collar, voices calling, shrill, sudden, crazy heat in the cheeks, a steady, unearthly, high-pitched whine. Something lowered upon my face.

Listen: courses are shaped on winds of unreason.

Surfacing I disbelieved, sure that I slept still, that the crossing continued, but becalmed, as if on unstirred lake. A tube in the arm, a throb in the head like a far off drip, not unpleasant—these were permission to float safe in the sound of sleep, eyes closed to brightness piercing like a sun set on incessant horizon.

But listen: we live on dirt.

Mother's voice beyond walls: a warning through fog.

"Doctor," she said.

I opened my eyes, slowly accepting: a white room, drawn curtains, steel rails around the bed.

"Doctor," she said, up-anchored, drifting. "Will my son," she said, and then, nothing at all.

Listen: words may fill us with terrible thirst.

"Walk?" said a voice, arid with mind.

"No," said my mother, poor mother, unmoored. "I want to know…the legs? How is it…they twist?"

Coming to, it is called. To where, I now wonder.

I sat up in the bed, at least I did try to. My body was weight, unresponsive, quite dumb. My elbows unbending, my feet simply refusing. I thrashed and I flailed like a netted fish, furious, and fought free the covers so snugly rigged.

They were white, these legs, so white—chalk rubbed on cement, pale blue veins, subterranean, suspect, and wan. The right leg, askew, falling short of the left, both splayed, fluky, random—not legs at all. No, slim banners unfurled in a sigh of wind, luffed, flaccid, irrevocably hinged to an unhelpful mast.

I didn't want them. Not these.

I wanted legs.

A scream began in my belly and filled my chest, my mouth, my mind. A scream filled the room. A scream came through the door on my mother's face and another when she saw the tossed aside sheets. A scream shook my shoulders and I can't remember now how I ever stopped crying.

Coming to, it is called. To where, I now wonder. That, and how did I leave?

For I cannot recall now tires skating pavement, the desperate whine of brakes, the metal, sharp, final, the thud of my body, or the dry snap of bone. No memory of falling or flying or my own gasp, stunned. The last time I walked. I could have been whistling. Did I roll? Could I crawl? Did I beg for God's pity?

My mind withholds it like the treasure of an ocean-downed ship, uncharted, unrecoverable, and a poor purse at best. This merciful mire, opaque as black paint, I've come to respect like unreasoning winds.

That they caught the man fails even to retain my interest. That his head swirled with liquid, not a surprise. That he went to jail for it is too sad to give comfort. Listen: whirlpools are things in which we're all caught.

Pain, you are water; you rise until flooding. Pain, you are water, deep most in the well. Pain, you pitch. You toss then ground, breaking on all shores, moon-risen, strong. Pain, you are water, most common of solvents. Clear. Colorless. Silent. Most innocent of all. You take the flavor from tea, make the whiskey take longer. Immersed, I was baptized, stinging, raw. Hard water, soft water, heavy, drinking, rain, ground water, spring water, steam water vapor. Every day you cloud sun, every day, pores to rivers. Pain, you are my mother's many tears. You are the mother we crawl from scratching towards dust. Your gray is unchanging, your shores never come.

Pain, pain, every day, every day, at breakfast in coffee, pain, pain every day, drip, drip, drip. You fill me, conform to the shape of my vessel. Extinguisher! You freeze and I cannot break you. Pain! How sweet! Fallen, so pretty, surface beaded. Gently soaking, seeping— then you deluge, then submerge. Pain, you rot! And I will ride you. You watch me. An old salt, I. Pain, you are water, most of me, every cell. Pain, you are water. There is no life without you.

book five

❖•❖•❖

Butter, dear

–22–

Jody   I'm looking at my foot. *My* foot! I got these red pumps, bright red, new, very high, very Italian. I got this hose, very nice, with sort of silver undertones. I get chills just looking. I thought everything was going so well.

But then the guy—the instructor—he says, "It just looks risky, Ms. Kochansky."

So yeah, I think, looking back up at the road. He makes a good point, but I'm not looking at my foot because I'm nervous. I'm looking because that's *my* foot. And it's on the gas pedal!

Anyway, I sit where I am.

"Go on," he says. "You'll be okay."

I check him out in the seat beside me. He's trying to be encouraging, you know, like he's paid to be. But what I get stuck on is how the words "Safety First" go up and down when he nods. See, he has them stitched onto this red patch on his cap. They sort of bounce along. A bad sign, I think. I don't know, I think safety should sort of sit still.

So then he leans into me. "You've got to make your intention known, Ms. Kochansky."

I've already told him it's "Miss." I lift my foot—and it feels something like lead just about now—up off the brake.

"That's right," he says. "Now go on, give 'er some gas."

I shift my foot and drop it. It's like the car leaps forward. Or is that my heart leaping into my throat? Or the Safety First guy leaping into the back seat? I don't know. Something definitely leapt though.

"Okay," he says. "Good." So what do you know? He's still there in the seat beside me. Though I notice his voice has gotten a little higher, a little fakey even. "Pull about half way into the intersection. Show the drivers coming toward you what you mean to do."

This guy, I should say, is my third instructor. I wore the other two out. The first gave up on my parallel parking, the second never came back after the lesson with my freeway merge. Now it's the left turn. Again. The left turn is something I already had checked off my list, but somehow... I don't know. I'm like in reverse.

"Gentle now," Mr. Third Instructor says, "gentle, gentle."

Like who's he trying to convince? I try again, gentle, gentle. This time it's okay. So I'm in it now, my nose is in the intersection.

"Good, very good," he says, but I notice his hands are drumming like crazy against his thigh. "Okay, do you think you should turn now?" he says.

I check ahead of me, my side view, my rear view, and to my right. I happen to be good on the "keep your eyes moving" part. I even enjoy it. I like thinking about what the other folks are doing, being part of it all. In Brooklyn the trains come and go. It don't matter if you get on them or not. And also, it's best if you just keep your eyes to yourself, if you know what I mean. But in traffic, people react to each other. Like the poor guy behind me on that turn who follows me out past the crosswalk, though this is not the nicest example. Anyway, there I am with my nose in the intersection and my eyes moving and the third Safety First guy talking to me in this tone like "Can you say 'intersection'?" I give what I think is the right answer. "No," I say, "someone's coming."

"Well, not for a while," he says. "You could have made it. But that's okay. Cautious is better than foolish."

"I could have made it?" I say.

"Yeah, sure."

"Should I go now?"

"No, no," he says, real jumpy. "No, not now. Too late."

"I missed it," I say.

"Yes."

He must think I am a complete... Jeesh, I don't even care what he thinks. *I* think I'm a complete whatever. So I take my foot from the brake again and roll slowly forward. I will not miss it a second time. I bite my lip and am immediately sorry. I am trying a new kind of lipstick, darker, a little more up to date, and I can taste it right away. So now, in addition to everything else, I probably have Revlon Plum Fantasia teeth. I try to keep my mind on the turn.

"How about after that green car?" I say.

"Looking good," he says.

This guy, you gotta hand it to him, he's upbeat.

And so I wait, determined. No more lip biting. No more car leaping. After the green car, I'll make my move. But then, wouldn't you know, the light goes to yellow. And there's the guy behind me—he's out in the intersection too, hanging out there over the line because he trusts me—and, I don't know, I panic I guess, something. I step on it.

So the guy coming at me honks like a train and somebody's brakes squeal and the Safety First guy says, "Oh, oh, oh." And me? I'm not sure if I say anything at all, just cross one hand over another and hurl myself into space. Sometimes you do a thing and, I don't know, you just do it like you mean it. And then I'm driving east.

The guy behind me passes real quick and flips a bird. This anyway, I think, is something like New York.

So now my driving instructor—he's sort of slumped down a bit, he's like, lower in the seat—he says, real quiet, "Um, Ms. Kochansky? What'd'ya say we, ah, pull over for a bit. Talk a little? Ms. Kochansky?"

"Miss," I say, "Miss, Miss." I am surprised by the whiny tone that has come into my voice. But, you know, it's not the first time I told this guy.

"Yes, well," he clears his throat. "Ah, how about over there?"

I pull over, careful, signaling first. I park and turn the engine off. I feel very much like I should look at him but I do not want to.

"Miss Kochansky," he says, all calm and professional, "you are certain that you want to drive?"

I never know what to say when people ask questions that aren't really questions. Do they want answers? I sigh, but even then I don't feel better. I admire my nice neat manicure against the steering wheel. Also Revlon Plum Fantasia, why buy no-names? It looks good. It looks adult.

Adult. So how's that for a word? But that's the way I always feel when I look into the mirror and put the stuff on. Except now it's coming off. It's amazing how fast make-up can be undone by tears. I can't help myself. Three weeks ago I could make a left turn and now I can't. I try to hide it. I don't want this Safety First guy to watch me break up over a turn. But he does. He does see me.

"Miss Kochansky?" He shifts in his seat and brings out a hand-kerchief. "Are you. . . " Then he hands me the cloth. It has the same stupid damn "Safety First" thing printed on it. I guess this sort of thing comes up a lot.

I pull myself together, sniff, make sure there are no mascara stains. "I'm from Brooklyn," I tell him.

"Yes?" he says. Always with the non-questions, this guy.

"So people from Brooklyn don't drive," I tell him.

"Ah," he says. And then he sits back against the seat and tilts the visor down over his face like he's gonna take a nap or something. Like he needs some privacy to consider this.

"Admit you don't drive here, it's like admitting you can't read," I say. He don't move. "I'm not exaggerating," I say.

This poor man—my victim—he stays there, hiding behind his cap, trying to cope with the idea that people someplace south of Mars might not drive. I take my first good look at him. His hair is red. I always think men with red hair look boyish. I don't know why. Anyway, I think he looks younger than me, though I hope not. Being so silly like that in front of some younger man, I don't know, it makes it worse somehow.

Finally he wakes up. "You never see a cab here," he says. Then he lifts his visor again so I can see him.

"No," I say, "you have to call them."

"You do that?"

"Sure," I tell him. "Sometimes. If I got big things to carry, or if there's no way to make a bus work out."

"But usually buses, right?"

I'm not sure what he's getting at. I shrug.

"Well, tell me," he says, getting very thoughtful now. "You can take a bus to work and all?"

"Yeah, well. . . yeah. I mean I have to get there kind of earlier than I'd like, and I never know what time I'm gonna get home."

"But is that really so bad?"

So that's it. He's giving up on me. Well, I'm thinking to myself, there are other driving schools in the Yellow Pages. I didn't have to use Safety First. I take off my seat belt and turn to him. "I'm like the only one on the buses between sixteen and like, maybe, seventy, who's not..." and here, you know, I'm not exactly sure how to go on. I want to say "retarded." It's what we always said at home, if we said anything at all, but this man, you know, he's a stranger. Deborah Steiner uses "developmentally disabled," but what is that, like ten syllables or something?

So I'm searching for a word and Mr. Safety First decides to help me out. "Crazy?" he says.

"Developmentally disabled," I say and I fix him but good with a look. 'Crazy.' Now there's a sensitive guy for you.

"Yeah, but is *that* so bad? If everyone used them we'd have cleaner air, less congestion..."

Oh, I think, so that's it. I mean I may have only been in California four months but already I know that The Environment is like a religion out here. As long as it's someone else taking the bus. So I say, "And a lot less fun, Mr. Rollin. At least I think I could be having a little more fun, you know?"

"Um," he nods a few times, letting that sink in, thinking deep thoughts. "I guess the way it is out there, not driving would be a little like not having any legs."

"Yeah?" I put my hands up on the wheel. "Well what's it like? Having an IQ of sixty or having to use a wheelchair?" It's not that I want to be sarcastic, or not exactly. But I sure do want to be something.

His eyes snap open wide, like "oops!" He stares at me. I watch this expression come over his face. I know this expression. I have seen it and seen it and seen it and seen it. Truth is, I feel bad for him. What can it be like for one of these p.c. environmental "dudes"— like Ryan used to say—to suddenly get it that they're in the middle of someone's "issue"—as June says? How was he to know? I just look like everyone else. And so what does Mr. Sensitive say? "Oh, I don't know. One or the other." This is true. This is what this man says. Hopeless. "One or the other." Same thing to this guy. No difference. And this, even after he thinks about it. I'm thinking tomorrow I'm gonna phone the U-Drive-2 company.

But right now, right now I know what I want and it's to not have to talk to this little man anymore. I straighten myself up and re-fasten my belt. You know what driving is? It's making your intention known. No apologies.

"Okay," I tell him, "I'm ready to drive now."

And I look down, and there it is: my beautiful red shoe. Now that I am an "executive," I get things at cost. I mean this is the best darn shoe I've ever had on my foot, and one of the best bargains. I pull out into the lane.

<h1 style="text-align:center">–23–</h1>

Ida   One last thing he wants and then finally, finally, he says, he will start with the sweater. And what a last thing.

He sits me down in the living room in the big blue chair. He don't say why, only that I should sit. He rolls up so close in front of me, our feet almost touch, a big grin across his face. Whatever it is, Danny likes this part. He shakes and twists one of those crazy bags he got tied to that chair of his, all this clunking going on, everything takes him such a long time, I can't imagine. At last Danny brings out a low flat box so big it almost covers his lap, and shaped like half a circle. Such a pretty, fancy box, you would think there would be chocolates in there. He holds it up, I should see. At first I think he got sequins glued on there, and beads, and maybe some little pebbles or stones, but then I can see that's not what they are. They are buttons, all glistening and glowing in a design so beautiful it could be one of those oriental rugs.

He sees he got my attention and winks at me. Slowly, he opens the box. What he got in there, Jacob, you won't believe, spool after spool after spool of different colored threads, every color you can think of and a few you probably can't. Small spools in a big box, tightly packed. I can't say why, but I reach for it.

Danny puts his arms around it. I want it worse. He shakes his head. "The way this works, Mrs. K., is that I hold up two spools at a time, one in each hand and you point to the one you prefer. Meanwhile, you talk about something else."

"*Ai*, what a bother, just let me—" and I reach for the box.

"Nope, nope, this is my special patented color selection method and there will be no altering the system."

"I just want to hold—"

"Have I ever told you anything about making a cookie?"

"All right, all right. You show, I talk." I sit up closer to the edge of the chair, I should see better.

"You point," he says. Leave it to Danny.

"And I point," I say. "All right then."

But I don't get to point. Instead Danny closes the box. He shifts in his chair which takes even more time than when I shift in my chair. All the times he's been here, I still can't watch. He brings out two gloves, black velvet and tight fitting. He makes a big show of putting them on. I'm just glad to see him smile. After last time when he was in so much pain, acting like he couldn't wait to get out. "Why don't you tell me one of your wonderful stories while you point, Mrs. K."

I don't know, what am I here? Some kind of story machine? You drop in a quarter; I talk?

"You do realize, I suppose, that above all, that's why I love to come here. Your cookies, of course, they're worth the trip, but the stories! Honey, that's why I stay!"

I giggle. This I mean exactly, Jacob; I *giggle*. I'm an old woman giggling because a man calls me 'Honey'. Well Danny—what can I tell you?—he got a way of making a woman giggle. He's looking up at me. Mrs. K., the storyteller. I got a reputation to uphold here. "About...?" I say.

"Well..." He taps his pencil on his pad. "I heard about your kitchen."

"Oh you did, eh?" He raises his eyebrows and I can just imagine what he's heard. "I didn't mean to be sharp," I say, "she's a guest in my house, but Danny, two-year-olds were easier to work with than your mother."

He laughs and says, "I also heard about the importance of sifting."

"Let me tell you about cookies, Danny. Cookies are little things, eh? So with cookies little things matter. Cookies take steps, one after another after another. You need air in the flour? You sift."

He puts up his hand, I should stop. I shrug and nod. He tries to grin but his face makes something else. That face must still hurt. He picks up two spools, green and red, and holds them in his black velvet hands. He looks at me and nods.

"I've told you already a little about, Sammy, eh?"

"Mm," he says, "Lila's kid. The lawyer."

Don't worry, Jacob, I am your good wife. I only say about Sammy what it is not too much shame to say. "So when he's done with the law school, big party, right?"

"Well, sure."

"Everybody's eating. Like they'll never see food again, they're eating. And what are they all eating?"

"Um, cookies?"

I turn to him and open my hands. "Of course, cookies. Who needs another dry Chicken Kiev?"

"Life's too short," he says.

I gotta laugh. Sometimes Jacob, Danny, he's so like you. "Exactly," I say, and point at lilac instead of mauve. "So everyone's going on, all these fancy-schmancy up-town law-school-shmaw-school types, 'Oh! What good cookies!' You know, like, big news, they got food over in Flatbush—"

"You were the hit of the party, Mrs. K.!" he says.

"Now one of these lawyer-schmoyers, he brought with some reporter who makes up every year a little book she calls *Ethnic Eats.*"

"Hey!" he says. "I have that book!"

I pretend I got a pain; I can look away. Danny shouldn't see how proud. I go on. "This woman decides she wants the Kochansky Family Bakery should go in her book. She asks me can she come by and talk about it. She don't have to ask twice, eh? I'm beside myself, such excitement. She comes over, I can't stop my mouth."

Danny's chuckle is not so nice. I go on.

"So the reporter, she asks about the macaroons at Pesach. I say, 'You got any idea how many kinds of macaroons there are?' She says, 'Chocolate, coconut...' I tell her, 'In the A&P in the middle of winter you see those. That's all anyone knows from, chocolate and coconut. Very limited. People just aren't exposed."

I like the gold he shows me better than the brown.

" 'A macaroon,' I tell her, 'for your information, is any kind of cookie—and you would be surprised how many—that only has egg white. You got your cinnamon, your citrus, your almond. The point is not chocolate or coconut or almond, the point is pyramid. Pyramid, you see? We made them because we were the slaves, eh? But on Pesach, we're not the slaves no more, so we gobble them down. You see how it works?' "

"Fascinating, Mrs. K., I never knew."

"That's what she said. So I told her how the cookies, they celebrate the meaning of the occasion. Eat honey on the high holy days—intense sweetness for the passing of time. Also erste sternen—the first stars—for Yom Kippur. This way, when the first stars come out we all give thanks and take a little something to sustain us until the big meal. Then on Rosh Hashanah, lots of seeds to begin the new year. My eyes were always on the next holiday. Sukkot, *oy*, that was the worst of all. You see, you could not always get things year round like today. The seasons used to mean more. So here we'd want to celebrate the harvest and all the new foods that we can all of a sudden have now, except I got to have lots and lots of some special ingredient *before* the season. I tell you, Sukkot, it made no sense."

"It's a paradox," Danny says, "but it's sense."

"A paradox I don't know from. A pain in the side..." I put up my hands.

Danny laughs, which he is supposed to. I go on. "The little book, it comes out, eh? And what do I see? A little star next to my name: This Year's Most Promising New Find."

"Hey!"

" 'Hey!' is right. Hey! Nobody can believe what good luck. Everybody wants all of a sudden cookies from the Kochansky Family Bakery. The phone never rang so much. We'd answer like a family, not like a business, eh? They'd think they got the wrong number. We had such fun with this!"

I can't decide, both those blues are really pretty. Danny closes his hand into a fist and then opens them again. I point.

"Now Lila," I say, "now that she's going to be the rich mother of a lawyer-schmoyer, she's thinking she might give up her little hat shop." I look at his face to see if I ever I mentioned Lila's shop.

"No big loss," he says.

"She never liked that shop anyway," I say. "She couldn't wait to be done with it. So she and that kid of hers, they get a big idea. Lila, she's gonna sell the shop; she's gonna put all the money into me!" I wait until he looks at me; Danny should understand what I'm saying. "I'm gonna be big business."

He makes a little applause. The gloves make a funny sound. We laugh.

I go on. "So first thing Sammy wants I should do is sit down with some friend, an accountant or something—someone smart with the numbers—we should know what things cost. Two days we sit, I don't bake. Paully goes crazy; he can never stand it, a day should go a little different. And I tell this friend of Sammy's what I pay for flour, what for butter, even how long during the day I keep my oven on. Next week, back he comes. It won't work, he says. What I got to do is choose cheaper ingredients."

Danny makes a noise like a horse snorting. You see, Jacob? Just like you! Right away he understands what a bad idea.

"So now," I say, "we got here some little man, probably never made a cookie in his life, and he's gonna tell me how to do it. And there I am, just listening quiet until he's all through. Not one word do I speak, not me or anyone else. What everyone does is look at me, and from their faces, I think maybe they are a little afraid of what I'm gonna say."

"I'll bet." He shows me two shades of green, one more ugly than the next.

"But I don't get a chance. My Jacob, he puts up his hand like this..." I show Danny how you looked, making sure everyone was listening. I showed him how you turned to Sammy's friend, closed your eyes and shook your head. I make my finger point, and I say, like you, 'My Ida makes something special here. Special. That's

what we got to sell—*more* special, not less. What we got to know is
how do we make what Ida does so special people will be happy to
pay.' "

"He's right," says Danny, who should know with his fancy
sweaters.

"Of course he's right," I say. "But what you got to know here is
that it was Jacob saying this. *Jacob*, you see? If I had said this, I could
still be saying it now, a lot of good this would do me."

Danny nods and shrugs. He didn't make the world either. He
shows me two grays so close I can't see the difference. I just point
and say, "At first, no one got any idea how to make *more* special
except Jody. She says we should put in with every kind a little explanation of why this cookie goes with this holiday."

"Exactly!" Danny says, which I just can't believe. He can see
I don't expect. "Everything you just told me, Mrs. K., about the
metaphor inherent in—"

"Meta-who?"

"All those secondary meanings—like in poetry. You bake poems,
Mrs. K."

Poems. Do you think, Jacob? Our Jody, she was a kid, and also,
a girl. What did she know? Me, what I knew was to bake. And
then that accountant of Sammy's, he drummed his fingers on top of
his numbers and said, 'printing costs, extra packaging...' We didn't
think twice. Instead we..."

Oh, my bright yellow kitchen, so much space wasted, so much
money, so much time, the family never the same. Could this have
been our mistake, my husband? That we didn't listen to our Jody?
Let's face it, our Jody knows a thing or two about how to sell, eh?
Maybe poems is what people pay for. I wipe my eyes with the bottom of my apron.

He says, real gentle, "May I assume you did not include explanations of—"

"It was Lila's idea. 'The religious,' she says, 'they're the one's
having all the babies. And everyone knows they got a little money
to spend, eh?' And Sammy, he's right away behind it. Let's go
kosher! Big business, kosher! Never mind to convert they're gonna

cut my living room in two, we shouldn't have any place to be a family. Kosher is what Sammy and Lila want and Sammy and Lila, it's their money.

"My Jacob, you should have seen, Danny. He wanted I should have the kitchen of my dreams. Every little thing he asked me, what did I want, how I can reach this or that, how much room do I need to put what. He'd either be asking me or out comparing the price of lumber. But I had work myself, every little corner of every little gadget had to be scrubbed 'till like new, or the thing had to be thrown out. Me and Paully worked all day and Jody when she got home. Lila and Sammy, what they did was sign the checks. Lots of money being spent. A lot of work, but *my* work. I'm not second to nobody."

Danny sits back a minute, doesn't reach for a spool. "I just was thinking of what my perfect kitchen would be. Everything down low, of course. It'd be fun to design. Right now we've got my mother's perfect kitchen: microwave, toaster oven, and a filing cabinet of delivery menus. My mother orders one meal from more than one place. She does this all the time, the Szechwan green beans from one place and the cashew chicken from another."

Poor Danny, my heart goes out. Maybe we shouldn't talk about his mother's cooking; it's upsetting. So I say, "I got a 'kosher' kitchen, Danny. Not the kitchen of my dreams."

Jody Changed everything. I like, started the job over.

Started on Sunday. Why not Sunday? I'm gonna stop hiding the Sundays. If it's good enough for Sharon, it's good enough for me.

I go by the Walgreen's first and pick up some cleaners, some plastic gloves, a dust mop and a bucket. At least I'll leave a tidy office for whoever it is they hire to replace me when they see the lousy figures from the Veterans' Day sale. I ran totally out of colors. They wear more colors on this coast.

What I do in my office is I just pick up piles, put them someplace else temporary, clean underneath them, hit the pile with the dust mop, then put it back neatly. I don't even try to see what's in them. I unplug the computer and put it up neat. There it is: one square foot of desk space! I order three big filing cabinets and a long folding table from the Home Office department. I get cardboard for a big sign to post above the time clock. I offer my girls unlimited hours at time-and-a-half for the next two weekends starting Friday night. At that wage, most of them are there every hour they can be. I tell them, "Let the Bali shipment stay in the boxes and let's get filing!"

So you know I had second—hey, I had third and fourth thoughts about setting up a situation where I'm spending hours with my girls, but it turns out, management-wise, this is maybe the best thing I've ever done. We work in blue jeans and T-shirts, the radio going, re- laxed, sorting and filing and throwing away. And all the time we're talking, you know how women are. It's not so nice to say but a lot of time we're talking about the one's who aren't there, which since I always am, I find kind of helpful.

I got to know the whole crew much better than I ever knew my last girls, even after working with them for years. We talk about movies and clothes and our families. Or they do. Me? I avoid that whole subject. They ask me why I don't got photos up in my office and I just say I can't find room for even one more thing! I just tell whoever asks I got one brother. I say his name is Paul. Then I ask about them.

Sometimes we play the radio. We talk about music—or they do, I don't know much—and TV. And also, like women everywhere, ev- ery minute, we talk and we talk and we talk about food. I mean, for most women this is like a hobby or something. They count calories the way some people know baseball statistics, always adding and subtracting and weighing percentages.

Which is not to say I'm not having fun. Even if I don't want to talk, I still like to listen. Also I got to keep pushing the work along. That's my job. At least I try to be funny about it.

I did lose my sense of humor once, though. The girls found a pile of their old schedules. Right away they're looking who got what last Christmas. Like I need to be reminded that I got only a couple of weeks until the big day after Thanksgiving onslaught. I tell them to turn off the radio and get those schedules filed.

End of the first Saturday, June pulls me aside. She wants to talk. So I say, "Talk then." But for her, that's not good enough. She wants it so private we got to go crowd in a dressing room—it's the only private place—and watch ourselves talk front and back view.

"Jody?" she says, a little bit timid.

I say, "Talk, June. Go on. Say what you got to say."

"Well, I know it's not my place. I, ah, wouldn't want to..."

And I say, "Who taught you to be so afraid of suggesting?" It's the kind of thing, I think, I've heard June say.

So she smiles and suggests, and what a suggestion! That June—I'm telling you, that one thinks on her feet. She thinks we should file what orders we can figure out separately from receipts so we'd have a crosscheck. She's right and I wish I had thought it myself.

"June," I say, as we both look in the mirror, "someday, I'm going to promote you." And right then, boom, I got me a worker who's both smart and loyal.

So we rearranged—a lot of work, but worth it—and I got no shame saying it's June's idea to the other girls and if they got any let's hear 'em and I mean that for always. I was glad they got to see that I wasn't one of those managers who took a few classes and walked in on the second floor. "No," I tell them, "I started in the basement and I wore my shoes out climbing." I tell them, "Push comes to shove, I walk with the union, 'cause that's who I am."

By now we know every movie everyone has seen and we know what everyone eats, how much, and at what time. They've been working hard. Everyone's getting a little fussy bumping into each other. Then, out of nowhere, Tonya sighs and says it will sure be good to have extra money with Christmas coming. Just hearing that makes my stomach clutch. But at least no one notices. They're all too busy saying what they'll do for Christmas. Then Beth, who don't say "boo" and everyone thinks is boring, tells us how on Christmas Eve she is playing bass in her punk rock band! She's gonna put blue paint on her face! Quiet little Beth! We all screamed! We had so much fun!

Later, over the pizza I had delivered, I got good and fed up with the constant food prattle, I sighed and I said to them, "This is what I think. What I think is you got to look at yourself and find what's good."

And one by one they start smiling like they like this notion, like it's an original thought or something.

"Like you," Amy says to me. "You got good eyes."

"I do?" I say. I'm sort of embarrassed.

"Beautiful," says Tonya. "Deep set."

"And so dark," says Marta.

So suddenly, you know, I am so self-conscious that everyone is looking at my eyes that all I can think to do is look away and when I do, I notice something odd.

"What is that behind there?" I say, and all the girls look. "Behind that bookcase. Hey, is that a door?"

So all at once everyone is clearing the shelves. It *is* a door! Marta and June and Beth heave the case away. The door is locked! The office key won't work. I stand there going through my ring of keys, all eyes on me. Finally I get a key to fit. The door opens. Everybody peers in. You'd think I was Geraldo in front of Al Capone's safe.

Amy says "eeyyoo." It is really cobwebby, but it's just a closet. Still I make a joke of going in there with my dust mop waving like I'm slaying some dragon.

What it turns out is in there are piles up to my shoulder. The whole closet, full! Order forms! I've found them!

My eyes well up. I'm moved by a pile of order forms; this is what it has come to!

Why are they here in this closet? And what's this stuff all over them? In the margins, on the backs, everywhere, little colored dots, red, blue, green, purple, orange. For brown she made 'X's because the brown has a way of looking a lot like the orange. Neatly typed numbers in the boxes—that's what they don't have. I think this time I actually will cry when Marta, that cop-to-be, calls out, "Hey, what the heck's this?"

And we all look at her standing there holding it up in her hand. One of those big round pens with like eight different colors of ink, hidden behind a pile like some pimply kid's dirty book. All I have to do is see it and it hits me immediately. I tell the girls, "I see why these papers are in here! They're quarantined. They've got the measles!"

The girls all come gather around. I say, "Girls, these are no doodles."

Marta says, "A code?"

I say, "Where's Sherlock Holmes when you need him?"

Everyone starts passing the top forms around. I ask if anyone's good at puzzles. Beth says, "I am, kinda." But when she takes a good look at it, she just shrugs. Tonya sings the theme from Dragnet.

I see it. One dot equals some quantity, and the color? Probably the discount. Something like that. I hold that pen in my hand, close my eyes. So all right, maybe Sherlock might have gotten it quicker, but then, he don't know Foundations like I do.

Ida   You got any idea what it is to make a kitchen kosher for business? All the seams, all the places where the corners come together, they could not be scrubbed, Danny. Scrubbed wasn't good enough. They had to be burned. All the surfaces had to have boiling water poured over. Poured. Lots of it—it can ruin your counters if you don't do just right. All the utensils had to be scalded and rinsed in a koshered sink, which—would you believe—can't be porcelain. Porcelain don't kosher. Don't ask me why. There's no reason for these rules, they just have them to see how many they can make you follow. You know for a family, eh?

"I know some," he says. " You have to have two different set-ups right? Two sets of dishes, two mixing bowls, two frying pans, one for dairy, one for meat."

I nod he should see I need all that. "But see here we got something different," I say. "For cookies I don't use meat, but I still got a family, don't I? I got to cook out of this kitchen. So one for the family and one for cookies. A special case. A million rules already, but also, all the extra rules for a business. You got no idea the headache. They make no sense these rules. For some reason, porcelain don't kosher. Why? Don't ask, just do. So that means we got to have a new sink; we can't have a new floor. The seam between the linoleum and the cabinet? For forty years it has never fit right. Always this ugly, broken crack I got there. It catches seeds and flour. I got to make Paully scrub on his knees; he whines and complains. Porcelain don't kosher! *Feh!*"

I point at the bright orange like I mean it. "But there is one thing, Danny..."

He holds a moment and waits for me.

"Automatic dishwashers!" I say. "Two of them!"

"Ooooh," he says, teasing.

Then he begins to pull out a few spools and make a little pile. I watch him. He covers the pile with his hand and says, "Go on."

So, I tell him how we had to knock down a wall, how every night you'd turn the room into a workshop and you and Izzy and Mort and your pa and Paully would make me a bakery. Then, next morning I'd turn it back into a family kitchen. We lived this way for months. The men in the kitchen and me and Lila, down at her shop counting hats for closeout.

I tell him about Paully and the way you showed him how to cut wood straight and hammer. Danny makes an odd look. I wonder if I've told him this before. So I tell him about the cookie sheets. I know I have not told about the cookie sheets, how they had to be coated every inch with oil and burned in a kosher oven, but how we couldn't kosher the oven until last because of some other rule and you thought to use the torch. You and Paully in the back yard, Paully holding the sheet out on some kind of grip thing you made him, while you torched. The sheets were shiny and new. They were like mirrors glowing back into the house. It was like the house was painted in fire. The whole side of the house, except for two big black wiggly reflections. You and Paully, one black shadow.

Danny, he stops with the pile all of a sudden. He folds his hands.

"What is it?" I say. "What's the matter?"

"Paully can also do construction work, Mrs. K.?"

Isn't this nice of Danny, he's gonna make a big deal how smart our boy is, so I say, not too puffed up, "Paully can do what ever his father teaches him."

"Mrs. K., there are fatherly men who would have taught Paully things."

"I don't understand what you are saying, Danny."

"No. I can see that you don't," he says. He shakes his head, real tut-tut. He picks up two shades of wine red and holds one out either side of my face. "That's beautiful about the cookie sheets, Mrs. K."

He don't want to tell me what's on his mind, who am I to ask? "I thought you would like that," I say. "An eye person like you."

He leans in again and holds a blue on either side of my face. So I go on. "Just to even talk to the rabbi that got to come and inspect is a very complicated business. The inspection you got to wait months for. Jacob wanted we should get on the list. We got some date in the future. We had no idea could we be done by then." I put my hands up and shake them.

"It was unnerving," he says.

"It was exciting," I say.

"Were you done?"

"We were done! We got Jody in a pink dress to open the door. She's gonna show him to the kitchen, he shouldn't look too much around the living room. We all run into the kitchen when he knocks and Jody, she opens.

"In comes the rabbi with his big hat and the long black beard and right behind him, Danny, some young guy from the health department."

"No."

I can see he sees where I'm going.

"So who knew he'd bring this guy? The health police. A whole different million rules we got to follow or he's gonna shut me down from selling at all, much less to the pious.

"Aw," he says.

"Sees how I use the same refrigerator for the family and the nuts for the cookies and says no good. What? We should have *three* refrigerators? And, of course, he don't like that the floor don't seal good. He got no problem with porcelain sinks though. Porcelain's okay by him.

"He hands Jacob a stack of notices. I can see on Jacob's face, he's thinking, 'With what money?' Two weeks later, the city shuts me down. The end."

"The end?"

"What? The end? So some kid from the city says it's the end, that means it's the end? I put the whole pile of papers on a cookie sheet with a little butter and burnt it to ashes."

"No!"

"I did. I koshered them but good. And then I changed the name on the label from the Kochansky Family Bakery to Ida's Cookies."

"Hey! Catchy!" he says.

"An improvement, if I may say so," I say.

What happened next, Jacob, maybe you never got old enough to understand. What I want is to show Danny the snazzy labels I got in the drawer of the sideboard, the ones that say "Ida's Cookies." But to do this, I would have to get up. It's a big deal now, to get up, especially from the blue chair. And anyway sitting right in front of me is Danny with the big spool box open on his lap. I can't ask him. With all those bags he got on there he couldn't even get between the table and the sideboard and he shouldn't have to explain himself. I'm stuck. I'm stuck in the chair.

Danny don't notice, he's too busy squinting at a pile of green spools in his hand. So all right, I won't be able to show him the labels, or maybe, if I remember, I'll show next visit; it's not the end of the world. But because I can't, I want to even more. I can't stand that I can't. It shouldn't be like this. Where is Jody when I need her? Off in her California.

Danny gives me a look like I'm a big puzzle. I think this has to do with the colors he's holding by my face, but what he says is, "You have the strangest look on your face, Mrs. K."

That's all he said. It's not like he handed me an engraved invitation. Don't matter. I'm out with it. I leave out the part he won't fit by the sideboard, but he can see for himself. I think he's gonna make a fuss, give it a try. He don't. He justs nods and shuts his eyes. Then he says, "A week or so ago, I was in the tub at home. I shouldn't use the tub there, Mrs. K. I'm much better off using the shower at the Vet's, but I enjoy it. I like to soak and listen to music now and then. But it's difficult—a difficult bathroom for me. So I draw the bath and I get myself all ready and a song comes on the radio. It's by Marvin Gaye, Mrs. K., and mmm, it just takes me back. I hadn't heard it in years. So I reached for the radio. I wanted it louder. Maybe I took a step. I don't know. I slipped. Banged my head against the toilet going down. That's how I hurt my face. It's all right. It didn't knock me out; I was okay. It's mostly healed and I'm glad nothing happened to my teeth. But now? Now I know I'm never gonna turn the music up again—you know?—not on a whim like that. Every time from now on that I even think of it, something adult—something sober—inside is going to stop me."

We sit quiet a long time, Danny and me. I'm not used to sitting so quiet with somebody, but Danny is easy to be quiet with, I don't feel nervous. I sigh. He sighs. I start to sigh again, but I don't. I say, "But Danny, this is your 'now' you love so much."

"Yes it is, Mrs. K. That's not one of our choices—that it not be 'now.' Our only choice is to let ourselves love it or not. I want to, Mrs. K.; I try."

–24–

Jody I don't bother with thongs, I leave my little robe, I push open the gate of the pool with wet hands. I slide open the glass door on my deck and drip on my rug. What I do not do, cannot let myself do, is think. I pull the phone onto the floor; I can't sit on the couch like this. I sit on the floor. Don't think, Jody, just dial. I dial. Then I think. I think: hang up. But no, it's got to be done. I've got to do it. No one else can.

"Ma?"

"Jody?" Every time.

I run my hand through my hair. Water flies from it onto the couch. Darn it.

"Blah, blah," she's saying.

"Ma. This is long distance." This always works.

Now it's my turn. But I can't. I just...I open my mouth. But...I close my eyes. Maybe I could write a letter.

"So?" Ma says, after a moment. "Maybe I should go then, eh?"

"No!" Oops! I shout this. I run my fingers through my hair again; I sit straighter, perkier. I smile. "Ma," I say, "guess what? Good news!"

"You're coming home!"

I close my eyes. Liar or worm. Worm or… "Nooo. No actually Ma, uh, what I wanted to tell you… They gave me a raise!" Well, at least it's true. "A big raise, Ma, a nice raise." I beat my free hand on the leg of the couch. This is it.

"Ma? You sitting? I think you should sit."

"You got a raise, Jody! I'm standing!"

"Sit, Ma."

"For a raise I should sit?"

"Sit, Ma." I stand. I pick up the phone and grip it tight. I walk little circles in front of my TV. "You sitting, Ma?"

"Right here, in the blue chair," she says.

Good. She's sitting.

So.

Go on, Jody. Say something.

I say something. "Ma," I say, "they didn't just give me a raise," and before she gets any chance to open her mouth, I rush on. "What they did Ma is they gave me a promotion. See Ma, what they gave me is something like the job I've been doing, but it's bigger, a real lot bigger."

"You already took this? You said yes?"

"Well, I…" I'm not sure where she's going with this. "They tell me they need an answer right away," I say. "Ma, they chose *me* to do it."

"So you say you want to think about it, eh? Smart girl."

Liar or… "Well, yes, I did say that but—"

"A good idea to talk to your mother before making such a big decision."

I have no idea what the right thing to say here is. Thing about Ma is though, that if I don't say anything, she'll just go on right ahead.

"Because I will tell you something, Jody, this sounds to me like when I tried to get the blessing for kosher."

Oh please, not this story. Though, I'll admit, she does tell it funny. In a different mood I would not at all mind listening to Ma tell a story I already know. Somewhere along the way maybe she'll find a new joke. It's worth a listen. Usually. Not now. Now I walk to my curtains and pull the chord aside and look at my pool.

I stayed in that pool even though I was getting achy. Even though my legs were trembling. My arms hurt too, my shoulders, my neck. My head, ringing and sniffly. Sleep would feel so good. But instead I stand by my window and half listen. It's so quiet out there. I just imagine Ryan screeching the gate open, trotting in, a nice neat dive. A real swimmer, that girl, no toe dipping there. Just dives right in and does.

"Ma," I say, right over whatever she's saying, "I was there, remember?" Not that saying it's gonna stop Ma.

I never know what to think when she does this. Maybe she don't hear. She's getting on and all, I know, but I think maybe it's just me she don't hear, you know? She's always been this way.

I'm losing my courage.

I still haven't decided what to tell her. Should I say that this new job has just come open and aren't I just the lucky one? Or will I tell her I always knew, that I came out here for this job and I always intended to stay. Maybe today. Maybe today will be the day I tell her.

"Ma," I say, "you're telling me a story I know on long distance."

"Oops," she says. I tell you, every time.

"Let me ask you something, Ma. Can I ask you something?"

"You got to ask if you can ask?"

"Just why are you telling me this story?"

"So you should learn from your mother's mistakes. This can happen. Everything is possible."

Maybe, I think. Probably not. But now she's got me, now I'm interested. I say, "Learn what, Ma?"

"Jody, darling, I don't want you should get bigger than you can handle. This causes misery. You listen to me. I know."

"Wait, Ma? You saying I can't handle this job?"

"So much responsibility, Jody—" she's saying.

I pull the phone from my ear. I stare at it. Who is she? What does she know about what I can handle? And my mama of all people! In the entire long history of Judaism, one mother got no ambition for her kid and lucky me, I get her.

Steiner   I'm in my parents' neighborhood when Danny Cohen taps on the window of a sweater boutique and waves me in. He folds while we talk.

"These are mine," he says, indicating with his eyes an area of shelves, "this corner."

He holds his gaze on me and, for a moment I think he might actually want me to help him fold his sweaters!

"These," he says, pointing ahead of him and leaning back, "and those up there."

He looks up there, then at me, then shrugs and returns to folding.

"Hey, good for you on Paul Kochansky," he says. "The rumor is you got him in permanently and he's doing contract work."

"Just a temporary, in-house program," I say. "He's pinning bows on dolls."

"Well, it sure helps that he can see to do it."

"You heard the story about his glasses, huh?"

"Pretty cool, Deborah."

That's Danny. Always in the loop.

"I'm afraid that may be it, though," I say. "It looks like contract work may be as far as I can take him."

"What do you mean? Isn't he a baker's assistant?"

"*Her* assistant," I say. "He can't seem to follow directions from anyone but her. He balks at it. And if you try again, Danny, you wouldn't believe the tantrums! He screams and smashes whatever's close."

"Whew, and Paully's a big guy!"

"Exactly! The center absolutely can't manage that behavior."

Danny pauses, arms in midair, holding up deep brown and gold half-folded sleeves. "Give up time," he says.

I assume I've heard him wrong and say, "Yeah. I hope I have it."

"No," he says, "I said give *up* time. Give it up. Let it go. You're not going to find him a job, Deborah. They don't all get jobs. And besides, if I remember right, it's not what the family asked for."

"Right. They asked for the moon."

I immediately regret saying it. I am in my parents' neighborhood. I am wearing jogging pants and a sweatshirt. I am supposed to be picking up orange juice. It's my day off from the Kochanskys."

"I've gotten to know Mrs. K. some."

"Have you?" I say. "She's never mentioned it."

"Well, I don't gather you two talk. Anyway, I thought you said they wanted housing—you know, safety, routine. A place. That's all he probably needs anyway."

"Paul is capable of much more. He deserves more."

Danny's brow furrows. He leans back in his chair to look at me. Then he says, "Deborah, I'm almost done here. It's just those up top."

He does that thing again, sort of freezes his gaze on me. "Um, Deborah, would you be so kind as to hand me those sweaters from that top shelf, please."

"Oh, sure!" I hand them down. He returns to his work, shaking his head.

"Deserves," he says, "now there's an interesting word. Are you saying you think it's not *fair*, Deborah?"

"Actually, I think it's a lot more than unfair. I think, in fact, it's criminal."

Danny puts down his sweater, closes his eyes, and opens them again, holding on me, wide-eyed.

"I mean it," I say, "under Right to Thrive laws. If it isn't, it should be."

Danny puts up his hand.

"Wait! Listen!" I rush on. "It should be! In most states laws make a parent culpable if a child 'fails to thrive,' right? Usually this means undernourished, but hasn't Paul Kochansky been denied the right to thrive? I mean social integration is vital."

"Deb—"

"Vital *literally*! Right to Thrive! Can't you see it?"

"You're seri—"

"I'm pretty sure that's the way to go. My case just isn't as strong under Right to Education. Laws are much more widely interpreted there. What I might consider unlawful, the state might call parental prerogative."

Danny has stopped still, blinking at me. He bites his lip, and lowers his gaze. Then he looks me in the eye and says, "Yeah, and you'd get your fifteen minutes."

Is that a joke? I study his face and I still don't know.

"Danny, you think this is about me?"

"No." This time he is openly sarcastic. "I think it's about helping Paul Kochansky and his family."

I turn from him. I look at our feet, mine on the floor and his against the pads of his chair. Neither of us speak. My parents will be wondering where I am. It's my day off. My eyes begin to fill.

"I've tried everything," I say, my hand rubbing the back of my neck. "Almost everything."

He nods. "Deborah," he says gently, "would you mind please helping me replace these sweaters up top?"

Danny hands me a whole armload which I have to lay upon the shelf and then smooth onto the pile. Meanwhile, he slowly twists and reaches into one of the bags he has tied on to the back of his chair. He brings out a notebook, the kind school kids use, and rips free a piece which he begins to carefully fold.

"What I think, Deborah," he says as he inspects his airplane, "is that the most important thing about knowing the ropes, is knowing that sometimes..." He squints and aims, "sometimes..." And then he lets it fly, saying, "the ropes just aren't there."

−25−

Jody Here's my plan. I'm gonna roll down the ramp into the food court, and hang a quick left. Then I'm gonna grab a hold on that brass bar they got in front of the Pretzel Palace—beats twisting my ankle again on the dumb brake thingys.

I check my pads again and leave go, and woah-oh-oh, smack, right into Sharon. We both rub our heads and look at each other. We check ourselves. We look at each other again and laugh. We look ridiculous, pads, helmets, Sharon's got a T-shirt that says "Skate-Rat Mom." Well, look at that! She skates! I had no idea. She says, "Yeah, few times around after work before I hit the freeway. Keeps me sane." I tell her I just started. She says, "Come on, let me give you a few tips."

She's got it all figured how to do the least amount of brick floor and the most amount of tile. She shows me how to lift and cross my leg and how I'm supposed to brake if I can ever learn to do it. She says she loves my new haircut and I tell her about the place a few blocks from here June told me about. I tell her they got a real good stylist there. She even taught me this up-to date way to do my eyes, no charge.

This makes Sharon start in on how she hates the cosmetics department. I couldn't agree more. They got it all, the staff, all the advertising money, that army of sprayers. "They all wear black," Sharon says. "They don't even wear my sportswear."

"True," I say, "and how many hours a day do you think they spend getting stuff back on hooks?"

Sharon just rolls her eyes. I tell how what I really lust after is hosiery. I *want* that floor space. I mean, do we really need to look at rows and rows of socks? What my department needs is a little bend over space. You know, a woman doesn't want to feel like she's gonna knock over things with her backside just because she bends to look at a tag.

I try to kind of show her what I mean, how high my displays are and how far apart, and I wind up hugging one of those heavy gold trashcans with the swinging lids. I apologize. Sharon laughs and says something like "Women who sweat don't apologize," and puts out her arm for me to lean on.

Half a mall later, she skates and I skate walk over to the water fountain. We take turns drinking. We drink a lot, smiling and wiping our mouths.

That's when I say, "Sharon, looked at your calendar for Friday?"

She says, "Friday?" Then, "Oh, Friday. Yeah, that's right. I saw someone wrote you on it."

"Me," I say. "I wrote me on it. Hope that's okay."

She takes another mouthful, nodding while she does it. She swallows and says, "Sure."

"But we could just take care of it now," I say.

She shrugs like that would be all right too. She leads out to the exit.

There's a little spot there with red bricks and shade trees and benches where I still wait for the bus. Not for long, though. The right car for me is gonna be in this weekend's paper. It's a gut thing. I just know it. I sit down next to my boss. It's dark already, but they got the courtyard lit with pretty, old-fashioned lamps.

Sitting down is better. It feels more like business. I take off the pads. I'm glad that she leaves hers on. It gives me an edge somehow. So then I do it. I lay it out. The hidden duplicates, the codes. "You two were friends I hear." I ask her what gives.

Sharon closes her eyes and sighs. "She swore me to secrecy. I'm really sorry..."

I say, "Tell your friend you were ambushed and could not resist."

She laughs. "Not friend—sister-in-law." And then she says—like this explains everything, "She was in my wedding party."

She looks at me and shrugs. "She's dyslexic," she says.

I tell her I have heard of this but I don't really know what it means. She says her sister-in-law has a real hard time reading and doing rows of numbers. Something about seeing symbols different. "She even has trouble with her own name—Nancy," Sharon says. "Always wants to make the diagonal on the 'N' go the other way."

"Huh," I say. Just that. I don't know what to think. "Well, if you say so, Sharon, but she still ran a real good department. Sales figures strong, the girls all seem happy enough. Everything's in pretty good shape."

"But she can't file worth a darn—"

"Um, I noticed!"

"And well, apparently she can't fill out the order forms either," she says.

"So how did she get the orders in, do you think?"

"Jody, if I knew... If I'd known! Jody! Why didn't you tell me?"

I mumble something about how they buy different on this coast. Then I say, "I didn't know how you'd take it. I didn't want you to fire me."

"Fire you? I'm thrilled to have found you! It's Nancy I would have loved to fire, but how could I? All the stores were going to computers and Nancy just could not keep up. She might not have gotten another job. And my brother was going to school..."

She's thrilled! I play it cool. "I see," I say, and sit back, taking it all in. "But you did know about the files," I say.

"Yes I did, I'm sorry. The sworn to secrecy thing—right? I mean, Macy's doesn't know. I never reported it."

I sigh. "That mess cost me a lot of Sundays," I say.

"I know, and I'm sorry—that's why I offered the overtime. For what it's worth, I've been very impressed. Me, I probably would have set a match to it all by now, but you have just been patiently working at it and working at it. And then turning your staff into a team! Jody, I'm so proud I was the one that hired you!"

I let this sink in.

Then I go for the close. "Sharon, there are some things I need."

I tell her that I want to promote June. I want her to handle schedules, some other administrative stuff. Then I tell her I want a spree for a Christmas sale staff incentive. She's never heard of it. So I tell her about mine. The store once gave me a three hundred dollar shopping spree as a bonus for doing a lot of extra work during an inventory. A very clever scheme, this. I got more than four hundred dollars worth of stuff when you factor in my discount and the store only pays cost, maybe—what?—a hundred and fifty or so. Not only is it smart, it's fun.

I tell her how I gave Ma half of it. Ma, she went crazy. Ma don't shop at Macy's usually, says it's too hoity-paloity. So this was, well, for her this was like winning the sweepstakes or something. She had such a great time. We bought matching hats and gloves and those silly animal slippers. Mine were puppies, Ma got bunnies. We got Paully a huge stuffed toy tiger.

"She sounds fun, your mother," says Sharon, and right away I'm kicking myself for talking too much to an employer. You would have thought I would have learned.

Then she invites me to join this group she goes to. She calls it her Old-Girls Network. They're professional women who raise money for some college scholarships they give every year. She says they're going to have an auction and that she always gets Macy's to donate

244 / Tracy Koretsky

the wild stuff off her displays. I flash on a whole room of women in beige suits bidding for Amy's little zippered leather thing. I tell her I'd love to go. That is, if it doesn't conflict...

And then I tell her that I left a few things unfinished in Brooklyn and that I got to go back there for at least a couple, three, weeks. I don't got that much time off coming yet, and we both know it, but still, I just say it flat out, no "I'm sorry," no "please."

She nods, thinking hard. I don't know if she's figuring how to work it or how to say "no" so I won't be mad. "Too bad," she says. "Christmas party's always a great time here. We'll miss you."

Ida   Danny asks about Lila and I do not say she fell over dead from the scandal—that rotten son of hers. I just say, dead four years now. He asks if I miss her and I tell him how it was years before that that Lila and us stopped talking. Somehow Lila thought she should have her money back. How this was supposed to work, I tell him, I guess he would have to ask Lila. We had no money. We had a kitchen and I was selling what I could make except not to the religious. Somehow this is not okay by Lila. And now her son's a lawyer, so..."

"Ah," says Danny, nodding. "Nothing destroys a family faster than even just talking about a law suit."

"Who talked! We screamed! Lila screamed at me and I screamed at Jacob and Jacob took a walk. I put Mama's cookbook on a sheet and poured oil on it, burnt it to ashes, the kitchen filling with smoke. 'You want to shut us down,' I screamed, 'let's do it faster!' Lila started weeping, calling Mama's name."

I know how much it hurt you, Jacob, to lose Sammy. For this, I am sorry.

"The family was never the same," I tell Danny. "We saw each other the High Holy Days, Hanukah, but it wasn't warm."

"And the rest of them?" he wants to know.

"All gone now," I tell him, "except Clara, Izzy's wife. She's in a rest home on Long Island. We were never close anyhow."

"Only your daughter now, Mrs. K.," he says, quietly, closing his box up.

"Out in that California," I say.

"She's been gone how long now, Mrs. K.?"

"More than four months."

"What does she say?"

"About what?"

"About what you're going to do?"

"What I'm going to do about what?"

"Mrs. K.!" Danny looks like he would like to stand up now. He opens his hands, still in those black gloves. "Your situation. Paully. Everything."

"Do?" I say.

"Are you planning on living forever, Mrs. K.?"

"Danny!"

"Surely, Mrs. K., you do think of this."

"When Jody comes home—"

"Are you sure she's coming home?"

"Of course she's coming home. My Jody's a good girl."

"I'm sure—"

"She'll come take care."

Danny puts his spools down. "She gave up her flat here, right? What makes you think—"

"She'll come. She'll take care," I say again.

"And then what? Then you can die?"

"If I ever get a second, maybe."

He looks away and laughs. He looks back at me and laughs again, shaking his head. "Always the joke, huh, Mrs. K.?"

"I should cry?"

"That would be your choice," he says. Then he waves his arms all around, a big show. Danny puts out his hand, fist up, turns it over and quick opens it so I can see next to the black velvet a small spool of the palest yellow. He smiles at me and nods. "Butter, Mrs. Kochansky," he says.

"No, no, a little brighter, Danny!" I say.

He shakes his head, he won't hear it. He says, "That was probably your perfect shade once, dear, but you're a little older now."

I look at it in his hand, nearly white. I don't know.

246 / Tracy Koretsky

"Ida, this is going to be a beautiful sweater. You'll enjoy it the rest of your days. Butter, dear, trust me. You'll pinken right up next to it."

So. Butter. I shrug. "What kind of buttons?" I say.

"I never even know myself until I put them on. Now..." He makes a cup of his hand and shows me I should do the same. He drops the spool in. My skin on my hands looks rosy and warm. He grins and settles back a moment then begins to put his spools in order. "You keep that," he says, "To remind you it's coming."

I'm going to have a butter sweater.

"And Mrs. K.," he says, "I don't mean the sweater."

Jody There comes a point when you have to stop floating. You think maybe you can do it forever, or at least, you want to. It feels so safe, so easy and quiet. But you can't. Something always happens. In my case, I hit my head. Bam. Right up against the side.

I climb out of the pool. I am dripping and goosebumped. I don't bother to dry. There comes a point.

"Ma," I say, shivering, "this is long distance." Then I say, "You'll never guess what I'm learning, Ma."

"Don't make me guess, Jody. Just tell."

"No," I say, "guess." I don't have to drag this out but I am enjoying it.

"I don't know. Something with that computer maybe."

"Nope. Try again." I gave it two days to make it look like I was thinking about what she said, but really just to cool off, I was so steamed.

"Well not how to drive your mother crazy. That you already know."

"No, but close."

"Close?"

"Not how to drive you crazy, Ma, just how to drive."

"You're learning how to drive?"

"Yep."

"You? You're learning how to drive."

"Yeah," I say. "Me."

This actually shuts her up. Maybe she's mad I didn't ask her permission first.

When she talks, she says, "Don't tell me this job you've taken is on Long Island."

"No, Ma, not—"

"Don't tell me Jersey, Jody. You didn't take a job there with all those chemicals, it's not good for you."

All of a sudden, I'm not having such a good time anymore.

"Ma," I say, "listen." She doesn't. "Ma," I say, "listen. Are you listening?"

"I'm listening," she says.

"Hey! Know what? I won't even have to change apartments."

"You can get your old place back?"

I look out my the calm blue pool, at the moon reflected in it. When I moved here, I could swim at this hour. I take a deep breath. "I mean this apartment, Ma. I mean the job is here."

Silence. I am expecting, I don't know, maybe tears. At least this sound she makes when she gets upset. There's nothing else like it. Like the eeeiyou you make when you see a dead worm except louder and for a long time. It's the kind of sound that makes you really not want to upset Ma again.

Finally she says, "What do you mean 'here'?"

"You know what I mean, 'here.' "

Here. My sunny apartment with the mauve wall-to-wall. My calendar. My magazines. My clicker by my chair.

There is a lot of static and pop. Suddenly nervous, I say, "You okay, Ma? You sitting?"

"Sitting? Of course I'm not sitting. Who could sit? You call, you got news like that! 'And by the way, Ma, I'm moving to the other side of the world. To where the crazies live yet! I'll send a postcard!' Just like that you call?"

And then, there it is, that sound. Shrill. I got to pull the phone away. And long! At least there's nothing wrong with her lungs! And then the tears. Tears and more tears.

So I'm blubbering too, "Aw, Mama. Mama, it will be all right."

"No, no, no," she's crying. "No, no, no."

And then I say, "It'll be like it was since I got here. You'll still talk to me and I'll—"

"No I won't!" she cries. "You never call!"

She's right. I call a lot less lately. This is because I've had an office full of girls. And, I'll admit, I have been avoiding her, but this secret has been so hard.

"All you got is work, work, work," she says.

She's right again. I don't know. I put the phone down and grab some Kleenex. Look what I've done. I'm killing my mother.

I pick up the phone. She's still talking. I say, "You don't know what I got, Ma." She don't hear me.

I let her go on for a while, just like I do with Paully when he's just crying because he's tired or something.

"Jody," she is saying, "I can't make it here all alone, me and Paully. There's too much. Jody, you can't do this."

I let her cry herself out. It's best. Finally she gets quieter, like whimpering, "I need you. I need you." I feel sick. I sit on my couch, hug a pillow, and shiver, and weep.

The worst is over. I set down the phone and quick run and throw on my bathrobe. Ma gave it to me last birthday, a nice color, a plum. My sweet Ma. She does try. I'm lucky to have her. Good company, and funny?

I come back to the phone. I say, "I'm back." It happens again. Ma don't even know I'm gone. Now her voice is like a pan of hot oil. "What happens when I die, eh? I should live forever so you can play fancy executive in California?"

On second thought, this robe is too heavy. I let it drop from my shoulders. "You can't do this, Jody," she is saying.

"Ma," I say, right over her, "I took this job six months ago. I knew when I left Brooklyn that I was leaving Brooklyn. I always knew and I did it anyway." I think she hears me. I never know with Ma.

There it is again—the sound. I set the phone down.

I slide open the glass door on my deck and walk in a straight line right down to the pool.

Neck long, shoulders back and dropped, ribs lifted, pelvis tucked just slightly, I take a long-legged active stride onto my deck. I look to my right; there's building ten. I look to my left, building eight, blue-green awnings over red stained decks. I place my hand on the rail, turned so my nail polish catches the light. I put no weight on it; it is only there to show the gently sloping lines of my arm to the camera. The invisible camera waiting by the pool, my secret game. I take the first step down, and strike a pose. I am wearing sweat pants and a T-shirt from employee appreciation day. I keep keeping my leg straight and long, and place it in front of the other, one stair lower like in the pin-ups. I tip my head, as glamorous as can be, showing off the profile of my new hairstyle. Then I take the next steps quick, light, like I have just seen that one very intriguing man across the ballroom. I swing open the chain-link gate to the pool like it was a door to a long white stretch limo. I keep my strides long, my ribs lifted.

Five stairs shaped like half-moons, each one wider, and divided by a silver rail, go down in the water. It's like something off an MGM. I take my step, lifted and graceful. Then I take another and another until I stand near waist deep at the bottom. I lower my arms so my fingertips touch the surface, then spread them, drawing smooth rainbows of ripples. I step forward, stretching, slow, smooth, like oil floating out on the water. I spread my arms and circle them back to me. The water caresses me in return. I spread them again.

And then I begin the long lovely stretch into swim, shimmering arm over head, bent at the elbow. Once, twice, my air leaving me in silver bubbles beneath the water; there is blue sky and jasmine above.

–26–

Danny Thursday at eleven, for eleven years, she still meets me at the door in a *peignoir*, though now it's something I've bought her, a flimsy straight drop from her shoulders, pooling at her feet, light colors that pick up the peroxide hair. She is sweet. She is gentle. Next to my mother she is what I think of as home. She is my

Thursday, my Marilyn, but she's as thick as petrified asphalt.

We usually kiss and spend a long while doing it. The whole thing takes some time to set up, it's best to go slow. We get that sort of cuddly-wuddly way and I roll her into the bedroom. Then we chat and catch up, while I get myself undressed and my tube in its bucket. We leave the catheter in, less risk of infection. Marilyn pops in porno, puts on one of my CDs. I go down the hall to the toilet to empty my bag. Marilyn's lit candles. It's about 11:30 a.m. A sweet time of day for taking time.

Soft, pink, Marilyn, rolls and rolls of squish with a body somewhere beneath. Those lolling blue eyes, innocent as an infant's. She says I'm the only one who does her, her other men take care of themselves. There is an older gentleman, a widower, and another, from Greece, and alone here. Now and then, there is another, but we're her livelihood. I plump her up on pillows, everything about Marilyn, soft. Her voice in passion: birdsong.

Then I close my eyes. Warm, soft, wet Marilyn does me, the way I learned from Rondee, lowering herself and keeping me in with her mother muscles until in a rush, my blood comes down. I cannot use my back. She must use her legs, but Marilyn is as generous a woman as can be. I watch the screen while she does it, or close my eyes.

After we do it, I roll back down the hall and clean up. Marilyn pops in a tape—she's partial to westerns, though I myself love the old elegant comedies. She brings a tray of stuff to nosh from the kitchen and we crawl in all cozy, she watches the movie while I mostly smell her, all the warm scent of woman I'll have for a week. When the credits roll, I get myself dressed. Her boy Tom's thirteen now, when he comes in I want to be respectable and ready to hang out with him a while. I used to do his homework with him. Now I just take an interest. There's only a few years left of school for Tom. Marilyn has been saving for his trade school. Her older gentleman used to be a banker. He's got her set up well it seems, so I don't worry.

Eleven years of Thursdays now, secret and held close. Eleven years of sharing and still feeling so empty. I owe so much to her, and am so glad for her, if only, if only, I could accept what I have.

I want a woman who is handsome. Square jawed, pouty, with a fistful of butt and lots of dark hair. A woman who will bend at the knee to address me like an adult and otherwise avoid addressing me at all. Who will know to do this without being asked.

I want a woman who knows *the* spot for veal *piccata* in Manhattan. I want a woman who laughs when she's alone.

I want a woman who condones my continued checks to Marilyn. I want a woman to read me to sleep.

I want a woman who's not afraid to sit on my lap when I'm wearing shorts and be photographed. I want her to kneel next to me and look at them straight on and then sit on my lap and be photographed.

I want a good girl. I want a woman whose Mommy and Daddy loved each other and lived to ripe old ages. I want a "B" student.

It's not enough that she love to wear sweaters. I want her to see them as objects in space. Those and big earrings that jangle my cheek when she's close, a faint smell of shampoo, nothing French or phony.

I want a woman who can handle mathematics. For me, none ever stuck, and I think some would be good. A woman who knows how to choose self-insurance is my idea of one fine babe any day of the week.

And oh, for a woman who likes to loll in a bathtub, my legs floating around her, swirling soap on her back.

I want a woman, and I always have, to share myself with, every day. I want a woman, and I always have, to take unto. I want a woman, mortal and aching, to care for and treasure above all else. I want a woman every night, every night into morning and, when day again, I thank God for dreams like sweet fruit fallen, and then I get on.

book six

❖•❖•❖

and while we are playing, the candles are burning low

–27–

Jody "I'm here," I call, poking my head in the door.

"You're here! You're here!" shouts Ma and comes at me, arms outstretched. Sweet Ma, I swear she's smaller since I last been here. When she hugs me, her head comes up to my breasts. This I always find a little embarrassing, to tell the truth, but I hug her a long time anyway. And then up comes Paully, bobbing and jumping and I try to get my arms around him too. Us three hugging, and I am home. 14th and Avenue M. Looks just the same, I know, but different too. Dingier, smaller, sadder, I don't know what. It feels different to me. I can't say. I hug my family and we all sway. They have no idea what I am about to do to them. I only hope I can. I close my eyes.

But then I hear something, a creaky hinge maybe, and I open them again. There, in my mother's living room, are a tall woman with short gray hair and a strange little man using a wheelchair.

Ma pulls away and turns to them. "She's here! She's here!"

"I can see that," the little man says.

"Ma?" I say. "Who are these people?"

"She never mentioned us?" asks the lady.

"No," I say. "Is there a reason she should have?"

"Jody," Ma says, puffing like a pigeon, "I would like to introduce you to my new friends—"

"Your what?" I say.

Meanwhile, the guy in the chair makes this comic face. He's like pretending to be offended. "I would have mentioned her," he says to the lady.

She waves him away. "Hush, Daniel," she says.

"My friends," says Ma, like she can't imagine why I might be even a little surprised that for the first time since I can't remember when there is someone in her living room that is not related to me.

"Sara Cohen," says the lady, hand out. I shake. "My son," she says with a tip of her head.

The guy in the chair kinda waves, big grin on his face. His arms aren't normal. "Danny," he says.

"You say you're her what?" I say, looking from one to the other.

"What's with the tone, Jody? These are my friends," Ma says, and I am so mad at her I can't even look at her. What? She's got no sense? She invites people in?

I bend down to look this Danny guy right in the face. "What's your game, Mister?" I say. "What are you hanging around my mother for?"

He's flustered; he didn't expect a question like this. And me, I know it ain't the time, but I can't help notice what blue, blue eyes he got. I look at his mother.

"Just 'cause Ma's alone here," I say, "don't mean nobody's looking after her."

"Jody!" Ma says. I can't even look at her. She never mentions these people.

"I'm sorry, I don't—" says this Danny.

I bend down again bumping Paully who's buzzing around when I stick my butt out. I yell for him to sit on that couch. Then I turn back to the eyes of my mother's new "friend." "You in real estate, or what?" I say.

"Jody!" Ma cries and this guy, he hoots.

"Right!" he says. "And I have six potential buyers standing in line for a place with a matchbox for a living room and two kitchens!"

Meantime, the mother goes over to the couch where she's got a handbag. She reaches in and brings out a wallet. She hands me her card: Sara Cohen, Daughters of Israel, Family Services, Outreach Volunteer.

Ah. No wonder Ma hasn't said. I rub my forehead. I am feeling very silly about what I have just done and tired from all my traveling and a little overwhelmed. The thought of what I've got to do here, what I've got to tell Ma, well, I haven't slept in a week.

Sara Cohen speaks gently, "But that's not what brings me here on the first eve of Hanukah." I look at her. I don't know what to think. I look at him. I know even less.

"I drive the bus," Danny says. "Those are my wheels parked in front." I had noticed a van and figured it belonged to the neighbors or something.

Ma is like tugging on my sleeve. She's saying, "He's the bus driver! The bus driver!"

"Oh, so there! She did mention me!" he says, satisfied.

"Yeah," I say, "once."

Then he tells me how he's been coming by every week and eating cookies and listening to Ma go on and how he actually enjoys doing this. And Sara puts her arm around Ma and talks about what an experience it is to make a new friend at this time in life and that, for the last month and a half, she's been coming by Thursday nights for dinner.

I'm looking at Ma. Ma's looking at the floor. Lunch hour after lunch hour, listening to Ma go on about how alone she is. I don't know what to believe.

"Why don't I know about this?" I say to her.

Ma shrugs. She don't look at me, only at the floor. She don't say anything for what seems like a long time. Then she does. She says, "And do I know everything about your life out there in California?"

The headache that has been coming on, hits. It's really pounding. I sit on the couch next to Paully who begins patting his hand on my thigh, saying "Jody, Jody." I put my hand over his and hold it there. I let my head fall back and look at the ceiling. I sigh.

"Maybe tonight's not good," Sara says. "Look, we can come back..."

"But Mother," Danny says, "I want to...you know." So what's this? Some kind of plan here? Now I'll get a chance to see what these two are all about.

"What?" I say, straightening up. "What do you want?"

Danny sighs. He's the kind of guy that expresses emotions big. You can just tell what he feels by the way he looks at you. "It was supposed to be a surprise," he says.

"Oh?" says Ma, rubbing her hands.

"I'll get it," says Sara, grabs up her purse and makes for the door.

"Oh! Oh!" Ma's saying. If she wasn't seventy-nine next month she'd be jumping up and down.

"I thought it would take longer..." Danny says.

"So soon? Oh!" Ma says. She's practically breathless. He rolls up to her and reaches out his hand. Ma takes it. Ma actually takes this guy's hand.

In comes Sara, no knock, no nothing. She's got a large box wrapped in gold foil with a big blue bow. "Wait 'till you see this!" she says.

Ma takes the box, no small deal—big box, little Ma. Her hands are shaking and she has no place to set it. She's all nervous and fluttery.

"Come on, Ma," I say and shove over on the couch onto Paully and I do what I can to help. Whatever it is, it's bulky, a sweater or a scarf maybe, soft and yellow. Little stitches, tight and smooth. Quality. The stitches so close together, good yarn with a little sheen to it.

Sara reaches in and holds up a sweater. It's long. Nicely made. Very nicely. The cuffs and bottom finished in a different yarn, maybe a linen. Sophisticated.

Ma claps her hands together, she's so happy. "Danny made this," she cries.

"You?" I say.

He's obviously proud of himself. "Mother helped," he says.

Sara waves. She does it real cute and I can't help but smile. Then it hits me to check out her sweater and I do. So it's high quality too, sure, but nothing special.

"Her's too?" I say.

"I just tell him I want them warm and washable," she says.

Danny smiles, like he's being patient with a child. "Mother looks good with a nice straight line in the back and a lot of shape to the neckline."

I study her. Yep. I could see that.

"And such a sweet collar!" Ma says, so we shouldn't forget her sweater for even a second.

"Peter Pan," Danny says. Peter Pan! Now there's something I haven't seen on a sweater in quite a while. I gotta say, it's a great choice for Ma with those chubby cheeks of hers. He even made little cords for a bow.

"Look! Look at my beautiful new sweater!" she's saying.

"Well come on, let's see it!" says Sara and helps Ma up and into the sweater.

"Oooh," says Danny, all delighted. "It's even better than I thought."

I have to admit, she is, well... darling. Everything about it. It fits like a coat, long, almost to her knees and loose. More like a dress. The color brightens her, the line gives her some figure again, the way the fabric falls from soft gathers at the shoulder. "Mama in a swing coat!" I say tearing my eyes from the vision of her and facing Danny who is rubbing his chin, thinking hard about it. I bend to him. "Who would have thought?" I say.

"And why not?" says Ma, all defensive for no reason.

"I wanted something she could throw an apron over and have it not bunch up," says Danny.

"Oh, but she'll never work in that," I say.

"Your mother will bake in anything she's got on," he says. "She won't even think about it until she's got flour on it."

I slide over on the couch so I can see him better. "You *have* been spending time with my mother," I say.

Ma interrupts. "As good as your Macy's?" she says.

"Oh Mama, much better than Macy's." I get up and check out the selvages. Cross-stitched with embroidery floss. "This is boutique stuff, Ma," I say. I say "Ma" but I look at Danny.

A quick something, I don't know what, comes over his face. It hits me he don't like to be looked down at. Anyway he turns back to studying his sweater. "Show it off, Ida. Come on. And make me look good, now."

Ma giggles. She giggles! Paully starts clapping his hands and Ma begins to shuffle around in a circle.

I go put myself on the floor next to Danny. "You sell," I say up to him.

"Um. A sideline," he says. So, of course, I am real curious what else he does, but this is Ma's time, so I sit back for the show.

"He wanted the details to have meanings," Sara says, "So, for example, the rows on the pocket? One for each member of your family."

Ma brings one pocket up closer to her eyes. On the other I can see a pattern, four rows of little raised leaves.

"Like with your cookies," Danny says.

"Metaphors," Ma says to Sara, pointing, a big inside joke. "You see? You see?" The three of them laugh and I feel as out of it as Paully.

"And I helped make the buttons!" says Sara.

"Oh yeah!" says Ma. "Yeah! The buttons!"

This I have to see. I huff and puff and get myself up and go to her. It's worth it. What buttons! The color of clay, the shape of leaves, of big oak leaves, each one different.

"You made these?" I say to Sara, and she holds up her hands and shakes her head.

"I just helped," she says.

"A little craft clay and a teeny-weenie cookie cutter," says Danny.

"Oh I can just see it!" laughs Ma. "I can just see you two!" And she starts laughing so hard I think she's going to hurt herself.

So Danny, smiling, says, "I know I got a little carried away with those, but... oh, Mrs. K."

Mama's teary face looks up at me. Then she turns to Sara for a hug. There is something about this hug—how easy it is. These two, they've hugged before.

"I painted the veins on," Sara says, real quiet. "With toothpicks!" I can tell that Sara cannot believe how clever she was to do this.

"Oh yes!" Ma says. "Yes. They're wonderful. Wonderful veins, Sara! Oh!"

Danny pretends he's jealous. "Enough with that already. Look inside!"

"Temperamental designers!" says Sara, stepping back.

Ma opens the sweater. "Look Jody!" she cries.

Inside on the right there is a long sewn-in pocket made of sturdy cotton.

"That's for your keys and some money, dear," Danny says. "Now, it's safe, not pretty; it does ruin the line of the sweater. So when you want to be pretty, you can remove it and carry a purse, okay?"

Ma's mouth is open looking at the thing. She's struck dumb by an inside pocket. And here I am, trying for years to get a word in edgewise. A removable inside pocket! What a darn clever thing.

"Look in it, Ida, look *in* it." Sara is like, beside herself. Ma digs her hand down and routes around. She brings out this whole bulgy pile of something, a handful of little clay leaves with shanks and painted veins.

"In case they break off, or chip..." says Danny.

They rattle one against another in Ma's hand. For a moment, I think, it makes us all notice how much those old hands shake. Finally it's Danny who speaks, softly, almost an apology. "They are fragile," he says.

Danny   In the homes of the religious it would now be time for the men to don hats and walk down to the synagogue. Meanwhile, the women, who are thought to serve God with the labor of their hands rather than their minds, would complete the preparation of a feast to open many days rejoicing. While the men sway and mumble their dactylic cadence, the women sing and dust their hands of the chopped parsley added last moment to the slow simmering soup. While the men finger tefillin, the women pat cool damp cloths to their foreheads. This is thought to be patriarchal male privilege by most on the outside. But when viewed from within, the appearance does change. With the men and their needs safely swept from the house, the shrewd women realize they can, at last, get something done.

And so, even Mrs. K.'s secular generation since, there remains a form to these evenings, unwritten or stated, but known and accepted nevertheless. I, a non-developmentally disabled male, am expected, past a certain set period of mixed-sex interaction, to evacuate the epicenter, where I most long to be. This simply because it moves to the kitchen. Thus, I am retired to paper or television, one more tedious than the other, when laughter and the smell of food escape the swinging door.

I am left to think old thoughts, to twiddle and grow disconcerted. This to justify, or at least try to, why it is in this mind, numbed and arrested, that, like a compulsive, I am oft moved to snoop.

I open drawers, medicine cabinets, stick my hands beneath cushions. I help myself to photographs, peek in back bedrooms. My movements are stealthy, planned and deliberate. I adore doing this. I have never been caught.

So, I'll just say, I am on my way to the, uh, bathroom, when I wheel myself behind Paully's open bedroom door. His sister, stocking footed, assigned to his care, picks up things, puts them down, and again rubs her forehead. He bounces on the bed, grunting his joy.

"Say," she says, teasing, biting her lip, "I bet I know a boy who'd like a new Captain and Tenille. A little Hanukah present? That is, if you've been good." And he wriggles as if tickled. And she laughs to see him so. "Have you been a good boy, Paully? You been behaving for Ma?" Then, on the bed beside him, "Paully, I think maybe you're not behaving for Ma."

He looks away, legs swinging, inattentive, nonchalant, seems suddenly to remember something, bounds up, goes to his shelves. I happen to know from previous, uh, visits, that the two small books on them contain photographs. One, old and frail now, snapshots of the family, the other, still fresh, a DOI yearbook. This second is Paully's most treasured possession. He has shown it to me each time he has seen me in his home. This time he lays it in his sister's curious hands.

"Oh! Pictures from school! Hey, you in any, Paully?" But now that the book has been given, Paully's interest ends, the same as each time he has shared it with me. "Paully, I'm asking. You in any of these?" Give up, Jody. It's useless. He'll be in next year. But if I am to remain ringside, I can't offer advice.

She sets the book down and rearranges the pillows. "Come over here, Paully. Let's have a talk." There is something in the way he crawls up to join her. How he knows how to lean, chin on her shoulder, stroking her arm. This is an old habit, and I see her sigh deeply, accepting his weight. She picks up the red and black checked wool blanket folded, as always, at the foot of the bed. "So you still got this, huh Paully?" and, when he says nothing, "Of course he's still got it, Jody. Here it is." She reaches across him. Her hand pats his shoulder, then picks balls from the blanket. "You been a good boy, Paully? Ma says you're not such a good boy lately." Paully begins to rock against her and hum.

Now Paully, as anyone who knows him has witnessed, does a fair amount of humming on any given day. But what he does here with his sister is, in some small way, different. There is a quality of effort, definite and concerted. I can see by his face, he wants to get it right. "Oh Paully," she says, "no. I need to talk to you now."

To which Paully responds by humming much louder.

"No, Paully," she says, "not now." But then, laughing, says, "Oh, okay, oh, all right." She sits up, breathes in, opens wide, and lets forth:

> In the jungle, the quiet jungle,
> the lion sleeps tonight.

This is the jazziest, most stylish, round-toned version of the line that I have ever heard. She continues. I grip the arms of my chair to keep myself from laughing. I mean these two are stellar. Big winning smiles. He's all over, but within a small range, reminiscent of a didgeridoo whining. She wemo-weps along until she finds something harmonizable between the original mock-calypso melody and Paully's accompaniment. Musicianship aside, her voice alone is a gift, a clear lucid bell. What a performance! Well chosen! Well performed! Well, well, well!

I am moved to applause, of course. Anyone would be. I even think momentarily that it might be worth discovery to do so. But just as she is entering the "hey-yupe highs" and I am about to bring my hands together and give it up for tonight's talent show winners, her smile disappears and she grabs him, suddenly, blindly, and with what I can see is a deep and desperate need. I lay my hands down.

Act II.

"Paully," she says. "Paully, sit up. Sit up. I need you." She pushes him off her and sits him up. Paully can be a rag doll sometimes—I've seen him that way at the center—pliable, never putting up a fight. Old positions. Habits. He sits looking at his lap.

"Paully," she says, again picking up the blanket. "You remember this don't you? Who gave you this, Paully? You remember that?"

Paully reaches for the blanket and takes it from her but says nothing.

"Did Pa give you that blanket?" she says. "Whose blanket is that?"

Paully ambles up and goes back to the shelf. He brings over the photograph album and opens it for Jody. Her breath catches as she touches the photo.

She exhales slowly, through her teeth, and sets down the album. "Yeah, that's right. You remember that, Paully? Pa giving you the blanket?" Paully buries his face in the blanket and rocks. Jody rubs his back. "That's good," she says. "That's what it's for. So's you'll remember."

She stands and begins to pace. There's not much room in Paully's room between the bed and his rocker, the dresser and tables for the TV and record player, but she uses what there is. I move more tightly against the wall.

"I remember the day he gave you that, Paully. I do," she says.

Paully looks at her.

"I know I wasn't there, I know. I had to go back to work, Paully. But I was there earlier that day. And, I tell you, I remember it. I remember it real good. One thing was that it was a real pretty day. You think stuff like that shouldn't happen on a pretty day, you know?" She watches him rock with his face in the blanket. She gives up trying to pace and sits on the edge of the bed. Paully crawls up and leans full against her. She sighs, runs her fingers through his hair and begins to speak. "We went up to the roof," she says, "of the hospital, Pa and I, to look at the view of Manhattan. It was a bright day, but fall, you know? The breeze never let up for a moment. I worried that Pa would be cold. He had so little hair left after all that chemo."

She stops speaking and gives her brother a little kiss on the shoulder, a slowness in this movement, a sad reluctance. "So I asked him," she said, "I said, 'Pa isn't it cold for you here? Don't you want to go in now?' And you know what he said?" She lowers her voice like a man's and says in a Yiddish accent, " 'In? I don't want in, Jody. All day I been in. I like this, this…cold. I like to feel…' " And then she stops, right there, mid-sentence, and stares at nothing at all. "His eyes," she says. "Paully, you should have seen them. Do you remember Pa's eyes, Paully? Remember how they were?"

She settles herself back onto the pillows and Paully crawls after her and curls himself on. "Pa's eyes," she says, stroking him, her voice set for a bedtime story. "Pa's eyes could look right through you. He knew how to look very deep. Pa had eyes that talked, Paully, that *talked*. I mean, hey, what can you expect of a man who spent his life waiting to get a word in around Ma, huh? Impatience. Sure, lots of that. And suffering? Oh, Paully! But you know, there was also something else. How can I say it? Glee. Glee, that's it. And, I guess you could say satisfaction. At least Pa always knew that when he finally did get that word in, it would be the word we would all remember later, so funny or simple or just turned around. Remember that, Paully? How funny Pa was?"

She looks at her brother, a man in his mid-fifties curled like a toddler, and kisses his head. "But they were angry a lot too, weren't they? He had a lot of anger he didn't speak. Only his eyes showed it. If you looked at them behind his paper, you could see it clear as anything. His eyes talked a lot if you knew how to listen."

She reaches down and hooks the blanket with one finger. She brings it to her and holds it tenderly. "But, you know Paully, that day, that day on the roof, I look down at Pa, he's sitting there in a wheel chair, he's got this blanket over him, and he looks up at me and his eyes are like…they're like all wet—not like he's gonna cry wet, not like that—but like milky, like clouded and so, so tired. Like…like they just wanted to be closed. That's how I knew, Paully. That's how I knew. You listening? You know what I'm saying?"

Her brother is silent and must be heavy on her. I can't tell if he's listening or dreaming. You can't tell with Paully. She folds the blanket over her chest and lets her eyes close.

"The pancreas. How does someone get cancer there? You know how you do, you look for an answer, right? The chemicals in New Jersey, something you ate. But there is no answer, is there Paully?

No one to blame, nothing to forgive. What can you do? I remember when the doctor told me, I looked up pancreas in the dictionary. I'm still not sure what it does."

Then she tries to move, to get the big lug off her. "Come on, Paully. Come on, get up." She tries to move him. "Come on, get up. Up! Oh! You're asleep, aren't you?" She struggles in frustration as he comes awake. "Useless," she says, as she finally gets free. "Jeesh, you are useless. Useless, useless!"

She moves to the edge of the bed, legs splayed in her skirt, hair half tumbled free of her pretty barrette, bent over her own lap. "What am I gonna do, Paully? What am I gonna say?" she asks her yawning brother, and then, back to her own lap, "What am I gonna do? I got to tell her, Paully. How?"

Paully, who is sulky because of the way she woke him, takes his blanket and huddles with it against the wall.

"Yeah. You like that blanket he gave you, huh?" she says, her voice an odd mixture: anger, tender love, something else. Fatalism? "It's nice, huh?" she says. She sits cross-legged on the bed, picks up the photo album, puts it on her lap. "It's a damn sight better than what you gave me," she tells the photo.

She tosses it aside, stands and faces her brother. "Tell me I'm doing the right thing, Paully. Just that. I won't ask nothing more. Just let me know somehow that this is the right thing by you. Paully... Paully, listen to me, now. You wanna be with people like at school, right? Like school, a place like school to live? 'Cause that's all I want too, Paully, so you can be happy. I just want you to be happy."

"I gowin' school," says Paully.

"Right! That's right. How'd you like to go there to live?"

"I gowin' school," he says, and his sister sighs.

"Okay, so I know what you're thinking," she says. "You're thinking, Jody, why now? Why not wait? But Paully, this can't go on forever. So when Ma's too tired or...whatever, then I could take her out by me. And you," she pauses a moment, "I could take you too, of course."

She looks long at her brother, a lump on the bed, puts her hands over her mouth and says through her fingers, "I know you're thinking: Jody, you can take us out there. By you." Her hands move up to cover her whole face. I can barely hear her. "And then I got here, except there."

She whirls to the bed and grabs up the photograph album. This time she speaks to it. "You're supposed to have a reason. Like you're supposed to be able to say *because* blah, blah, blah, and I don't got a blah, blah, blah, or I do, but it's not the kind of thing other people can see or even understand and sure I know it's gonna knock the wind out of Ma. She's not gonna know what hit her. But what you don't see is that this is something I am doing. You see? I am *doing* it. It's not like, oops! This is happening to me like things just do and it's good or bad or whatever. This is something else. This is something *I* am doing. Me. Because, you know it's gonna make my life… well, it's gonna make my life… normal. Just… normal."

She drops the album onto the bed, still open. She stands above it, her hands on her hips, looking down at it. "Oh, so you think my life *is* normal. So you think nobody got a perfect life and everybody got responsibilities and people they got to do for. Well okay. Maybe they do. Maybe they do. But I been thinking about this, about other people and all, and I noticed something. You listening, Paully? I figured out something that everybody else got that I don't got."

She turns to face him. He looks up at her. "They got the right to expect," she says. "That's it. That's the difference. They expect. I don't. They think they can have something for themselves. But me? Me, you know, I never in my life, never, expected nothing. Just to take care of you, that's all, for my whole life."

She turns back to the photo, persuading. "I just know, I just… *know* that the minute I do this thing, this thing that I, Jody Kochansky, am doing—on purpose—I tell you, that's when I'm gonna start expecting, I don't know—something. Something for myself. And I just want to know from you…" she says, turning back to her brother. "Show me, Paully. Show me I'm doing the right thing. Don't just sit there! Show me, Paully. Don't just sit there like a… useless…"

She picks up a pillow and lunges for him, hair flying, but she backs off, sits back hard and socks the pillow into her own middle, punching and punching, arms flailing, taking pain, avoiding pain, creating pain, protecting herself.

Paully crawls up behind and circles her neck with his arms.

"No Paully! Get...Jeesh, get off! I mean it. Paully get —" and she pushes him off with real force, her face flushing. "I don't want you on me, Paully. Just..." she fixes him with a look, which instantly softens. "You hurt me sometimes," she says gently, "when you hang like that."

Ida Do we got a spread! You know me; I love to lay it all out on the sideboard and just look: brisket, latkies, kishke, beets, my mama's water pitcher. Danny brought flowers. And I gotta tell you, everything Sara Cohen don't know about baking, she knows about shopping. All sorts of things from specialty stores she brings: Japanese crackers and cheese from France, Russian pickled eggs and wrinkled up Greek olives. And for every one of them, she found just the right dish. Good taste, that Sara—class. From California, Jody schlepped oranges and some fruit called a mango and one of her fancy teas; you know how she likes that stuff.

I baked, of course, many things, people should have a choice. I always like to lay them out with the rest so that everybody remembers they should leave room. It looks...pretty don't say it, and oh, it smells so good. I made the challot myself. I haven't in years.

So when I call everyone together, I do it like a song. Two notes: "din-ner." I don't even got to tell you, I don't have to do this twice.

"Mama! Ma'amool!" Jody brings her hands to her cheeks like she used to when she was just a little girl. "Ma'amool are my...mmmm!" she says.

Danny edges in so fast we have to step aside to make room. He reaches for one. Jody real quick looks at me. What can I do? He's a guest.

He holds one up and looks at it that way he does. He studies it. Many people have never seen a cookie like a Ma'amool, shaped like some kind of desert flower.

"Shortbread," he says, no question in his mind, "but what's—"

"Dates," I say. "Stewed dates."

"Really," says Sara and I tell you Jacob, she can't elbow her way up to the sideboard fast enough.

Then Danny lifts the plate and offers them to Jody. She quick looks at me; she knows better. But then she looks back at Danny and then at that plate and real timid, picks one up. What the heck. I take two and give one to Paully.

"I stew them nearly a whole day," I say. "No shortcuts, no water. They should feel like sand against the top of the mouth."

"Um," says Danny.

"Um-hmm," says Sara, and turns it over in her hand.

Still Jody has not taken a bite. Danny smiles at her and nods. She makes a little nibble. Her eyes close.

"Cloves," says Danny, and he points a finger.

"Walnuts," says Sara, and nods.

"Cinnamon," I say, "a drop of good vanilla."

Paully wants another. I say, "Be a good boy."

And then, not another word. We all stand there nodding, eating very slow.

Sara licks her fingertips and reaches for the plate. Real quick, Jody looks at me. You see how our daughter knows not before dinner? But what can I do? Sara don't take one though. Just looks. "Their shapes," she says. "What would you call them?" She hands the plate to Danny, he should get a better look.

"Why don't we sit?" I say.

"A press?" Danny says. That Danny. Too sharp for his own good.

"Good guess," says Jody. "It's called a tabis."

"Why don't we sit?" I say.

"Mama got hers from Israel," Jody says. "Aunt Lila bought it for her."

I look sharp at Jody who should know better. Lila and Sammy I do not even want to hear about anyway, but especially not here with Sara and Danny. These two, they never miss a thing. "Why don't we sit?" I say.

Jody, she don't notice, she says, "My cousin Sammy sent her there. She's the only person I know who's ever been."

Sara snaps her finger. "That's right," she says. "Sammy! I know Lila's gone but where's Sammy this Hanukah eve?"

I look at the floor. Such a good boy he sends his mother to Israel. Then he kills her with his scandal.

Jody makes a face like, oop! She says, "Why don't we sit?"

"It's Hanukah," I say, same time, "the menorah!"

"Uh-huh," says Danny, mostly to Sara, and rolls himself backward.

We gather around your mama's old brass menorah. I have been lighting it at Hanukah for almost sixty years. And now for the first time in nine of those years, Jacob, I got a bar mitzvahed man here to do it the way it's supposed to be done. So many years, so many, this was a happy home.

So just when I think nothing is ever gonna change again. It's like what you said about dropping your tuchas into a chair, eh? And at my age!

You wouldn't recognize your son, Jacob. And I don't just mean the hotshot new clothes. All the time, ninety times a day, with the "gowin' schoo, gowin' schoo." And all right, so I hate to admit it, but what I would give to say, "Yes. Yes you are," and mean it. But he's not—that's the problem. They got the place closed for two weeks—a Hanukah break they call it. First they get him all stirred up, then they say see you later.

And then—would you believe—the daughter who can't wait to move away from her mama, I don't even gotta ask. She tells me! For a couple weeks she's staying! Now Jody, Paully will listen to. He's been so excited; he's been Windexing that teapot. He's been acting a whole week now like every minute she'll walk through the door. It's mashuga, but nice mashuga.

And, I don't got to tell you, there haven't been so many people all together in this living room since your funeral. Since your funeral! I never expected there would be again.

And I am wearing this beautiful thing—the last beautiful thing I will ever own. A whole coat! I hadn't thought! And so soft and a color all my own. This beautiful thing, so new it still smells a little like the leather on the hands that made it.

Danny davens as he says the prayer and lights. Then Sara, she asks will he maybe say a little more. I gotta smile. That Sara. Says she's not so Jewish. Ha!

Danny looks at the floor, clears his throat, bows his head. "By these lights," he says, "we are most blessed, for they come at a time when the days grow shorter, drawing us inward, drawing us home, making us face another white season. Let us cherish them, and, each other."

"Amen," says Sara, and puts her hand on his shoulder. He lays his over hers. I have never seen them do this, but I can see, it is something they do.

Jody, she stammers, "Amen," like she just got nudged, which reminds me. Prayer. This don't happen in my house every day.

Then Danny turns his face up, big smile at his mama, and says, maybe a little too loud, "But enough! Words! They are so limiting! What I'd really like," and then he sort of shoots his eyes over, Sara should look at Jody, "really, really like," he says, "is that song. You know, the only Hanukah song anyone ever bothered to compose."

Sara raises her eyebrows. I don't think she thinks much of that song.

"I haven't heard it in years," Danny says.

"Well sing it," she says, eyebrows still up there.

"Oh yes," I say. "Do."

And Paully, he's bobbing. You know, we're gonna have some fun now.

"Oh no, no," says Danny, "my voice would give us all pain."

"Jody sings!" I say.

And Paully starts in with the "sing-sing the record player" business.

"No! Ma!" Jody says and steps backward, right into Paully.

"Yes, yes!" I say, and then to Sara, "Oh, Jody sings so good."

"Really? Oh sing, Jody!" says Danny. "Just one. It's just what we need." He does that shooting thing with his eyes again.

Sara says, a little flat, "Oh please do, Jody. We'd all like it so very much."

"Ma, why'd you have to say that?" Her voice is a loud whisper, like everyone don't hear.

"The Hanukah song, Jody!" Sara says. She makes polite applause.

"Pleeeeese," Danny says.

So Jody sings. The little Hanukah song. To be truthful, she don't start so good; she's all shy and nervous, not like when she's just around us. She starts like a little peepy bird. But I tell you, I can't take my eyes off her, Jacob. For one thing, there's a lot less of her. I don't know what they've been feeding her out there but she's been trimming down. She got a new haircut, just straight and simple and brushed back into a silver barrette—no more of those frizzy curls— even a different way to do her make-up. And the clothes! So simple! None of the ruffles and trim she always had to have. Very classy. She still should lose that tush of hers, but let me tell you, she's looking very smart these days, very smart.

Then, who can say what goes on in her mind, but suddenly our Jody decides she can sing. She closes her eyes and makes a beautiful thing, a sweet long moment, out of that line:

> and while we are playing,
> the candles are burning low

and then—oh no!—she stops. Just stops! Has she forgotten the words? She just stands there looking at the candles.

Danny helps her. "One for each night..." and she picks it up, and they sing together, "...they shed a sweet light."

I don't know what he's talking, Jacob. His voice sounds all right to me.

And then, of all things, there is a knock at the door.

–28–

Steiner   I am astonished when Sara Cohen opens the door. Jody had said nothing about another guest. And as I step in, I see Danny seated next to Mrs. Kochansky. On the couch, there is a woman with her head in her hands.

"You must be Jody." I offer my hand.

She doesn't look up to see it. "I'm so sorry," she says to her lap. Then, in a sort of a stage whisper, "I got caught up here, and—"

Sara takes my coat and the cake I've brought and leaves the room.

"You don't call on a holiday eve?" says the mother, coming up to me.

I was beginning to understand. "It was *her* idea," I say, indicating Jody. " 'Just show up,' she says. " 'Don't call. If you do Ma is just gonna watch the TV and say uh-huh into phone now and then.' "

"Well, she would!" says Jody.

"Sounds about right," says Danny, grinning, enjoying this altogether too much.

"Besides," I say, addressing Jody, "that approach worked so well the first time!"

Jody rubs her forehead. "I didn't know my mother would have guests." She drops her head back and looks at the ceiling. "Heck, I didn't even know my mother *knew* guests!"

Duped again! Jody asked me here at this time and I will be late for my own family's party because of it. There's a short list of things she's to have spoken to her mother about by the time of this visit.

"What's this?" says Danny, coming toward me, and, before I realize what he's doing, he has taken the book from under my arm. "*Directory of Residential Facilities,*" he reads.

Jody closes her eyes as the mother makes that odd sound she sometimes makes, almost a spit, something like, "*fa!*"

Sara returns with my cake on a plate and sets it on the sideboard.

Danny claps his hands together in glee. "You bring a cake to Mrs. K.'s!"

"I can see this was a bad idea," I say. "Sara, I wonder where you put my coat?"

Jody holds up her hand to halt Sara. She takes a big breath. "Mama," she says, "I've done something about Paully."

"Paully. Since when is it your business to do something about Paully?"

"Since when, Ma? Since when?"

"So you tell me, Jody, did you go to one of these places? You take the day off work, God forbid, and actually go?"

"Well not to one of those places, but I—"

"Mama understands that you think you're being a good girl," she says. "You think that by picking up a phone you can make a good thing happen. But, what? Suddenly you believe some shiny brochure they hand you with the nurses with the perfect teeth and the size eight. You don't know better?"

Mrs. Kochansky is slowly working into a frenzy, moving from person to person.

"She saw a little TV show, maybe?" the mother says, pulling on Sara's arm. "They go in there, they clean up everything for one day, they give the children some new clothes, and in come the cameras."

And then, to Danny, "Suddenly she stops being a smart shopper?"

"These places, Jody?" She stands before her daughter, hands behind her hips, leaning up, as close to her daughter's face as she can be. "You think I don't know? I know. Not for dogs, Jody. Not for dogs."

I cut in. "Excuse me, Mrs. Kochansky," I say, a little more forcefully than I intend. "Did *you* go?"

She whirls and steps up to me. There is nothing else like Ida Kochansky's face in anger, all the lines emanating from the sharp nose, the eyes narrow and intent.

I can't imagine what my own face looks like, but seeing it, Sara jumps right in, stepping towards us, her arm out. "I don't think this is the time or place."

But something inside me tells me Sara is wrong. This is the time and place. This is it. I look over at the daughter's face. She is slightly wincing, like she's afraid to get slapped. Then I look at the mother, right down into her eyes. "What I can't understand is *why*?" I say.

At which point, Sara, who has somehow insinuated herself between us, a hand on each of our backs, says to me "Deborah, have you forgotten Willowbrook?"

"What? That place in Staten Island?" the mother says, suddenly disarmed.

Aha! So she has heard of it! That was the first I'd learned.

Danny says to Jody, "An exposé by a young Geraldo Rivera," and then to Mrs. Kochansky, "Mother's not speaking of the place, she's speaking of an event."

"That was twenty years ago, Danny," I say.

The mother is stirring up again. "That gray place!" Then to Jody, "Your father said it smelled like a rag no one washed!"

Jody says, "Pa?". And Sara lays her hand firmly on the mother's arm, sadly, solemnly, nodding. Amazingly, Mrs. Kochansky calms down.

"Twenty-five," Sara says to me, right over the mother's head.

"So big deal," Mrs. Kochansky says, this time to me, "I remember that too. A Kennedy goes in, all the TV cameras follow. A few days later, it's old news."

"Old news!" I cry. "To whom? That visit started a revolution! One that I am fighting today!"

"A revolution!" says Danny. "Comrade!"

Mrs. Kochansky turns back to Sara and says, louder than me, "The wonderful new world of being a retarded person." She opens her hands towards me in case Sara found the implication too subtle.

"All she wants is he should earn a paycheck," she says to her guests. "All I want is he should be happy." Then she points at me, "This is what a mother is. You wouldn't know."

Something. Something about this. I will not be pointed at. "How happy was he plugged into the TV and locked in his room?" I say.

"Plu—wha? I got no locks!" she cries.

"Is that where you've put him right now?"

"What kind of idea is this you got in your head?" the mother says.

"I saw! In his room! All the headphones!"

"Since when do you know anything about Paully's room?"

"The rocker ten inches from the TV."

"So he likes to sit close."

"Maybe he couldn't see it, Mrs. Kochansky!"

She looks at the floor, then at me. "I'll tell you what I see," she says. "I see a little girl who should be taught some manners." Then, to everyone else, "She snoops!"

It is Danny Cohen, to my surprise, who comes to my defense, "The door was probably just open, Mrs. K."

The mother seems flustered by this. "He was never a burden to nobody," she says, though it is unclear to whom.

I think her daughter might beg to differ. I restrain myself from saying this.

Danny raises his hand. "I have a question, Deborah."

"Sure," I say, glad to have an ally.

"Well let's see, if Willowbrook was twenty- five years ago and Paul is now fifty-five, then um, how old would Paul have been at the time of Willowbrook? That would be..." and he pretends to do the math on his fingers.

"Thirty, Danny."

"Yes, thirty."

"There were waiting lists," I say.

"No there weren't." Both Danny and Sara say it, same time.

Jody holds up her hands as if she'd like us to all slow down a little bit. "So, if this big exposé broke twenty-five years ago," she says, "when did places like Paully's center happen?"

"Not for another ten years or so," says Danny. Sara leaves the room.

"The late seventies, early eighties was the height of such things," I say.

Jody's eyes look past me as she thinks, then return to mine. "So when my brother was maybe thirty-eight, thirty-nine?"

Mrs. Kochansky makes that odd sound again.

"Miss Steiner," says Jody, "I think we may have our answer to *why*?"

The mother takes this as her cue and steps up to me. "Very nice," she says. "Very fancy college girl, you. What? They didn't teach you any history?"

"And since then?" I can feel my cheeks redden. "You're going to tell me that no one has ever approached you, Mrs. Kochansky?"

"Not that I know of," says Jody, and at the same time, Danny, "Why go looking for trouble?" and the mother, louder than both of them, "Those cookies wouldn't have gotten baked with out him."

Sara steps forward with my coat. "It's the first night of Hanu-kah," she says, gently, "and we're all hungry."

Ida   Because he takes the most room, Danny always sort of leads the way. Tonight though, he does more than that. He blocks the table. No one can get to it. He struggles up to pull out a chair, which is not so easy for him. Then he puts out his hand, Jody should sit. She accepts, big sweet smile.

We gather round. When I take your place at the head of the table, Jody is to my left, Paully I tell to sit at my right and Sara takes the seat across from Danny.

Jody, that bad girl, is talking so fast so everyone should get the taste of that visit out of their mouths. I am so mad I can't even listen.

Something is going on with Danny. With me, well—you will forgive me, this is not a nice thing to say about a guest in the house—but with me Danny sometimes eats a little sloppy. So, he's relaxed. Also, I think, it's hard for him to reach the table with those arms of his. But tonight, next to Jody, he eats slowly with one hand in his lap. He holds the bowl real nice when she's taking the beets. Like a fine gentleman he behaves to her.

For a while everyone is busy taking food from the bowls onto their plates. I'm fussing that it got cold while we discussed history with the mashugana maven but Sara says food always tastes better just a little bit cooler and Jody says she thinks that too, which never in my life did I know she thought.

I push my plate aside and take Paully's. I start to cut his brisket.

Jody stops her mouth for two seconds and looks at me like she hasn't seen me cut Paully's meat all her life, but then just starts talking again, on and on like there was never a knock on the door.

"Ma, you should see the grocery stores in California! I tell you, these are something amazing. Huge! You need socks? Aisle six. Screw driver? Aisle thirty-seven, over by the olive bar. The olive bar! You ever heard of such a thing? Or maybe you want water," she says to everyone, fork waving, "you know, in a bottle? Will that be mountain or artesian spring? In glass or in plastic, six, thirty-two, or sixty-four ounce size, lime, kiwi-strawberry, or mandarin orange? Not just orange, yet. Mandarin orange. They got two delis, a bakery, a butcher, a fish counter, a liquor store, and a video rental place. They got more stuff than on your average block in Brooklyn and you can hand them plastic at the register and some kid will help you carry your bags!"

So Danny says California grocery stores sound just great to him. And Jody, you know—always with the work, work, work—she says, "Oh yeah. I love this. I mean for a person in retail, super markets are always interesting. They think of everything first, special music programming, closed circuit TV, point of sale, signage, height of display—"

"Height of display. That's what bugs me," Danny says. "They always got stuff for kids down at my level."

I don't know what to do when Danny says things like that, calling attention like that. I look at Jody. She looks Danny straight in the eye, but all she says is, "Huh." Sara, of course, she don't even notice.

So I say, "Big deal. I want a little carton of milk and some butter, I should walk forever?"

Jody shrugs. She knows truth when she hears. She eats her beets. Then, all of a sudden, she gets all braggy. "Well, Ma's right. I mean I do have to drive there."

She wants I should make a big deal. I shrug.

"I just got a 1984 Datsun!" she says, "but it's not the car, Ma." She says, 'Ma' but she's talking to Danny. "It's the driving."

"You like driving?" Danny says, and Jody blinks; she didn't expect. Danny sees and says, "New York's a hard place to drive."

And off Jody goes again. You'd think she was brought up in Jersey, the way she loves driving. "When you drive, you pull right up, you walk inside," she says. "You miss your block? Make a U-turn. No crossing empty platforms at night feeling like a fool 'cause you daydreamed through your stop. Drivers are in control. Drivers, drivers, drivers," she says.

I can't get over how she talks now. She don't stop to let anyone get a word in. Since when does Jody talk so much? So I say, "California, California, California. If it's such a big time there, what are you doing here?"

"Visiting you! Oh Ma! I'm sorry, it's just I got so much to say here. I've missed you so much. I have. I'm sorry. You're right. I won't talk about California any more tonight." Which is a relief, but it don't mean she talks any less. "Actually though," she goes on, still nobody else gets a word in, "there are a lot of things I want to do here. Get over to the Macy's for one. And I thought I should, you know, look up Evelyn Kaufman."

"Don't bother," I say, "you can look at her through your bedroom window."

"Across the street? Evelyn's home?"

"She lives there now, she and the boys and Sylvia." Jody avoids my eyes. She don't want to know whether I think this is a good thing or not. So what she does is she turns to Paully and asks how he likes that school of his.

Now it's his turn, gabbling, no one really understands altogether what he means when he gets all excited like that. He wants to show off how neat he eats soup now with the new teeth, no dribbling, but he can't do it, he's too excited. I just want he should calm down and eat his supper. I take another piece of brisket and start to cut it for him. Jody gives me that look again. She clears her throat. "He's got hands, Ma," Jody says. "He can use a knife."

"Since when do you know? You've seen so much of Paully these days!" I look at Sara. "Paully can only use a knife standing up next to a cutting board."

"Ma, he can cut his own—"

"No! Paully don't cut meat!" I turn to Sara. "He don't know how!"

"Well you could let him try, Ma," says Jody. "You've got to let him try more things for himself. We've got to.""

"So now suddenly I got a maven for a daughter too?" I tell her real good. I point my finger. "Don't you tell me what I should and shouldn't, little girl. This is a nice dinner Sara and I put together all afternoon. You talk nice when you eat it. You come all the way from California to ruin my dinner? Thank you very much. This kind of visit I don't need. You come here and invite your maven friend to bring her drug store coffeecake and I won't even mention that awful book."

She looks at her plate. Suddenly she's got nothing to say.

Paully is spreading the beet juice across his plate in four lines with a fork, you know, like he does, and it makes a squeak. For a moment we all watch, then Danny says, "Ahem, and speaking of Ms. Steiner—I love the way she always uses your full names!—I got a great story about her."

Sara says, "You're such a gossip, Daniel." He ignores her; he's too busy looking at Jody.

"Actually, I enjoy her," says Danny in that lecture voice he has sometimes. "She can talk about Genetics."

"Genetics?" says Jody. "You mean like chromosomes and stuff?"

"Right. She has what I'd call a deep layman's interest and I have a technologically outdated university degree."

"No kidding," Jody says. "I'd sure love to know more about that." That's what she says. Since when our daughter got an interest in anything but selling bras, I don't know, but that's what she says.

So quick, before Danny takes it into his mind to tell her everything about what ever it is, I figure I better save my dinner party. "I thought you had a story," I say.

"A joke actually," he says. "See, earlier that day my friend Saul had told me a joke that I was still chuckling over. And when I ran into Deborah, well, I just had this feeling it would be her kind of joke."

"A Deborah sort of a joke?" Sara says, and I say, same time, "No such thing."

Sara says, "You'd better prove it."

"So, there are these three rabbis, right?" he starts, and Sara and Jody laugh. Me, I'm not in the mood for jokes.

He goes on, "They're sitting on a hill, it's a beautiful day, the sky is clear in every direction. So here these guys are, rubbing their beards, twirling their ringlocks and arguing about something or other in the Talmud."

"Well, that's what they do," says Sara. These two, they're always good together.

"That's right. So there they are. Arguing. Two great big rabbis against one little scrawny one. And the little one just can't score any points with these guys so finally he just raises his arms to the sky and he says, 'God, if I'm right, give me a sign.' And suddenly, whoa, thunder breaks. Then lightening, then pouring rain, right from the clear blue sky. The littlest rabbi is jumping around. He can't believe he's been heard!

"The other guys though, they see no connection. What's the little guy jumping around over coincidences for? So the little guy falls to his knees and says, 'Still God, they will not listen. Won't you give me another sign?' Now keep in mind that this is two signs from God inside of fifteen minutes that this guy is asking for."

"Chutzpah," says Sara, leaning toward him.

"But, for whatever reason, bang, there it is: nightfall, shooting stars and great winds. So the medium-sized rabbi says to the bigger one, 'Well maybe he's got a point.' But the bigger one says, 'Aw, that's nothing. I heard about a sign from God in Sheboygan that made that look like a fine day in May.'

"So the little guy falls back onto the grass and beats the ground with his fists and cries to the heaven, 'They won't hear me, Lord. Tell them I'm right.' And a voice comes up as if out of every limb of every tree, down from the sky itself and up through every blade of grass. 'He's right,' the voice says. So the big rabbi says to the medium one. 'All right, two against two. We're tied!' "

Even Danny laughs. Even Paully laughs. Me, I don't laugh.

"Two against two!" says Jody.

"We're tied!" says Danny.

"So what does Deborah say?" says Sara.

"She says"—and he changes his voice to that snippy way she's got, and says —" 'Well actually, it is essential to the Jewish character to question, even to question God.' "

"Essential to the Jewish character?" Sara shakes her head. I tell her and tell her about Steiner. She never believes.

Danny nods, his lips together, he don't want to bust out into a big laugh.

"She *is* a Jewish character," Jody says, and Danny stops trying to hold out.

"Jocularly challenged," he says when he can.

"I don't know," says Sara. "I suppose I'm rather glad that Columbia is still putting them out that way. She's a deep thinker, that young woman."

"I don't know, Mother. I'll give you that she's a deep thinker," he says, "but is she a complex one?"

"That's it," Jody says, snapping her fingers. "Everything's too neat for her."

"What I can't stand," he says to Jody—everything he says tonight is to Jody—"is that she sees me and she sees a wheelchair. I'm not a wheelchair. I'm not a man in a chair. I am a man who designs sweaters and tutors the bar mitzvah and has lots of various interests who also happens to use a wheelchair." He stops to drink some water. He has gotten worked up saying this. "When she looks at Paully, all she sees is...I don't know..."

"The eyes," Jody says.

I look at my son. "She's right. The eyes."

"And then she just assumes your brother is the same as every other person with Down's."

Jody nods. "And she will save him through her 'system.' "

Danny shakes his head, "Her brave new system."

"The little Nazi," I say.

Jacob, what was it that you used to say? "You can't unstir the pot." Everyone begins talking all at once. The Nazis killed people like Paully. They killed people like Danny. This is no way to treat wonderful, wonderful Deborah Steiner. I should only be grateful. Our whole dinner party, we're going to talk about that girl. Then Jody and Danny begin to tell me how to live my life and Sarah wants I should take another latke and Paully, in the middle of everything, starts to sing—Old McDonald. No one listens to me at my own dinner table that you bought for me. So I stand, which works good, because everyone suddenly got nothing to say. Sarah reaches out her hand and lays it on my arm but then she takes it away. Everyone, even Paully, leans in close.

I clear my throat, very dramatic for once, and then look at each person at the table, real solemn, real serious, one by one. First I look at Sara. She's biting her lip. Then Danny, who can't meet my eye; he's such a bad boy. Our Jody's got both hands flat against the table, holding on.. Then I look over at my babaleh who thinks I want he should sit up straight. So he sits up real fast and what happens? He spills his milk all over the table. Everywhere there's milk, on Jody's skirt, on the plate of latkies. He had a full glass, of course. At a time like this, you would expect an empty glass?

Sara and Danny can't wait to go get something to clean. And you think Danny can get out without shaking the table? You think again. So now we got a mess on Paully. He gets upset, and I turn to take him to the bathroom.

"Oh, no. Let me, Mrs. K.," Danny says, he's the big helper all of a sudden, but before he goes he gives a little wink at Jody and says, "Good luck," which I do not think is very nice at all. So I stand there, the big villain in my own house, looking at a plate of soggy latkies and my daughter rubbing her skirt with a napkin. What can I do?

"It's time for *Jeopardy*," I say. I go to the living room.

Danny   Upon reflection, perhaps it was a bit of an ambush. But a man like me, I've lost many chances. I wanted to speak; there was so little time left. So I pulled myself between the fridge and counter and waited through the spill-cleaning flurry until I had her alone in the kitchen. She whirled at my whisper, looked down, looked curious, nearly crept over, carefully quiet.

"I expect Mother and I will go now," I say, *sotto voce*. She instantly agrees. "I just—if you have a moment—well, I'd like a word." She kneels beside to better meet my eyes. She likes a musky sort of perfume. I would have taken her for violets.

"Your mother," I say, "I know she seems perfectly here tonight— like, 'hello, earth to Ida' sort of here—but when I visit alone, early afternoon usually, Jody, she does sometimes sort of...fade in and out. I mean mostly she seems to go into one of her rehearsed stories or defends her expertise in cookies —"

"Yep. That's Ma."

"But the rest of the time, that is, when I'm not here, she just... talks."

"Out loud?"

"All day."

"To herself?"

"Well, no. I wouldn't say that. I would say, mostly it seems, she is speaking to your father."

Jody closes her eyes. Poor thing, she's feeling guilty as hell, I can just tell. Then her expression changes. She folds her arms, studying me. "And just how do you know this?"

"Well, I visit her, like she said. Your mother doesn't lie—about that—this *is* my usual krechen joint—and I don't, you know, want to frighten an old woman with my noise so I sort of..." I show her how I can creep, stealthy as a cat. "She leaves the window open a crack," I say. "I hear her."

"You always go around eavesdropping?"

"Often," I say. She is taken aback. Good. "But only because I love to! I mean, Jody, I'm so good at it! Between the people who don't see me all the way down here and the ones who would rather not look, there's just so much opportunity..."

She shoots me a sideways look, rolling with the joke.

"Yeah," I say, getting her back for before, "besides, it really gives me a chance to appraise prime real estate like this."

"All right, all right." she says, a good sport. "This *is* New York."

"There are as many good people in New York as bad."

"More." She smiles, lips closed, pressed tight, meeting my eyes. "Thank you," she says.

"For listening to your mother?"

She nods, quickly, her earrings brush her collar. She's got those eyes closed again, maybe holding back.

"It's a dirty job," I say, more gently than I mean to, "but someone's got to eat all those krechen."

She rolls her eyes. Good. "You got any idea how much is she baking now?"

"A dozen a day, maybe two."

"Jeesh, you would think it was five times that, the way she talks."

The door swings open. Mother looking in. Mrs. K. is in the living room with the TV blasting. We can speak in normal tones. Paully's in his room and we can leave any time. I tell her we are talking. One look at me, Mother says, "Take your time." When she leaves, it is clear that Jody is through joking.

"What are you telling me, Danny? That I should stay here? In Brooklyn?"

"No, of course not. I'm telling you that, for what it's worth, I can see that all the choices here are difficult and imperfect, but something needs to be done and you are a smart and caring person, and you have to trust yourself to do it."

She meets my eyes. "I flew out of here, Danny." It is a confession.

"You just needed what all of us do. Something to hold onto."

"Danny," she says. That's all she says. Flat and expressionless. She stands up, brushes off her knees for no reason, then says, "Yeah," and after a moment, "Hey. Thank you."

"What? You find it so hard to believe that someone should want to listen to your own mother's stories?" I say, in my best imitation.

She laughs. "Well, to you, at least they're new."

"Not anymore," I say.

And then she sighs. And what a sigh. Her whole body seems to give. I think of her in that bedroom with Paully, the pillow. She'd just gotten off a plane. "Anyway, I meant thank you for me." She leans against the counter, starring down. "I'm beat," she says.

"Not at all," I say, and then—ready, set, go—I do it. I say, "Honey, I'd like to make you sigh all night."

What can I say? The first line? It's always a disaster.

She hears it. She thinks she doesn't. She licks her lips looking far left. She is asking herself if she heard right; I can just tell.

"Forgive me," I say quickly, before she looks, "I have to do this. It's difficult, and awkward—hey, for me too, believe me—but it's necessary."

She turns her head, taking me in.

"See it's hard for a guy like me," I say, "to get a woman thinking in the right direction, that is, to be open to me, and to it—that is, the idea of me as a sexual person."

She continues to stand, motionless except for her blinking. I'm in it now. "So what I've discovered," I say, "is that sometimes I need to give the women a sort of kick start, sort of starting on a higher gear. But this can backfire; I can get the timing wrong. It's a rough call to guess the degree of subtlety versus, say, raunch, sincerity versus sophistication, that a particular woman needs to hear her first sexual advance through."

"Sexual?" She turns to me, her arms folded over her chest, brow furrowed.

"Exactly. I wish I could say I got it right more often. I mean I find a fair number of women willing to go out with me. I'm fun. I like to talk about anything at all. I'm a gentleman. I can pay. I've been told, once or twice, that I'm all right to look at. I'm even novel to look at!"

She laughs, I keep talking, "Through a whole meal, the way I eat. But, well, so many dates, Jody, so few lovers."

I hate this part, my set shtick.

"Would I be different if the roles were reversed?" I say. "I don't know. But so often, most of the time, when it comes down to it, to the nitty-gritty, there's always some reason, some character flaw about me that she'll make up if she has to just so she can stop at the zipper. The zipper. It's always the zipper. Even if I do the zipper, it's the zipper. She's suddenly just too far in and she's afraid of getting further."

I can see her gulp. I know this reaction. Acceptance. I gulp. I go for it. "I can, you know," I tell her.

"Can what?" And then, maybe to spare me, maybe because curiosity gets the best of her, "Can...like what? Everything?"

"Yeah sure...everything. I mean, like, you know, I work."

"Yeah?" She gives me a strange look, coy. Her eyes narrow, her full lips poised in preparation for a grin or a sneer. I wish I knew. I clear my throat.

"Yeah. Sure," I say. I'm trying to sound confident, maybe even a soupçon debonair. "Everything, ah, holds up real good."

She laughs, her head thrown back. Embarrassed, I think. "I'll, ah, keep that in mind," she says.

"And I'll keep you in mind. It will be easy." And then, I don't know, what the hell, I'm in this far. "Besides," I say, "a knitter like me, nimble fingers, steady pressure, a loving appreciation of soft folds. You'd think I'd be a very popular man."

I've used this line once before, on a woman far more sophisticated than Jody who thought it wry. Jody, it shocks. Good. She'll think about it later no matter how busy she is this coming week.

And then I say, hoping I am managing to suppress my smile, "I apologize. I know this has been so rushed—for me too! I would have liked to let it develop."

She shakes her head, still recovering.

"But I didn't want to leave you tonight just thinking of me as some odd but nice man who visits your mother," I say.

"I wouldn't say odd—"

"Jody?" I say. "Would you happen to have a favorite place for veal *piccata*?"

"Veal? What?"

"I'm sworn to trying every veal *piccata* in the five borough area. One of my life's lesser ambitions. Say you'll help me."

She doesn't know what to say. Puts her arms up, drops them down. Opens her mouth, closes it. Then, in a single flustered rush says, "I know I'm little right now but all the magazines say my weight will probably come back."

Aw. What a thing to say. She can't look at me.

"And my bones will continue to shrink," I say, softly. "So I'll rest my feet on yours and you'll tuck me beneath your fragrant and precious shelf of breast and off we will waltz."

"I've never been to college," she says, about to bust into tears.

"I've never worked an honest day in my life."

She busts out laughing instead, relieved, I suppose. A big, honest laugh, nothing feminine or shy about it. And then she cried. "It's not all it's cracked up to be," she says, sniffing.

I roll myself next to her. "Say yes, Jody. Tomorrow night?"

And she shrugs and she nods and I am very, very happy. I pop a wheelie, make a gesture something like tipping a hat, and back myself out the kitchen door.

−29−

Jody   As I walk Sarah and Danny to the door, Ma turns up the volume for Double Jeopardy.

I swallow hard and look at her on that sorry old couch, that jaw of hers sticking out like some kind of trap waiting to spring. Get rid of that couch, I think. It will be such a pleasure. The floor beneath it is thick with dust. Without Paully here every day, she can't keep this place up. I am doing the right thing. I am.

"Mama," I say, "I want for us to talk."

"So who's stopping you?" she says.

"Well, do we have to have the TV?"

"In two seconds they got a commercial, then you tell me what you got to say."

"Mama, turn off the TV."

"From Deborah Steiner you learn to make orders at your mother?"

I stand up and walk in front of the TV. Then I do it again, the other way. Finally I turn it off and rest against it.

"That's enough, Ma. That's it. Now I have something to say and you're going to listen. Do you understand?"

"You mean you got something to repeat..."

"*Sha*, Mama! Don't you talk. I talk. I talk, and when I'm through, you talk. Do—you—under—stand?"

For a moment, I think we are both startled. I say, low, like a lullaby, "What I was thinking, Mama..." and then I pause. I fold my arms over my chest. I know I am doing the right thing.

When I speak again, my voice means business. I even surprise myself. "What I have decided..."

I wait for her to look at me. I want to know that she has heard the word 'decided.' She has.

I go on, "Is that after we get Paully settled, you can come out by me."

Her head is shaking hard, side to side. Her eyes are closed. I try to tell her about the senior community two stops south of me on 101.

"It won't be all at once," I tell her. "You can get used to it slow."

"This is what you come up with, all your big months of scheming with your little mavenla friend?" she says. "This is what you got? Just move everything around, like all this is your business? Paully in some terrible...I shouldn't even speak, such a terrible thing...and me? In your California! No, Jody. No."

I sit next to her on the couch, or no, I like fall onto the couch.

"You tell me then," I say. "You got something better? You're so full of all the answers. You tell me!"

"Come home!" she cries. "Jody! Come home!"

This orange vinyl couch, it's horrible. It looks like a Dunkin' Donuts in here. And half the time, it smells like one. This is what Ma wants for me. Ma didn't even like it when I moved out of here three blocks away. She said, "What's wrong with your room? It's not good enough anymore?" That I should sleep in the room she dies in with Paully in the next room, that's what my Mama wants for me. How can she want that? I should not have asked her. I have lost ground.

"Mama," I say, "sometimes once you know an opportunity exists you get all kinds of ideas for how to make it possible. Don't say no. Say maybe."

"Save your sales talk," she says.

I am losing my courage. I stare out ahead of me looking at nothing. You've got to make your intentions known, Miss Kochansky.

"I looked into getting Paully into some place out in California, Ma; I did. The lists were as long as my arm. They got babies on the list, Ma. Two-year-old babies. Here too, you know? Long lists. But here, see, he's already in with the Daughters of Israel. He knows people there, Mama. Paully's got friends now. You've seen. Paully's in. He's happy there. Am I right?"

"So good for Paully. Paully likes his school. So all right." She hushes up, looking at me head to foot slow. I don't know what she sees when she looks, but I feel shame somehow.

"And that has something to do with these big changes you think you decided on. I should leave this home your father gave me?"

It wasn't supposed to come out this way. I don't know how it was supposed to, but not like this.

And that is when the phone rings. I can't believe it. *Now*? When I am finally...

Ma looks at me and then at the phone. I am supposed to pick it up. It's her house but I am supposed to pick it up. That's just the way it is with Ma.

"I'm not gonna," I say.

"What?"

"You heard me. You heard."

She crosses her arms over that yellow sweater and sits there, chin stuck out. The phone rings again.

My first reaction is to be afraid. I don't know why, it just is. And then I think again. I have done nothing, nothing for years but take care of her. I have done nothing wrong. Nothing. Suddenly it hits me that all the things that I was going to say to Ma, all the times I laid it out in my mind, those things sound an awful lot like apologies. I have done nothing wrong, and I have nothing to say that doesn't sound like I have.

She looks at the phone. She looks at me. It rings. Ma got no answering machine. This could go on a while.

" 'Jody, get that phone,' " I say. I say it like her, in her impatient, harassed voice. I do this perfect. I have been hearing this voice so long, it's part of me. " 'That phone is gonna make me mashuga,' " I say.

Paully comes out of his room. He looks at the phone and bites his hand.

"He's the one don't like the phone, Ma. Not you. He can't use it; he don't understand it. So every time the phone rings in this house, every time, my whole life, I got to stop what I'm doing and grab it up quick, we shouldn't upset Paully. Grab it before the next ring. Hurry, Jody, hurry. And God forbid I should get a call. I get a call from a friend, Paully got to come into the kitchen and start banging around. And what do you do? You say, 'Let Paully clean, Jody. Let Paully sit.' God forbid I should ever be able to talk on the phone at my own house."

"*My* house," she says.

The phone rings again. Paully jumps around. I don't care. I fold

my arms, just like her. I stick out my chin. " 'Let Paully,' " I say in
her voice. " 'Let Paully.' What about 'Let Jody,' Ma?" Yeah I know.
I know. 'Let Jody get it; let Jody pick it up on her way home; let
Jody take him to the movie, let Jody babysit. Let Jody babysit and
babysit and babysit and babysit. Babysitters get paid, Ma. Did you
ever think to pay me, Ma? I didn't have to ask every time I needed
anything. Pay *me*!"

Ma is blinking at me, her mouth open. I know I should stop, but
I can't. It is like being at the peak of my swimming. I point at Paully.
"That's no baby, Ma. That's no baby and I'm no baby-sitter."

The phone rings. I look at Paully and point at his room. He sees I
mean it. It's hopeless. With difficult people, you can negotiate. With
impossible people, it's hopeless. There is no negotiation anyway.
There is only telling Ma what I have done.

I get up. I pick up the phone. I tell whoever is selling whatever
that we're not interested.

The expression on Ma's face has changed. She is not shocked
any more, anything but. I can see by Ma's face that she's got all the
answers now. It's a face I know. Final.

" Take an old woman's life savings! That's what she wants. This
is how this little girl makes her living, Jody! This is who you want
to believe?"

" Ma," I say. "Mama, listen—"

"Listen? You want listen? You listen to this. Over—"

"Mama, please. . ."

"my—"

"Mama, stop."

"dead—"

"Mama, no! Don't say that! Don't!" When it comes on full I grab
a pillow and dig so I don't touch myself. Mama stops. I drop my
head onto the pillow and just let go. I hear her get up in her slow,
awful looking way. I hear the kitchen door swing. I lay out on the
couch and wait for my heart to slow down, my stomach to release.
14th and Avenue M. My inheritance.

I stand up and follow my mother into her kitchen. What I got
to say, I say to her back. I tell her how it was his eyes that first told

me. He had wanted me to see it, Pa. He wanted me to see he knew he was dying. And when he could see that I could see, that's when he did it. He reached under his red and black checkered blanket, and brought out the old case, this odd looking thing, bulging green leather and a long brass zipper. His hands were shaking while he tugged on it, fussy. Suddenly Pa, such a frail old man. It happened too fast. It was so hard to watch. I wanted to jump in there and help, but I just closed my eyes. He showed me the key to the safety deposit, the forms I got to do for Paully's disability, the papers for the cemetery plots he got for himself and Ma and Paully. For me, he said, he still had hope. God bless him. He had a little AT&T, a little U. S. Steel, a few bonds, a worn passbook. He had this and that. He worked hard. He did. I promised him I'd try to stretch it out, make it last. I promised him I'd always be there anyway I could...

I look at my mama, at her back. Her new pretty sweater. It's hanging on her now like a popped yellow balloon. I squeeze my eyes shut.

Oh, God, I'm sorry, Pa. I'm so, so sorry. But you know, even then, when I took it from you and closed it and put it in my bag. Even then, Pa, on my shoulder? It pulled like a ton. Even then I had to set it down.

I walk the few steps to my mama slowly. I don't want noise. I lay my hands on her shoulders. There was a very quiet moment in my house. Quiet and long.

"Mama, Pa gave this house to me. It's mine. And I am going to do with it what I have to."

Ida   I am sorry, my Jacob. To my grave I meant to carry this, but now... now I talk or I lose.

"So, Pa gave you this house? So of course he did! At last he should get what he wants; Paully should be shut away—"

"Ma," she says, "Ma." She never lets me finish.

"You think this surprises me, Jody? You got to make a big production? Eh? This don't surprise me. All Paully's life, Pa hated him. Why not in the grave?"

Jody sighs. A big sigh, a big long sigh she gives her mother's troubles.

"What? Am I boring you little girl? Your mother's struggles are boring to you? Of course. Of course they're boring. They're boring to me also. Fifty-five years I been bored with this trouble. You would rather talk maybe to Miss Maven-of-Miserable. She can tell you something about these fifty-five years I can't?"

Jody looks at her shoes. She takes a big breath and talks so fast and so soft I can't even get the details, all I get is "wonderful opportunity," and we got to "act immediately" for this "one-time offer."

"I said save your sales talk!"

Jody can't even look at me, Jacob! She cannot even meet my eyes. All the time, she thinks they should take Paully. I should have no one. I should sit here alone. I look at my daughter in the smart uptown outfit, sitting there staring at the nails she still bites.

"Fifty-five years ago," I tell her, "years before you was even thought up, my little babeleh, my first—mine son, Jody—was handed to me by the man I loved, *loved*, Jody, like I only wish you could know, and this man would not even look into my eyes. This is how ashamed he was of this son I gave him."

"Now, Ma. Ashamed? Pa was not ashamed!" she says.

"Pa was not ashamed? Pa? *Not* ashamed? Wanted to lock the boy away! Wanted him in the yard, in the other room. What fights I got you should never know."

"What fights, Ma? He lived at home. No one bothered—"

"Of course! Of course he lived at home with his family. You think this was nothing? You think this was easy? A mother got no fights?"

"Ma," she says, "Ma—" She never lets me finish.

"Listen to you, Miss-Grown-Up-I-Know-Everything-Now!" I turn and look up at her. My arms around myself, I can feel Danny's sweater. "Your brother Paully," I tell her, "he never waits for nothing, eh? He comes, middle of the night."

Jody shrugs and goes to the table. She slumps in a chair and stares at her hands.

Maybe I shouldn't have started. Such a shandra you should not repeat. But there is no turning back. The time has come. "I was so excited," I tell her, "you would not believe. The last few weeks,

Jody? These feel like forever. And then I was late, Paully was taking his time, and it was hot in August, so when I finally felt it, I was so excited. I grabbed on your father's arm and just cried out. No words, just sound, not loud, but so he would know. So your father, he hears. He was not sleeping so well at that time. The fathers, they wait too, eh? And what does he do? This Jody, I will never forget. He kisses me, full on the lips, and long—a very special kiss, like I should take from him life and breath. And then he lights the candle."

Jody turns her chair and rests her head against the wall. I can see she will listen quiet now. I don't need to hurry.

"That kiss and the pain, Jody, how can I explain to you? Like a special wine, they mix inside, like a sound, like a buzzing. For a moment I feel like I have risen up from earth and then, slam. I'm back down on it. The pain takes me again. With such pain your mind cannot think. People began to wake up and come in and out of the room. My mama, your Bubbe Kochansky, Lila, Aunt Sylvia, and all the time I'm waiting for Mrs. Shilovitch."

"Who's this Shilovitch?" she says, her eyes still closed.

"Mrs. *Shilovitch*! Only the woman who pulled my babies from me and brought you onto this earth." I look at her long enough to see she understands. I put my hands flat on the counter; I should feel something solid. "I am worried they don't know where she is. Someone else's baby, maybe? But then she comes and I know I will be all right. I let things happen. This is how it is, you got to let it happen."

Jody nods and I go on. "Your pa comes in and lifts me and my mama spreads blankets and towels over my bed. The rabbi comes and goes. Never in my life did I feel pain like this. Mrs. Shilovitch makes an herb tea, it smells like wet wool, I'll never forget. Then Mama holds my head up while I sip. It calms me. I'm so tired. I fall back and begin to let my baby come. But it's not like that. You can't just let it happen. You also got to work. You got to push."

"Ah," she says, which is more like "aha!" And then, "hmm."

And suddenly I can't go on. Why am I telling her this, Jacob? A forty-two year old woman you would think would know these things. What has happened to our daughter?

I go on. "I don't know how many hours. This tea, it is very strong. It is not something to sip for pleasure, this tea. The last part, I don't even remember. Can you believe that I cannot remember such a thing? I felt like things were happening to me. Do you understand this? I could not stop what was happening to me and it's not that I wanted them to stop, but it was scary not to be able to. I remember they called my name. I cannot answer. I try. I want to. I tell my mouth to open and cry out, but nothing. Nothing! I feel like I am being pulled down, fast down, into a black, black pit. I go out. I black out. Can you believe? A mother who does not feel the moment that her baby is free! Such a moment to miss! Where did I go? *Ai* ! I don't know, I don't know for how long, but when I wake up—the light in the room?—a very special kind of light in the room—cool dawn kind of light, silver and blue. There is a smell liked it rained in the night. I look around at all the things, the dresser with my hairbrush and combs, Pa's tray with the long straight-edged razor he used then, the chair pulled up next to the bed, and there a teacup and the dregs of leaves, a bowl of water, a small blue cloth. I see the wardrobe. It's a little bit open. There's a white sheet spilling out of it. I see your pa's blue work clothes. I am home, I think. I am in my bed. My head is pounding like I am wearing a pot and someone is banging on it.

"Then I hear it. A cry. A cry like it should come from me but I can't feel my own mouth make it. A long, long cry. Open. I open. I cry. Then the door opens, the room for a moment is filled with light, and my small bundle is given to me.

"Oh Jody, is there a word for the moment when a mother is handed her baby? Do the doctors got a name for this? They should make a special word. There is nothing else like this, Jody. This is a hunger. Ha! A hunger to feed. There is no other name."

"Aw, Ma," she says, looking at me now, "that's really beautiful."

"Like you would not believe," I say. I grab me a box of Kleenex from the pantry and rip the top off. I go on. "So I take my precious, my little babeleh boy, and I lay him on the bed next to me. And so excited, so happy, I pull up my gown. I don't care who looks, such a hunger I have. I take the rough cloth out like Mrs. Shilovitch told me, like I have been doing every day for months, and I rub, you know, here..." I pat my breasts. Jody nods.

"I am in such a hurry. I don't know why. But I want so much, so, so much. I don't care, I am rough with myself. I rub and I squeeze and I push the first... the first, ah,... out."

"What? Milk?"

My poor Jody. She don't know nothing. "It's not milk," I say, "not the *first*, Jody. It's awful. It's... you don't want to know this can come from your body."

"Really?" she says. Forty-two. My little girl.

I sigh and go on. "I do this as fast as I can, even too fast; I hurt myself. But I want to be ready for the baby, because finally, finally Jody, how can I tell you? Like a sigh, like a release it is, to let down a breast to a baby. And I want to do this but I hate to do this. I want to see, eh? As much as I want to feed him I want to look at him. And all I can see is my breast! And then there are the tears, everything such a happy blur. So I catch his fingers. Such small delicate fingers he got; they make a little dance in the air. I find his toes, his tush, his little... ah..."

"It's a penis, Ma."

"It's a little funny, pointy thing, Jody, you can't believe how sweet. And the other part? Like a little hazel nut! Wonderful! So wonderful! I felt myself pour down. Wonderful, oh Jodeleh, how can I tell you? So wonderful.

"But Jody? Jody are you listening to me?"

"Mama, I'm here," she says, "I'm here. Go on."

"Jody he don't... Paully! Ai!" I put my hands out to her. Will she understand? "I got my breast," I say. "I can feel... Oh! All on the bed, my milk. He's not... oh God, Jody!"

"Mama? I don't under-... Mama, please."

"He don't suck! What kind of baby don't suck? I push into him. Oh God, Jody, I can feel myself pulse, once, twice, like blood. It is smearing, all on his face, his neck, my hands, the bed. There is not so much, but it's oily, it spreads. It's warm, sticky. The smell— like milk and burning sugar, like custard for the homentashen. I got it everywhere but in the baby. I push his tummy, he don't suck! I tip up his head! I pick him up. Jody! He don't suck. I cannot understand what I am doing wrong. What kind of woman cannot feed her own baby?

"Then I feel the bed move. I see my Jacob's hand. And then, on the pillow next to me, I see his face. Such a dear face, too pale, so pale I've never seen, and so unhappy. 'Jacob,' I cry! 'I can't! Oh God! Oh look!' I let Paully's head drop back. Maybe this way, I think, oh God, oh please! I try everything I can think as fast as I can think. I cannot make it work.

"But Pa—and this, Jody, this is so surprising to me—Pa is calm. He puts his hand on my cheek. 'Ida' he says, 'Ida, if it can't eat, it shouldn't live.'

"It. It! This is what your father said about this sweet baby I have just given him—'it.' "

"Oh, Mama," Jody says, sorry like she should be and I know, for once, she is listening to her mother.

"I think maybe I just don't hear right. I slap the baby's back. Your pa—I cannot, even now I cannot believe what—Jody, he tries to pull my hand away. Is this what he wants I should do? I don't understand. I look at him. His lips are pressed together, he draws them inside. His eyes are shut very tight. 'What is it? Jacob! My darling! What?' I cry. Still he does not open his eyes. He does not do anything. I cannot even take a breath.

"The door opens again. A glow from a lamp surrounds my mama. Can you believe this? The room is getting darker. The light from the window is fading. It is not dawn. How? How long can I have been sleeping? And this little one at my breast, how long has he needed his mama?

"Mine own mama, God rest her, she looks so tired and so old standing there, her braids all loose and long. You see how I remember? I was so alive then, so awake, my head still boom, boom, boom. Quickly Mama puts the lamp on the table beside me and lays her hand on my shoulder. And I know, Jody, somehow I just know, that baby is going to suck and I am going to be a good mother. I cannot say how. But I know this for truth. I feel strong. I feel calmer. I can speak.

" 'Mama?' I say, and I feel like my mouth is full of cotton.

"'I am here, babaleh.'

"'I am so thirsty.'

"And then I hear her quiet steps again. And when she is gone I look up into my Jacob's suffering face. 'Jacob,' I say, 'I must know. Now.'

" "His face, *ai*! Such a look! So much pain. So closed, so tight. Never have I seen a face so lost. And then he opens his eyes and nods, quickly, many times. But even then, me, he will not look at. 'Our son,' he says. He don't say more. His mouth is open. I think maybe he will make words if he has them. But he has no words. My husband, my new baby's father, he reaches for that baby, that creature I have just smeared all over his little body with my useless milk, all slippery and wet and awful, and pulls that baby from my arms, and lifts him, his limbs dangling down, like he's a rag doll, so I should take a good look. So I look. I see an infant, a thin, wrinkled infant. He is white like a pearl. He is sloppy with my milk, oily, blue like skim. His head is flopped and heavy, his mouth wide open, crying, high, sharp, scary cries. And, there is something, somehow, I don't know, something, different, something not right— something..."

"The eyes," says Jody.

"The eyes," I say. "This is always it, eh? So again the door opens. My mama stands with the water, stopped still, watching me watch my husband.

"'Jacob,' she says, 'You must put him down.'

"But what you got to see here, Jody, is that it was not what she said. It was her voice. This pleading, like she is afraid of what my husband might do to my son. I sit up quick. I raise my hand to Jacob to stop him. I want to see. I want to know. And then I understand. Such people I had not seen much before—a few times maybe—in all my life. Such odd fat slow people. Like children always. How? I think. How can this be possible? This is my son?

"Oh, how I need to hold him. And God forgive me, how I want to throw him, to hurl him away with all the strength that is in me.

I am very awake. My insides so empty, so roomy. I want to push him back in. Wait a little longer. Get it right. I have not done it right. I have made a mistake. What an ugly baby, an ugly hateful droop-headed monster. Why me? Dear God, why me?"

My daughter is blinking at me, her eyes round and bright, her lips pressed together. It is a look I have seen her make since she was two. Whenever the world gives Jody something new, this is the look she makes.

"You got to understand, Jody," I say, "this takes longer, much longer, to tell you than it did to happen. To love and to hate a baby like this? It takes just a moment, that's all. And then that moment? It lasts as long as you live."

"I know, Mama," Jody says, and strange enough, I don't know how, but she sounds like she does.

I go on. "But then he cried, eh? The baby cries and the mama remembers who she is. I grab Paully. I grab him by the throat."

"By the throat, Mama?"

"By the throat!" I say. "And then I shove. I do. I shove into his mouth and I force it. With my fingers, I force it. And I force his tongue down, away from his throat. I do this hard. I don't know what I am doing but I have done everything else. So I force. And Jody? Oh Jody, I can feel it! I feel myself pulse into him. From me into him! My baby, my sweet precious, he is taking my milk at last! I raise my eyes to your pa's; he should see what a thing! What a miracle! And he says, oh God, Jody, he says..."

"What, Mama? It's okay."

But it is not okay. I press my hands into the countertop, I close my eyes very tight. "'Let it die, Ida,' he says. 'Let it die.'"

Yes. I told her. Forgive me, my Jacob, may you rest well at last, I know you loved your son. I know you did not blame me. But I did not know so then, my womb still stretched, still healing.

"No. No, Mama," Jody says. "You must not have heard right."

"But I did! I did hear right! I think this too. I think, this he could not have said. But then he says again, 'Let it die,' and then louder, very loud—I never have heard your pa beg before this—'Ida, Ida please. Let it die.'"

Jody   I blow my nose. I toss the Kleenex in the trash with all the others. Not a trace of mascara left.

Ma says, "Oh what, what have I done now?" She comes to me, her hands out. "The baby cries and the mama remembers who she is, eh?"

I stand and put my arms all the way around her. Sometimes my mama can be so sweet she melts me.

"Jodeleh," she says, "this is wrong. What have I done here? I shouldn't speak, I know. I know. 'Memory is silent,' your pa used to say, and he was right. When we speak, we re-create. For this reason we say the kaddish, eh? Oh your father, he was wise."

"No," I say, my voice comes out of me like a little girl. "No, it's good, Mama. We shouldn't have secrets."

Mama gets all stiff and uncomfortable. We almost never hug, and I am sure we have never hugged like this. I think I would like to do it for a long time. But even as I think this, I can feel her back away.

"'We shouldn't have secrets,'" she says, mimicking me, and then laughs. "What can a daughter begin to know about her mother's secrets?" She looks up at me. And when she does, she got a look on her face I have never seen. At first I can't figure it, and then I do. My mother, she's not looking at me like a mother looks at her daughter. She's looking at me like one adult looks at another. And maybe something else too, maybe a little fear, a little careful. It is *my* house.

"Jody," she says, one brow raising, "you listening to me now, Sunshine?"

"Yes, Mama," I say right away, still like a little girl.

"Jody," she says, "I don't want Paully with no strangers."

"What?" I say. "Oh no, Mama. No. Not strangers. That's what I've been trying to—"

"What, Jody? You don't listen all this time to what your mama tells you?"

I look close at her face, my mama's face, lined and covered with an old lady's soft down. Every part of it, all the lines and muscles, all of it, drawn together and staring up at me. And then I see. I see how much I matter. I see why she told me.

Forty-two years I have been listening to my mama's stories. My mama's remarkable stories. She has made me feel them like they were my own. I have tasted them and smelled them. Forty-two years, I have been put to sleep with stories, eaten my meals with stories, had all my questions answered by stories, been shown how to live and how not to, listened all the way to the end and thought I understood only to see later that I did not. That the story had answered something for her, but not for me. So much of herself, her life, that she has shared with those wonderful, endless, repeated stories, her voice as much a part of me as my teeth and hair. And yet, I have never heard this one. This one—this secret—she has held on to. A secret is a heavy burden we carry as if inside a sack. No one else can even guess what's inside. But when we swing that bag at someone who doesn't know how heavy it is, a secret is a weapon. For forty-two years my mother has won with her stories—every battle.

I turn away from her. How can my mother do this to me? How can she want this for me? I remember that despite everything I have done and worked for, all the hours, the calls, the faxes, the negotiations, what ever I want, whatever I feel, whatever I *own*, nothing can begin without her signature at the bottom of a release. What matters is that she is the mother and the legal guardian, that's all.

"Ma," I say to her, baby voice all gone now, "I'm listening to you tell me how much you wanted your baby to live."

"You see? You see how hard a mother fights?"

"I do. I see and, Ma, I'm proud of you. But Ma? It's time to fight again and, this time, I'm here. This time I'm going to help you. We've got to see how much Paully can do. He's going to surprise us, Ma."

"Jody," she says, "for a mother and daughter, I think, we are very close, but still to me your mind is a mystery."

She has said this before. Whenever I come up with a different answer than the one she comes up with she says this. "Yeah?" I say. "Oh yeah?" I don't say nothing else, even though I could. Usually I can't get a word in around Ma's talking. Now she's finally not saying anything, I'm too mad to talk. I huff out of the kitchen into that stupid, ugly living room. Jeesh, I hope they tear that wall paper down first thing. I turn back into the kitchen. Ma hasn't moved. "And that makes it wrong, or what?" I say.

She looks at me. I can see she's not putting it together.

"It's a mystery to you, so like what, automatically it's wrong?" I turn and leave that kitchen again. I don't know where I'm going. This time, Ma follows. Any second now—I just know it—any second, she's gonna start talking.

"Don't you talk, Mama," I say. "Just don't you..." and then I stop because I see her. My poor mama, a tired little old lady now, worried and scared; she don't even know what's happening to her life all at once, standing there in her little yellow sweater, like a china doll, so white and tiny. My mama, my best friend. If I could only make her understand...

I drop onto the blue chair and put my head in my hands. I hear the squeak of that awful vinyl on the couch while Mama sits. Any second now, she's gonna start.

"Mama, look," I say. "There is one thing you got to know. Or, I don't know, maybe you already do know this but that don't mean I don't got to say it. Because I do. And you got to hear.

"Mama, when I went to Santa Clara, I knew it was for good. Right from the start, I knew it was for good. I didn't know how or why. I just knew I had to go. I had to. But now I do know why. It's because I'm not his mother, Mama, you are."

I look up at her to see if she's listening. She is biting her lip. I have never seen my mama afraid of me. I wish she wasn't.

"I know you didn't ask for your life, Mama. Poor, sad Ma, I used to think, she gotta stay in with Paully all day. I know you would have liked to be out in the world. I know that about you. So I'd tell myself, 'Grow up, Miss Kochansky, Ma didn't ask for that. Life isn't fair for you? So who said life was fair?' And I let you do it, Ma. I let you make me feel guilty.

"I mean, in some ways, I did kind of think it was my fault. The way Paully used to break stuff? I know why. I do. Before then Paully never really noticed he was different from other people, you know? There was just us and we treated him like himself, and that's just the way things were. But, there I was, twelve years old, I was beginning to have a few friends of my own from school. Sometimes the phone would ring for me, or maybe someone would come by. I never had anyone in, you know. Anyone could see that wasn't such a great idea. But still, Paully, he saw. I know he saw. And what I think is that maybe then he figured out that things were different for him. We all went out, we knew other people and, you know, did the normal things that normal people do. And I think he was really mad about it. Mad at us, I guess, maybe at himself, I don't know. For a while, he just seemed mad all the time. So, in a way, I guess, it was my fault Paully broke all that stuff. I felt really bad. Poor Ma, poor Paully. So what did I do? So I never brought a friend home. Well, I wanted to protect him too. I helped. Sure I'll take Paully to the movies, Ma. Like I don't want to flirt with the boys like all the other girls, like Evelyn. Sure I'll come over, Ma, I'll take care of things, you got enough to do. Sure, sure, sure. I'm not saying it's all your fault I had to go, Ma. I'm just saying I had to."

I get up from the chair. Ma never takes her eyes off of me. I don't know what she sees. I move next to her on the couch. "Had to," she says, just flat.

For a mother and daughter, we are very close, but still to me her mind is a mystery.

"Maybe you understand that, Mama. Maybe you don't. Maybe you will someday. I don't know." I wish my mother and I hugged more. I wish I could put my arms around her little shoulders without her shrinking away. "All I know, Mama, is that Pa, he left me...." and then, of all things, I start laughing, a low chuckle. My inheritance. I mean, what a joke. Mama can't figure me; her chin trembles. "I've been trying to do the right thing, Mama," I say. "It hasn't been easy."

"He gave you my house!" she cries, like she stopped listening a half-hour ago. "My house that he bought for me! Because he hated Paully, Jody. He wanted him shut away!"

"But Mama!" I say, "Paully *is* shut away! Right here! He's been shut up in this house my whole life."

"No! Paully is with his mother!" She buries her face in my shoulder. I circle her in my arms.

She starts shaking with sobs. "Jody, I can't let you do this, Jody." I have never seen my mama like this.

"Mama, you don't even know what I'm doing! You haven't even let me tell you!"

This is going so much worse than the worst I'd imagined.

"You can't anymore!" I cry. "Paully's too much for you now. The house is too big."

"No!" she is screaming. She is actually screaming.

"Mama, that's what it's for, the house, the savings—it's for when you can't anymore, please Mama."

"I won't," she sobs. She is hanging on me. "You can't"; "No, no, no"; "Never."

She pulls away from me, looking up at me, her jaw stuck out. She's talking fast, the same stuff, "No, no, no," and "I'll never let you," but it's low now, like a hiss. She tries to stand, but she can't somehow. This is all too much for her. I'm killing my mother. She starts in again with the "my dead body" stuff. I can't. I just...I promised myself again that I wouldn't. I said I never would again. I said I would let the state sue her first, anything. Anything but going back to that. And then I do. I beg. I actually fall to my knees before my mother and beg. "Please, Mama, please. Listen to me."

And then, bang! We both look. Paully's door slamming open. He runs right for the kitchen, whooping and bobbing. I know what he's up to. Mama cries out, "Jody!" I run after.

He knows. Paully knows much more than we think he does. Already he's in the recipe file. One big bunch, he pulls them out. He's letting cards drop to the floor, they get under his feet, they bend. I try and go for him, he throws some. More drop out. "Make him stop, Jody!" Mama cries. She's trying to catch him, calling him a bad boy. He's jumping and swinging. One card lands in the sink. Ruined. "Make him stop, Jody!" Mama yells. He's too fast.

He shouts and runs the way he does, like a skip, into the living room, down the hall, back again, throwing cards. I go after, my barrette flies out. Mama yells when she steps on it. I look back at her. She can't even bend down to pick it up.

"I don't want that boy in the bathroom," she cries. So you know right where he goes. He knows. Nobody can say he don't. I run after him into the bathroom, shouting. "No, Paully don—oh!" Two cards float into the toilet.

I get him trapped in the shower and lean on the doors Pa put on there because Paully could never remember to pull the curtain in. I can see him bobbing behind, trying to get out, shouting sounds that make no sense.

Mama finally gets here. She says, in this low voice, "I don't want him in there with that water." Like I can do something about it. I make a motion with my head toward the toilet. She should quick get her cards before the ink runs so bad she can never make it out again.

She gets her cards, then puts the cover down on the toilet and sits. "Orejas de Hammon and Linzer Torte," she says, "maybe ruined." She puts her head in her hands and says, "What has happened all of a sudden to my life?" Always so dramatic, Ma. Can't she see I need help? I make with my eyes, she should look over by the door. She does, but then she just looks back at me.

"Lights, Ma," I whisper. "Get the lights."

Now she gets it. Up she goes. Poor Ma. Getting herself up and down takes forever. Finally she gets there. She flips them off.

Then, just like Pa, I start in. "Paully," I say, slower, down low, right there in the dark, just like Pa, "now it is night. When the lights come on it will be a new day and you can start over like a good boy. Nobody will be mad at you and you can go to your room and be good. A brand new day, Paully. Here it comes." This works. He misses Pa. That's what makes him quiet. Well, all right then, as long as it works. Ma flips on the lights. Through the shower doors I can see Paully standing there, calm. I open the door and put out my hand. "All right, Paully," I say, "give me the cards."

Paully holds them back, up over his head. He looks past me, right over my shoulder. He's looking at Ma. His mouth is working, making gibberish sounds. Maybe I was too fast with the lights; he's not calmed down yet. He's pointing at Ma. This is new; I've never seen him point at people. His mouth is working. Then he starts up with "school, school. I go school tomorrah," over and over. Then he stops. He closes his eyes. His mouth works. He's trying to say something, I don't know what. I didn't even know he could actually say anything. Not really, anyway. But he's trying, that's for sure. I say, "It's okay, Paully. Go ahead."

"I want school. Live there. Go there. Live. I want!"

Mama looks like she's gonna fall over, no exaggeration. She's got her hands out for balance. I run quick and get my arm around her. She leans on me. "He don't," she says. "He never..." I get her sitting on the toilet. "I thought my heart would stop," she says. Ma. So dramatic. "He never..."

I lean into her, next to her ear. I say, "I need you to sign the papers, Mama. That's all you have to do. I'll take care of everything else."

I hold my breath until I'm about blue. But she says it. It's soft, but she says it. I hear her. I let my breath go in a great wind.

I am kneeling there on the tile in front of a toilet my mother is sitting on. Mama's face like a frightened child; she can't believe what she's done. Paully can't get out; I'm in the way. I don't care. I let my head fall onto her lap. "Did I hear you, Mama? Did I hear you?"

Her hand comes down on my head, pushing the hair away, shaking. "You heard me, Sunshine," she says, and this time no one could miss it. "I said 'all right.' "

"Oh Mama," I say, "oh God, Mama." I circle her legs with my arms and hold tight. "A house just lifted off my shoulders."

book seven

❖•❖•❖

"What a big room!"

–30–

Steiner   That the house was unusual actually came as a surprise to me. Mrs. Kochansky had never invited me into her inner sanctum, and I hadn't realized. It gave me an idea.

Since the living area was sacrificed to accommodate that industrial kitchen, the appraised value came in well below the neighborhood norm. Therefore my boss was able to justify the purchase to the funding entities.

Jody negotiated a deal whereby she would sell her mother's house to the Daughters of Israel for just beneath that appraised value. In exchange, Paul would be housed and cared for until his death.

Several weeks later, upon receiving the final papers, which reflected changes made by our center's lawyers, Jody reneged. She had assumed that her brother would reside in the house. In fact, Paul, because he did not meet the employment requirement, would take a place vacated by one of the prospective tenants. This would be a nice shared room in just the sort of facility Jody had once pressed for. Now it seemed, she'd set her sights on more.

Meanwhile, I concentrated on the mother. I contacted some of my professors at Columbia who contacted other professors at Columbia, and a different deal was crafted. The graduate student who would take on the project of interviewing Ida Kochansky and compiling her recipes was completing a Ph.D. in food anthropology.

One week later Jody phoned, no trace of anger, rather urgency, as ever, and a long list of questions. What was the difference between what the law required Paul to have and what the DOI was able to provide? Answer: full-time, in-house staff. Fiscally impossible. She understood with no further explanation. How much would their salaries cost, she wondered. How much their board?

On the day I came by to introduce Mrs. Kochansky to Alice Katz—her biographer!—I made sure to call first.

Alice made it clear that I was the one who brought them together and Mrs. Kochansky actually invited me to sit down and join them. Like Danny, Alice thought Mrs. Kochansky quite funny and with all her laughter I didn't have to say much.

But when Alice excused herself to use the bathroom, Mrs. Kochansky and I were able to have our first useful talk.

She wanted to know how and how often the word "normal" is used.

"Normal?" I say. "Well it's used in the social sciences for a particular statistical—"

"But what about *normal*?" She looks at the floor. "Like, um, *sub-normal*."

I tell her I haven't used the word normal since graduate school and that 'sub-normal' is new to me.

"I knew it!" she said and then, just as I was opening my mouth to say "Guess what, Mrs. Kochansky. I quit my job today!" Alice returned.

Jody's offer, when it came, I would call a thing of beauty, figures juggled into elegant balance. She'd projected salaries with increases, equity, non-profit property tax, a dozen things or more I would have needed two classes to make me aware of.

At the core, the proposal was this: to offset the extra required funds, the deed to her house, reappraised for high market, would be presented to the DOI in exchange for one dollar. It was completely original, full of integrity. It was her entire inheritance. I was very impressed.

Not a moment was wasted. Staffing was re-drawn. An architect commissioned to design a two-story addition for twenty. Twenty! Ten small private bedrooms on each floor, plus requisite plumbing. The room that had served as Mrs. Kochansky's bedroom would become a small studio apartment for the use of on-duty residential workers. Jody's old room, the facility office. The kitchen, of course, was easily adequate.

To meet the legal requirement that Paul be employed, he was assigned facility maintenance, the vacuuming and weed trimming he'd been doing for forty-odd years. And there he would remain, just behind his mother's kitchen, for the rest of his natural life.

As Vicki, my new supervisor, shows me around that first day, she asks if I'm planning to wear what I'm wearing—slacks and a sweater. When I say "yes," she bites her upper lip. "We mostly wear these," she says, opening her own locker. She hands me a light yellow smock with an old-fashioned Peter Pan type collar. "You can wear any kind you like. Or, nothing, if that's what you want, but, ah, I think you might want to."

None of the staff have a chance to talk to me until just before the first lunch shift and then they all seem friendly but in a hurry. New Yorkers. Vicky tells everyone to be sure to show me the ropes. Some one laughs and says, "The only ropes around here are used to tie wheelchairs into the van."

Which brings me once again to wonder about that particular ex-pression. Where did it come from? What does it actually mean? As I take my first lunchtime stroll around Harlem, I consider the possi-bilities.

Perhaps it is nautical. Or maybe from sport, the fighter's ring or the competition pool. Or could it have come from the pinrail of the theater or bodies hanging from trees? So many kinds of ropes. But to know them? That is the faith of the acrobat who makes a leap.

–31–

Jody To tell the truth, just thinking about these last months, it's like, "Uh-oh! Break out the Alka-Seltzer." After all, I'll be forty-three years old next month; I'm no kid.

Back when I was a kid I used to love to pretend I could fly away. I used to love speed and spin, like at any moment I could just be hurled right off into space and grow wings and off I'd go.

I remember those old merry-go-rounds they used to have on the playgrounds, the one's shaped like stop signs with all the different

colors. Oh, I loved them best. If I opened my eyes—if I dared—
I'd see all the colors blur together, the playground, the fence, the
buildings, all blurred together. And maybe I'd be able to hold my
eyes on the kid-next-to-me's face, but only for a minute, before it
would also begin to smear.

Usually, I would stand along side and push Paully. Then, when
it'd get fast enough, I'd jump on and take the rest of the ride. But
how I loved for someone to push.

There was this one day though; what can I say? This big kid
comes along—I don't know, maybe a sixth-grader—and says to me
that he'll push for a while if I just want to ride. So I jump right on.
And off he goes, pushing and pushing, faster and faster and—I tell
you—it's the greatest thing. I mean, I am flying so fast it takes my
breath, and for a minute or two, I can't even hear Paully's cries.

Now when Paully gets ignored, he's, well, really shrill. He
shrieks. And he's shrieking and I'm yelling for the kid to cut it out,
but this kid, he don't. And then the world goes soft, you know,
swimmy. Suddenly I start thinking maybe I'll be sick; I'm all sweaty
and scared. I'm so whirly I can't even scream no more, just hold on;
that's all I can do.

And then, slam—the thing comes to a stop. And there's Pa's legs.

He pulls this kid up to him, hard up, by the collar, fast as a snap,
and looks down on that kid, like...I don't know what like...like an
eagle looks. Serious. The kid, he just hangs there, you know? My
Pa, he lifted sacks for a living. So then he drops the kid and the kid,
he runs like heck of course. Me? I crawl off that thing. I want to feel
land with my hands first. I don't know how Paully got off. When
I can finally look up I see him sort of trotting behind Pa as he goes
back to his bench beneath the trees and his Sunday paper.

I think to go over and sit with them. Really by that time all I
want is to sort of sit on the bench nice and quiet and think a bit,
maybe read the funnies. But there's something, I can't say—a gut
thing—tells me I should stay where I'm at.

And I'm right, of course, because Pa is just sitting over there
stewing, working up a good mad. I hear about it later though, walking home.

He says, "Jody, what were you thinking? Why'd you let that boy push?"

"He said he would," I tell him. I don't know why it's such a big deal.

But to Pa this is a big deal. He stops right there in the street to lecture me. He's waving his arms all around. "You don't ask any questions? You just let some boy push?"

"Pa," I say, pulling on his arm. Pa don't usually like to stop on the street with Paully. People look. They do.

He's yelling at me. I mean, he's yelling. Pa never yells. "You don't look after Paully?"

"Pa," I say. I tug on his sleeve. "Pa, let's go home."

And he does. He starts walking and he says, "Yes, let's go home."

So we walk, him first, then Paully, and me a half a block behind. I can't get any speed up. It feels like it's the last seven blocks of my life. Not that I'm afraid he'll hit. They finished with that when I was real little. But if Ma gets into it, she won't drop it for weeks. It will be all I hear about. It's like, exhausting, you know? So this is what I'm really scared of.

But it's not so bad once we get in. Pa was a man who liked to think about things before he said them. I guess that's what he does on the walk home.

We get in, he takes my jacket and says, "We won't tell Mama about this, eh?"

Ha! I hadn't thought of that. She'd probably have a few words for him too. That sure cooled Pa off.

So I nod and add the merry-go-round to the list of things not to tell Ma. Like we don't say that lots of times we'll throw out the lunch Ma packs us and have hot dogs and ice cream cones instead. Or that when we do homework it's me who's showing Pa the math and not the other way around. Or—most secret of all—that sometimes Pa will meet my cousin Sammy in the park and they'll sit talking. I have kept these secrets well for a long time. Pa knows he can trust me.

So phew, I can breathe. Then, of all things, he gets on his knee.

This way he can look right in my face. And he says, "Jody, come here. Come listen to your Pa."

I go over to him and he circles me with his arm. This is not a usual thing with Pa.

"Jody," he says, "listen good to what I tell you now. Jody, if you don't know who's pushing you, you don't know where you're going."

That was my Pa.

I get all sniffy. "I'm sorry, Pa." Sniff, sniff.

"You just think next time, eh?" he says.

And I am sorry. I realize it was, like, not a real bright thing to do, but, I'm not sorry too.

See, I already decided, on that seven blocks home, that if someone offered to push tomorrow, I'd take it. I mean, Pa wasn't pushing. Pa was sitting behind his paper where he always was. If I was gonna do any riding at all, that's the way it had to be. Because, hey, if I just listened to Pa all I'd ever get to do is wait for Paully to slow down so I could finish the ride.

Well, look at me, Pa! I'm riding now! Hey, I'm cruisin'. Going seventy down a long smooth, wide California highway with my foot on the pedal.

Six months—just six months—and yet in my mind so much clearer than all the other time that went before it. I left the department ready to set sales records this Christmas. Plus, I got Stage One of OME—Operation Move Everybody—(that's what Danny calls it!) started in Brooklyn and when I go back, I'm gonna have the first date I've had on my birthday since I was twenty-something.

I got going. Before I left the first time for Brooklyn I took the girls to the Olive Garden to celebrate the Christmas sale being set up. We ordered a couple of bowls of their artichoke-spinach dip and when we all had some, I tapped my beer. I made a little speech. I thanked them all and I asked them to thank each other. Then the big news: the spree. I tell them what it is, and of course, everybody's into it. I tell them it goes to the top seller for the pre-Christmas sale and can be used immediately after Christmas. It was like a ripple went through them; this was excitement. Beth didn't care, of course, too

part-time, or June, because she knew already, but everyone else—
even Meena—got a glint. Amy though, she was the one who'd get
it. I knew that. I told them, and especially her, that I hoped they'd
remember to have fun with this so we could have a few more sales
meetings at the Olive Garden. I let that sink in.

Then I told them, the spree would cover the time I'd be gone.
That got their attention. I tapped my beer again and lifted it and
announced that June was in charge in my absence by virtue of her
promotion. Everyone was happy for June. No one else wanted this
and she's going to be such a help. This way I could go back to New
York a lot over the next several months. Sharon fixed me up with
some family leave time. It is unpaid, but at least I can have it as I
need it. It's something anyway—flexible.

So there we are, congratulating June, and who should come up
but Mr. Rollins. Mr. Rollins of Safety First. I couldn't place him
right away, but then—that hair. I show him my car keys. He says,
"You're driving." Still with the non-questions, Rollins. I tell him
that I can't get enough of it. He says "Well, hey!" He scratches his
head and looks at me. He shakes my hand. So of course, my girls
want to know who this guy is and I have had just enough beer to
say, "Oh, you know, somebody I gave a little thrill to once!" I let the
girls look at one another and think what they will. But I do push my
beer aside, 'cause if I'd say a thing like that to the girls I work with,
maybe I'd better not drink anymore before I'm gonna drive.

When the food comes, Meena asks Beth about her Christmas Eve
gig because maybe her son will go, and Beth launches into some
long story about how they're not going to play after all because
someone's girlfriend will be in from college and can't see him with
someone else. It takes me back. I can see it on some of the other
women's faces too, some of them sort of smile, some roll their eyes.
Except Amy. She looks ready to jump in with advice. That Beth, she
grows on you.

So after she's got this whole cockamamie story laid out, and she's
the center of attention, she looks at me—of course I've got linguini
half way in my mouth—and says, "At Halloween I got to see a lot of
my friends from high school who went away to college." I nod and

chew. Turns out the college kids had a lot more to talk about than the guys in the band, and she has decided it's time for her to go too.

Marta raises a fist and says "Yes!" I guess she has been trying to talk Beth into this. Amy too, it looks like.

Then right there, in front of every one Beth asks me to write her a letter of recommendation. Turns out she wants to go to a Jesuit college. Me, I just make a joke to cover up how flattered I feel. I say, "I may not be Hemingway but I been told I got a way with the words." I know it's not funny. The thing is, I say it like Ma. Say something like Ma, everyone will laugh. Guaranteed.

Ma. It's good to be laughing again with her. It's the best. It's what I missed most of all. Not only did I get arrangements started for the house and get OME in motion, but I went back to my old department. It looked so old and gray to me now, not a drop of natural light. Parker retired four months ago and instead of Eckhart from Shoes—the guy everyone thought would get it—the store hired some teacher from the Fashion Institute. Lots of changes. No one was happy.

Speaking of which, poor Evelyn. Back at her mother's with the boys. Ev went to college but she never did anything with it. Now she's got some money from the insurance, but she has no idea what to do with herself. Her mother is driving her crazy. She feels trapped. Poor, poor Ev. I didn't tell her I'd started skating.

No, that I told Danny, over veal *piccata*. He knew the place already, really knew it—the owner came out to say hi. He ordered everything done just right. I keep thinking back on that meal. I'm sure I think of it every day. This was the first dinner date I've gone on since before Pa died. Before that, a salesman now and then, but just a meal, nothing to even think about the next day. But this? It was so unexpected. I didn't have anything to wear to something like that, and no time to shop either. I put my hair so many ways it was just a staticy mess. A dinner date! I was so nervous, everything about that van, everything about Danny's chair made me nervous. How was I supposed to eat?

But Danny? Danny is a great talker. He'll talk about anything. And there are a lot of things he really knows about too. He made me so comfortable. He really did. Comfortable, but ah, upset too. In a good way, upset, if you know what I mean. Our heads so close together, I tell you, it made me woozy. And Danny, you know, I think he could see that, and he didn't do nothing about it. A perfect gentleman. He'd even change the subject maybe, let me recover myself. He gave me a little lesson in chromosomes. At one point he made like two chromosomes talking to each other, some silly voice, and I just giggled. I mean, giggled. I haven't giggled in years, even with Ryan I didn't giggle. But sometimes, my eyes would fall on his body, and I can't help it, I'd get this chill. I wouldn't mean to, it just happened, like I'd be surprised all over again somehow. Anyway, Danny didn't do nothing but hold my hand and kiss me on the cheek good night.

And then he called my name, the silly name he has for me: My Lady of Sighs. I get kinda embarrassed just saying.

He came by or called every day that I was home, but I was very busy all the time with arrangements and we only had time to duck out once for a quick coffee. I swear, we're all gonna spend all of 1991 moving. It's all set up like dominoes. We start with Ma and Paully moving to Sara's. They're gonna share a room until we can move Paully back into his own room. Paully's been sleeping at the Cohen's three, four nights a week now, getting used to it. Ma has slept there a few times too. Actually, it was Ma more than anyone who worked out all the sleeping arrangements. She was the only one of us who had lived in a big extended family and she just had a knack for it.

After that, I go home for two weeks, I help Ma pack. One pile to take with her, one to leave for some crew the DOI arranged for. They'll put it into storage for the group house. The whole kitchen we don't have to even touch. It's all done. It's just helping Ma decide what to keep, and keeping it down, you know. She's gonna go stay with Sara and Danny until they're through building there. She can see what every bit is like—I made sure of that—they promised me up and down they'd pick her up and take her if she wants to see the place any time. It's part of the deal. And then, I go back again, first there's Ma and Sara's move, and then there's Danny's.

So I call Ma twice a day now, a little at lunch, a little when I get home, she can't wait to find out what's in my mail. Every day there's stuff about the plans for the house and the money the DOI is raising. Plus, this women's group of Sharon's got their thumbs in every pie in the South Bay. They got way more events than I got time, and—don't ask me why—Ma likes me to read her the flyers. She thinks they are so funny. But what this call is about—what Ma can't sit still until tomorrow for—is whatever Danny's got waiting for me. He sends me things: postcards, key rings, food labels, stuff from the paper, little in-jokes. He knows that I share these with Ma; he keeps that in mind. It's good to laugh with Ma again. It's the best.

Though there are still plenty of things that I won't tell her, plenty of things. For one, the light pink envelope I got from Ryan. That I just set aside. She wrote:

Dear Jody,

I asked my Aunt Lucy what to write a letter to you about and she said something that I thought was funny that happened since I came here to Seattle. So here is my letter.

A girl in my school has a cat and it's her grandmother's cat and it's always in the room with her grandmother. But it always tries to sneak out. And they catch it in the house and give it back to their grandmother. But that's not the funny part. The cat gets out once when the front door is open and the cat runs out. And it just stops there with this look on its face like "What a big room!" That's how my girlfriend said it, and I thought that it was funny. The weather is nice here in Seattle. I think about swimming with you a lot.

Love,

Ryan

I sent the sweetest little California Otter they had at The Nature Company to the address on the envelope, but I never heard back. I'm going to tell Danny about her. I haven't yet, not yet. I got to work up to it.

I talk to him late—real late out there—sometimes he's just in the mood to listen. I try to think up sayings for him—like Pa's. I sit there in traffic and work to come up with them. I tell him it's best to swim on top of the water. The lower you let yourself sink, the harder it is to go forward. And another thing, I say, if you want to walk any distance, you need the right shoes. I try to make him laugh. He's easy.

But some nights he's got more energy, we talk about everything, Ma and Sara and Paully and Steiner and Macy's and the boys he's teaching and the Old Boys Supper Club and just everything else. When you think that my last two best friends... well, one was retarded and the other was nine! I tell you, I just pinch myself sometimes talking to Danny. I keep thinking one day I will wake up and, kaboom, it will all be over.

I tell him this late one night; I just can't help it. He understands. He says this is a thing with being Jewish. You can never just enjoy anything without remembering all the people who got pain and suffering to deal with and can't be enjoying it too. Danny tells me this takes practice—to just let yourself enjoy.

Then, this time more than just teasing, he calls me my pet name again. I've been waiting for this. I tell him how I read in last month's *Healthy Life* that sighing adds oxygen to the brain and that there is no way a person can sigh without relaxing their muscles. He says that may be true, but it's also resignation, relaxing instead of bracing for the fight.

So we made a deal, Danny and I, every time I catch myself sighing, I've promised him, right away I gotta say, right out loud, "Well—it's possible."

−32−

Danny Dear reader, listen. I hope you can hear how gentle the soft coming and leaving of air. Sigh now, go ahead, sound, fill your belly like a round happy Buddha, and sound. I hope you are comfortable. I hope you are warm. Or, if you are not now, then that you have been, as you have followed these pages, comfortable I hope, feet raised, afghan-draped or, perhaps, felined, your warm cup of something a short arm's reach away. Or better, the rise and fall of air taken by one you love near you, the only sound in the room. I hope you were there once, as we followed these pages. I hope you are there now, and notice, and are glad.

For it is coming. It is. If it has not come yet. And it will take you and rake you and sure leave you changed. Though daily you live and daily you face it, or mask with night, and thus do not live.

But it is the sun, and the sun again tomorrow and rise again you do, as the constant lungs demand. You can, for you must, for we all do who live. So reader, fill, fill. Take this air which makes possible the sound of rejoicing, of song, of the lover's release, but now, for now, sigh, sigh—a prayer that says "I accept."

And you will know then the sighs of my Jewish people. The long terrible shudders emanating deep from the chest that sing "I am old, I am old, and the world is a heavy wearing place." The sighs of the knees, little whimpers that ask, "all this for me to carry?" and those of the belly, "so much food, so little time," and also those which slip embarrassed through the smile at the darling child who makes us all proud. There are the sighs for morning that say good-bye dreams, and the sighs for evening that mourn another sun setting. And too, we know the sighs of all people, of the lost love remembered, or the wonder of a mountain's daunting hugeness. Here indeed, a vocabulary as rich and complex as any language, as evocative as music. Two old men sharing a bench can pass a full morning sighing and they will understand one another, a communication of the lungs and heart.

And if one should luck into a sure fire one liner, then I hope he does share it, and thank God, and get on.

For it is coming. It is. If it has not come yet. Faulty chromosome mitosis, viral infection, the madness of mobs, the bus turning the corner, a war no one understood, all blown unfettered as falling snow, faintly, falling. Hear it falling. Snow, over all of us, ever, equally, ever, the living and the dead. Listen.

−33−

Ida I think it works like this: you got all these different ingredients and alone, they're not so good. Who would want to
nosh a cup of flour? Even a fistful of sugar don't sound so nice.
And you ever tasted shortening? It's only when you mix them all
together they begin to make sense. But if you don't give it time to
work in a warm safe place, you eat just a little, you get sick. Bake too
long, they go hard and brittle. You see, time and hard work, that's
the way I think it goes.

Now, work, I can tell you, I know something about. But
time? At my age, you would think. Still so many surprises, Jacob!
Still, I can't believe, more to do. So this much about time, I can tell
you: it don't move in straight lines. Time moves like the filo in a
paglech, some layers big and long and smooth, almost no bumps or
bubbles at all, some layers short and ready to snap off, whole years
stuck together so you cannot pull them apart, some melting beneath
the touch of your fingertips.

Forgive me, my husband, I should leave the philosophy to
you. This was your special gift, like our Jody's beautiful singing
voice and, if I may say so, my way with a cookie. This is how God
touched you.. Always quiet, always thinking, I feel lucky to have
found you.

Me? I do my best. I fill the layers with honey, walnuts,
poppy seeds, chopped dates. They disappear inside. Sweet little
lifetimes of dough, into the drain, into the drain. What can you do?
You live. You learn. You wait. Time is a thing you cannot control.

Fifty-five years you spend with a person and suddenly they
go. I only thought that I would wait, Jacob. That's all I thought.
Who knew this child could live so long?

And you are gone and Jody is gone and Mama and Papa and
Lila and Izzy and my own body and soon, Jacob, soon my own life,
gone, gone, gone.

They showed me a drawing of what they'll do. Everyone
gets their own little room, and then some big bathrooms with the
bars and all that. Our room will be for the people who work there

and stay overnight and all. The kitchen, they're not going to change a thing! I leave all my bowls and cookie sheets and cutting boards, my measures, my sifters, my heavy leavening bowls... But, Jacob! The spice grinder, the shape cutter, the letter cutters, the little candy cup molds, my kitchen! Where will that go? Where will that be!

Shh, shh, Ida! Don't wake, Paully. Look at him smile. What's he got to dream? You should see him, Jacob, with the dentures. You would be proud, Jacob.

They say they're gonna make a garden in the back. These children love to garden, they tell me. I don't know. I could only get Paully to weed right for two minutes. He's got friends there, Jacob, children like him. What can I say? He wants to go. They got more choices today, retarded people, a lot more choices. And our Paully, he made one. Nobody could miss that.

And while I'm at it, they got a few more for mothers too, eh? Is that Sara clever? She's had her eye on that place all along. She's got figured right away how to do it, how to afford. My Social, hers, plus the rent from Danny's friend Monty or whoever he's gonna live with.

So how do you like that, Lila! I'm going to die in your Florida. I am. Not you. What kind of mother is it that dies of shame? Stock fraud. Is that all? You had not been tested enough, Lila. Poor you, my son only got Down's, your's got greed and stupidity. You would think he hadn't had such a fine uncle. *Feh!* I'll tell you, Paully's room's a lot nicer than that cell Sammy got.

A lot nicer. What did that maven-of-miserable know? Paully got everything he likes here. We did right, Jacob, raising our boy at home.

Our home. We had together thirty-four years, this home. And now I lived here nine without you! Nine without you, Jacob. I bought myself a VCR and waited. When I think I'm not going to die here in my home, in our home...

But I will be buried next to you. I will be buried here in Brooklyn. Our Jody can use that phone of hers and get me delivered. All right, I know our good girl will do right by me. The best all the way, nothing cheap. I know she will. And they will lay me down next to you, my Jacob, because you were my husband almost my whole life, Jacob, married forty-nine years.

Do you know, Jacob, that I still remember clear the first time I saw you? I was a girl. Sixteen. I just finished school, not graduated, just left. Well, this is the way it was done. I was lucky to go that long. I got the job at the factory that made bread and crackers. It was factory, not bakery, eh? Very different. No smell. For my job I had to paste the labels straight. What can I say? Boring work. So when I can, I go with the other girls. We go out by the back doors— back where they got the loading docks—maybe we'd bring an apple, we'd talk. A little break. A little sunshine. And, so what? We'd have a little talk with the boys working back there, mostly being polite of course, seeing as we were in the same space. So sue me, I noticed you. A big man, with your sacks of flour. How strong! Reaching, your muscles taking the weight, your hands. So big! You could hide an apple in them. An afternoon in the fall, a cold breeze on my arms. I thought you were special. I thought, different. You kept taking off your cap and knocking off the dust. The other men? They could care less, their caps were dusty, so what? But you? You liked things just so, eh?

So I knew who you were when you asked me. A little dance they gave at the B'nai Brith. Your friend, Hershel Reuven, asked my friend to dance and since we were both left there, standing alone, you asked me. "Luck" you think, Jacob? Maybe. Maybe "luck" is right. Herschel and my friend, one dance was all they got. They were like Sara. She says, "Who buys without shopping?" Me. I do, Jacob, when I see what I want. Still—what can I say?—all these many years later—I still have a girl's heart. Forgive me. Still I wish I could say different. I wish that it was all your idea and that you walked across that room and chose me. So all right. You had other ideas later, eh? You made other choices.

But then, who had time to wish? Once I got older, I was never one for dancing. I like to listen to the music, maybe clap along. Dancing, I think, is just the most embarrassing thing. So to say I was nervous, that alone does not say it. All I could see was the third button on your shirt. A white shirt, a bow tie of all things, your broad chest. So strong. You weren't tall for a man, I know, but to me, you were tall. To look up into your face, I would have lost the steps all together.

Before you asked my pa, you knelt before me. I know you remember, Jacob. Who could forget? You said that when you looked down on me that night, down next to you, in your arms—my hair just washed and floating up, settling against your white, white shirt —you said you knew right then you didn't want to let go. And then came Paully.

Alone and never alone. And outside, the sky is getting light.

So our life together was not what you'd call an adventure. It was a life; that is all. But if I know nothing else, I know this. Don't expect too much; you won't be disappointed. So maybe my daughter wouldn't want to live a life like mine, but she would be missing something. You were a strong man and a gentle one and a thinker. Never did words just fall from your lips. You were a fine and loving man. I respected you and I never really loved anyone else. You were not perfect; none of us are. You gave me a good life.

But Jacob—can you believe?—it's not over for our Jody. It's Danny, Jacob. Danny! There's something big happening there between those two, alevai. You would think they was teen-agers! I don't know, neither one is really talking to me about it.

You know, I think maybe I was wrong about God. Maybe some people He makes wait until they really got the time to enjoy happiness. I don't know, maybe for me, he was just waiting for me to quit talking! Like you used to say, Jacob, "When you complain, you are no longer alone with misery."

What Danny says is that I should pray. He's teaching me! At my age, eh? Still so much to learn. When I was a girl, they taught only the boys to pray. The girls were taught to cook. And so a Jewish home was made. But Danny, he says it's not done that way anymore. He says, if I'm gonna talk I might as well talk to God because God, at least, is there and you, Jacob, are, well, you are dead. God, at least, can answer. Danny says time is a brokhe and we must spend it with the living.

So what Danny's doing is he's giving me a few hints for getting through to God. The first rule, he says, is that every day you got to practice. Then what you got to do is think first about what you want to say. With God, you don't open your mouth until you have found the right words. Much more intense to speak this way. I asked Jody about this, she said, "I think the thing is, Ma, you got to go in knowing your bottom line."

So, if you'll excuse me a minute, Jacob. Dear Lord, here it is: thank you. Thank you that Paully's illness was easy and for sending me a friend to show me that it could have been worse. Thank you for my good daughter, such a loyal girl who loves her mother. Thank you for sending me home my Jacob a better man. And also, for putting my recipe file into the hands of someone who sifts. A scholar you sent me, no less—a very great gift. But as for this sense of humor you cursed me with, well all right, I admit the knife got two blades. I can make Jody and the mailman and the butcher and Jacob and Lila and Sarah and Danny and always, thank you dear Lord, always myself a darned good laugh.

Though I tell you God, if this is what you give people who would do anything to be funny, I would hate to know what you did to Lucille Ball.

Which brings me to my bottom line. I thought just maybe—if you don't mind a little suggestion, Lord—I was thinking that when the time comes, you could let me die laughing. Just send in Paully to do his Pavarotti. So why not? I deserve it and with your sense of irony and my sense of timing... well, think about it anyway

That's all I ask, God. That and never to have to hear that Steiner-girl's name in my own house again. The rest, I think, we can leave to Jody.

And now, it is coming. The sun is pouring in. Paully rolls over again. All night I have been up with this worry and what does it change? Soon Paully will wake up, he'll need this, he'll need that. And the hands will do what they do every day. So, if you don't mind, I really gotta stop my mouth and think for once. I got to make, every day, cream puffs. Cream puffs I haven't made in years. But before Jody comes to put away my kitchen, I want I should make the perfect recipe. I want they should float, Jacob, they should float like clouds. Sara told me they got a tradition in the Cohen family, they got cream puffs at the wedding. So maybe our Danny can take a mother's hint.

— ACKNOWLEDGEMENTS —

Ropeless is a work of fiction based upon research. Special thanks to Karen Prestwidge and Scott Walker of the New York City Office of Mental Retardation and Developmental Disabilities, and to Dr. Allen Shifferman of the Brooklyn Jewish Family Services Home for the Retarded, who took time from their busy schedules to grant me interviews and tours. The following books were invaluable as well: *Sexual Options for Paraplegics and Quadriplegics* by Thomas O. Mooney, Theodore M. Cole, and Richard A. Chilgren; *Maternal Acceptance of Sub-Normal Babies* (an unpublished dissertation) by Cynthia Wayne-Bestrow Ph.D.; and *Cookies from The Jewish Holiday Cookbook: An International Collection of Recipes and Customs* by Gloria Kaufer Greene.

I would like to thank everyone who has believed in this novel and encouraged me, particularly my agent Nancy Ellis—a true force of nature—and her patient, efficient staff. I am proud that *Ropeless* has been recognized in numerous contests. Coordinating and judging these competitions is a daunting, and often thankless, endeavor.

The beautiful cover of this edition was created by Sherry Bloom (bloomsherry@hotmail.com) specializing in covers and websites for authors.

Finally, ineffable and enduring gratitude to Ken and Jezebel for making me feel loved and valued each and every day.